THE TALENT CONTINUUM, BOOK ONE:

A
DISCOVERY
OF
TALENTS

Phoenix McDonald

ISBNs: 9788991805902 (eBook); 9788991805919, 9798991805964 (Paperback); 9798991805926 (Hardcover)

Cover Design by Dany Rivera
danyriverarts.com

Editing by Lindz McCleod
lindzmcleod.co.uk

Line editing by Charlie Knight
cknightwritesediting.carrd.co

Proofreading by Alexandria Anderson
anandersonauthor.com

Formatting by A.M. Weald
amweald.com

Published by Phoenix Rises Publishing, LLC
Portland, Oregon

For Tadpole

CHAPTERS & CONTENT

Prologue: Old Friends and New Beginnings..........................1

Chapter 1: Marcus..16

Chapter 2: Cornus...30

Chapter 3: Secrets and Disappearances.......................37

Chapter 4: A Message Arrives.....................................50

Chapter 5: Return to Lysomnus..................................63

Chapter 6: Thicce Colpat...77

Chapter 7: Hitting the Trail..98

Chapter 8: A Talent Emerges....................................136

Chapter 9: The Fyrtudo...164

Chapter 10: The Price of Her Name..........................198

Chapter 11: Splitting Up..210

Chapter 12: The Lost Languages of Lysomnus..........220

Chapter 13: Fisc..225

Chapter 14: Return to Thicce Colpat.........................255

Chapter 15: Grasian..266

Chapter 16: Power Evolves.......................................285

Chapter 17: Hostage..301

Chapter 18: Faceoff...320

Chapter 19: Joining the Fight....................................340

Chapter 20: Friends to the End.................................349

Chapter 21: Home..368

Pronunciation of Names and Places..........................383

Acknowledgments..385

About the Author...387

Other Works by the Author.......................................389

OLD FRIENDS AND NEW BEGINNINGS

Malcolm

Malcolm Talent woke up to see the evening sky of Lysomnus above him, rays of sunlight breaking between the trees' broad green leaves. Pushing himself to his feet, he walked along a familiar path that wound through the Grenewud, the expansive forest of this world, to say goodbye to his best friend. Tears ran down Malcolm's face as he realized that this would be the last time he would see her.

Malcolm had noticed signs in his son that indicated the boy would soon begin traveling to Lysomnus. When Deacon traveled for the first time, Malcolm would no longer be able to visit this planet that felt as much like home as his own. The thought of losing the ability pierced Malcolm's heart with unbearable pain, but he had known this was coming for some time now. He had done his best to say his goodbyes.

He walked faster toward Thicce Colpat, the home of the Scrybb, and his dearest friend on Lysomnus, Berberis. The thought of wasting a moment of the time he had left was unbearable.

Malcolm and Berberis had met in the days when he first traveled to Lysomnus. He had been found and welcomed by her people, the Scrybb. They were leaf-covered people who closely resembled Earth's shrubs, They were Malcolm's first family on Lysomnus. Malcolm had met a Scrybb girl about his age who was shorter than him and covered in beautiful rose-colored leaves. Twigs formed her facial features beneath those leaves. Glowing orange eyes lit up her face. She showed him around and helped him to learn about her people. Most Scrybb were welcoming and friendly, although some were standoffish and not happy to see him. His mother said it had always been that way; many of the Scrybb did not like humans. Malcolm understood that not everyone was going to like him, especially in a world where he was the only human.

Now, Malcolm reached the end of the path and entered Thicce Colpat. He headed for the school, a wide building constructed of wood over a base of sand-colored stone. Berberis had been elevated to the position of Teacher after her Travel year, a period of time when young Scrybb journeyed and learned about their homeworld after a sheltered childhood.

Malcolm trailed a hand over the rough stone of the wall before he opened the door and stepped inside. He looked up at the elaborately carved ceiling with designs added by generations of Scrybb crafters. Voices echoed in the hallway through open doors along the hall. Most of the students in the classrooms at the near end were approaching their Travel year, but Malcolm would find

Berberis teaching a new class of young Scrybb at the far end of the hall.

Without warning, young Scrybb dashed out of the classrooms, some eyeing Malcolm curiously as they ran by. The sound of rustling leaves swept around him, along with the scent of fresh greenery. The susurration was soon drowned out by excited chattering as Scrybb children rushed past him.

Berberis was leaning against the doorway of her classroom with her back to Malcolm, shaking her head and laughing, watching her own diminutive students hurrying away in the opposite direction. The youngest Scrybb returned immediately to the nursery after class, where they lived under the watchful eyes of Scrybb tenders.

"Berberis!" Malcolm called out, hands around his mouth to be heard over the cacophony in the hallway. Berberis's rosy leaves fluttered as she turned in response.

"Malcolm!" she cried, hurrying down the emptying hallway with her arms extended. "What a wonderful surprise." Malcolm eyed the vines that constructed her limbs warily; they were covered in small, sharp thorns.

He shrugged to himself, unable to resist embracing her. Wincing as she hugged him, he found himself savoring the pain of the small punctures today. It would probably be the last time he would ever feel them.

"Is it time, Malcolm?" Berberis asked, her orange eyes meeting his.

"I believe so," he said, "and I want to spend these

final hours with you. If Deacon travels tonight or before I am able to return again, I want us to take time for a proper goodbye."

"We must not spend these hours in sorrow, my friend," she said, carefully wiping his tears away. Her leaves, covering the thorns beneath, were soft against his skin. "We will go to my rooms and have one of our famous discussions—well, famous to *us* at least." She nudged him affectionately with her elbow.

"And bring some delicious selections from the dining hall," Malcolm chuckled. He carefully offered a companionable arm to his friend as they made their way to the large building where a congregate meal was served every evening.

Carrying a tray laden with roast meat, savory vegetables, bowls of rich stew, and plates of sweet fruit, they made their way to Berberis's home in the dormitory.

"Remember when I started teaching and telling my students all I learned on my Travels, Malcolm?"

"I do. Cassiope was none too happy with you. I never have understood why the Scrybb insist on keeping the outside world out and the children uninformed until their Travels."

Berberis looked away. She popped a piece of meat into her mouth. Malcolm waited patiently, knowing she was stalling for time.

"Malcolm, you must understand. The Scrybb are a private people, and we have our reasons for keeping to ourselves. You know there are several people here who are not happy because *you* are allowed to visit and stay here."

"Yes, but—"

"There is a very good reason for that, and for the times I have met you outside of Thicce Colpat and asked you to stay away."

"I wish you would tell me more, Berberis. Perhaps I could have helped."

She lowered her head, hiding her orange eyes.

"No one can, not even you. But please, let us move on to happier topics."

"All right," Malcolm said, not wanting to spoil their time with an argument. "I am very excited for everyone in Lysomnus to meet Deacon."

"I will be happy to meet him and extend him the same hospitality I have always shown to his father," Berberis said, looking back up at Malcolm with a smile. "I know he will love it here. How could we not welcome the son of Malcolm Talent?" Her smile wavered for a moment. Malcolm looked away before the sadness in her eyes could add to the pain in his own heart.

They continued reminiscing about their many adventures over the past decades and even some of the disagreements they'd had over the years. Malcolm told Berberis of the visits he had made to his friends among the rest of the people of Lysomnus. Each one had been more difficult than the last. He had saved this special trip to see Berberis for what he believed would be his final visit to Lysomnus.

The day before he had first traveled to Lysomnus, he had suddenly become clumsy, unfocused, and overwhelmed by exhaustion accompanied by a mild sense of euphoria. He was seeing some of those same signs in Deacon. He shared this with his friend and told her Deacon could begin traveling as soon as the very next night on Earth.

As the light outside began to dim, a deep ache settled in Malcolm's chest. Tears welled in Berberis's eyes. Each was deeply aware of the end of their lifelong friendship—not by choice, but by the limitations of Malcolm's bloodline.

Finally, as deepening darkness outside indicated the ending of the day, Malcolm stood up.

Berberis looked up, tears spilling over and trickling down the leaves below her orange eyes. Malcolm tried to blink away his own tears, only to feel one escape and run down his face to hang, trembling, from his jaw. He wiped it away.

"Must you go?" Berberis asked wistfully.

"It is inevitable, my dear friend. I have loved you and your world for my entire life, but my time here is at an end. I must give way to my son now, just as my mother did for me. It is Deacon's turn to explore Lysomnus and learn to love its people."

She smiled, spilling more tears out of her eyes. Malcolm watched as they trickled from leaf to leaf until falling to the floor.

"Of course, Malcolm," Berberis said with a catch in her voice. "Your son will be welcome here. I hope he loves our world and the people in it as much as you have. You have a beautiful soul. What else could the son of Malcolm Talent be but a kind and gentle person?"

Malcolm reached out and grabbed Berberis by the hand, unmindful of the thorns which pierced his skin.

"Please, walk with me to the edge of Thicce Colpat to say goodbye."

The walk was too short, and they were embracing at the opening of the path into the Grenewud. Alone, Malcolm trudged into the darkness beneath the trees. He struggled to keep from looking back, knowing he would lose control if he did. At last, he turned, and the sight of Berberis watching broke him. He buried his face in his hands and wept.

Malcolm woke up sobbing. He muffled the sound by burying his face in his pillow. Linda slept on peacefully in her bed across the room. The two of them slept separately, as those in his family always had, so wives and husbands would not become aware of their spouse's disappearance when they traveled to Lysomnus.

Malcolm noticed immediately the next morning that Deacon was not his normally pleasant self the next day. The sixteen-year-old boy was irritable at breakfast, snapping at his mother when she spilled a little juice on his hand. It took a sharp word from Malcolm before he would apologize. He seemed calmer after school but complained about every perceived hardship from pop quizzes to homework. While grabbing a snack in the kitchen, he broke a plate, swearing and stomping out of the room. Linda was visibly shaken.

That evening, Deacon got into a fight with his girlfriend on the telephone. Something felt wrong to Malcolm. The day before *he* had traveled to Lysomnus, he had been happy, even though he had been clumsy and awkward. The feeling of buoyancy Malcolm had felt before his own travels was missing in Deacon. Malcolm wondered if he was wrong about the timing of his son's traveling.

After dinner, the teen announced he was going to bed earlier than usual. That, at least, was consistent with what Malcolm remembered from his own experience. He remembered being exhausted, almost unable to keep his eyes open.

Malcolm waited until Linda was asleep before grabbing two items from his nightstand and creeping out of their bedroom. He grabbed a chair from the hallway and sidled into Deacon's room, turning the chair so he could sit with his arms resting on the back. Moonlight streamed through the window, highlighting the boy's dark red hair and large freckles. Malcolm rested his chin on his hands and admired Deacon's striking features. His son was tall, rangy, square-jawed. He was a good-looking boy. What was Malcolm missing here at home while distracted in Lysomnus? He realized he hadn't taken the time to notice his son in quite a while—not since Deacon had been younger.

Was this really the night Deacon would travel to Lysomnus? Many of the signs were present, so he waited patiently in the dim moonlight. It was important to be here if his son did travel to Lysomnus to help him understand everything about traveling. His mother had been there for him, and he remembered just how much he had needed her calm guidance after returning from the sudden visit to a foreign world in his sleep.

Before long, he was struggling to stay awake. Staying alert was arduous work in the quiet hours of the night. At last, he lost the battle, chin resting on his crossed arms, snoring softly. He didn't notice when Deacon disappeared, the blankets settling silently into the empty space where the boy's body had been.

A few minutes later, Deacon reappeared in the bed. The boy sat up with a loud gasp, bringing Malcolm to his feet. He caught the tipping chair before it could clatter to the floor, then sat on the bed and gripped his son's shoulder firmly. "It's okay, Deacon. You're home now."

The boy looked up at his father, eyes wide. "Dad? I had the craziest dream! I was in the strangest place, and it felt like I was actually there!"

"You did go to that world, son. It wasn't a dream. Let me explain everything to you." Malcolm looked into his son's wide blue eyes and took a deep breath.

"All the members of our bloodline—the Talents— have a special ability. We call it traveling. We leave Earth at night, in our sleep, to visit another planet called Lysomnus."

"Lysomnus? What do you mean, another planet?" Deacon said incredulously. "You've got to be kidding me.

Come on, Dad. You're telling me I went to another world in my *sleep*? That sounds like bullcrap! Now I'm supposed to believe it was real? Why wouldn't you tell me about this?"

"Listen, son," Malcolm said, trying to be patient. "If I sat you down yesterday and told you to prepare to travel to another world in your sleep tonight, would you have believed a word I said? Or would you have thought I was crazy? But if I'm making it up, how did I know what happened?"

Deacon pulled his knees up under the blankets and laughed against his crossed arms.

"But the answer is yes. Your body was gone from Earth and appeared on Lysomnus. Did you meet anyone while you were there? Talk to any of the people who live there?"

The boy grimaced.

"There were some strange animals there. They made noises. Maybe they were trying to talk."

Malcolm frowned, confused. "Animals? I don't know of any animals that talk in Lysomnus. Describe them to me."

"Well," Deacon said, biting his arm nervously, "they were tall and muscular, but they looked a little like those little brown animals that pop up and look around on nature shows. Groundhogs? I dunno, or kangaroos, but they didn't hop. They just made funny noises, and they kept waving their arms all over the place."

Malcolm tented a hand on his forehead, frustrated. He took a deep breath, trying to stay calm.

"I don't know why you look upset, Dad," Deacon said. "They were just dumb animals. When I tried walking down the road, they poked me with sticks and started getting excited. I ran the other way to get away from them. I could feel the pokes and smell the dust. It was so real."

Malcolm's face was burning, flushed with anger.

"Boy, those were *not* animals. They are *people* called the Cativera, and they communicate using sign language."

"Who thinks giant groundhog squirrels are going to try to talk to them? And in a dream? I don't know how you can even call them people. They're giant, hairy animals that carry sticks and can't even talk."

"Listen, just because you don't understand them doesn't mean you have the right to decide they aren't people. You will be traveling to Lysomnus frequently from now on, and part of your responsibility is to get to know the people there and treat them with dignity and respect." He held out one of the objects he'd carried inn. "You need to put this on."

"This is so awesome! It must be worth so much money," Deacon held up the bracelet of heavy silver links, and it clinked softly, gleaming in the moonlight.

"It's called a Stikke."

"Stee-kuh?" Deacon parroted.

Malcolm spelled it for him. "It's a special Talisman that keeps you from traveling every night."

The boy clasped the Stikke onto his wrist. "It fits!"

"It always fits any member of our family who wears it."

"Why would I want to keep myself from traveling, Dad?"

"It's to keep you from traveling in case you need to stay here on Earth." Next, Malcolm pulled a small crystal cube from the pocket of the t-shirt he was wearing. A small flame, bright blue at the base and fading to yellow at the tip, flickering inside. "This is the Halfriez. You can heal injuries with it."

"Wow!" Deacon exclaimed, taking the cube from his father. "It's cold!"

"One more thing, son. Everyone in our family eventually develops some kind of power."

The teen looked really excited for the first time. "Power? What kind of power? How strong?"

Malcolm shrugged. "There's no way to know. Some members of our family have developed stronger powers; others have less. They're useful abilities, not things to be used against anyone on that planet, son. And when your power manifests, you have to practice getting better with it. You don't just master it the first time it shows up. Your abilities won't work here on Earth, only on Lysomnus."

Deacon still looked excited. "What's your power, Dad?"

Malcolm tried to relax, remembering how excited he had been when first learning about the world of Lysomnus from his mother.

"I have the ability to make plants grow very quickly."

Deacon looked disappointed.

"Don't think lightly of my skill, son. I helped the Scrybb extensively and even the Cativera, who grow and harvest grain. We developed new varieties of plants together and increased production to provide food for many people across all of Lysomnus."

"The Scrybb?" his son looked confused.

"Oh, you'll meet them soon enough," Malcolm said, a bittersweet smile just touching the corners of his mouth. "Some of my favorite Lysomnians are Scrybb."

"As you travel around Lysomnus, you will meet many different people of all types. Please keep an open mind and be friendly and kind. The people of this world are intelligent, wonderful, and gracious."

"Different," the boy said. "You mean—different like those groundhog things."

"*Deacon*," Malcolm said firmly. "Stop calling the Cativera groundhogs. The people of Lysomnus don't look anything like Earth creatures. They are complex and incredible, each one of them. They deserve your respect and admiration. Do not waste this gift with a biased mind. I have been waiting to share Lysomnus with you, to be able to see it through your eyes. Don't let that vision be an ugly one." He sighed. "You've been given an incredible gift, son. You will be visiting an entirely different planet, getting to know and befriend new and interesting people, and tasting new and incredible food. I've spent an enormous portion of my life there."

Deacon blinked. "Does Mom know about any of this?"

Malcolm shook his head. "No, and you can never tell her. No one who isn't a genetic Talent is allowed to know. That's why your mother and I sleep in separate beds and why you and your wife will have to do the same. She can never know your body is gone at night."

He reached out and touched the links of the Stikke gently with one fingertip. "I couldn't travel much when you were born, or your mother would have known, getting up with you during the wee hours." He chuckled, reaching and grasping his son's hand. "Please, son, take the time to get to know the people of Lysomnus. I know you will come to love them as I have. With each bruwe you visit, you will find more to love about this new world."

"Broo-way?" Deacon repeated. "What is a broo-way?"

"Bruwe," the older man said. "It's the Lysomnian word for village. The Cativeran bruwe is Grasian. You were probably close to it if you saw them."

"I think I might have heard them make a sound like that," Deacon said. "But mostly, they just waved their arms around. How was I supposed to know?"

"I suggest you visit them and take the time to learn their sign language so you can communicate with them since you're going to be spending many years traveling to Lysomnus," Malcolm said.

Deacon's eyes shifted. "I'll definitely take the time to get around and meet more people. Why don't you just show me around? Introduce me to all the people you know there?"

His father shook his head, anguish deepening the lines in his face. "It doesn't work like that, son. Once the younger Talent begins to travel, the older Talent loses the ability. That's one reason I couldn't go with you when you traveled tonight. I had to wait for you to travel and come back. It was the same for your Grandma Ruby when I first traveled." Malcolm released Deacon's hand and patted him on the shoulder. "I'm glad you'll be traveling now. We'll be able to compare our experiences, and you can get to meet the same people I know. Please take the time to enjoy yourself and be kind to the people.

"We have a lot to talk about tonight. I want to fill you in on all the things you need to watch out for—there are dangers there—as well as ways to behave so you don't offend people. We'll talk as much as we can now, and we can continue to compare experiences as you travel to help you learn everything you need to know.

"Please, appreciate your time in Lysomnus—it goes by a lot faster than you think. Before you know it, you'll be talking to your own child about their first travels."

Deacon snorted. "That's a long way off."

Malcolm grabbed the chair and set it next to the boy's bed. It was going to be a long night. "Time goes by faster than you expect, son. Treasure every moment you spend there because before you know it, you'll be having this same discussion at your own child's bedside, and your time in Lysomnus will only be memories."

CHAPTER ONE

MARCUS

Marcus Talent turned from his computer and reached for his cell phone to text his best friend. The screen stayed dark. He must have laid the phone on his desk the previous night instead of the charging pad. He hadn't even checked when he got up to finish his homework so his weekend would be free. He frowned. How was he supposed to text Leopold?

He unplugged the charging pad and plugged the phone in directly, hoping to charge it faster. They were supposed to hang out today, with a cookout planned at Marcus's house that evening.

It took Marcus longer to get ready for the day than most sixteen-year-old boys. His dresser was next to his bed to make it easier for him to get dressed. He'd climbed out of bed that morning and unplugged the bebionic prosthetic arm that was always charging overnight on the dresser. After donning a fresh t-shirt, Marcus had put his prosthetic on and jumped right onto the computer to finish his homework. Now he moved carefully to the dresser, opening drawers and pulling out more clean clothes.

This bebionic arm was just one of several prosthetics he had used since he lost his right arm just above the elbow in a car accident when he was nine years old. His right arm ended in a residual stump just below his t-shirt sleeve. He finally stood with a grimace and stepped away from his desk.

It only took a minute to put on his current myoelectric prosthesis. He might have forgotten to charge his phone, but at least he'd remembered to charge the prosthetic. It sensed his muscle movements and, with a few clicks of the controls on the prosthesis, it would perform most of the functions his right hand could have achieved.

Marcus sat carefully on his desk chair to put on the rest of his clothes. He pulled a stiff blue cloth that resembled a hammock from a drawer with long canvas straps attached. One at a time, he pulled his socks over the end of the hammock and lowered it until he could rest his foot in it. With a smooth motion, he pulled the sock onto his foot. He put his other sock on. With a grimace, he lowered his jeans until he could lift his feet high enough to get them into the legs.

After he pulled them up, he groaned in pain and pushed his left hand against his lower back. In the years since the accident, six surgeries had restored some of his ability to sit, reach, and walk, but he was still limited. He often found the pain and loss of mobility from the surgeries to be more limiting than the loss of his arm. It was necessary for him to use a cane to walk, and for longer trips, he sometimes still used a wheelchair. Marcus had taken pain medication in the past, but his doctor and parents weren't comfortable with that. Instead, he'd learned to adjust to living with pain and used tools to offer accessibility when needed.

He used a long shoehorn to slide his feet into tennis shoes with special stretch laces. He pulled his phone off the charger, slid it into a pocket, and grabbed his cane. He almost tripped over the cane while hurrying down the hall to the kitchen. He wondered how late he was for the breakfast he could already smell. Marcus's mom, Kate, was a nurse and occasionally worked weekends and still insisted on making breakfast for him even on the days she worked. She hadn't called down the hall to him, so at least he wasn't too late.

"There you are!" Marcus's mom said when he entered the kitchen. "By the way, I forgot to grab bacon at the store yesterday, so I was only able to make pancakes."

He looked at his phone. The battery had gained a sliver of charge, so he sent Leopold a quick text. *You still coming over?*

"You know you don't have to do that. I can make my own breakfast."

"I know, Marcus. I do it because I enjoy it." She set his plate on the table, then reached up and grasped his face in her hands. "Look how tall you are. You're growing up too fast."

Marcus put his hand over hers. He had passed her in height over the last year, and it still felt strange to look down at her. They shared the same hazel eyes, delicate bone structure, and light brown skin that always looked like they had a tan. He was glad he had her black hair, too, instead of his dad's dark red hair, although he shared the older man's tumble of wild curls.

It hurt Marcus's heart to see the burn scars on his mom's face and neck, a memento from the same car accident that had disabled him. She gave his face an affectionate shake and pulled him down to kiss him on the cheek before letting him go.

"I really appreciate it, you know," he said. "No one makes pancakes like you, Mom."

She scoffed as she turned away, but the hint of a smile quirked the corner of her mouth.

His cell phone vibrated with a reply from Leopold. *On my way.* Marcus plugged the phone into the charger on the counter.

A rumble vibrated the entire house as Marcus sat down to eat. "What's that?"

"New neighbors, I think," His mom straightened her scrub top as she came back into the kitchen. "Now where did I put my purse? Oh, there it is." She grabbed it off the table and patted Marcus on the shoulder as she walked by. "I'm only working an eight-hour shift today, so I should be home in plenty of time before the cookout tonight."

"Bye, Mom," he called after her.

After he had finished eating, Marcus put his plate in the sink and made his way out the door to check out the new neighbors. Taking a seat in a chair on the porch, he propped his cane against the wall. Several people carried furniture from a long truck into the house next door. His own driveway was empty; his father usually left early for work. Deacon Talent worked most weekends and wasn't home often.

A pretty girl with long, wavy black hair came out of the house and glanced in his direction. She considered him with dark, angular eyes and then smiled. Marcus smiled back. He felt a faint sense of alarm when she started walking in his direction.

"Hi," she said. "I'm Sadie, your new neighbor, as you can see," she laughed self-consciously, gesturing toward the commotion next door.

"Hello," he replied, embarrassed as he heard the shakiness in his voice. He found it difficult to talk to new people, particularly kids his own age. Their discomfort around his disabilities made him nervous. "I'm Marcus. Welcome to the neighborhood."

"Thanks," she said, her face lighting up with a smile. Marcus felt his heart speed up a little. He worried she would hear it thumping, even though he knew that was preposterous.

"Sadie!" A woman who looked similar to the girl called, hands on her hips. "We need your help here."

"Oh, I gotta go," she said, a flush climbing her face as she looked over her shoulder. "Be right there, Mom!" she called.

"Sure," Marcus replied. "Hey, we're having a cookout tonight. Why don't you and your family come over and join us? Kind of a 'get to know the neighbors' kind of thing?"

"Um, sure, that sounds great," Sadie said. "I'll mention it to my mom and dad." She turned and jogged back toward the truck.

Marcus rubbed his left hand up the side of his face, then rested his forehead in a shaky palm. He was surprised by his own boldness, inviting Sadie and her family over. He was normally introverted. Leopold was the only person he typically hung out with. Other kids hadn't always been very nice to him.

As if thinking about his friend had conjured him out of thin air, Leopold rode into the driveway and parked his bike in front of the porch while glancing at the activity next door. "Hey, bro," he said, a broad grin dimpling his cheeks as Marcus smiled. Leopold was the polar opposite of his best friend. He was shorter and stockier with bright blue eyes and messy blond hair.

"New neighbors?" he asked, climbing the stairs. He stood

in front of Marcus and shadow-boxed the air, hopping from foot to foot. Marcus leaned to one side, trying to see around Leopold.

"Yeah, they're just moving in today." Marcus continued to watch the family walking back and forth from house to truck. It looked as if all the furniture was in the house; everyone was now moving boxes. Sadie walked down the ramp at the rear of the truck carrying a cardboard box with KITCHEN scrawled across it in black marker. A younger boy followed behind her.

"Ah, the plot thickens," Leopold said, seeing the look on Marcus's face as he watched the pretty, dark-haired girl make her way up the driveway.

"Oh, shut up," Marcus said, looking at Leopold for the first time.

Leopold grinned, dropping into the chair next to Marcus on the porch. "Have you met her yet?"

"Yes," Marcus replied, his face heating up as he struggled not to smile. "Her name is Sadie. I invited her and her family to come by for the cookout tonight."

Leopold smirked. "Oh, *Sadie!*" He teased lightly.

"It's not like that." The warmth of his flush deepened and spread. "I was just trying to be nice. I'm sure my parents will want to get to know her parents too."

"Sure, I guess," Leopold said. "And I'll be *so* happy to make her acquaintance." He clutched his hands beneath his chin and fluttered his eyelashes. Marcus finally lost the battle and burst out laughing; Leopold always cracked him up.

"Are you gonna let your parents know about their extra guests?" Leopold asked.

"Oh—yeah. I should text my dad." He looked around,

then realized he had left his cell on the kitchen counter. "Ugh, I left my phone in the kitchen, and it's charging. What is wrong with me today?"

"C'mon, let's just go inside," Leopold said, handing Marcus his cane. "Besides, we need to get back to Elden Ring." He opened the door and followed Marcus inside, laughing as he saw his friend glance back over his shoulder.

Once Marcus had switched his phone to the charger in the living room, Marcus texted his dad to let him know about the extra guests. The boys sprawled on the couch, game controllers in hand, lost in the Lands Between. Marcus's double PS5 setup let him start the game and then pull Leopold in on multiplayer mode.

Marcus struggled to play the game. He found himself frustrated to the point that he wanted to quit. It hadn't been easy to learn to use a gaming controller with the bebionic prosthetic, but he had learned to adapt and usually played quite skillfully. Today, however, he was getting killed every five minutes by weak zombies or random skeleton dogs.. Leopold kept glancing at him. "What's up with you today, bro? I thought this was the day we were going to take on Malenia? That's not going to happen, the way you're playing."

Marcus sighed, pausing the game and setting his controller aside. "I don't know. It's been a weird day. I feel off, somehow. Not in a bad way, just strange. It's like I can't even hit the right controls." He held the prosthesis up. "My hand is slipping off the sticks, and I can't even hit the right buttons. It's like I'm suddenly so clumsy."

Leopold hesitated for a moment, looking puzzled. Then a prankish smile creased his face. "Dude, if you gotta make an excuse for sucking so bad, just say so," he laughed. A serious note behind his eyes told Marcus his friend understood.

Marcus sighed and picked up his controller. He tossed unruly black curls out of his eyes. "Come on, let's keep playing. I'll do my best to keep it together. I worked too hard to get over 120 to give up now."

Deacon's booming voice startled them later as he entered the house. "Boys, can I get a hand here?"

Leopold leapt off the couch, reaching back automatically to catch Marcus's outstretched left hand and pull him to his feet. Snatching up his cane as he rose, Marcus followed his friend out of the living room to find Deacon hanging up his keys. Reusable shopping bags lay on the bench by the front door. "Take these to the kitchen," Deacon said, running thick fingers through his dark red curls. "There's more in the car."

"Holy cow, Dad," Marcus exclaimed. "How much food did you buy?"

"Well, someone sprung a bunch of surprise guests on me at the last minute." Deacon grunted, loosening his tie. A grimace crossed his face as he gestured in the direction of the neighboring house. "I picked up burgers, bratwurst, some hot dogs..." He looked down at Marcus with a strange look of consideration. "Uh, son...are you sure they're going to want to eat our food with us?"

Marcus saw a thunderstruck expression darken Leopold's face even as he felt his own flush with embarrassed understanding. "What? Wh—why would you say that?"

"Well," Deacon hesitated, "I don't know if burgers are the kind of food people like them eat, Marcus. Didn't you notice?"

"You can't be serious. That's racist, Dad!" Marcus said.

"You should know better. I—I'll go and tell Sadie to forget it." He flung the door open so hard it bounced off the wall behind it.

Deacon caught the door and Marcus's shoulder before he could leave.

"Just wait, son. I'm sorry. I spoke without thinking. You know what, I'll go over there myself, right now. Introduce myself and have a conversation. I feel like a real ass." Deacon was rambling, and Marcus could tell he was embarrassed. The strange sense of cheerfulness he had been feeling all day helped him relax and made him want to cut his dad a break for what he'd said. "You boys can bring the rest of the stuff in. I'm sure your mother will be home soon."

Leopold and Marcus followed Deacon out and grabbed more bags. Just as they were climbing the porch stairs, Marcus's mom pulled into the driveway.

Kate stepped out of her car and greeted the boys, but when she saw Deacon standing in the driveway of the house next door talking to Sadie's parents, she walked over to join them. Marcus and Leopold returned to the house.

"Wow. I never took your dad for that kind of person," Leopold said, breaking the uncomfortable silence.

Marcus began digging through the food in the bags. "I didn't either." He screwed up his face, thinking hard. "Though I don't know if the topic has ever come up before."

"Well," Leopold said, gesturing at Marcus with a blue-and-white package, "at least he got Oreos. Everyone likes Oreos, don't they?"

Marcus laughed and snatched the package out of his friend's hand. "Let's take all this food out to the deck," he said, pointing at the bag of bratwurst and premade hamburger patties for Leopold to carry while he stuffed the

Oreos back into a bag with several kinds of chips in it and followed his friend outside.

"Why don't you sit down?" Leopold suggested when the bags were on the table. "I'll go back for the rest. You need to take a break so you can sit and visit with everyone. And *Sadie.*"

Marcus swung his cane at Leopold as he went back into the house. He was secretly relieved. With a sigh, he sat down and opened a bag of Fritos. Crunching on some of the corn chips, he leaned back and relaxed. Leopold brought out another handful of bags just as Marcus managed to lose his grip on the chips and dump Fritos all over the table and deck. He couldn't help but laugh as Leopold caught the bag and rescued the chips that were left. Marcus picked a couple off the table and popped them into his mouth.

The gate next to their garage opened and Deacon and Kate escorted the new neighbors into the backyard. Marcus sucked in a breath as he caught sight of Sadie, her wavy black hair blown away from her face by a slight breeze. Her dark eyes met his, and she quickened her pace.

Hopping up the steps, she took a seat next to Marcus. "Hi!"

"Hey," he responded, scrambling to think of something to say. He grabbed the package of Oreos in desperation. "Want a cookie?"

"Ooh, Oreos," she said, grabbing the package and tearing it open. "I love these things." Twisting one of the chocolate cookies in half, she scraped off the white icing with her teeth. With one crumb-covered finger, she pointed at the package. "You'll probably have to take these away from me."

Marcus laughed. "I eat them that exact same way," he said.

"Weirdos," Leopold said, dropping into another chair with a sigh. He set several cans of soda on the table. "Oreos are supposed to be dunked in milk."

"Bleh." Sadie grimaced. "Then they get all soggy and half of the cookie—"

"—falls to the bottom of the glass!" Marcus and Sadie finished together. They looked at each other and laughed.

Leopold rolled his eyes and cracked open a Dr. Pepper. "You two are going to get along just fine," he said after taking a long swallow. His cheeks puffed out as he belched.

"Nice," Marcus said. Sadie laughed again.

"Incoming," Leopold warned under his breath. Marcus looked up to see his parents walking up the steps with Sadie's parents and the young boy Marcus had seen with Sadie before. Marcus noticed Sadie's mom and dad looked slightly uncomfortable.

"Hello, Leopold," Kate said with a smile at her son's friend. She shifted her gaze to the pretty girl sitting next to her son. "And we haven't met yet?"

"Mom, this is Sadie."

"Hello, Sadie," Kate said graciously, holding out her hand. Sadie raised her cookie-free hand and Kate took it, folding her other hand gently around it. "It's so lovely to meet you. I'm Kate."

Sadie smiled shyly while Deacon ushered Sadie's parents to the table. Marcus looked at them curiously. Sadie took after her mother with the same pale golden skin and dark eyes, but the older woman's hair was straight and shoulder-length. Sadie's father was a compact man with neatly styled black hair tinged with gray. Sadie's brother looked like a younger version of her right down to the long, wavy hair.

Deacon's formidable bulk overshadowed all of them.

"Boys, this is Sadie's dad, Travis Kim. And that's his mom, Yuni."

"Yumi," the woman corrected gently.

Deacon frowned, looking slightly annoyed. "I'm so sorry," he said. "I've just never heard such an unusual name before."

Marcus and Leopold exchanged glances while Sadie shifted in her chair. "It turns out Travis is a home-grown American, born right in California, Marcus," Deacon said, clapping a large hand to the shorter man's shoulder. Kate looked at her husband sharply. Marcus saw the same anger cross Leopold's face that he felt on his own. What was *wrong* with his dad today?

Sadie cleared her throat and looked fiercely up at Deacon, a flush creeping up her neck to suffuse her face. "My mother, *Yumi*, is also an American. After she married my father, she moved to the States with him and became a US citizen," she said stiffly. Marcus heard a firm note of pride enter her voice as she spoke.

"I apologize for any assumptions," Deacon said brusquely to the young girl glaring up at him. "I'm going to light the grill." He walked off heavily across the deck.

Sadie grabbed the younger boy's hand. "And this is my brother, Steven." Pointing around the table, she said each new person's name as she signed to Steven. "He was born deaf, so we all speak with him in sign language." She continued to sign as she spoke, explaining that this kept her brother included in the conversation.

Steven smiled at them all when Sadie stopped and then signed something back. "He said hello, and please pass the Oreos," Sadie translated.

They all laughed together. Marcus noticed Deacon had

turned away from the grill and was staring at Sadie and Steven, frowning. When he saw Marcus looking at him, he turned back to the sizzling meat.

Marcus and Leopold stood and shook hands with the adult Kims before introducing themselves. He was so embarrassed by his father's behavior. He never expected his father would exhibit racism in the way he had today. He noticed a look of consternation on his mother's face, as well. He guessed his parents would be having an uncomfortable conversation later that night.

Marcus noticed while they were eating that while the Kims occasionally glanced at his prosthetic arm and the cane leaning against his chair, they did not stare or ask questions. He felt more at ease with Sadie and her family than he had around other people in a long time.

He had just taken a big bite of his remaining burger when the patty slid from the bun and landed in his lap. Ketchup and mayonnaise splattered everywhere. Marcus could only laugh at his own predicament, watching Sadie giggle with one hand over her mouth. Leopold laughed even as he grabbed the roll of paper towels and handed a few to Marcus.

"Got a little somethin' on ya there, brah," he snorted.

"Thanks," Marcus said, trying to scowl but unable to keep a straight face.

Marcus looked across the table to see Deacon watching him despondently. He wondered if Deacon felt bad about all the blunders he had made with Sadie's parents.

By the time everyone had finished eating and the food was put away, twilight had fallen, and Marcus found himself yawning. Deacon rested a hand on his shoulder. "Maybe it's time for you to head to bed, Marcus. You look exhausted."

Marcus caught a melancholy note in his father's voice.

"I am pretty tired. Maybe I will, after everyone has gone home."

Yumi overheard this last remark and stepped to Marcus's side, calling Sadie to join her.

"It is time to say our goodbyes for tonight, Marcus. You are tired, and our families will have plenty of time to get to know each other."

Sadie smiled at Marcus and said goodbye to Leopold. She followed her family through the gate in the fence. Leopold elbowed Marcus gently. "That looked like a pretty special smile. I think she likes you, my man."

Marcus shook his head. "She's just being nice." He did like Sadie, even though they had just met that morning. She was funny and really nice. He hoped he would get another chance to talk to her the next day before they had to go back to school. His dad would be working, so he could at least avoid any further embarrassment on that front.

Leopold followed his shadow across the grass to the gate. He turned back with a jaunty wave as he left the yard. "See ya, bro!"

Marcus grabbed his cane and made his way inside. He made sure to put his phone on the charger, then toed off his shoes. After leaning his cane against the wall, he slowly changed into his sleep shorts, not bothering to remove his t-shirt. He was so tired, he could barely keep his eyes open. With a sigh of relief, he turned to his bed and had just enough time to pull the covers back before collapsing onto his pillow.

CHAPTER TWO

CORNUS

Marcus opened his eyes. He was curled up on his side on the ground in broad daylight. Green leaves were strewn everywhere around him. His back ached miserably.

Was he dreaming? It didn't feel like it. The texture of the dirt and leaves on his skin felt more real than any dream he'd ever had. He grabbed a handful of leaves and brought it to his face. The rich odor of moldering leaves and damp soil filled his nose.

The sensation of pain in his body was something he didn't usually experience in dreams. Now, he felt all the agony of lying on the ground. Sudden panic tightened his throat.

Where was he? He pushed himself to his knees, realizing as he did so that he was still wearing his bebionic arm. He always took it off and plugged it in at night. Had he forgotten? Marcus fought to remember. He was so confused. He looked around for his cane, but it was nowhere in sight. He was wearing the sleep shorts and the ketchup-stained t-shirt he had fallen asleep in.

With a groan of effort, he stood up, took a step, and promptly caught his foot under a root and fell heavily to one knee. Pain jolted up his back at the impact. Only the knowledge that getting back up would be nearly impossible stopped him from curling up in a ball and crying from the pain. He was finally able to see his bare foot bleeding where it had been scratched by the root. With a sigh, he braced against a tree and made it back to his feet.

He looked around. There were trees surrounding him and little else as far as he could see. As a kid who grew up in the city, he knew very little about the woods. Everywhere around him, trees soared toward the sky. Branches extended out everywhere, heavily laden with thick, shiny green leaves. The trunks were smooth with pale green bark covered in soft, patchy moss. He couldn't imagine where he was or how he had gotten there.

From some distant point in his memory, Marcus recalled his father telling him, "All trees that grow in the forest have one root that points to the north. Look for those, and you will find your way." For the first time, he wondered why his father—who was as much of a city dad as Marcus was a city kid—would have known such a thing.

Marcus looked at the ground around the trees near him. Sure enough, there was one thick root that came up out of the ground on the same side of each tree and pointed in the same direction. In fact, the root he had tripped over was one of these. He decided it couldn't hurt to follow them. It was somewhere to go, wasn't it?

As he made his way from tree to tree, fear clawed at Marcus's chest. He had no idea where he was. He didn't have his cane. He *did* have his prosthesis, which he'd gone to bed wearing. He had been exhausted, but now he felt as refreshed as if he'd had a full night's sleep. Marcus wondered if the presence of the prosthesis and his clothes, which he'd been wearing, and the absence of his cane, which he'd dropped as he stumbled into bed, meant something important.

Leaves crackled underfoot as he made his way through the trees. His footsteps released the sharp scent of the leaves into the air around him. He could almost smell the water that trickled audibly nearby.

Underfoot, the forest floor was slowly changing. The flat, leaf-covered soil where he had first awakened grew into a gradual incline, with small streams of trickling water, downed branches, and rocks. If his dad had been right about the roots, then the land must be rising toward the north. The rough terrain made it exceedingly difficult for Marcus to lift his feet and force his way uphill, and the pain in his back only grew worse. The surrounding area was now filled with patches of dark green brush and undergrowth.

He pulled himself from tree to tree, occasionally stopping to rest and take several slow breaths, hoping the pain would subside. As he rested, the crack of a snapping twig startled him. He paused as he heard something moving through the brush. Branches and leaves undulated wildly nearby. Fear turned his deep breaths into trembling gasps.

Marcus tried to ease himself carefully behind a broad-trunked tree to watch. He hoped it was just a small animal. Then, a large section of one bush moved away from the others. He gasped as he saw a small, person-shaped figure covered entirely with dark green leaves. Heart thumping wildly, Marcus carefully stepped away from the tree, staring. He was afraid to turn his back on the strange creature.

It abruptly stopped walking. Marcus froze.

The creature appeared to Marcus's eyes to be a walking version of the dogwood bushes in front of his house. Bright orange eyes stared at Marcus.

"Um... hello?" Marcus said, stepping further away from the tree. He immediately felt foolish, talking to a walking bush. It probably spoke leaf or something.

At the sound of his voice, the creature looked directly at him, blinked, and said, "Hello!"

Marcus stumbled in surprise and nearly fell over. "You… speak English?"

"I do not know what 'English' is," the leaf-covered creature replied. "I speak the language of Lysomnus. Why are you staring at me like that?"

"I've just never seen anything like you!"

"I am not a thing. I am a Scrybb! And my name is Cornus."

"A Scrybb? I've never heard of that before. It's just—I've never seen a bush walking around!"

"How dare you call me a bush!" The leaf-covered creature spun around indignantly and stormed away, audible sounds of annoyance floating back to his burning ears.

"Wait!" Marcus called after him. "Cornus? I'm sorry!"

The leafy boy stopped and lowered his head with an audible sigh.

He slowly turned and walked back up to Marcus's side. "You are clearly in need of assistance." Marcus looked down into the Scrybb's bright orange eyes. The top of Cornus's leaf-covered head came to Marcus's chest.

Cornus held out one stubby hand, comprised of twigs covered in more leaves. Marcus was reluctant to take it at first, fearing he'd be scratched, but he didn't want to offend the Scrybb again. He took the small leafy hand in his own. To his surprise, it didn't feel scratchy or sharp at all. The leaves that covered the boy's palm protected Marcus's from the twiggy framework beneath. Cornus carefully led Marcus up the incline. Marcus winced and held his breath in pain. He was glad Cornus was shorter and matched his own slow pace.

"What's your name?" Cornus asked.

"Marcus. Marcus Talent."

At this, Cornus looked up sharply.

"Talent, you say?"

"Yes, that's my last name," Marcus said, stepping carefully over a large rock that jutted from the forest floor.

"Do you know any others with the second name of Talent?"

"Of course I do. It's my dad's last name."

"Dad? What is a dad?" Cornus asked, the leaf-covered twigs that formed his lips curving downward in a confused frown.

"He's my father. My father's last name is Talent."

"Your 'father'?" Cornus sounded out the word. He tugged on Marcus's hand. "This 'father's' name would not happen to be *Deacon* Talent, would it?"

Marcus stopped walking, surprised. "How would you know that?"

Cornus peered up at Marcus through his leaves. "Deacon Talent is very well known here. He has been a visitor to our world for many years."

A shock ran through Marcus's body. "Cornus, can you tell me where I am? I just woke up here, and I'm so confused."

"This world is called Lysomnus, Marcus. I heard you arrive and came looking for you."

"This *world*? You *heard* me arrive? That doesn't make any sense. What do you mean?"

"Come on," Cornus said, taking Marcus's hand again. "We should keep moving. I will feel better once I find us in a familiar place. Then we can talk more." The Scrybb peered around, leaning as if to look beyond the trees that surrounded them. Marcus wondered if Cornus was unfamiliar with the area.

Together, they made their way up the hill, where the trees finally ended. Cornus stopped abruptly with an unhappy exclamation. Marcus released the Scrybb's hand to lean against a nearby tree, waiting for the pain to subside. Beyond the tree line where they stood, a rectangular field of dirt spread before them, strewn with small rocks and gravel as if carelessly tossed there by some giant hand.

"We must go back. I have brought you the wrong way," Cornus said. "It is not safe for a human to walk onto a Brynar."

"A Brynar? What's that?"

"This is a very dangerous place. You will be attacked out there." Cornus's voice was shaky, and his leaves rustled as he indicated the bare patch of ground.

"*Me*? Why?" Marcus was puzzled by his new friend's fear. The barren field before them was the last place that Marcus would have called dangerous—there wasn't even a breeze to blow the dust around. He stepped cautiously onto the rock-strewn dirt. Cornus tried to seize his hand again, but Marcus just pulled away and stepped out from the trees.

"No!" Cornus cried out, reaching out in an attempt to grab Marcus's hand one more time and pull him back, but it was too late.

A shrieking howl like nothing Marcus had ever heard tore through the air behind him. He whirled to go back to the safety of the trees, but the air between himself and Cornus was shimmering.

"What is that?" he yelled to Cornus as loudly as he could in order to be heard over the shrieking noise.

Cornus shook his head hopelessly. "It is the arrival of a

<<null>>," Cornus yelled back.

Marcus couldn't make sense of the word Cornus said. "What?" he yelled over the noise. "I can't hear you!"

Before Cornus could answer, the shimmering area twisted, tearing a black void in the world. Out of the void rolled a black *thing*, and then the black hole disappeared. There was a popping sound, and the howling abruptly stopped.

Cornus leapt in front of him, arms spread wide ."Marcus! Run!" he shouted. Marcus spun, but without his cane, he could barely manage to stay upright.

The thing that had rolled out of the void exploded into the most frightening creature Marcus could possibly have imagined. He stared at the amalgam of constantly shifting tentacles, glaring white eyes, and howling mouths. His mind was unable to make sense of what he was seeing. Some of the mouths had teeth, while others swam with drool. He watched one with razor-sharp edges spin past his face in terror.

Marcus couldn't move. His limbs felt as if they were immensely heavy, and a cold sensation of dread ran down his spine. He knew he was about to die, but he felt almost sleepy despite his brain screaming at him to run. The creature shoved Cornus to the side with one tentacle, lunging straight for Marcus. Despite the weight of his fear, Marcus shuddered as he sucked in a breath and forced himself to move. He managed to take a few steps. A sudden violent wrench spun him around. The creature had his prosthetic grasped in a thick tentacle and pulled it into a sharp-toothed mouth. Marcus shrieked in terror. The world around him disappeared, and everything went dark.

CHAPTER THREE

SECRETS AND DISAPPEARANCES

Marcus opened his eyes, quaking with fear. Had he screamed out loud?

He scrambled to a sitting position, surprised to be alive. His bebionic prosthetic was gone, and he was bleeding from ragged gashes on the end of his residual arm. Slime dripped from his skin onto his legs.

"It wasn't a dream," he said to himself out loud as he stared at the slime and blood. The shaking worsened, and his teeth began to chatter.

Deacon slipped into Marcus's room, closing the door quietly behind himself before turning the light on. "Oh, Marcus," he said, moving to his son's side and sitting down. "I'm sorry I wasn't here when you woke up. I suspected you might begin traveling tonight. What happened? You look terrified!"

"Dad!" Marcus lifted his bleeding residual arm, his entire body shaking. "I thought I was dreaming at first, but everything felt so real... and I was attacked!"

"Attacked?" Deacon frowned. "That shouldn't happen when you visit Lysomnus." A look of horror appeared on his face as he noticed Marcus's residual limb and the blood. "What happened to your arm?"

"Wait, you know about that strange place I went to?"

Marcus said, watching as his father wiped his arm with a grimace, inspecting the tears and cuts on his arm carefully.

"I should have just listened to Cornus. He warned me to stay out of the B-Brynar," Marcus struggled to get the words out as his body shuddered and his teeth continued to chatter.

"A Brynar!" Deacon exclaimed, looking at him sharply. "You went onto a Brynar? Tell me everything."

Marcus told him what had happened from the start of his experience in the other world to waking up back in his own bed. Deacon's face grew increasingly alarmed. "You were incredibly lucky. I didn't think it was possible for a human to survive a phantasm attack. How terrifying that during your first journey to Lysomnus, you wandered onto a Brynar." He sighed. "Marcus, I can explain where you went and why if you'll just be patient with me."

"What do you mean?""

"I knew you were going to travel tonight. And I'm sorry I didn't tell you it was going to happen, but I really couldn't."

"*You knew*? Why couldn't you tell me? And why did it happen?"

"That is a complicated story," Deacon said. He pulled a clear stone out of his pocket. It looked like ice, with a flicker of flame right in the center.

"This Halfriez, Marcus, is a very important item. It's very old. It has been handed down in our family for many generations. It's a talisman that helps us heal injuries. Let me show you."

Deacon held the Halfriez against Marcus's right arm, at the end of his residual limb. He closed his eyes. Marcus felt heat build in the stone and his own arm and watched with alarm and then wonder as the bleeding stopped and the ragged tears in his skin closed up and faded. Soon, they looked as old as his other scars.

"This is yours now," Deacon said as he placed the stone into Marcus's hand. "When you go back to Lysomnus, you will find the Halfriez very useful. It's one of only two Talismans that works both in this world and that one."

"*Back?* Why would I want to go back? I almost died!" Marcus exclaimed.

"It's a very complicated story, so it will be better to wait and let me tell you all at once."

"Does Mom know about this?"

A mixed expression of guilt and sadness crossed Deacon's face. "No, and you can't say anything to her or anyone else about it."

"What about my arm?"

"You'll have to use your body-powered backup for now. You can tell Mom the bebionic wouldn't charge when she asks and that I took it to work with me to drop it off for service."

"Okay."

"Now that you have been there, I can finally tell you about Lysomnus and the Talent bloodline. We have a special gift passed down from parent to child. We travel in our sleep to that world."

Marcus looked at his sodden t-shirt.

"Maybe too realistic," he said. "Seems like a dangerous place."

"It's not supposed to be like that, son. When we travel there, it's supposed to be wonderful—meeting the people and enjoying the food and all that world has to offer. While your body was physically gone from this bed, you should have had the opportunity to experience those things, not get attacked. What happens there will affect you here because your body physically travels." Deacon said, a serious look on his face. "That's why when you woke up, your prosthetic was gone."

"Oh no! Cornus!" Marcus cried out. "That thing probably killed him after I left!"

"Who's Cornus, son?" Deacon asked.

"He said he was a Scrybb. I met him in the woods where I first woke up."

"You found yourself in a much better place than I did on my first time in Lysomnus," Deacon said bitterly.

"So you know the Scrybb?"

"Yes, they are friends. How tall was Cornus?" Deacon asked.

"Pretty short. He came up to my chest." Marcus held his left hand against his chest at the level where the top of Cornus's head had reached.

"Your Cornus was a young Scrybb," Deacon explained. "Adult Scrybb are about your height." He looked puzzled for a moment, then snapped his fingers. "He must have been on his first Travels. That would explain why he didn't know there was a Brynar up that hill. I assure you, he is quite safe." He smiled, squeezing Marcus's shoulder. "Brynar—and the phantasms that appear there—are only dangerous to humans. The one that attacked you probably left right after you did." He rubbed at his eyes with his fingers, suddenly looking old to Marcus. "Cornus must have lost his way if he so easily stumbled across that Brynar without knowing it was there. An adult Scrybb would know better. Young Scrybb are sent out to Travel around their world when they come of age, and I suspect that your Cornus is on his first Travels and left the path."

"Dad, Cornus called the monster something I couldn't understand. It didn't even sound like a real word."

"It isn't a word we can understand. The creatures that threaten humans on the Brynar aren't there until they sense an opportunity to attack one of us. The people of that world call them something that refers to where they come from—a negative dimension between our planet and theirs. We can't seem to understand it, much less say it. I've always called them phantasms—that's what my father called them, as well."

"It looked like there was a hole in the world!" Marcus exclaimed. He remembered the howling he'd heard while that hole was open and shivered at the thought.

"That's exactly what it was, Marcus. The phantasms exist outside of either world, in another dimension. I believe they can only access Lysomnus through a Brynar. When humans are foolish enough to try to cross a Brynar, a phantasm slips out and attacks." The muscles in Deacon's face jumped as he clenched his jaw.

"Why don't they come and get us here in our world?" Marcus asked.

"The phantasms can only enter a world through a Brynar. There aren't any on Earth. And there aren't many in Lysomnus. I am shocked that you came across one on your first trip there."

"Lysomnus," Marcus murmured, testing the word. "That's what Cornus called it, too."

"We travel to Lysomnus for the first time right about your age, though we never know exactly when. There are signs that it will happen. Grandpa was waiting for me after my first trip there when I was about your age."

"He didn't tell you first?"

"Would you have believed me if I had told you about all of this before you went there? I know I wouldn't have believed my father. I almost didn't believe him even after he explained everything to me."

"I guess it would have been hard to believe—but then why didn't you just come with me? I would have been safer if you were there to help me, Dad!"

Deacon shook his head. "It doesn't work like that. Once you start traveling, I can't anymore. I tried to say as many goodbyes as I could during my last few trips because I knew you would be traveling soon, and I wouldn't be able to see my fa—my friends anymore."

The sadness on his father's face nearly brought Marcus to tears again. "I'm sorry, Dad. Did you have a lot of friends there?"

"Yes." Deacon covered his face with his hands and turned away from Marcus for a moment. He cleared his throat, and his voice sounded different as he began to speak again.

"I'm not really ready to talk about a lot of that yet," he said. "I can tell you a lot more about Lysomnus and how things work there, but I'd like to wait until tomorrow after I get home from work. Your mom will be working a twelve-hour shift at the hospital, and we'll have time to talk about everything. Don't mention anything about this to your mother or any of your friends at school, okay?" He held out his hand, upon which rested a bracelet of heavy silver links. "I have one more thing to give to you tonight. It's called a Stikke. When you wear it, it keeps you from going to Lysomnus. I think you should just sleep the rest of tonight and hang out with your friends tomorrow. I'll come home from work early, and we'll talk then."

Marcus reached out and took the Stikke. It linked together easily and fit comfortably on his wrist. "This fits *you*, Dad?" he asked, eyeing Deacon's large arm.

"It always fits whoever wears it. Regardless of who needs it, in our bloodline, it always fits." Deacon stood with his hands in his pants pockets and walked to the door. He turned and looked at his son. "Whatever happens, I'm glad you're a part of this now, Marcus. Since we lost Grandpa Malcolm's memory to Alzheimer's, I've felt alone, with no one to talk to about Lysomnus. We'll talk tomorrow. I need to get some sleep before work. For now, just get back to sleep too, son."

The light turned off. As Deacon opened the door, he turned his head and spoke in the dimness. "I'm happy for you and the start of your adventures." The door closed firmly behind him.

Marcus felt a chill at the sudden insincerity in his father's voice.

Marcus was sure he would never be able to sleep, thinking about Lysomnus and his new ability to travel to a different world—in such a short time, he had gone from feeling terrified to excited—but instead, he fell asleep almost as soon as his dad closed the bedroom door.

When he opened his eyes, Marcus had no idea what time it was. The sun shining through his bedroom window told him he had slept much later than usual. He struggled out of bed with real effort. His whole body still ached—more proof that his exertions during his short time in Lysomnus were very real. He seized his cane, gasping at a muscle spasm in his overtaxed back. With a sigh, he headed for the closet, where he kept the body-powered prosthesis he used as a backup when his bebionic arm wasn't charged or needed repair. He would need the limb sock that went beneath the prosthesis to protect his residual limb, as well.

Marcus was well aware of his privilege—his parents both made good money and could afford to purchase the most effective prosthetic equipment for him. Inconvenience wasn't something he was used to, even if the stigma of being disabled did cause him loneliness when he was ostracized by many of his classmates.

His body-powered prosthesis had a harness that fit across his shoulders, and a few well-practiced motions would open the hook that helped him grasp and manipulate objects. It wasn't nearly as useful or as convenient as the bebionic prosthetic, but it was definitely better than nothing —he had not adapted well to living without a prosthesis like some disabled people he had met.

As he held the prosthesis, Marcus looked with a feeling of wonder at his residual arm, for once glad he didn't have a physical arm. If the "phantasm" had torn away an actual arm, he would probably have bled to death. It was just sheer luck it had gotten the prosthetic instead. The Stikke on his wrist jangled slightly as he moved his left arm..

He slung clean clothes over his shoulder and walked across the hall to his bathroom. Today, he had the house to himself. His mom was working a twelve-hour shift at the hospital. His dad always worked weekends unless there was a special occasion. Sometimes, Marcus got the feeling that Deacon would rather not be home with his family.

As Marcus showered, all he could think about was Cornus. While his time spent with the Scrybb had been short, he had felt a bond with the friendly boy. Marcus wondered if he had just vanished in front of Cornus. The other boy must have been so frightened when that happened! Did he think Marcus was dead, consumed by the monster from another dimension? He hoped that he could find the young Scrybb again when he returned to Lysomnus. He also wanted to ask his dad if there was a way to control where he arrived when he went to Lysomnus; he didn't want to end up anywhere near a Brynar again.

Once he was ready for the day, Marcus made himself oatmeal. He ate quickly, thinking about all the questions he wanted to ask his dad. There was so much to learn about Lysomnus! What other kinds of people or creatures might live there? What kind of place was it—an entire planet like Earth, or something else?

After washing up his dishes, Marcus wandered into the hallway. He thought about taking a look toward Sadie's house to see if anyone was up over there. He looked forward to getting to know her better; she was the first person his own age who had been friendly ,even nice to him, other than Leopold. Marcus had to admit to himself he found Sadie attractive, but he was sure his disabilities were off-putting enough to keep her from reciprocating any interest. Still, though, he was sure they could become good friends. Finally, he decided to walk over and see if she was up.

When he opened the front door, Marcus nearly tripped over his cane at the sight of his dad's Buick in the driveway, gleaming bright green in the late summer sun. A dark form slumped in the front seat. With a sense of unease, he stepped outside and felt a wave of relief when he saw it was just a jacket.

Marcus carefully made his way down the steps and over to the car. When he opened the door, he saw Deacon's gray sport coat draped over the headrest of the driver's seat as if tossed hastily into the car. His father's briefcase leaned against the passenger door. It wasn't like his father to be so sloppy with his work attire. He closed the car door and leaned his forehead on the warm roof of the car. When he shuffled his feet, he heard a jangle of metal. Taking several steps back, he leaned carefully to the side and peered into the shadows under the car. His father's car keys were lying just beneath the car door.

Unease coiled in Marcus's belly. His father would never leave the important papers he kept in his briefcase in an unlocked car, and he would never leave his keys somewhere they could be found.

Panic made it hard to breathe. Marcus turned and started back toward the house. He needed to call his father's cell phone and see where he was. There had to be a rational explanation. "Hey, Dad?" he called as he reentered the house, then shook his head at his own lack of logic. He had been sitting here eating breakfast for several minutes; he would surely have heard Deacon if he were in the house. Unless... he laughed to himself as he finally realized where his dad must be. Sitting down at the kitchen table, he waited for his dad to finish up in the bathroom and come downstairs. He must have urgently needed to go and dropped his keys in his haste.

After waiting a few minutes, Marcus started to think he was wrong. Walking upstairs was painful for Marcus, but he had to see if his father was up there. Maybe something had happened to him. *What if he had a heart attack?* Marcus thought fearfully. He made his way up the stairs with difficulty and called out again.

"Dad?" He received no response.

His parents' bedroom stood empty, beds neatly made and the master bathroom spotless. The spare bedroom and bathroom were also empty. He made his way slowly back down the stairs, cold fear crawling up his spine.

He remembered he needed to call his dad's cell phone. He pulled his own phone out of his pocket and called his dad's number. He heard the muffled ring of his dad's cell through the front door he had left standing open. As he walked out, his dad's voicemail picked up, and the phone stopped ringing. Impatiently, Marcus hung up and called again. This time, the ringing led him to the car, where he realized it was coming from inside his dad's briefcase.

His fear turned to anger, and he had to stop himself from throwing his own phone to the ground in frustration. Instead, he returned to the house to get his grabber—a tool he used to retrieve objects from the floor he wasn't able to reach—and got the keys from under the car. He pulled the other items from the car, as well.

Marcus could not shake the feeling that this had something to do with Lysomnus. It couldn't be a coincidence that his dad went missing after the first day Marcus had traveled. He returned to the house, placing the briefcase on the bench and hanging his dad's keys up. Somehow, it made him feel better.

Marcus's next thought was his grandfather. Unfortunately, Malcolm wouldn't even know who Marcus was. The poor man didn't even recognize Deacon anymore. The last time they had all visited, his grandfather asked about someone named Berberis and cried when Deacon told him she wasn't there.

The sick feeling in Marcus's stomach just got worse and worse. He had to talk to *someone* about this and figure out what to do. Deacon had said Marcus's mom didn't know about Lysomnus, and Kate wouldn't even be home from work for hours. The only person other than his mom that Marcus felt he could trust with a secret this big was Leopold.

He tried his friend's cell first. Straight to voicemail. He would have to call the house and hope his friend was home. Marcus waited impatiently as the phone rang.

"Hello?" Leopold's mom answered. Marcus closed his eyes in relief.

"Hi, Mrs. Larson. Is Leopold home?" he swallowed as he tried to keep the shakiness out of his voice. "I really need to talk to him."

"Oh, hello, Marcus," Mrs. Larson said. "Leopold's out in the garage with his dad. He must have left his cell in his room. Hold on." Marcus waited while he listened to her footsteps, the rustling of the phone against her ear. Kirsty's voice piped in the background over the babble of cartoons. Marcus had to fight not to ask her to hurry up. Why could he still hear Leopold's sister talking? Their house wasn't *that* big. Finally, a door opened, and he heard Leopold's and his dad's voices echoing in the garage. Metal clanked on metal.

He could hear brief murmuring in the background as Mrs. Larson handed Leopold the phone.

"Hey, Marcus, what's up?"

"Leo, hey! I need your help," Marcus burst out. Leopold hated being called *Leo* and would instantly know something was wrong.

"Uh, dude, are you okay?"

"Can you come over right away? It's an emergency."

"Of course, bro—anytime. Just let me check with my parents." A few seconds later, Leopold said he'd be right over and hung up.

While he waited, Marcus wished he could pace the way other people did to get rid of nervous energy. Instead, he walked slowly out the back door and stood on the deck, staring at the tall wooden playset he had stopped using after the accident that had changed his life forever. The swings swayed back and forth, jangling the chains that held them up. Marcus shivered as he watched them.

A few minutes later, the doorbell rang. When Marcus opened the door, he was surprised to see Sadie smiling at him, with Leopold standing behind her.

"Uh, hi, Sadie. What are you doing here?" he asked, then mentally chastised himself for sounding rude.

"I thought I'd stop by and see if you wanted to hang for a while. When I saw Leopold riding up, I thought we could all get to know each other better."

The stocky blond boy rolled his eyes.

"Um, so, okay, well," Marcus babbled, trying to think of a good excuse, "Leopold and I were going to start working on this project together today. I—"

"Awesome!" Sadie grabbed Leopold's arm and led him into the house. "I'd love to be a part of it."

Leopold pulled his arm away from Sadie's and looked at Marcus. "Is your dad home already? Why is his car here? He was supposed to be at work all weekend. What's going on, dude?"

Marcus sighed. "Okay. You know what? I'm just going to tell you everything. You're probably going to think I'm insane, but I really need help, and I don't know what else to do. Just...come sit in the kitchen, and let's get this over with."

CHAPTER FOUR

A MESSAGE ARRIVES

Marcus sat down in one of the chairs, facing Leopold and Sadie. "Okay, I'm going to tell you what's happened, and it's going to sound kind of crazy. But I swear it's all true."

Leopold waited, a curious look on his face. He knew Marcus better than anyone—maybe even his parents did. Marcus could tell Leopold was waiting to see if there was something *really* wrong or if Marcus was just blowing something out of proportion. Sadie stood awkwardly, one arm across her body and holding her opposite elbow. She looked intrigued.

Marcus took a deep breath. "So, last night, something happened to me. It's supposed to be a family secret, but now, I don't know what to do."

A vertical line creased the skin between Sadie's eyebrows. She looked from Marcus to Leopold as if wondering if this was a private joke between them. Leopold's solemn expression made it clear he saw nothing funny about what his friend was saying. If anything, he looked concerned.

"Sorry. It's hard to explain, and you're both going to think I'm nuts." Marcus held his hand up as if to stave off a jumble of questions that weren't being asked. "I traveled to a different planet in my sleep last night, then I found out from my dad that it's a special ability that runs in my family, and now he's missing." Sadie laughed and then stopped abruptly, realizing Marcus was serious.

Leopold stared with his mouth open. "You're kidding me, right? C'mon, bro. I've known you your whole life, and you've never said anything about this. Are you feeling okay?"

"Dude, I swear. It just happened for the first time last night. Apparently, it doesn't happen until a certain age." Marcus held out his body-powered prosthetic. "When was the last time you saw me wearing this? I had to get it out because the other one... Well, it's kind of a long story."

"I mean, you using that arm is unusual, but it's not exactly proof that you *went to another planet*." Leopold pulled a chair out for Sadie and sat down on the one next to his friend. "Seriously, do you have any kind of real proof?"

"I *do* have proof," Marcus said. He walked back to his room and saw the Halfriez lying next to his laptop. He seized the talisman in his left hand.

"Here it is," he cried, curling his fingers around it and bringing it back to the kitchen. "This is called a Halfriez—I remember now." He held it up, showing the others the clear cube with the flickering flame caught in the center.

"Wow," the blond boy breathed, reaching for the beautiful talisman. "Oh, it's cold!" He passed it to Sadie, who gasped, running her fingers along the cube's crystalline sides.

"My dad said it can be used for healing—and it can. I got hurt while I was in that other world. This cube healed me."

Leopold was staring at the crystal cube in his hand. "Tell us more about this place where you went?"

"It's called Lysomnus. I don't know that much about it. My dad was supposed to tell me more about it today, so he was going to come home early. I only went there for the first time last night, and I had no idea it was even going to happen. He said he couldn't tell me anything about it until after I traveled for the first time, or I wouldn't believe him." Marcus briefly told the others about his adventures the night before.

"Yeah," Leopold said, letting out a shaky breath. "It's more than a little hard to believe."

"It would be hard to make something like that up, though," Sadie said.

"I wasn't even there very long, just enough to meet Cornus and then get attacked by this—this phantasm thing. Then I woke up here, and my dad told me a little about it and gave me these." Marcus indicated the Halfriez, then held up his left hand where the Stikke that had kept him from traveling the rest of the night before rattled on his wrist.

"What is that?" Leopold asked, grabbing his arm and admiring the heavy, shining silver links of the bracelet. "I can't believe I didn't even notice you wearing this bling, dude."

"It's a Stikke. A special bracelet that stops me from going to Lysomnus if I have it on. He wanted me to wear it so I would stay here on Earth until we had a chance to talk today. Now I don't know what to do or where he could be."

"You said you have proof that Halfriez thing can heal?" Sadie asked.

"Yes," Marcus said. He slipped off his shirt, avoiding Sadie's eyes. Then he removed the prosthesis and limb sock, showing them the new pink scars where the phantasm had torn his skin while pulling the bebionic prosthetic from his arm. "When it tore off my prosthesis last night, it did this. I had these injuries that were torn open and bleeding, but my dad used the Halfriez, and it healed me. Just like that." He snapped his fingers.

Sadie reached out and trailed her fingers lightly up the scars on his residual arm, sending shivers through his body. She bit her lower lip, closing her eyes and sighing as if the weight of his words bore down on her mind. "It's crazy, but... I believe you," she said.

Leopold lightly punched his friend on his other shoulder. "Let's be practical about this. Put your clothes back on so we can grab something to eat. We'll talk more about what to do in the kitchen."

Marcus wanted to act, not talk, but he knew there wasn't anything they could do until they had some ideas. He followed his friends down the hall to the kitchen and looked to see what was available for snacks. A bag of pizza rolls he found lurking in the freezer seemed to be the best option, so he pulled them out and threw them into the air fryer. While they waited, they munched on leftover Fritos from the cookout.

"So," Leopold began, grabbing a handful of corn chips, "You said you met a person in this other world?"

"Yeah, Cornus. He was this bush person I met. Although I think he'd be mad if he heard me calling him a bush person." Marcus smiled at the memory of Cornus's indignant response to being called a bush.

"Bush person? You mean like from the rainforest?" Leopold crunched Fritos with his mouth open, which drove Marcus bananas.

"No, not like that at all. He's a Scrybb. He's kind of like a person, but he has leaves covering him instead of skin. Um, and twigs, kind of?"

Leopold's eyes were wide as he sat and stared at Marcus. Frito crumbs sat on his tongue.

"You're pulling my leg now. He's made of leaves and twigs?"

"*That's* the part you don't believe? Really, Leopold? I mean, for Pete's sake. And close your mouth, it's gross." Marcus rolled his eyes and got up to get the pizza rolls, which had just finished cooking. While Marcus put the sizzling snacks on a plate, Leopold grabbed sodas out of the refrigerator.

"Hey, you got any ranch dressing in here?" he asked, bending down to get a better look inside.

"It's in the door. Probably bite you if it had teeth." Leopold gave him a dirty look as he grabbed the bottle.

Sadie grabbed the plate from Marcus and nodded for him to get the paper towels off the counter while Leopold scrounged for the dressing. She had passed on the Fritos but was happy to share in the pizza rolls.

Watching his friends move about, performing the ordinary tasks of preparing snacks, Marcus couldn't help but feel an overwhelming sense of relief. He had shared an incredible story with his friends, and they believed him. Now, they were ready to start figuring out how to help him find his dad.

The grease was still hot enough to burn their fingers as they impatiently tried to grab the snacks and eat them. Marcus bit one in half and dropped it out of his mouth onto a paper towel, sucking in air rapidly after the hot filling burned his tongue.

"Some ranch would help cool that down for you,"

Leopold advised.

"Nah, I don't really like ranch," Marcus said.

"You must be crazy—everyone likes ranch! And I've seen you eat it lots of times at my house."

"Just trying to be polite. It's the only kind of salad dressing you guys ever have."

Leopold rolled his eyes. "Y'know, you *can* say you don't like something. I've known you for eleven years! How have you never told me this? *Dude.*"

"I don't really like ranch either," Sadie said. "I'm more of a blue cheese fan."

"Me too!" Marcus said.

"Ugh, gross. Ranch is the best dressing. Everyone knows that." the blond boy said, rolling his eyes.

"*Anyway*, back to our topic, *Leopold.*"

"I wonder why they call them *condiments*," Leopold pondered. "Seems like *complements* would be a better name, don't you think? They complement what you eat, and you wouldn't really eat the stuff on their own."

Marcus glowered at Leopold.

"Okay, okay, I'm sorry." Leopold held his hands up in surrender. "So, if you can't talk to your dad, what about your other family? You said this was a family thing, right?"

"I thought of that too. You remember my grandfather has early-onset Alzheimer's, right? It's only been a few years since he was diagnosed, but it's pretty bad already. He doesn't even remember us anymore. My dad still goes to visit him, but he doesn't take me anymore."

Leopold looked glum as he took a pizza roll and drew circles in the ranch dressing on his plate with it. Finally, he popped it into his mouth and chewed thoughtfully. "We're basically flying blind here. I mean, you don't know anything other than that your dad isn't here in your house. He could have just gone for a walk, for all we know."

"But he'd never leave his briefcase in the car and the car unlocked," Marcus insisted. "And the keys were on the ground under the car. He'd never do that."

Leopold held up one ranch and pizza-sauce covered finger. "On an ordinary day. But today is not ordinary. For one thing, we know he was going to tell you about Lysolis or whatever it's called. And he either came home early or was still home, neither of which is normal for him on a Sunday.

So, what happened that caused him to leave his car unlocked and his briefcase inside? It seems like whatever it was must have happened while he was standing right by the car, probably with the door open. And it must have left him no time to react because he left his important things behind."

"Is it possible anyone else knows about Lysomnus? Someone who would want to stop your father from telling you more about it?" Sadie asked.

Now Marcus was really concerned. He hadn't really thought any of this through earlier; he had been worried about it in an abstract kind of way. Now that his friends had outlined the specifics of his concerns, he felt even more sick.

"Let's go out and look at the car again," Leopold said as Marcus's fear grew. "Just in case there's something you didn't see."

They hurried back outside to look at the car again. Marcus could see nothing that looked any different from before. Or from any other day when his dad parked it here.

"Any new or unusual marks on it?" Leopold asked.

Marcus walked around the car, looking carefully at the car's finish. It was only a year old, and his father had taken good care of it, so it was in pristine condition.

"It doesn't make sense," he said. "His jacket and briefcase were in the car like they were just tossed in there. His keys were on the ground like he dropped them. But the door was shut, and he's just...gone?"

"My parents said they heard a weird noise this morning," Sadie said. She pointed at the window closest to Marcus's driveway.

Marcus's mind was a whirl of emotions, thoughts, and confusion. He could hardly think straight, much less figure out what to do. Before he could reply, the same howl he had heard only once before, on the Brynar in Lysomnus, began to build right behind them. The air shimmered and twisted around them. Marcus grabbed Leopold and tugged him away from the noise.

"Sadie! We have to run!" He had no idea how a phantasm could be coming through *here* when his dad had insisted it was impossible, but he wasn't going to stand around and find out.

Sadie whirled and ran toward the house while Leopold stood staring slack-jawed at the shimmering air, oblivious to the deafening howl shrieking all around them. Marcus pulled on Leopold, desperate to get his friend to move. "*We have to move!*"

The shimmer spun open to reveal the same black hole in the world Marcus had seen in Lysomnus. He knew it was too late. The phantasm would come out and attack them, and they would be defenseless against it. Before the opening grew large enough for a phantasm to emerge, a long ivory object flew out of the hole, and then the whirling blackness vanished, leaving a silence so sudden it seemed loud. On the ground at their feet lay a rolled-up scroll, neatly tied with string. Marcus stared down at it, terror seeping out of his body, leaving him numb.

Sadie's parents came running out of the house and looked frantically around the neighborhood. Sadie's mom dashed over to the kids when she caught sight of them.

"Did you hear that terrible noise? It sounded like a tornado or something! But the sky is clear!" Yumi exclaimed. Sadie had returned to the driveway and stood next to Marcus.

"Yeah!" Leopold said convincingly, staring up into the sky as Sadie slid the scroll surreptitiously under the car with her foot. "We were just sitting around in the kitchen when we heard it and ran outside to look. But we didn't see anything. Crazy, huh?"

Travis looked into the sky, then up and down the street again. Other neighbors had also stepped out of their homes to look around.

"Guess there's no way to know what it was," Marcus said with a shrug. "Maybe some new supersonic military jet or something."

Yumi looked at Marcus doubtfully but nodded and walked back to her house. Travis glanced occasionally up at the sky as he waited for her.

"What the hell *was* that?" Leopold said, whirling on Marcus when the adults were finally out of sight. Sadie bent to retrieve the scroll from beneath Deacon's car.

"That is the same dimensional void that appeared when the phantasm attacked me when I walked out onto the Brynar. Except it isn't supposed to happen here!"

"I think you'd better tell us everything," Leopold said. "We're clearly missing a lot of details."

While they walked into the house, Marcus filled in the

few details his dad had given him before he'd gone back to sleep.

Leopold whistled. "That's terrifying, bro. What's on this scroll? Did you get a message from a phantasm?"

"Let's find out." Marcus took the scroll from Sadie's outstretched hand, pulled the string, and unrolled it. Rolled up, it had looked like some ancient paper, but once he unrolled it, it had a thicker, oilier feel. Marcus thought it must be some type of animal skin. There were only a few words marked across its surface:

IF YOU WANT HIM, COME AND FIND HIM

"What the hell?" Marcus dropped the scroll on the floor. Leopold bent and retrieved it gingerly, unrolled it, and read it again. Sadie stepped over to look too.

"'Come and find him'? Come where? Not that howling crazy place?" Her breath tickled Marcus's ear as she read it over his shoulder.

"I don't know. I can't go there, and that's where the phantasms are. If they had him, he would be dead. I can only hope he's somewhere in Lysomnus."

Leopold grabbed Marcus's arm. "Didn't you just tell me that he can't go there anymore? How is that possible?"

"I don't know. Maybe someone from there has him?" Marcus trembled with frustration and fear. "I don't know anything! He should have told me everything last night. Now I just... I don't know anything." He covered his face with his hand, pressing hard enough to see stars behind his closed eyelids.

"Okay, Marcus. Okay. I'm sorry. Hey, maybe your friend there, Cornus, maybe he can help you. Or his people." Leopold babbled, desperate to say something that might help.

"I've got to try to go back there," Marcus said, thinking out loud. "Yeah. I'll go there and find Cornus, maybe see what the Scrybb know. My dad said they could be trusted and were helpful."

"How will you get there? Can you fall asleep right now and just... go there?" Sadie asked.

Marcus had never felt less like sleeping in his life. He wasn't sure how he could make himself fall asleep so he could return to Lysomnus, and he didn't want to wait until tonight to go—who knew what could happen in the time it took to get there?

"I have to leave my mom a note," he said. She would wonder where his father was, too. He wished Deacon had told him something before this happened. "I don't know what to say, but she deserves something."

He went into the kitchen and grabbed a dry erase marker for the message board. He pondered what to say but finally just wrote: *Going to be gone with Dad for a while. Love you, Marcus.*

He went to his room. Leopold and Sadie followed him down the hall. Looking around, he couldn't think of anything that could help him sleep. He knew it was dangerous to take medication, and he was afraid if he did so, he might not wake up right away if there was danger nearby when he got to Lysomnus. He just didn't know how any of this worked. His muscles were thrumming along with the buzzing in his head from frustration, which made him feel even less like sleeping.

"Did your dad say that the Halfriez cube was just for healing?" Leopold asked. "Maybe it has some other magical properties—like one that can help you sleep."

Marcus thought back to the previous night. "He did say

that it was for healing, but he didn't tell me how to use it or anything. I'm not sure. It might be risky to use an item without knowing much about it."

"You have to try something. In stories, there are always talismans with many powers. Maybe try it, and if it doesn't feel right, then stop," Sadie suggested.

Marcus got as comfortable as possible, lying on his back on his bed. This time, he made sure he had his cane in his hand. He took the Halfriez from Leopold and lifted it toward his head. A clink on his wrist stopped him short. "Won't do me much good to fall asleep if I have this on," he said, holding up his wrist.

Leopold took the bracelet. "Good catch."

Marcus held the Halfriez against his forehead. He felt nothing. "I feel kind of stupid."

"Maybe try to move it around on your forehead and think about what you want it to do," Leopold said.

"Seems like you're the one who should have been blessed with this ability," Marcus said irritably. "I don't seem to be as adept at it as you would be."

"Just shut up and try it."

"Fine."

Sadie put her hand on his right arm. Her light touch made him feel tingly and yet relaxed, so he focused on that. He pressed the Halfriez to his forehead and moved it slowly back and forth. When it crossed his temple, he noticed a sudden change in temperature in the previously cold stone. He stopped moving it, and it continued to warm, producing a soothing sensation against his skin. Before long, he could hardly keep his hand there, and he felt Leopold take the Halfriez and gently move his hand down to his side.

Drifting in the murky sea of sleep, Marcus dimly heard

noises as if they were miles away: the clink of the Stikke he had given to Leopold, the call of birds outside his window, the howl of the phantasms' netherworld, and Sadie's voice calling him.

CHAPTER FIVE

RETURN TO LYSOMNUS

Marcus groaned and rolled onto his side, opening his eyes. Leopold lay nearby with his head on one arm. Marcus gasped in surprise when he saw his friend. Why was Leopold here?

He looked around quickly. They were both lying on sand-covered ground, and he could see the edge of the forest. The trees were shorter and closer together here. He rose to his knees with the aid of the cane he still held in his hand. "Dude," he said, poking his friend with the tip of his cane. "Hey, Leopold!"

"Unnh..." the boy's blue eyes were slow to open at first, but when he saw the strange world around them, he sat up quickly. "Holy shit!" he exclaimed, then clapped a dirt-stained hand over his mouth. He pointed. Marcus turned and looked. Sadie was lying on the ground just a few feet behind him. "Is this it? Lysomnus?" Leopold asked, eyes wide. Marcus nodded. "Why are *we* here?"

Marcus shrugged. "I thought maybe you'd tell me."

"Bro, I have no idea. I was watching you fall asleep, and OH MY GOD—" Leopold put his hand back over his wide-open mouth.

Marcus couldn't help himself and dissolved into laughter at his friend's discomfiture.

"Dude, I was *holding your hand*," Leopold whispered. "I took the Halfriez, and I hadn't let go because you squeezed my hand. Sadie still had her hand on your arm."

"Oh—*oh*. Huh. Guess that might have been one of the things my dad would have told me about? But then wouldn't my mom have...OH! My parents sleep in separate beds. Same room but separate beds. My dad always said it was because he has restless leg syndrome. But it must be to keep him from taking—well, bringing—her with him to Lysomnus. So, that's why he said she couldn't know about traveling at all." Marcus sighed. "Just another one of the things I expect my dad would have told me about today."

Leopold frowned, digging into his pants pocket.

"Something is poking me!" he cried out, then pulled the Halfriez and the Stikke from his pocket.

"How could you have gotten the Stikke through when it's supposed to make me stay on Earth?" Marcus was thoroughly confused, but he took the items as Leopold held them out.

"Maybe it only does that when you actually *wear* it? And maybe you can bring it through so it can make you stay on this side?"

"Huh, I never thought of that. I don't even know how I went back home last time; I just woke up there when I got hurt. If I'm going to find my dad, I'm going to want to stay here without returning unexpectedly." He held it out so his friend could clasp it back onto his arm.

"Yeah, and don't be doing that without your good friends Leopold and Sadie, okay? I'd rather not be trapped here."

"Let's wake Sadie up and start looking for Cornus. We've gotta get into those trees and find the Scrybb." He could hear the sound of waves breaking onto the shore not far behind them, and the scent of salt filled the damp air.

Sadie was disoriented when the boys shook her awake. She looked around wide-eyed and clapped her hands over her mouth with a small cry when she realized she had traveled with Marcus to Lysomnus. She chewed at her thumbnail nervously as they made their way toward the treeline.

The terrain was uneven and rocky, with huge boulders that stood high above the sand. Occasionally, it gave way to wide gaps where Marcus would get bogged down with his cane. The monotonous crashing of the waves on the shore behind them slowly diminished as they made their way toward the tall trees in the distance. The sky was overcast, with grim, dark gray clouds looming oppressively low in the sky. The wind blew steadily, tossing sand in their faces that kept them blinking tears away. It was cool enough that Marcus wished he had a sweatshirt. The smell of salt was everywhere.

"What a lovely world you've found for us to explore," Leopold cracked, but his ordinarily sharp wit was dulled by the oppressive surroundings and the fear they all felt.

"Hey, at least we have our shoes on," Marcus said. "Those big rocks would be hell to walk across barefoot like I was last time." In his head, Marcus couldn't help but think of how painful it was going to be for him to walk across them at all. He needed help each time they came to another wide cluster of boulders to climb up and make his way across. The uneven piles of rocks were wide enough it was impossible to stay at ground level and walk around them.

"How do you know we're even heading the right way?" Sadie asked.

"Well," Marcus tried to keep his annoyance in check,

frustrated by his friends' complaints, "That way is nothing but ocean," he pointed back the way they'd come. "We need to get to the woods so we can find the Scrybb. I found Cornus in the woods the first time I came here, and I'd like to find him again. My dad said the Scrybb are good people."

As they approached the forest, Marcus was relieved to find that there was less sand and gravel to pull him down. There were only a few of the large boulders to climb across. The chilly, salty breeze blew Leopold's already messy hair around in swirls that Sadie laughed at. All three of them brushed sand from their hands constantly, even while it slipped into every crevice of their clothing.

It was when they were climbing across the last rock pile that Leopold slipped. His foot plunged between two big boulders. His body swung forward with the force of his own momentum. He reached out desperately for anything to hold onto.

A crack of breaking bone was accompanied by Leopold's agonized scream.

"Leopold!" Marcus yelled, reaching for his friend from behind the gap. The stocky blond boy had managed to catch himself and was braced on his hands against the two boulders. His face was waxy and pale. Tears trickled uncontrollably down his cheeks. Sadie knelt and looked down into the crevice, then shook her head at Marcus with a sick look of dread on her face.

"Marcus, I'm stuck! I think my leg is broken."

Marcus lay down and peered down, trying to see in the waning daylight. He could just see Leopold's leg. His pants were ripped, and the jagged edges of white bone tore through his skin. Dark blood covered his shoe and painted the rocks red.

Marcus patted his pocket.

"The Halfriez!" he exclaimed. "But I don't know if it will work while your leg is broken like that. I think we have to try to pull you out, Leopold." Marcus looked up. "It's going to hurt because we have to pull and the bone is broken."

"Okay," Leopold whispered. "Do what you have to."

Marcus climbed back up, and he and Sadie slid their arms under Leopold's, pulling up firmly and carefully. Marcus gasped as pain lanced up his back but ignored it as best he could. Helping his friend was more important right now. As they pulled, Leopold cried out. Marcus tried to see if the leg was moving at all.

"I don't think we're able to lift him out by ourselves, Marcus," Sadie said, a desperate look on her face.

He tried to pull one more time as hard as he could. Leopold's body slipped to one side and he screamed so loudly Marcus's ears rang. Leopold wrenched his arms away from them.

"Stop! Stop! I can't take it." Sobs tore from Leopold's throat as he buried his face in his bent arm.

"This isn't working," Marcus said. He clenched his teeth in frustration. It was tearing him apart, listening to his best friend cry in pain. "I'm just going to climb down there and heal it through the rocks. There's no way I'm leaving you in this much pain, bro."

Marcus was still on his knees. He began to turn carefully so he could ease himself down to the ground. With a *clink!* the Halfriez slipped from his hand and vanished into the darkness.

Sadie cried out, leaning so far to try to catch the healing stone she nearly fell into the crack headfirst. Marcus reached out desperately to try to catch her, but she caught herself, pulling back into a sitting position with tears standing in her eyes.

Marcus slowly made his way down to the ground. He peered between the rocks but could see nothing save for a glimpse of Leopold's bleeding foot. With his left hand, he groped around, careful not to bump his injured friend, but could not feel the cube. Shouldn't the crystal be shining in the darkness or something? There was nothing to see. Marcus felt sick at losing their only hope of helping Leopold.

He leaned against the boulder and stared out toward the ocean. The clouds had begun to break up, and a warped reflection of the setting sun was visible on the turbulent water. Alarmed by the idea of being stuck here in the dark, he couldn't imagine what this was like for Leopold. The badly injured boy was shaking violently, teeth chattering. He didn't answer when Marcus asked him how he felt. Sadie came down and helped Marcus back up. Together, they tried to lay close to Leopold to keep him warm.

Filled with dread, Marcus and Sadie watched the skies darken. Leopold stopped responding to their questions. Guilt overwhelmed him because he had brought Leopold to this alien world. Marcus couldn't live with the idea that Leopold might die here. If only he knew where to find the Scrybb, he could head toward the trees by himself to try and find them.

Cold fingers of fear squeezed Marcus's chest as he heard a noise in the trees. It sounded like a crowd of people was walking toward them. The hiss of the sibilants came to his ears first, then louder chatter followed. He exchanged an apprehensive glance with Sadie and carefully slid to the ground in front of the boulders, facing the woods.

A second later, Sadie landed beside Marcus with a

thump. Marcus reached out with his hand, and she took it, squeezing tightly with her cold fingers. There was movement among the trees. In the dwindling light, he wasn't quite sure what he was seeing. Dim figures approached across the sand. He had no weapons except the rocks strewn around him on the sand, so if these were hostile people, he and his friends were defenseless.

As the figures grew closer, orange eyes glowed at different heights. Squinting in the waning light, Marcus recognized a familiar voice. "Cornus?"

"Marcus!" called the voice of the young Scrybb.

Relief flooded his aching body, his knees going weak. Cornus would know some way to help, he was sure. "I'm so glad to see you safe. I'm sorry I left you alone yesterday."

"Marcus, I am relieved to see *you* are safe. I thought the <<null>> had mortally wounded you. But I heard you arrive today and came to investigate."

"My friend really needs your help, if you can do anything." Marcus stepped back and pointed to the top of the rocks.

The young Scrybb seemed confused. "Your friend? You brought someone with you?"

"I have two friends with me today," Marcus explained. "One of them is badly hurt and needs help. I don't know what to do."

Cornus came to his side and saw Leopold trapped in the rocks. "Oh, a bad break. Your friend is in trouble." Cornus returned to the shadowy group and held a quick muttered conference, followed by rustling and footsteps all around him.

"What's going on?" Leopold said weakly.

Marcus sighed with relief to hear his friend's voice

speaking clearly for the first time in hours. "Cornus and the Scrybb are here to help, Leopold, so please try to hold on."

From behind the rocks where Leopold had fallen came the sound of rustling and crackling like branches in a high wind. It was difficult in the darkness, but in the orange glow of the Scrybbs' eyes, he could see vines extend from the arms of the Scrybb who surrounded the rocks, reaching over the boulders to twine around Leopold's body and legs. Sadie, who had come to stand beside Marcus, reached out to take his hand again. He tucked his cane under his right arm and squeezed her hand gratefully.

"Tell your friend this will hurt a great deal," Cornus told Marcus.

"Yeah, I heard," Leopold said hoarsely. "Just please get me out of here."

Cornus stood by the base of the rocks where Leopold was stuck, and as the vines wrapped around his body pulled him up, another Scrybb who had extended vines from his hands around Leopold's foot and broken leg pulled them out of the crevice where it was stuck. Leopold screamed once and was silent.

"Leopold!" yelled Marcus. "What happened?"

"He was given a strong drink for the pain first, and now he has lost consciousness," Cornus said. "He can rest now while Healers look at his leg."

Marcus was relieved to see his friend free of the rocks he had been trapped in for so long. He felt weak. "How can his leg be fixed?" he asked Cornus.

The young Scrybb looked at him sidelong. "Do you not have the Halfriez your father carried? He should have passed it on to you."

Tears filled Marcus's eyes.

"I tried, Cornus. But we couldn't get him out, and then when I was going to just try to heal him anyway, I dropped it. It's gone."

"Your friend could not be healed until he was out of the rocks and his leg cleaned and straightened. If you had healed him while he was still in the rocks, it might have been necessary to break the bone again as it would have been poorly knit together."

One of the other Scrybb approached. "He is ready for healing now." He held out the Halfriez. "This was near the rocks."

Marcus sighed in relief, took the Halfriez, and lowered himself to his knees next to Leopold. The Scrybb had removed the bloody shoe from Leopold's foot, cut the material of his jeans and pulled it back, and cleaned the blood, dirt, and sand from the swollen, reddened area where Leopold's shattered bone had ripped through his skin when it broke. Blood still soaked the fabric of his friend's torn jeans. It made Marcus feel sick to look at the tortured skin around the sharp ends of the bone.

The Halfriez felt cold in Marcus's shaking fingers. He placed it against Leopold's leg, hoping that it would work, though he had no idea how to use it. He closed his eyes and focused on healing his friend.

The Scrybb standing around him straightened the break, pulling the bone back into place. Now the Halfriez began to warm, and Marcus felt the leg straighten further. He opened his eyes to see the skin knitting itself back together, leaving deep purple dimples where the worst of the injury had been. The Halfriez got much hotter than it had when he used it to sleep, the light of the flame inside the cube flaring out enough to light the entire area around them.

"It's hot, Cornus!" Marcus exclaimed, worried.

"I do not know much about it," Cornus replied. "I expect the energy to heal must relate to the damage done."

That made sense. The light was dimming now, and Marcus could see that even the purple scars were filling in.

Cornus's and the other Scrybbs' orange eyes were glowing more brightly now that the sun's light was completely gone. The rest of the rocky beach had vanished back into the darkness, but Marcus could still hear the waves crashing onto the shore. It was eerie, seeing the orange eyes of the Scrybb float at different heights in the darkness. "Cornus, what do we do now? We don't have anywhere to stay or any supplies. It will be really difficult for me to walk very far and painful for me to sleep on the ground."

"Be calm, my friend. We will take you back to our bruwe, Thicce Colpat. There, we can feed you, and you will rest. I will walk slowly with you and help you find the safest route." Cornus attempted to take Marcus's hand as he had done when they first met in the forest.

"I'm sorry, Cornus, I'll need you to take hold of my prosthesis—my other arm—to lead me. I need my left hand to walk with my cane."

Cornus looked with surprise at Marcus's prosthetic arm and the hook on the end of it. "But you had a hand the last time you were here! Did the <<null>> take it?"

"Well, it did take my hand, but that was not a real hand either. I lost my right arm in an accident several years ago." Cornus looked at Marcus oddly but reached out and took the prosthesis in his hand. They fell in behind the rest of the Scrybb; Marcus could hear the rustle of their leaves just ahead. Sadie was walking beside one of the Scrybb adults, talking quietly.

"Leopold is sleeping now," Cornus said. "Some of the other Scrybb are carrying him."

"Thank you. I can't tell you how much this means. You saved us."

"I am happy to be able to help you. I was relieved to see that you were alive and had returned."

Marcus had the disadvantage of being unable to see in the darkness and was dependent on the Scrybb boy's guidance. "Cornus, I can't see anything. Don't you have any way for us to see the way there? Light a torch or something?" A collective gasp rose from the Scrybb ahead of them at Marcus's words.

Cornus stopped walking, and his orange eyes widened. "Light a torch? Fire? Marcus, fire is deadly to my people!"

"Oh! Oh, I'm sorry, I didn't think. I'm stupid. Of course you wouldn't use fire!" Marcus could feel his face burning in the darkness. He was sure Cornus could see his embarrassment despite the lack of illumination.

"We do not need to carry light, Marcus. We can see as well in the night as we can in the day—we just see differently. I know humans cannot see the light we see at night."

"Different light? What's it look like?"

"The color is gone, but we can see clearly."

"Oh, I'll bet it's infrared! We learned about that in school." Marcus said. "With infrared light you can see in the dark. I've seen that on reality shows, where they film what people are doing at night. You Scrybb must be able to see the infrared spectrum at night."

Cornus retrieved Marcus's prosthesis and tugged to start him walking again. "I have no idea what you are talking about, but we are falling behind."

As they walked further toward the forest, Marcus tripped over a jutting rock, although Cornus had been leading him around the worst of them. He fell, and his shin struck the sharp edge hard enough to draw blood. His back burned with agony from the jolt. "Damn it!" He held his hand to the tear in his pants as blood trickled into his shoe.

"I apologize, Marcus. It is my fault." Cornus's orange eyes dimmed with anxiety as he looked at Marcus's leg. "It is not deep, just a small cut. The Halfriez will make short work of it."

Marcus pulled the Halfriez out and quickly healed his leg, wishing the stone could clean up blood as easily as it closed flesh. The tacky feeling of cooling blood in his shoe was unpleasant. The pain in his back had subsided with the use of the Halfriez as well. "It's okay, Cornus."

"I assure you, we are close to the path. You will be much happier when we arrive in Thicce Colpat." Cornus was obviously excited at the prospect. His leaves rustled as if the young Scrybb were experiencing strong emotion.

"Bruwe?" Marcus asked, carefully standing up. "What is a bruwe?"

"Didn't your father tell you anything about Lysomnus?" Cornus sounded irritated. "It's where we live, our home."

Marcus soon felt the sensation of being closed in, and the ground beneath his feet felt much easier to walk on.

"Cornus? What changed?" He asked.

"We have entered the Grenewud. The Scrybb care for the great forest of Lysomnus. You are now walking on a path that is maintained and kept clear for travelers by Scrybb. It will be much easier for you to walk now."

The rich scent of moldering leaves filled his nose again as they walked, reminding him of the loamy smell that he had first noticed when he woke up on the ground when first arriving in Lysomnus. The comfort of the familiar scent, reminiscent of those fallen green leaves, gradually overrode the smell of salt. While he still could not see, he could almost sense the trees arching overhead as he and Cornus walked. They were moving a little faster now that there were no obstacles underfoot for him to trip over.

"Hey, the first time we met, everything was different. There were bushes and roots and small springs to watch out for. Why isn't there any of that here?"

"Because we are on the path to our bruwe, Thicce Colpat." A note of embarrassment had crept into Cornus's voice. "I was lost when I found you because I left the path."

"I'm glad you did."

"If you could see, you would notice the archway the trees of the Grenewud are creating overhead and flowers that grow beside the path to mark the way."

"Aren't you afraid of being attacked?" Marcus asked.

"Attacked? By whom? And why?"

"Well, I...I'm not sure. I guess I thought...maybe if you had an enemy or something?"

"Enemy! Why? No one has any reason to be an enemy of the Scrybb." Cornus sounded aghast at the idea.

"Well, the first time I came here, we were both attacked and injured. I meant to ask before if you were all right," Marcus said.

"I am fine. A Scrybb has nothing to fear on a Brynar. Once you were gone, the <<null>> left immediately." Then Cornus looked up at him. "We were not both attacked that day. *You* foolishly went into the Brynar and were attacked. I tried to stop you. The <<null>> are not a danger to the Scrybb, Marcus. Only to humans."

They started walking again. Marcus was about to ask another question when he realized that he could see light ahead. "What is that?"

"We might be able to see at night without light, but that does not mean we do not have any other source of light," Cornus chuckled.

"What do you use?" Marcus asked.

"We do not *use* anything," Cornus responded a bit frostily. "It is the Vosfyren. When a Scrybb has reached the end of our life cycle, it is an honor to host the life cycle of the Vosfyren. They live on the Scrybb who have passed on, and there is light in the darkness."

As this conversation had continued, Marcus and Cornus approached what must be Thicce Colpat. A blue-green glow had brightened until Marcus could see quite clearly.

The forest path ended, and they entered a bustling area where many Scrybb hurried around. Marcus saw what appeared to him to be rows of stationary Scrybb. He shook Cornus's arm to get his attention. "Do Scrybb sleep outside? Are those sleeping Scrybb?" He indicated the stationary bushes.

Cornus snorted and pulled his hand away.

"You really are the most insulting human. Those are not Scrybb! Those are bushes and plants! We do not stand around in rows. Is this not sufficient light for you to see anything yet?"

Cornus walked away angrily. Marcus wished he had just kept his big mouth shut; every time he opened it, he seemed to put both feet in.

THICCE COLPAT

Marcus stood awkwardly at the end of the path, taking in the Scrybb domain. The path where they had just entered Thicce Colpat ended abruptly, and the tree line extended in both directions and surrounded the bruwe. Marcus had expected to see some kind of rustic village, but this 'bruwe' was nothing like that.

To the right, rows of bushes continued as far as Marcus was able to make out in the dim blue-green light. The light itself, Marcus saw, came from individual, free-standing Scrybb completely barren of leaves standing at intervals along the edge of the trees, and he could also see them at various places farther into Thicce Colpat. Pebbled pathways meandered through the bruwe. Buildings made of stone stood ahead and to the left—large ones to the outside, smaller to the inside—leaving a wide communal area in the center. Those with a second story had walls of sturdy wood logs. The air was now filled with the sharp green scent of growing plants and flowers.

He took a closer look at the glowing Scrybb nearest to him. It stood about his height, though the eyes were closed. Most of the leaves were gone, and the blue-green glow emanated from thick lichen growing along the vines that made up the creature's body. Without its leaves, Marcus could see that the Scrybb were similar to humans. Thick vines formed limbs that wound into the torso, leading up to the head. Features like fingers, ears, and lips were formed from curving twigs and sticks. As he stepped behind the creature, he saw something interesting: a small indent resembling a navel centered in the lower back. While he was examining it, he heard a high-pitched humming, and the lichen glowed brighter in front of him.

"Child, please come out of there." A stern voice said from in front of the lichen-covered Scrybb.

Marcus jumped. He stepped around from behind the dead Scrybb to see an adult Scrybb woman glaring at him.

"Um—I'm Marcus," he gulped. "I'm sorry. I came here with Cornus?"

"I am aware of who you are. It is not appropriate to interfere with the dead. Where is Cornus?"

"I'm afraid I upset him," Marcus said, embarrassed.

"Mmm." She frowned. "I am Cassiope, one of the Teachers here. You should come with me until Cornus can be located."

"Yes, ma'am," he said. She stalked away, clearly expecting him to follow. Cassiope was as tall as he, but instead of leaves like Cornus, she was covered in spiny needles that draped along her body. White bell-shaped flowers cascaded down the back of her head like hair. Cassiope led him away from the rows of bushes along pebbled pathways lit by glowing Scrybb and approached a tall building made of stone and wood.

"Do you know where Leopold is, ma'am? Or Sadie?" Marcus asked. "We fell behind, and I didn't see where they went by the time I got here."

"Your injured friend is resting; the girl is getting some

refreshments. Are you hungry?"

"Um—yes, actually," Marcus stammered, suddenly realizing he was starving. It had been hours since the snacks they had eaten in his kitchen earlier that day.

"You must eat," Cassiope said emphatically, turning and marching toward a large building. "Then you will sleep." She was very stern, making Marcus as anxious as if he were reprimanded by a teacher in school back home.

Inside the building, Marcus saw rows of wood tables. Vosfyren, glowing from the limbs of dead Scrybb, relieved the darkness here as well, and he was glad for their light. Scrybb were seated randomly at several of the tables. Cassiope led Marcus to a long table where he found smooth wooden plates and bowls, and metal utensils. Delicious odors wafted up from several large pots and serving dishes.

"Help yourself, and then I will see to your rest."

"Thank you," Marcus tucked his cane under his right arm, took a plate, and stacked a bowl on it along with utensils. He tripped as he attempted to serve himself. When Cassiope saw him struggling, she held his dishes for him.

He was surprised to find meat on the table. There was a rich-smelling stew and pieces of something that looked like chicken. He found warm bread, several varieties of roasted vegetables, and fresh fruit. Marcus spooned some of the stew into the bowl Cassiope held, put several vegetables along with the meat on the plate, and a large piece of soft fruit with smooth, purple skin. The rich, hearty smell of the food was making it hard to keep from drooling. When he turned and scanned the room, he saw Sadie waving from a table nearby and made his way over to her. Cassiope placed his dishes in front of him as he sat down.

The stew was delicious. It had a thick gravy with a spicy

kick and soft, sweet vegetables that offset the spice. Chunks of meat filled his mouth with every spoonful. He couldn't identify the meat—it had a gamey, more intense flavor than beef—but it tasted wonderful, and the roasted variety was so tender it fell apart in his mouth. He sopped up the rich brown gravy with the soft bread and took another bite, savoring the flavors of a roasted spicy green and orange striated vegetable.

"Isn't this food amazing, Marcus?" Sadie asked as he swallowed. She was licking gravy from the back of her spoon with relish. Despite her delight in the food, he could see dark circles beneath Sadie's eyes. It was clear the strain of the day had exhausted her. Still, he tried to muster his enthusiasm at the delicious food to bolster her mood.

"It's wonderful!" he replied. "I feel kind of guilty eating without Leopold."

"I know," Sadie said. "I was wondering where you were, too, until I saw you come in with that Scrybb woman. The man who brought me here just told me to come in and get some food and left. I think he's some sort of leader. He was very brusque with me and wouldn't answer any of my questions." She spooned up another bite of stew.

Marcus was chewing a mouthful of food when someone sat down beside him and plunked a wooden mug next to his plate. Liquid sloshed over the side. "You look like you could use a drink," said a deep voice. A large Scrybb man loomed over him. The man had heart-shaped leaves and orange flowers that grew in square patterns on his head and in intricate patterns on his body.

"Hello," Marcus said, swallowing quickly.

"I am Abutilon." said the newcomer, gesturing at the stein. "Have a drink, child."

"What is it?" Marcus asked, tentatively picking it up and smelling it. A sweet, fruity aroma filled his nose. An unfamiliar scent, but one that immediately made him thirsty. He was unable to see the contents in the dimly lit room.

Abutilon blinked. "It is only fruit juice. You are not a very trusting person, are you?"

"I'm sorry." Marcus tipped the stein to his lips. The sweet taste of the juice filled his mouth. "Oh, it's good!"

"Of course it is. Scrybb made it!" Abutilon laughed. He patted Marcus on the back. "Finish up, young one. There is enough to share with your friend." He winked at Sadie, then stood and walked toward another table, calling, "Buddleja! Come outside with me, my love."

A delicate Scrybb woman rose and took Abutilon's hand. She had long, thin leaves and purple clusters of flowers concentrated about her head, with several in particular places on her head and body as if she wore jewelry.

Marcus shared the juice with Sadie and was laying his utensils on his empty plate when Cassiope reappeared. "Come, children. Leave your dishes. We have a place ready for you to rest, and I have located Cornus. He has been chastised for abandoning you."

"Oh, no," Marcus said guiltily. He hadn't meant to get the young Scrybb in trouble. "It was my fault. I kept saying offensive things."

"No, Cornus has been thoroughly schooled in etiquette. It is a requirement for all Scrybb prior to leaving on Travels. Regardless, we must get you to rest. You are both to sleep yourselves out; you have been through much this day." Exhausted from their exertions and with his belly full, Marcus didn't even look around while they walked; he just blindly followed Cassiope.

Marcus felt as if he would pass out at any second; exhaustion pulled at every part of his aching body. Every step was agony. He had thought that it would be a simple matter to come back to Lysomnus and find his father. Now he realized that Lysomnus, while its people seemed welcoming enough, could still be a hazardous place. He wanted to ask Cassiope about his dad, but since she had been so stern with him and had punished Cornus, he was afraid to say anything.

Cassiope stopped Marcus with a hand on his shoulder. "Young man, please get some sleep. You are safe in Thicce Colpat." She indicated a soft-looking bed with a thick quilt pulled back invitingly. Next to it, he saw Leopold asleep in another bed. Sadie was crawling into a bed on his right.

"Thank you, Cassiope," Marcus said, trying to swallow around a lump in his throat. He tried to blink away the tears, but they spilled over and ran down his cheeks. Sitting down and kicking off his shoes, he crawled under the quilt. The bed was as soft as it had looked. Cassiope pulled the quilt over Marcus's shoulders and walked out. Marcus couldn't help but think of his mother, who was probably worried about him, not knowing where he was or why he was gone. He wondered anxiously who might have his father and if he was safe.

Marcus looked over at Leopold, who was sleeping soundly. One hand was dangling from beneath the quilt. Marcus reached out and grabbed it, gripping tightly as sleep overtook him.

When he awoke, bright light spilled into the room through the windows. He had never been so happy to see daylight. He looked at the other beds, but they were empty, quilts thrown back haphazardly. He sat up and looked around. There were more beds in the room, but the others were all neatly made. He looked for his shoes, but they were nowhere to be found. He grimaced at the sight of his bloody sock, now dry and stiff. Using his toes, he peeled the filthy thing off, then did the same with his other sock.

"Leopold? Sadie?" he called. "Hello?" No one answered. When he stood, he felt light-headed. He reached out and seized his cane, which was leaning against the wall. "Hello? Is anyone here?" he called again. No answer. Every part of his body cried out in pain as he made his way to the door of the bedroom. He groaned when he saw he was at the top of a flight of stairs. He didn't remember climbing stairs on his way to bed.

Step by step, leaning his back against the wall, he carefully made his way down the stairs. When he was finally down, he closed his eyes in relief and rested before opening the door.

He stepped out onto a porch, where Leopold was waiting in a chair. "Well, it's about time, sleepyhead," the blond boy said, his hair in its usual state of disarray.

"How long have you guys been up?"

"Marcus, you must have been really tired. You slept for nearly two days," Leopold said..

Marcus looked carefully at his face to see if he was joking. The amusement on his friend's face was disconcerting. "I really slept for that long?"

"Yep. Yesterday, last night, and part of today, too. It's past lunchtime already!"

"Where's Sadie?"

"Over in the gardens, I think, with another Scrybb,

a Grower by the name of Malberis. That is one Scrybb who is *very* interested in meeting you, actually. I guess her family line is linked to yours somehow? Anyway, I told them I'd come get them as soon as you woke up. Oh, and I'm taking you to the baths. Good thing, too, because brother, *you stink.*" Leopold dissolved into gales of laughter.

"Ha, ha," Marcus said sourly. "Wait—the Scrybb have bathing facilities for humans? That seems odd. People with leaves need a bath?"

"Right, that's what I said! It turns out this bruwe has this bunkhouse here and also bathing facilities for human visitors. Who those visitors might be, I don't know. The Scrybb are *very* reluctant to talk about it for some reason. But let's get you cleaned up, man! There are human *clothes* over there, too."

Leopold led Marcus along gray-pebbled paths that wound through small buildings. The small, smooth pebbles felt cool under Marcus's bare feet. They passed many different varieties of plants and flowering trees. They looked unfamiliar to him, but the heady fragrance of every flower filled his nose as he slowly followed his friend. While his pain was as present as it was every day of his life, it was wonderful to breathe the air of this world. He had never noticed just how bad Earth smelled before, and he enjoyed the sweet perfume of the clear air.

"So, will my clothes look like that?" he asked, eyeing Leopold's new garments. "You look like a character from medieval times, or something." Leopold wore close-fitting gray pants with black ankle boots and a collarless white shirt with a vest that matched the pants.

"There are a lot of clothes to choose from. I thought this looked kind of cool." Leopold shrugged. "You'll see when you get there."

Marcus was curious about the clothing in this 'bathhouse.' Where did it come from? Why was it here? People so closely related to plants clearly would not need to bathe, and he had seen no Scrybb wearing clothing. Deacon might have explained this if he hadn't so inconveniently disappeared. Marcus felt annoyed toward his father for the first time since this whole situation began. His father wasn't around much even on Earth.

"Oh, hey. How does your leg feel?" he asked Leopold. "I'm glad I was able to heal it with the Halfriez, but since it's the first time I ever tried it, I wondered how well it worked."

"It's great! I can't believe you were able to fix such a bad break. Cornus told me the bone was actually sticking out through my skin! I wish I could have seen it."

"I don't know if you would have wanted to," Marcus said, grimacing as he remembered the devastating, gory injury.

Marcus felt so guilty for bringing his friends with him to Lysomnus. If Marcus had just left his friend back on Earth, the broken leg would never have happened.

"I dunno, man. I hope your dad will be the one to answer that after we find him. Speaking of your dad... Marcus, I was talking to Cassiope about this whole 'Deacon has been kidnapped' situation, and she said we should meet with all of the Teachers this afternoon to discuss it."

Marcus frowned. He didn't know what to expect from such a meeting. Cassiope had seemed cold and standoffish when he had met her.

Leopold stopped and pointed at the small building in front of them. "This is the bathhouse. You'll find clothes in the first room on the left. The towels are in the second room, and the bath is all the way in the back. You're going to love it, I promise. I'll wait for you in case you need anything."

Marcus started toward the door, then stopped. "Hang on to this for me, will you?" Marcus handed the Halfriez to Leopold, who slipped the clear cube into a small pocket inside his vest.

The temperature increased as soon as Marcus entered the bathhouse. The first room to the left contained many types of clothing. Everything was stacked neatly along one side of the room. He found pants similar to those Leopold had been wearing, but in black, and grabbed them. He chose a red shirt with small snaps he could close with one hand. He was relieved to find stout black boots he could step into without help. While he didn't have his sock tool with him, he knew he could do it himself if he sat down and used one of several tricks he had developed over the years. He'd just have to deal with the pain. There were even undergarments. Marcus piled everything on a bench near the door.

The next room contained stacks of warm, fluffy towels; the flowery scent in the room grew even stronger as Marcus lifted one from the closest pile. He bunched the towel to his face, breathing in the scent, before draping it over his prosthesis.

Finally, Marcus entered the last room.

An oval bath the size of a small pool sunk into the center of a rough stone floor. The scents of jasmine and honeysuckle were carried on billowing steam. He saw a bench to sit on and carefully stripped off his clothing. He set his cane and prosthesis next to the edge and descended several steps into the steaming water. He would need to clean the harness for his prosthesis, too, since it was as dirty as he was.

He found soap when he reached the opposite side of the tub. The scents of cedar and orange filled his nose as he lathered up.

After giving himself a good scrubbing, Marcus washed his limb sock, laid the harness to his prosthesis out on the side of the bathtub, and scrubbed it well. Then, he rinsed it, rinsed off the soap, and returned it to the side of the tub. Then he gave his cane a good scrubbing. Sand had gotten into the adjustable holes in the sides and was rattling inside. Even the rubber foot was filthier than usual.

The towel waiting for him on the ledge was still warm. Marcus dried himself off thoroughly, wiping down the prosthesis and harness. He wrung out his limb sock as much as he could, then draped it over one shoulder. It needed to dry as much as possible before he put it back on.

When he had first entered the bathhouse, it had felt quite warm, but now that he was leaving the steamy room, it felt cooler. His limb sock was still a bit damp, but he put it on under his prosthesis. He would have to dry it out more later to be safe.

After dressing in the rest of the new clothes he had picked out, he stamped into the new boots.

Leopold was waiting for Marcus outside and nodded in approval as he looked Marcus up and down. "Not bad," he said.

"Great," Marcus said sarcastically. "I was just dying to get your approval."

"Sadie and Malberis are meeting us at the dining hall," Leopold said. "Malberis said it would be rude for them to wait here by the bathhouse." At the mention of the dining hall, Marcus realized he was starving again after sleeping for two days.

As they approached the large building, Marcus saw Sadie standing near the entrance with a tall Scrybb girl who had lovely rose-colored leaves. Sadie wore loose, high-waisted silver pants and a cropped navy-blue shirt with billowy sleeves. Her wavy black hair shone in the sun. Marcus's heart skipped a beat.

"Marcus!" she cried out, running toward them and grabbing him by the prosthetic. "I want you to meet someone." Sadie turned toward the Scrybb girl. "This is Malberis. The Scrybb don't usually keep track of family lines and parentage, but Malberis's family has a connection to the Talents. Her, um...well...I'm not sure what the lineage would be. She has an older relative who was a close friend of a member of your family. Malcolm Talent was his name."

Marcus felt a shock jolt through his body. Every time he and his mom had gone with Deacon to visit his father, Malcolm asked about someone named Berberis and was so devastated he wept when he was told she wasn't coming. Berberis was a Scrybb? The one person his grandfather remembered was a Scrybb he would never see again? Marcus was gutted. Deacon stopped taking them to visit the older man because he was afraid Malcolm might give away the family secret?

"Malberis, it's wonderful to meet you," Marcus said when his emotions were under control. "Your relative must be Berberis?"

Malberis broke into a beautiful smile.

"Yes! Does Malcolm still speak of her?"

Marcus swallowed past a lump in his throat.

"Yeah," he said. "He talks about her every time I see him. You must be named after the two of them."

"I am," Malberis said with a small chuckle. "It is quite

unusual for a Scrybb to be named after anything other than their plant lineage. But Berberis insisted. She will be so pleased to hear he still remembers her after all this time. Several members of my family asked Deacon about Malcolm, but Deacon refused to talk about him."

Nausea churned in Marcus's belly. He wasn't sure if it was from missing meals for two days or fury at his father for never giving these people a simple answer about his grandfather. Deacon was well aware that his father missed his Scrybb friend. The sheer cruelty of it simmered like a bed of hot coals in Marcus's chest. "I'm so sorry, Malberis. Malcolm does speak of Berberis frequently and longs to see her even though he can no longer travel to Lysomnus. Please pass on his love."

Malberis's leaves drooped for a moment, and she looked miserable. Marcus had the feeling her relative, Berberis, felt the same way. Then she smiled and looked up at them, ignoring the tear that ran from leaf to leaf down her face. "I will do that, Marcus. Thank you so much. Now," she took a deep breath, "do not let me hold you up from nourishment I know you so badly need." She turned to lead the way inside. Marcus reached for her hand, but Sadie grabbed his arm.

"Don't do that, Marcus," she laughed. "You'll regret it." Sadie pointed at the numerous thorns that lined the branches forming Malberis's limbs.

As Marcus and the others turned to approach the doorway, a small figure dashed out.

"Marcus! I am so sorry for leaving you alone the other night," the young Scrybb said. He stopped in front of Marcus and reached out with his hands. Marcus handed his cane to Leopold and reached out to Cornus. The Scrybb boy threw his arms around Marcus, who hugged him back.

"No, Cornus. I'm the one who should be apologizing. I said so many stupid things. It's no wonder you wanted to get away from me for a while."

Cornus let go of Marcus but led him inside while Leopold handed the cane back with a smile. "I broke the rules, though. It is my duty to provide aid to any in need I meet during my Travels. I should never have left you, especially over something you did not understand."

"Let's just forgive each other and forget the whole thing, Cornus. I'm glad we're still friends."

"Agreed, Marcus!" The young Scrybb looked delighted.

Sunlight streaming in the windows of the banquet hall made it much easier to see than on Marcus's previous visit. The tables were beautiful, made of wood and polished to a high shine. The benches that lined both sides of each table matched them. There was a wider, longer table at one end of the room that held a large variety of food. Marcus took a moment to really appreciate the beautiful craftsmanship of the room now that he could see it in daylight. With Cornus's help, Marcus made his way to the serving table, and the Scrybb boy filled a plate and a bowl with Marcus's selections. After he grabbed utensils, he turned to see Cornus was carrying his meal to a table nearby, where Leopold and Sadie waited with Malberis. They had left the seat at the end of the bench open just for Marcus so he could slide in easily.

Cornus sat opposite him. The young Scrybb shook his head in amusement as Marcus started stuffing himself with delicious stew and fresh, warm bread. When Marcus felt sated, he looked up at the others who were watching him eat with amusement. He flushed and picked up a piece of fruit.

"So, Cornus, I really don't want to offend anyone again.

Can I ask some questions about you and the Scrybbs?"

"Of course. I would be happy to answer your questions. But we are 'Scrybb,' both singular and plural." Cornus looked steadily at Marcus across the polished surface of the table.

"Oh, I'm sorry. I wanted to ask... I was surprised to find that you eat meat here. It just seems kind of...strange to think of meat-eating plants?"

"We are not plants, Marcus. We are people. We may look different from humans, but we have many similarities—our emotions, our communication. We are more alike than you think."

"I guess you're right. I just wasn't thinking of it that way. Making assumptions is wrong, and I shouldn't have done that to you."

Leopold interrupted. "Where does the meat come from? I mean, we've seen the bushes and plants for a lot of the fruit and veggies, but not animals."

"We trade for it. Scrybb are growers and crafters, not hunters. The Grenewud, the forest around Thicce Colpat, is a peaceful place, and while there are animals nearby, they are not the kind that can be consumed. The meat that we eat is obtained by trade with people in other bruwe, and we trade some of our produce and crafted goods with them. It is the same for many of the items you see here."

"Can I ask how you cook the meat?" Sadie said. "That's been on my mind all day! I know how the Scrybb feel about fire, so how can you cook meat and vegetables or make stew?"

"Oh," Cornus said, "we use the emeristan, heavy iron stones that stay hot for a very long time. We trade for them with the people who live near the burning mountains—the Beornan Rokk."

Marcus was chewing thoughtfully while listening to Cornus. He looked down at his plate; he wiped at the gravy with the last of his bread, exposing some of the pattern in the wood plate. "These plates are beautiful too. For some reason, I feel like I've seen one before."

"Seriously, Marcus, you think you've seen a plate from a planet you just came to for the first time two days ago?" Leopold laughed and swirled his finger around his ear.

"What does it mean, this?" Cornus imitated Leopold's gesture.

"It means crazy. Like Marcus is losing his marbles."

"Marbles?"

"Um, never mind. Just going crazy, like his mind is all mixed up."

"But what are marbles?"

"Well, they're these really pretty glass balls that kids used to play with, I think."

"And why does it make a person go crazy to lose these marbles?" Cornus asked, sounding puzzled.

Sadie burst out laughing.

"Oh. Uh, I really don't know why. It's just a saying in our world." Leopold shifted uncomfortably. "Marcus, I'm going to get you some juice."

Marcus had been having a hard time keeping a straight face. It wasn't too often Leopold ended up the butt of his own joke.

When Leopold returned, he had a cup of juice in his hand. Marcus drank it quickly and then put the cup on the table.

"Let's go, Marcus!" Leopold said, already halfway to the door.

"Wait! What about our dishes? Shouldn't we clear the

table?"

"It's okay!" Sadie replied. "There are Scrybb who do it."

Cornus nodded, taking Marcus's prosthesis in his hand. "Everyone has their own job to do here."

As they stood to leave, Marcus noticed Malberis did not follow to join them.

"Aren't you coming?"

She shook her head. "As much as I would like to join you, I am also part of the meal staff. I must remain here and complete my duties." Marcus was sorry to leave her behind so soon after meeting her. She was the descendant of his grandfather's friend, after all. He waved to her as he followed his friends.

They walked along the paths together, moving through Thicce Colpat as quickly as Marcus could go. It was obvious that Sadie and Leopold knew their way through the bruwe already. He tried to look around as they walked along the pebbled paths that wove from one building to another. There were flowering plants along each border and Vosfyren on every corner. The largest buildings, neatly constructed of logs above stone, were on the outer perimeters of the bruwe: the dining hall they had just come from was one of them. There was another to the left that loomed over a smaller structure.

"Cornus? What's that building?" Marcus called out.

The young Scrybb turned to see where he was pointing. "Oh, that's the children's dormitory."

Marcus wanted to take his time and explore more, but his friends were rushing ahead, and he had fallen too far behind to ask them to stop. He could only glance around as they hurried along, and he struggled to keep up. He saw the bathhouse and the bunkhouse where they had slept and another building in front of the children's dormitory that he thought might be a school. Smaller buildings toward the center of the bruwe, he assumed, must be homes where the adults lived. The center of the bruwe had a large, open area that must be used for gatherings. Several times, they had to move off the path to get around a startled adult, and exclamations followed them, telling them to stop acting so foolishly. Finally, the group of young people reached the forest edge and slipped under the shadow of the trees. "You could have waited for me," Marcus said breathlessly as he caught up. Cornus and Sadie looked surprised, but Leopold looked guilty.

"I'm sorry, man. I know better than that. I think I just got carried away."

Sadie's eyes darted between the two of them, finally meeting Marcus's. "I didn't even stop to think, Marcus, and I apologize. Of course we should have waited for you. It was rude of us not to walk slow enough for you to keep up."

"I apologize also, my friend. I continue to add to the things I do to cause you harm." Cornus looked mortified.

"Okay, guys. It's fine. I just wanted you to realize I need you to wait for me when we're walking together." Marcus said. "Now, Cornus, why does it look different here than where we came in the other night?"

"That is because we are on the opposite side of the bruwe from where you and I entered Thicce Colpat," Cornus replied. "On this side, the path leads to the burning mountains—the Beornan Rokk. The path we arrived on comes from the ocean where we found you, the Diluvium. Thicce Colpat is near to the Diluvium, but it is a longer journey to the Beornan Rokk. The forest ends close to the foot of the mountains, and we trade with the people who live there."

"What people are those? More Scrybb?" Marcus asked.

"Of course not. All Scrybb live here, in Thicce Colpat. There are other people who live in their own bruwe in other parts of Lysomnus. We only see them when we go on our Travels or when we go there to trade."

"Who are they?" asked Leopold.

"Well, I...I know their names. The Fyrtudo live in Palaga, near Beornan Rokk. Then there are the Muirnati, who live in Fisc, near the Diluvium. And the Cativera live in the bruwe of Grasian, to the south." Cornus sounded as if he was reciting lessons.

The three humans exchanged a glance. "Cornus," Marcus said, "what do you actually know about these other people?"

"Erm, well, we are *supposed* to get to know more about them on our Travels, to be honest. Our Teachers do not give us a lot of information about them other than where they live and what we trade with them. I have not heard much about them from recent Travelers who have returned—it is as if no one is visiting them anymore."

The path they walked on felt like the one they had been on the night Leopold had been injured.

"Who keeps the paths so clear?" Marcus asked.

"Scrybb, of course," Cornus said.

"So, everyone has their own different job to do? Do you have money in your world?"

"Money?" Cornus looked confused.

"Yeah, like when someone does their job, they get money for it. Then, when they have enough to buy something they want, they give the money for that thing," Marcus explained.

Cornus still looked puzzled. "When someone does their job? Everyone does their job because it needs to be done."

"For no pay? What about paying the bills?" Leopold said.

"Who are the Bills?" Cornus asked.

Marcus burst out laughing.

"Hang on, hang on," he said with his hand on his knee, catching his breath. "Cornus, how do your people get stuff they want or need? Like individual people?"

"Well, we just have it available. I mentioned before that our people trade goods for things with other people. Everyone in Thicce Colpat can have anything in Thicce Colpat. Any Scrybb or any visitor."

"No stealing? No crime?" Leopold looked dumbfounded. "Does anyone ever try to come and take the things you produce without trading?"

Cornus looked offended. "Absolutely not. No one would. Just as we would never do such a thing to them."

Leopold grabbed Marcus by the arm. "Do you realize this world is like a paradise? No money, no poverty, no crime?'

"Right, except for the murderous phantasms and the fact that my father is missing. I'd call that a crime."

Leopold's smile vanished. "Yeah, I'm sorry. It's just—to see a world where that stuff doesn't happen is pretty cool."

"I'm sorry, Leopold. I know that's important. But man, we gotta survive this 'paradise' first. We've only seen a little bit of it to already assume it's perfect."

Cornus had been watching this exchange silently until now. "I believe we should return to Thicce Colpat to meet with Cassiope and the other Teachers."

The five of them began to walk back slowly along the forest path. Sadie put her arm around Leopold's waist.

"It *is* a pretty amazing world where no one goes hungry

and no one fears being stolen from," she said. "But Marcus is right, you know. We haven't seen much of this world yet to know just how safe it really is, Leopold."

"I know," he said, leaning his head against hers. "It's just so nice to see a place where need and poverty aren't killing people the way they are back home."

"I know," she said. "Let's just enjoy that for the moment."

CHAPTER SEVEN

HITTING THE TRAIL

Marcus followed Cornus to the building near the children's dormitory, which he had guessed was a school earlier. Leopold and Sadie followed right behind. As they entered, Malberis hurried around the corner of the building and joined them. "They're already inside," she whispered. "They seem upset."

As their group walked down the hall, Marcus heard voices coming from one of the classrooms ahead. They all stopped, uneasy; the voices were hushed and sounded angry.

"You know we should not help them," a man's voice, barely discernible, reached their ears. They pressed against the wall beside the classroom door; Marcus stood the closest.

"While I agree with you, they are just children, and they deserve some assistance, even if Deacon is involved. I do not believe there is any risk. We have always welcomed members of the Talent family," replied another voice—a woman—that Marcus found familiar.

"That's Cassiope," Leopold whispered. He had spent the days Marcus slept discussing their situation with the stern Teacher.

Marcus wondered why the Teachers would hesitate to help them if Deacon was involved.

"Deacon's father helped us a great deal and was a close friend," said another woman. Marcus wondered who this Teacher could be.

"If Nun the Wiser and the other humans were to find out, we could all be in great danger." said a man angrily. The voices suddenly all shouted together in an uproar.

Other humans? Marcus looked accusingly at Cornus and Malberis. Cornus looked guilty; Malberis, confused.

"I do not know how she would find out, without you foolishly saying her name," Cassiope snapped.

Abruptly, cries of fear echoed into the hallway. Goosebumps rose on Marcus's skin at the sound.

"Do you conspire against me, Scrybb?" rasped a new voice. Marcus edged right up to the door and peered inside to see a gaunt woman in a black robe standing in the front of the classroom, facing the group of frightened Scrybb. A black hood concealed most of her face, and dark red hair streamed out of it to her waist. When she gestured toward the frightened Scrybb, Marcus saw that her right hand was nothing but bare bones. The flesh of the other was dead white, with blackened finger tips that ended in talon-like nails.

"Have you forgotten I hear you every time you say my name? Never forget what I can do to you." Flames flared in the palm of her pale-fleshed hand as a bony finger pointed towards a Scrybb, and the man began to scream. He pawed at himself as the leaves of his face burst into flames. The delicate edges of the leaves on the hand he was beating against his face turned a crisp brown and curled inward. The fire petered out as other Teachers threw water on him. The evil figure laughed.

"Don't cross me again," In the blink of an eye, she disappeared. A *pop* sounded as air collapsed into the space where she had been standing.

"As I was saying," Cassiope snapped as she worked with the others in assisting the burned Scrybb to a seat. "You know better than to say her name, Clieris. *Ever.*"

Marcus stepped back as the acrid scent of burnt greenery drifted out of the doorway. His friends looked horrified as he whispered to them what he'd just witnessed.

"And you know better than to get involved in the affairs of humans," said another man.

"You all know how tired I am of humans and the problems they continue to bring to our midst," Cassiope said. "But I don't feel right abandoning these young people who are alone and lost in our world."

"We cannot simply leave them to their own devices," said the other woman who had spoken earlier. She looked very much like Malberis—the same pink leaves and thorny vines. Marcus was certain she had to be Berberis, his grandfather's friend. "Malcolm would never wish such a thing. He was a good friend to us. We cannot blame these children for the shortcomings of his son, Deacon, and our mistreatment by the other humans."

Marcus felt his face burn with humiliation. His father was *not* liked by the Scrybb?

"The decision to help them and any repercussions that arise from it are placed firmly on your heads," the burned Scrybb's voice rasped; it grew louder as rustling footsteps approached the door. "The rest of us are not in support of this."

The man suddenly appeared in the hallway and glared at Marcus and his friends as he hurried past them. Marcus felt a chill when the man's angry gaze met his eyes. A strong odor of burned vegetation filled Marcus's nose as he passed. A group of other Scrybb adults followed him out of the room, most of whom avoided looking at him. Berberis patted him lightly on the shoulder and nodded to Malberis as she passed.

As they entered the classroom, the teens found Cassiope waiting for them. She was tapping one foot impatiently at the front of the room, which was filled with small tables and chairs. "You are late, Cornus. You were supposed to bring your human friends in time to attend the meeting."

Cornus lowered his head. "My apologies, Teacher. We were afraid to enter after what we heard as we approached."

"For a youth on his Travel year, you are undisciplined, Cornus. You must accept further assignments."

"Further assignments!" Cornus protested, looking helplessly at his friends.

"Cornus!" Cassiope snapped. "You have completed little more than one month of your Travels thus far. I have decided you are to accompany Marcus, Sadie, and Leopold to go find Marcus's father."

"But I had hoped to—oh, wait. Accompany them?" He looked down at the floor again. "Oh, yes, ma'am."

Malberis begged to go with them, but Cassiope said firmly that since she already had Traveled and received her adult assignment, she would not be allowed to leave the bruwe.

Malberis's shoulders slumped at the news, and tears welled in her eyes. Sadie embraced her carefully. Marcus whispered to her, "Please tell Berberis that Malcolm sends his love." She nodded with tears in her eyes and walked slowly out the door.

Cassiope followed her briskly.

"Cassiope! Wait!" Marcus called out.

The Teacher stopped, one hand on the doorframe.

Marcus had to edge around her stiff body to face her.

"I don't know if Leopold told you everything while I was sleeping. Cornus said when we first met that my father is well known here. Now he's missing, and I strongly feel that he has been kidnapped—taken by someone in Lysomnus. That he's being held hostage somewhere... I was hoping to discuss what the Scrybb might know. Especially about these 'other humans' you mentioned."

Cassiope put a hand to her forehead as if she had a headache. "Marcus, you do not know everything that is involved with your father and his life here. Or with the other humans in Lysomnus. I do not wish to discuss any of this."

"Who was that woman who came into the room at the end of your meeting? That Nu—"

Cassiope clapped her hand over Marcus's mouth.

"Do *not* say that name. You have just seen what happens when you do. You are asking for more trouble than you know." Cassiope took a deep breath. "I have already said far too much." Her stern expression changed for just a moment, and Marcus glimpsed fear in her eyes. "I am aware you heard the end of the meeting. We will simply not get involved any further. Allowing Cornus to accompany you is the most that we will do. Cassiope removed her hand from Marcus's mouth.

"You will need to make your way to the Fyrtudo and see if they can help you. They might have information about the whereabouts of Deacon or have heard news of... the other humans and their leader." With a deep sigh, she turned and walked slowly down the hall, her back stiff. Marcus thought she might look back as she exited through the door leading outside, but there was a resolute set to her back as she left without hesitation.

Once Cassiope was gone, Marcus rejoined his friends. He wasn't feeling overly confident. He hadn't exactly hoped for a map with an X to mark where his father was, but he had hoped that the Scrybb might guess where his father could be. He was taken aback that they would only provide Cornus's guidance as their assistance. He thought uneasily of their first meeting when Cornus had been lost in the woods. Was the young Scrybb capable of assisting them on a journey across Lysomnus? Particularly as it was obvious that Cassiope and the other Teachers knew more than they were saying.

The foursome walked out of the school building, and Marcus met Leopold's eyes. It was daunting to think of traveling through a world where they'd never been before. With his disabilities, Marcus knew he was in for a difficult time. Leopold was the only one who understood just how challenging things would be for him.

"Cornus," Marcus began, "how will we be traveling? How do the Scrybb get around during their Travels?"

"Oh, we walk," Cornus answered, much to Marcus's dismay.

He sighed. About as bad as he had expected. "But what about supplies? Food, water, clothing?"

"Well, Scrybb do not need clothing, as you can see. And we are exceptionally good at foraging when we Travel. It is one of our tasks—to prove that we can provide for ourselves out in the world. Foraging, as well as creating connections with the other people of Lysomnus, are a part of that."

"The three of us will need more clothing, Cornus," Marcus pointed out.

"I can procure packs for you. You can carry a change of clothing, and when we stop to rest, you can change and rinse out the clothes you have worn."

While Marcus, Leopold, and Sadie made their way to the bathhouse to grab additional clothing, Cornus brought small packs for them. Unfortunately, they were only able to fit one set of clothing in each pack. Once they were prepared, the four of them walked toward the edge of the bruwe together. They saw Abutilon waiting for them a short distance down the path. He gestured to them and called, "Come along, children!"

Marcus whispered to Cornus, "Does someone always see you off like this?"

"No, usually we just leave. This is most unusual."

They followed Abutilon to the edge of the forest path, where they found Buddleja waiting next to a small, four-wheeled wagon. A seat with a back on it faced forward. A hinged bar extended from the front of it, with a two-sided handle to pull the wagon lying on the ground.

Buddleja showed them a box behind the seat and opened it to reveal a supply of fruit and vegetables. "I know Cornus is supposed to forage on his Travels, but no one said anything about you three. And who will know if you share?" She smiled at them shyly. Sadie reached out to take the pretty Scrybb woman's hands gently in her own, thanking her. Buddleja nodded.

Abutilon patted Cornus on the shoulder. "It was not too many years ago that I set out on my own Travels. It can be nerve-wracking to Travel this world alone, even with new friends. And we would not have you start out with a strike against you. Young Marcus will have an easier journey if he can ride when he is tired or in pain."

Cornus hugged Abutilon for a moment. The tall Scrybb cleared his throat and patted the boy's shoulder. "Yes, well.

It is time for you to go." He gently pushed Cornus away, stepping back and sliding one arm around Buddleja's waist.

Embarrassed, Cornus thanked Abutilon and Buddleja again, and the three humans echoed him. Leopold and Cornus each grasped one side of the handle and pulled; the wagon rolled easily. Marcus wanted to walk for as long as he could and followed behind using his cane with Sadie at his side. After a few minutes, all of them stopped and looked back to see Abutilon still standing at the end of the path. They all waved. Abutilon returned the gesture, then turned and walked back into Thicce Colpat.

"Cornus, did Abutilon make this for us?" Marcus asked from behind the cart.

"It is possible. He is a very talented Crafter. I have seen the Crafters build wagons to carry our produce to other people for trade and to bring back other goods to Thicce Colpat. But I have never seen one so small or with a seat on it before."

"It must be something he shouldn't have done... Is that why they gave it to us in the forest, where no one could see?"

"A Scrybb can certainly give any of his work to anyone they please, but to help a young Scrybb that is leaving for his Travels is forbidden. I believe they are trying to circumvent that rule by giving the wagon and food to the three of you. It is possible it would be allowed, but rather than risk being denied the favor, he did not ask."

"Better to ask for forgiveness than permission, in this situation, I suppose," Marcus said.

"Hmm, I like that saying," Cornus said.

"Hey, guys? I have a question," Leopold interjected. He was pulling alongside Cornus, listening to the conversation.

"Where are we right now, and where are we going? I remember Cornus here saying this path led to some burning rock mountains. I'm just wondering how that helps us find your dad, Marcus."

"Right now, we are entering the Grenewud, the great forest that covers much of our world," Cornus said. "The trees of the Grenewud are old, soaring high above the forest floors and protecting those who travel below. They help to guide those who are lost with their roots, which emerge from the soil to point to the north at the foot of every tree."

Marcus now realized where his father had gotten the information he had given Marcus about finding his way through the forest, although that information had nearly gotten him killed.

"Hang on a sec, buddy," Leopold said. He stopped pulling, climbed onto the wagon, and settled on the seat, legs stretched out before him. "This sounds like it might take a while." He grinned at Cornus. "Continue."

Marcus rolled his eyes. "Be quiet. Leopold," he said, then gestured at Cornus, who had waited patiently during the interruption. "Please, go on."

"Yes. The Grenewud stretches from the Diluvium in the west to Beornan Rokk in the north to the region in the south where the Cativera live. To the east is also the Diluvium, but we don't go there. We have paths that lead in many directions, and this one leads toward Beornan Rokk. The Scrybb do not go into the mountains—that is where the Fyrtudo live. They are miners and forgers, and we trade with them for their goods. They give us the emeristan and other items."

"So, what is our plan, then? How will going to see these Fyrtudo help me find my dad?"

"I do not have the answer to that, Marcus. I can only escort you to the other people of Lysomnus and see what they may know."

"So, you think we should start with these people by the Bo—Beornan…" Marcus stammered.

"Beornan Rokk, yes. It is a few days' journey, but we must start with the closest people and move on from there."

Marcus looked up at Leopold, who was munching on a piece of fruit. "Hey! That has to last us a while, you know."

Leopold winked at him. "Nah, Cornus is gonna teach us how to forage. And produce spoils if you don't eat it soon enough. Right, dude?"

Cornus smiled. "You do have a point, Leopold. I would enjoy a piece of fruit. Would you be so kind as to give me a pellod? It is the soft purple one."

Leopold reached back into the box, scrounged around, and held up a round purple fruit slightly larger than his fist with a pink hue on one side. "This one?"

"Yes, that is the one. Thank you." Leopold tossed him the fruit.

Marcus sighed. "You might as well give me something, too. Seems like a good time for it."

"Any kind in particular?"

"Surprise me."

Marcus grunted when a blue fruit the size of his head thumped him in the chest. He barely had time to react and catch it. "What is this, a watermelon?"

"Who would eat a fruit made of water?" Cornus said with his mouth full.

Leopold snorted. "You'll like it," he said to Marcus. "It's a sartine, and it's kind of like a big orange, except it's blue.

You open it, and it comes apart in sections. Doesn't taste like an orange, though. But nothing here tastes like things back home!"

Marcus hoisted himself onto the front of the wagon to peel his fruit. It was odd to see a fruit that was blue; as his mom liked to point out, "no food in nature is blue." Apparently, here in Lysomnus, that wasn't true. He tried to work the fingernails of his left hand into the thick rind but couldn't seem to make much headway.

"Uh, guys? Is there some kind of secret to getting into this fruit?"

"Oh, yes." Cornus came around to stand next to him. "The sartine seems impervious unless you know the secret to opening it. Here," he said, holding out his leafy hands. Marcus lowered the fruit to his waiting palms.

Cornus began to roll the large fruit between his hands. The Scrybb boy was so small and the sartine so large that it appeared he would drop it at any moment. Marcus looked up at Sadie and Leopold, who were grinning. In that instant, the sartine made a popping noise, and the fruit split open in eight equal sections. Cornus set it down, and it spread to reveal the flesh inside. Sadie began to pass out segments around to everyone, taking a big bite from one herself. Marcus was holding what looked like an orange segment but was bright blue, and as large as a slice of watermelon.

"Oh, I missed something! I looked away right when you opened it." Marcus was disappointed.

"It is not so hard," Cornus said. "You will do the next one yourself, and you will see there is no special trick."

"It's fun, Marcus," Sadie said.

Marcus bit into his section of the sartine. The rich, sweet taste was familiar, and he realized that the juice Abutilon had given him in the banquet hall in Thicce Colpat was made from this fruit. He removed a few flat white seeds as he ate the tender flesh.

"What should we do with the peel and the seeds, Cornus? Bury them somewhere?" Sadie asked.

"Yes, that is appropriate. Near the path so that when the vine grows and produces fruit, it will provide nourishment for other travelers."

Leopold began to look for a stick. Once he had found one sturdy enough to dig a hole, Marcus joined him, using his cane to help dig in the soft soil, and the two buried their seeds close to the trail. Marcus saw Cornus doing the same with the small black seeds from his pellod. The Scrybb boy used only his strong, woody fingers to dig a trench.

Marcus watched as Cornus dropped his handful of seeds and pulled the dirt overtop, patting it down. "Hey, Cornus, your people use tools. I mean, the utensils you have for eating and the wagons and stuff that the Crafters make. Why don't you get to take any with you on your Travels?"

Cornus stood, brushing the soil from the twigs and leaves of his hands, "Scrybb are expected to learn how to manage without supplies like tools and stored food. Of course, in our daily lives, we have access to such things, but life is not always so easy. It is important to be able to manage in the worst of situations."

"But you're so young. I mean, at least it seems like you are. Hey, how old are you? Is it okay to ask that?"

Cornus stood up and returned to the wagon, shaking his hands to remove the dirt. "Yes, it is perfectly fine, Marcus. I am eighteen years old. Different Scrybb grow and mature at different rates. I will reach full growth in the next couple of years and begin to flower soon after that."

Marcus noticed Cornus's eyes glow brighter as he spoke of flowering.

"Does *flowering* mean the same thing to Scrybb as puberty does to humans?" he asked.

"I do not know what 'puberty' is, but for a Scrybb, flowering is the final step to reaching adulthood. We are considered fully mature and functional to mate once we have flowered," Cornus explained seriously. "We should continue on our journey." He walked back to the front of the wagon and lifted the handle, waiting patiently for someone to join him.

"You want to ride for a while?' Leopold asked Marcus as he slid off to the ground and took his side of the handle.

Marcus nodded. "I probably should. The pain is pretty bad, and if I push too hard, it's just going to get worse."

"Good idea, bro."

"Why do you call each other these words?" Cornus asked. "They are not your names, and yet you use them often when talking to each other."

Leopold laughed. "They're just affectionate nicknames people from our world use when talking to friends."

"Oh," Cornus said, but he still looked mystified.

"Let me know when one of you wants a break," Sadie chimed in. "I can take a turn on the handle as well. I don't mind pulling my share of the weight."

The path was wide enough for all three to walk abreast as Leopold and Cornus pulled the wagon behind them.

"So, Cornus, flowering does sound similar to human puberty, I think," Leopold continued. "I mean, for humans, it's when our bodies get physically ready for having kids."

"Yes, it is similar then. We must complete our Travels first, and when a Scrybb has returned, he is assigned an adult position and can mate when flowering is complete."

"So do female Scrybb go on Travels?" Sadie asked.

"Oh, yes. Every Scrybb does. Most of the Scrybb from my year are out Traveling now. Some are due to return home soon, and some will still be out for a while. I am the only one who has just recently begun," Cornus said, seeming a bit embarrassed.

"Did you do something wrong?" Marcus asked, looking over Cornus's head at Leopold, who shrugged.

"When we met for the first time, I had only been on my Travels for a month. After what happened, I did not know what to do when you were injured and left, so I returned to Thicce Colpat. The Teachers were upset with me for not continuing along my way. They said there was nothing more I could have done, and there was no way to know if you had even survived."

"But you found us when Leopold was injured!" Marcus exclaimed.

"And I, for one, am very grateful," Leopold added.

"Yes. I had only been back in Thicce Colpat for a brief time, talking to the Teachers about what had happened when we heard you return. The Teachers had some debate about whether we should help you this time. By the time I convinced them that you were just a child with little knowledge of Lysomnus, it was nearly dark. Of course, I had no idea that Sadie and Leopold were with you or of Leopold's injury."

Something Cornus said struck Marcus as odd, but he couldn't put his finger on what it was. He looked at Leopold, but his friend's blue eyes were locked on Cornus's, intent on what the Scrybb boy was saying. "Why wouldn't you have helped me, Cornus?" Marcus asked, puzzled.

"It was a complicated subject, and I was not included in all of their discussions. I informed the Teachers about you, and they met in private. I was finally able to talk to Cassiope alone, and that helped. She is more compassionate than some of the others."

Marcus pictured the stern Scrybb who had been so brusque and unwilling to talk to him. Compassionate? Only Berberis had acted compassionate of all the Teachers he had encountered in Thicce Colpat. He thought about the angry Scrybb man they had overheard in the school building and realized he must have been one of the other Teachers. Marcus shuddered internally, realizing Cornus must be right about Cassiope having *some* compassion. She and Berberis might be the only reason they had received any help at all.

Leopold said, "So you would have come sooner if you had known that I was injured? That would have been nice. It was the longest day of my life."

"Yes, the Teachers did feel bad about that. They would have come immediately if they had been aware that you were in need of help. Especially as you could have been attacked during that time."

Leopold stopped walking. "Attacked! I thought you said there was nothing dangerous here!"

Cornus turned to look at Leopold, who started walking again. "I have never said there is nothing dangerous here. There are creatures here that could kill you and eat you, or attack you and leave you to die, or find other ways of ending your life. We may not need *money* to *Pay the Bills*, but we do live in a world where you must be careful and know what you are doing."

Leopold tripped over a root beside the path. Sadie snorted. "Or maybe just watch where you're going?"

The four of them laughed, the tension broken.

Cornus called a stop for the day as twilight began to descend. "We must stop to eat and rest."

"Finally! I'm beat." Leopold said with a sigh of relief.

The others turned to look at Marcus, who was sitting on the seat of the wagon behind them. He had gotten down and tried to walk with them earlier before giving in to his growing discomfort and fatigue and climbing back on to ride. He had pushed far past what he was comfortable with, hoping to spare his friends the extra weight.

"Yeah, let's get some rest, guys. And some chow," Leopold said.

"Chow?" Cornus echoed. "What is...chow?"

"Just an expression. It means food, dinner, y'know. Chow."

Marcus was already turning to open the box behind him and pull out some of the food that Abutilon and Buddleja had stocked for them.

"Why not just say 'food' if that is what you mean?" Cornus sounded a bit irritable.

"Sorry, Cornus," Marcus said, handing food to the others. "Leopold is the king of expressions, substitutions, you name it. Takes some getting used to."

Cornus frowned. "I am not sure I really want to get used to it."

"Aw, c'mon, Corny ol' pal!" Leopold teased.

"Please do not call me 'Corny,' Leopold. My name is 'Cornus.'"

Marcus reached down and hooked Leopold's arm with his prosthesis. "Hey. You of all people should know better than that... Right, *Leo?*"

"Okay, okay." Leopold shook off Marcus's prosthesis and

grabbed some food, scowling. Sadie took a few vegetables as Leopold handed them to her, along with a pellod.

"Hey, guys," Sadie said. "I think we're all testy from walking for so long. Let's try to get along, okay?"

Cornus was inspecting a plant on the side of the path, and he turned to smile at her. "You are correct, my friend. We should not let our weariness affect our mood."

"Yeah, you're right. I'm sorry, Cornus. Peace, okay?" Leopold walked over and held his hand out to the Scrybb boy.

Cornus turned to Leopold and looked at his hand. "Peace?" He looked up at Leopold's earnest face with a confused expression. "I am sorry, I am not aware of this custom."

Leopold laughed. "Put out your hand, bro. Like mine!" He shook his open hand for emphasis. Cornus lifted his open hand. Leopold seized it gently in his own and shook it up and down. "It's a gentlemen's agreement!"

Cornus looked delighted. "I like this custom!" He grasped Leopold's hand more firmly and shook it. The two boys laughed.

Sadie rolled her eyes and said something in a language Marcus didn't understand. Then she said, "The 'Gentlemen's Agreement' was an ugly part of American history that affected Southeast Asian people in a very negative way."

"Uh, what did you say?" said Marcus.

Sadie looked at him with an angry expression on her face. He shrugged helplessly.

Cornus shook his head. "Sometimes, I am so confused by the things you all say."

"Uh," Leopold said. "I don't know what she said either, Cornus."

Cornus looked at Marcus and Leopold. "So you didn't understand what Sadie said either? Do humans not all speak this same language in your world?"

"No, we speak different languages depending on where we come from, Cornus," Sadie said. "You might have noticed that I look a little different than Leopold and Marcus. People like me come from another part of our planet. And my people speak a different language than Marcus or Leopold."

"Do you speak more than one language, Sadie?" Leopold asked hesitantly. He and Cornus were still shaking hands. Marcus tried not to laugh, but he couldn't help it. When Sadie looked at him, face still clouded with anger, he pointed at them, and her shoulders shook as she dissolved into giggles. The two boys looked down at themselves and hastily released each others' hands. Leopold flushed.

Sadie got her laughter under control. "Well, you know I speak three already, Leopold. English, Korean, and ASL—American Sign Language."

"That's really dope. You must be so smart, Sadie," Marcus said. "So, is sign language the same here as it is in Korea, or are they different?"

"Actually, the two are different, and there used to be two forms of sign language in South Korea. My parents had to fight for Steven to learn Korean Sign Language and not the old version—Korean Standard Sign Language, which was just a coded form of verbal Korean language. It's hard to learn and affects the literacy of the deaf person. South Korea passed legislation in 2015 making Korean Sign Language an official language in the country."

"So, you speak four languages," Leopold said. "That's really impressive."

"Half of my family lives in South Korea. I was raised speaking Mandarin and Korean because of my grandparents, so actually, I speak five languages."

Cornus looked dazed. "What is 'sign language'?" he asked.

"My brother, Steven, can't hear, so we all learned to speak with signs we make with our hands and arms," Sadie explained, signing at the same time. "I just signed the same thing I said at the same time."

Leopold shook his head. "Five languages. That's unbelievable. I can barely remember how to speak one language the right way."

Marcus laughed.

"We should try and find some water. It's been a long day without anything to hydrate our bodies other than the juice of the fruit we have consumed," Cornus said. "The leaves of this plant right here make excellent vessels for holding water, and I believe I hear a stream nearby."

"You must have some great hearing, Cornus," Leopold said. "Sadie and I can keep watch while you get some water."

Cornus showed Marcus how the leaves of the plant he had found could be rolled into the shape of a large funnel. He then tore one side of the leaf, waiting until a sticky fluid leaked from inside. This fluid sealed the funnel along the seam as he pressed the torn edge against the curled opposite side, forming a closed cup in which to carry water.

The shallow stream Cornus had heard was not too far from the path. Marcus was a little surprised he hadn't heard it himself since it was rippling cheerfully over a bed of stones. A few large boulders stuck out far enough that a person could walk across the stream without getting their feet wet, but Cornus ignored these and waded into the deeper water, standing in the water while they both drank. Marcus didn't know if he'd ever tasted water so refreshing.

"Are there fish in these streams, Cornus?" he asked when his thirst was slaked.

"Fish? In the Grenewud? No. Fish are found only in the Diluvium. They only live in the undrinkable water." Cornus shuddered at the thought while refilling the cups to take water back to the others.

"Oh. In our world, there are fish in our ocean, but also in streams and lakes, too."

"Then you have living creatures in your drinkable water? How unsanitary!"

"I guess... Yeah, we have water treatment plants, and I know people will get sick if they drink water without a way to filter it. Companies started selling these filters for people to start carrying with them in case they were stuck somewhere without clean water," Marcus explained.

"I do not know what that means," Cornus said.

"Never mind," he said. Then he turned, ready to head back and bring the water to the others, but Cornus still stood in the stream. "Aren't you coming?" Marcus asked. Cornus lifted one foot from the stream. Waving roots extended from the bottom of his feet.

"I need to hydrate myself by taking in water through my roots every day this way. Drinking water is good, but root hydration is also important.

Marcus sat down on a nearby stump and waited until his friend said he had taken in enough water, and they made their way back to the others.

"Finally!" Leopold exclaimed. "I thought I'd die of thirst. You would come back, and Sadie and I would just be dried-out husks lying on the path."

"Don't be so dramatic," Sadie said as she took her leaf full of water, but Marcus saw her smile in the shadow of the leaf as she lifted it to her lips.

Cornus, however, looked alarmed. "Could that happen? I do not want to endanger any of you by taking too long while hydrating. I can take less time to protect your health."

Marcus snorted and punched Leopold lightly on the arm, spilling some of the water onto his shirt. "Don't listen to this fool, Cornus. Take all the time you need when hydrating. He's just messing with you, making a joke as he always does."

"All of these jokes—should I not believe what Leopold says to me anymore?" Cornus looked earnestly at Marcus.

"No, Cornus. Leopold just thinks he's funny and likes to make people laugh. I'm sure he'll try to be more sincere from now on." Marcus looked with consternation at Leopold as Sadie gave him an elbow.

Leopold looked chastised as he promised he'd try harder to joke less with Cornus from now on. Marcus saw a twinkle in his friend's eye that told him differently.

Later, they sat with their backs against the broad trees beside the path. It was after nightfall and getting dark. All the humans could see was each other's shadowy silhouettes and Cornus's glowing, orange eyes. The lack of light wasn't so bad now that they weren't trying to go anywhere.

"Cornus?" Marcus said in the failing light. "What are the people like who live by the Beornan Rokk? The ones we will meet soon?"

"The Fyrtudo? I have never met them, as I had not made it far on my Travels and was not headed in their direction. We learn about all the people of Lysomnus from the Teachers, but I cannot tell you much more than I already have. Young Scrybb do not leave Thicce Colpat until they are ready for Travels and can experience the world for themselves."

"Wait, what?" Leopold asked, incredulous. "And then you're just supposed to go wandering around by yourselves for a year?"

"It has always been so. We spend many years with the Teachers, learning about Lysomnus, the people, the dangers, and how to survive on our own."

"It doesn't really sound that thorough, Cornus," Sadie said. "You know the names of the other people and their locations, but you don't really seem to know anything else about them other than what your people trade with them. It's as if you're expected to learn everything else when you Travel. It feels like you're not very well prepared for such a journey into the unknown."

Cornus's leaves rustled as he squirmed uncomfortably. "I do not know what to say other than this is how it has always been."

"Cornus," Marcus broke in, "do you live with your parents and go to school with the Teachers during the day like we humans do?"

Cornus's bright orange eyes turned toward him. "No. I know of the family units in which other people live, but Scrybb do not live in this way. Scrybb couples mate and have numerous offspring. The young offspring are raised in a nursery and then begin schooling. The Teachers guide the young Scrybb in all things."

"Don't you ever see your parents? Don't you miss them?" Marcus thought of his own mother and felt a deep throb of homesickness. He thought of her smile, the sound of her laugh, the feel of her strong hands on his face as she remarked on his height just a few days ago.

"As I said, we do not know each other as a family unit. I was separated from them as soon as I sprouted. If we have anyone to whom we are close, it is the other Scrybb in our Teaching year. I have some close friends from my year, but we are all Traveling."

Marcus realized this was why Cornus was so friendly with him when they met, holding his hand to guide him. He was obviously most comfortable with people near his own age or maturity.

"Do you have different Teachers? Some who teach one lesson, and some another?" Leopold asked.

Marcus bet he knew the answer to this one. "Cassiope is the Teacher for your entire year, isn't she?" he guessed.

"Yes," Cornus replied. "Every Scrybb year has their own Teacher, and Cassiope is mine. She has been kind. I can only hope I have not caused her trouble or embarrassed her with my errors." His leaves rustled again. "We should try to sleep now and travel at first light. It will be several days before we reach the Beornan Rokk."

The humans were now glad for the packs they had been carrying all day, as they made excellent pillows. Cornus merely sat with his back against a tree and fell asleep that way. Judging by the leaves carpeting the ground, Marcus would have guessed the season to be mid to late autumn, but the warm temperature made him wonder if it was instead late summer here. Slowly, he drifted off to sleep.

He woke a few hours later, realizing he could see better as soon as he opened his eyes. Looking up toward the sky, he noticed hazy light shining through the leaves of the trees. He shifted painfully so he was facing the sky at a better angle. Through a wide gap in the leaves, he saw a moon shining in the sky above. Rather than the round satellite of Earth he was familiar with at home, the moon he saw above him now was cracked into two pieces—one smaller, the other larger than the top half. Large chunks of debris trailed behind it across the sky. Despite the damage, this planet's moon still reflected enough light to illuminate the darkness.

When Marcus looked around in the moonlight, he saw Cornus was now lying curled up on his side on the ground. Leopold had rolled away from his backpack pillow, using his own arm as a replacement. Sadie was lying against a tree nearby. As he looked at her, Marcus realized her dark eyes were open, catching a glint from the moon above. She smiled at him sleepily and adjusted her head on her backpack to a more comfortable position. He smiled back, feeling warmth in his chest at the curve of her lips in the moonlight, a special moment shared just between them.

Marcus was still tired, but the pain in his back and legs made it impossible to go back to sleep. He watched his friends, thinking about how strange it was that just a few days ago, he'd been living a regular life on Earth. Embarrassing himself in front of the new neighbor girl. Struggling with a video game, as if that mattered. That night he had traveled here, to another planet, and then he had come back from Lysomnus with an injury after an attack that could have killed him. He ran his fingers over the cool metal of the hook on his prosthesis, thinking about his dad. Now that Marcus knew Deacon had been coming to Lysomnus all these years, he wondered: why would someone want to bring his dad back after he had to *stop* traveling here? Did Deacon know about the other humans here? That terrifying woman? Would he have told Marcus about all of this if he hadn't been kidnapped?

He groaned and tried to find a comfortable position. He had to try to go back to sleep so they could get as far as possible the next day. Who knew how long it would take to find any clues as to where his dad might be, and what if he was hurt? Although, since the message seemed to indicate that Marcus was supposed to come find him, maybe that meant they wouldn't hurt his dad. Now that he thought about it, that was odd, wasn't it? Why would someone want to get Marcus to come to them, using his dad as bait? What was so special about him? Was it just that he could travel to Lysomnus? Although, obviously, whoever they were could travel too. None of it made any sense. Finally, he curled up with his head on his pack and fell asleep, waking to his name being called repeatedly.

A foot was prodding Marcus's leg, none too gently. "Get *up*, lazybones!"

"Ugh." He rolled onto his back and blinked to see Leopold standing over him, arms crossed, blond hair still tousled from sleep.

"You gonna sleep all day, bro?"

"Nah, I'm awake." He held up his hand, and Leopold carefully helped him to his feet.

Cornus was near a bushy tree on the other side of the path, pulling purple orbs from its branches. He turned and carried an armful of fruit to the wagon. "Pellod," he said, winking at Marcus.

Leopold climbed up beside Sadie, who had just pulled the rest of the food supplies from the box and was replacing them with Cornus's harvest. She had made a neat stack of wortang—the spicy, green and orange striated root vegetable Marcus had eaten back in Thicce Colpat. It had been delicious roasted but was also tasty eaten raw.

"Let's eat some breakfast and get on the move." Leopold handed Marcus and Cornus a wortang, and the last one he took for himself. Sadie was just finishing one she'd taken from the box as she worked. "That's all the veggies, guys. We're down to just a few fruits. I'm guessing they didn't want to take too much from stores and give themselves away for helping us."

"We will be fine. I will find more," Cornus reassured them.

Marcus swallowed the last of his wortang, then bit into the purple flesh of a sweet pellod. The tangy flavor of the fruit was so different from anything he'd ever had back home, and he didn't think he could ever get tired of it.

Stomachs full, they buried the seeds beside the path before Sadie and Cornus seized the handle once more. Marcus kept pace alongside them with his cane, body aching as his muscles warmed up. He wasn't used to this kind of physical activity. Leopold walked beside him, looking concerned.

"You know you can't keep walking this much," he said quietly to Marcus. "Back home, you would already be in your wheelchair. You should be riding."

"Yeah, but sometimes you gotta work a little harder when circumstances change, right?" Marcus said, looking into Leopold's eyes. It was something his friend had said to him when he had wanted to give up not long after one of his early surgeries. Leopold smiled and put a hand on Marcus's shoulder. His blue eyes shone more than normal.

"You're right, buddy. You're the strongest guy I know. Keep walking as long as you can, and I'll pull you the rest of the way." Leopold walked a little bit ahead, swallowing hard. He tapped Sadie on the shoulder, and they traded places on the handle. Sadie dropped back to walk with Marcus.

"So, Cornus," Leopold said, "you started telling us about the people who live in the Beornan Rokk last night. We got sidetracked, and you didn't get to finish." Marcus listened closely.

"Yes, the Fyrtudo. Not many of the people of Lysomnus could live near the Beornan Rokk, but the Fyrtudo can. Our Teacher, Cassiope, said it is because of their physical structure. Like I said before, they burrow beneath the mountains for iron and the emeristan, which they trade with us and many other people of Lysomnus to use for cooking, heating, and other things. In return, we trade craft goods, food, and other items that we make."

"These Fyrtudo...did Cassiope tell you what they look like or anything?"

"Not really. They are quite different from us. And I imagine from humans, as well. They must be extraordinarily strong to live and work near the Beornan Rokk. I believe they are much larger than our people. Most of the people of Lysomnus do not wander far from their homes except to trade, so we do not meet them until we Travel. For some, it is impossible to come to us to trade, so we go to them."

Marcus and Sadie exchanged a wary glance. It was clear Cornus didn't know enough about the Fyrtudo to help them get a clear picture. As they walked on, Marcus felt the back of Sadie's hand brush his own. He glanced quickly at Sadie. Her cheeks were flushed. Pressure began to build in Marcus's chest as he plucked up the courage to do something he had never done before. He swallowed hard, put his cane surreptitiously under his right arm, then slid his fingers into Sadie's. They squeezed each other's hands tightly. A relieved sigh escaped both of them at the same time, and they looked at each other with smiles that turned quickly into stifled laughter.

"Haven't they ever come to your bruwe to trade? Do the Scrybb always travel to trade with the other people of Lysomnus?" Leopold continued to question Cornus, unaware of anything happening behind him.

"Well," Cornus said, sounding a bit reluctant, "I think other people used to, but our Teachers asked them to wait for our Traders to come to them. Cassiope mentioned that the Scrybb prefer this now."

"I'm surprised you're even still sent out on Travels. It sounds as if the Scrybb are purposefully isolating themselves from the other people of Lysomnus."

"That is something I have never considered. We have to have contact with the other people of Lysomnus for trade."

"Why don't the Teachers want any of the other people to come to your bruwe anymore, Cornus?" Sadie asked. "Do you know?"

"No, I do not," Cornus replied.

That morning's walk seemed incredibly long to the group; even Cornus, who had anticipated a year of Traveling on foot around Lysomnus, found their walking pace frustrating. Marcus moved to the seat of the wagon early, both for his own relief and because he knew the others could move faster without needing to walk slowly for him. His only regret was releasing Sadie's hand. Part of him wished he could ask her to come sit with him, but she was taking a turn pulling with Leopold.

Cornus told his companions he estimated it would take approximately ten more days to reach Palaga, the Fyrtudos' bruwe at the base of the Beornan Rokk.

"Ten days!" exclaimed Marcus. "I thought it was closer than that." He saw just what an undertaking it might be to find his father in a world that was, inconveniently, world-sized. Particularly when they had to walk everywhere they went. He realized just how much he had taken fast, modern transportation for granted back home.

"Aren't there horses or something we can ride?" Leopold asked.

"I do not know what a 'horse' is. We have the wagon for you to ride if you are too tired to walk, Leopold. Sadie and I can pull both you and Marcus."

"Uh, no—I—uh, that is—a horse is an animal, Cornus," Leopold stammered.

Marcus snorted at his friend's discomfiture. Sadie laughed, a merry sound that made Marcus smile.

"What Leopold is trying to say, Cornus, is that in our world, there are animals that people sit on, and they move faster than we can. It makes traveling easier."

"Oh. No, I do not know of any people in Lysomnus who ride on other living creatures. That seems cruel. Do your 'horses' like you to ride on them? Do you ask them if you can do it?"

"Well, I think it's kind of a friendly relationship most of the time? Like, the people who own horses care for them and feed them and stuff, and the horses are trained to let the people ride on them."

Cornus peered into the shadowy forest to their left. "Do you have a horse, Leopold?"

"Well, no. We live in the city, and most, uh, people who have horses live in the country. I don't really think there are a lot of people who have horses where we live..." Leopold trailed off as it became obvious Cornus wasn't really listening to him anymore.

"What are you looking at, Cornus?" Sadie asked. Their pace slowed as Cornus stared intently into the woods until they had nearly stopped.

"Something is moving toward us through the trees," Cornus said in a low voice.

"Are there any dangerous animals in these woods?" Leopold asked, clambering ungracefully onto the wagon at Marcus's feet. Sadie stared at him, holding the handle loosely in one hand with an amused expression on her face as he climbed out of potential harm's way.

"Yes, but I do not believe that is what I am seeing. Most of the Grenewud around this area is inhabited by smaller creatures that stay hidden when people are moving about. I am seeing something larger than that."

Marcus also caught sight of movement through the trees. A shadow flitted toward them from tree to tree. The thought that something dangerous might be approaching them was frightening despite Cornus's reassurances. Then he realized the sound of brush rattling in the woods was familiar—he had heard it the first time he had met Cornus. The shadow was another Scrybb!

She emerged from the trees onto the path with a few light, dancing steps. This Scrybb looked like a younger version of Buddleja, except the flowers decorating her body were white instead of purple.

"Davidia!" Cornus exclaimed.

Catching Cornus's hands, the new Scrybb pulled him into an embrace. She was taller than Cornus but appeared quite youthful.

"Cornus, my friend! Greetings! I am happy to see you."

Cornus hugged the Scrybb girl back just as enthusiastically, stepping back to look at her but keeping his hold on her hands. "I did not expect to see you until I returned from my Travels. What brings you to us?"

"A warning. I arrived home and heard you were Traveling with three humans. You need to be alert—there is a new Brynar ahead. You will reach it today." The smile on her face changed to one of concern as she warned him of the danger.

"A Brynar!" he exclaimed. "On this trail? Are you absolutely certain?"

"Yes. I crossed it while returning home from my own Travels and returned, hoping to catch you before you reached it when I heard you were Traveling with humans."

Cornus looked surprised. "Why did you come through the woods?"

Davidia shivered so vigorously that her leaves rustled. "Something doesn't feel right about this one. A new Brynar, on a Scrybb path, where there was none before? I went ahead to check it out again. I felt all shivery while I was near it. You should *all* avoid it, even you, Cornus."

Cornus shook his head. "You are being ridiculous. We will have to detour around the Brynar, of course, but only for the safety of my human companions." He held out a leafy hand to indicate his friends.

The three friends waved to Davidia from their respective places next to and on the wagon as she looked at them.

"Hello," they said in unison as Marcus began to descend carefully. Leopold followed with a sheepish expression on his face. Sadie shook her head at him.

"Oh, they are so cute!" Davidia exclaimed. She sauntered over and threw her arms around Marcus, who was now standing next to the wagon. His arms were pinned to his sides beneath hers, so he just awkwardly bent his left arm up and patted her on the back.

She stepped back and looked at him, her eyes glowing. "What is your name?"

"M-Marcus," he stammered, unsure of why he suddenly felt so shy.

Leopold stepped up next to Marcus and threw his arms out, saying, "And I'm Leopold!"

"Well, you are a bold one," laughed Davidia, giving Leopold a hug too.

She turned to Sadie. "Hello, lovely girl," she said. "What is your name?"

"I'm Sadie."

"And I am Davidia!" said the Scrybb girl, stepping over the handle and embracing Sadie as enthusiastically as she had the boys. Sadie's eyes widened in surprise, but she laughed and hugged the Scrybb girl back. After the way they had been treated by so many other Scrybb, it was refreshing to meet one so friendly.

"Davidia, we do not have time for this," Cornus said stiffly.

"Oh, Cornus, you are always so stuffy. Too much like Cassiope, if you ask me." Davidia waved a leafy hand in his direction. "I am just taking a moment to meet your friends. What is the rush?"

"We need to reach the Fyrtudo as quickly as possible. The father of my friend, Marcus, is missing, and it is particularly important that we do what we can to help him."

"*Your* father is missing?" Davidia looked at Marcus quizzically. "Why?"

"My father is Deacon Talent," Marcus said. "He was

kidnapped a few days ago, and I need to find him as soon as possible."

"Why did someone take him?" Davidia asked.

"I don't know," he replied. "That's the mystery. I got a message through the same kind of portal that the phantasms use telling me to come and find him."

"Phantasms?" Davidia looked confusedly at Cornus.

"<<Null>>," Cornus said.

"Oh! Oh, that is very strange, who could do that? And if they want you to come get *him*, does that mean they really want *you*?"

Sadie, Leopold, and Cornus all looked at Marcus. "Hm," Leopold said as if considering the idea for the first time. "Why would they want you, bro?"

"I have no idea," Marcus said. "I already thought of that, but I can't think of any reason why someone would want me badly enough to kidnap my father as bait. After all, I'm new here."

"Okay," Davidia said, hands on her leafy hips. "I am going to accompany you to the new Brynar and help you make your way around it. Once you have reached Beornan Rokk and we have heard if the Fyrtudo know anything about your father, I will turn around and head back to Thicce Colpat."

"Davidia," Cornus said rigidly, "we do not need your help. These are my Travels and my friends, and we can make it just fine without you."

Davidia rolled her eyes. "Cornus, stop being so stubborn. Your Travels will not count any less if I help you with this one part. Dragging humans around with you is not even part of Travels to begin with." Over her shoulder, to the humans, she added, "No offense to you all."

Startled, Marcus said, "None taken." Leopold started to say something else, but Marcus silenced him with an elbow to the ribs.

"Fine," Cornus said, turning and stomping quickly ahead of them up the path. Davidia shrugged, grabbed the handle with a nod to Leopold, and they pulled at a speed Marcus could keep up with. Sadie walked beside him, holding his hand again and looking concerned.

Leopold watched Cornus get farther and farther ahead. "Should I, like, try to catch up to him and talk to him or something?" he asked Davidia.

"Oh, I do not think that will help. He is very stubborn. We must let him walk off his anger, and then we can talk about this," Davidia said. "It will not take him long to reach the Brynar; he will have to stop and wait for us so we can all detour around it. That will not be so easy with this wagon." She shook the handle they were both holding.

"So you were in Cornus's Teaching year?" Marcus asked. "It sounds as if you grew up together."

"Yes, we did. There are twenty of us in our year. That is a smaller number than usual, and we are all very close. Cornus is a favorite of mine."

"It looked like he was so excited to see you at first, but now he's so mad," Leopold said. "I don't get it."

Davidia rolled her eyes. "Cornus has always been the *serious* person in our year. He is smaller than everyone else, will bloom later than everyone else, is starting his Travels later, too, so he feels that he must prove himself. No one else cares about those things, but he does."

"Well, he did have to come back after he started his Travels," Marcus said.

"Oh, no! Why, what happened?"

"It's really my fault," Marcus said and explained to her what had occurred when he had first come to Lysomnus and again when he and the others came back to find his father.

"That is quite the story," Davidia said, growing more serious as she looked back at Marcus. "Cornus did not really do anything wrong, but I can see why he is upset. He so desperately wants to prove himself a proper Scrybb, and to have these things happen on his Travels must be so frustrating."

"Davidia," Sadie asked, "Forgive me for asking, but you look remarkably similar to Buddleja. Are you sisters or somehow related?"

Davidia smiled. "It can seem complicated to people from outside Scrybb society. Davidia and I look similar because we have a shared flowering line. I do not know if both of the Scrybb who created us were the same ones, but they were the same 'species,' as we say. So, we look alike, except we have different colored flowers."

Then, she abruptly changed the subject, shaking the handle in her hand, "I am surprised to see this wagon since it is forbidden to use anything on our Travels to carry anything with us or use any tools."

"Oh, this is *ours*," Marcus said. "Abutilon gave it to *us*, not to Cornus."

"Hmm. That is one way to get around the restriction. Then again, as humans, you *are* too weak to last on a Travel year without some assistance."

"Hey!" Marcus cried out. "I resent that. I'm able to take care of myself."

"Of course you are," Davidia said dryly, eyeing his cane and prosthesis. "Of course you are."

"Davidia," Sadie said tightly. "Marcus is stronger than

you know. He may appear weak and have physical limitations, but don't assume that he is not as capable as you or I."

"Look," Leopold said, interrupting their burgeoning argument. "There's Cornus."

The small Scrybb was sitting forlornly on a log beside the path. About twenty yards beyond him, the path opened on to another of the barren, rock-strewn patches that Marcus had seen on his first visit to Lysomnus. Cornus stood up at their approach and reached for Davidia's hand. She released the handle and took Cornus's outstretched hand with her own. "My dearest friend," he said, pulling her close and wrapping his arms around her. "Please accept my apology for my behavior. I know you are only trying to help us."

Davidia sat down on the log, and Cornus sat back down beside her, leaning his head on her shoulder. "Cornus, I forgave you the moment you walked away." Davidia released Cornus's leafy hand and wrapped her arms around him. "I can never stay mad at you."

Leopold was walking toward the Brynar.

"Leopold! Stop!" Davidia, Cornus, and Marcus cried out in unison. It might have been amusing if not for the fear in their voices. Sadie flinched, staring out toward the barren dirt.

The blond boy stopped, turning toward them. "I understand it's not safe out there. I just want to look."

They all joined him, being careful not to step past the tree line. "Not much to see, is there?" Marcus said.

The sun had warmed the air above the flat, dark surface of the Brynar. Sweat beaded up on Marcus's face almost immediately. A breeze swirled idly across the flat surface of the deadly space, stirring up dust devils. Clumps of dirt and rocks were strewn across the Brynar.

"Hard to believe there's something that wants to kill us out there," Leopold replied.

"There is nothing 'out there' right now," Cornus said. "The <<null>> only enter Lysomnus once they sense that a human has stepped foot on a Brynar."

"Whoa, what did you just say?" Leopold exclaimed.

"Was that even a word? It's almost like I couldn't hear it!" Sadie added.

"I told you, we can't understand their word for the creature," Marcus reminded them. "My dad said that's why he calls them phantasms."

"The <<null>> are called so because of the dimension from which they come, which exists between your world and Lysomnus," Davidia told them. "For some reason, the Brynar seem to be weak points where they can break through to Lysomnus, but they only do so when they sense a human. They kill and then leave."

"Wait a minute," Leopold said, frowning. "If my buddy Marcus here has this special Talent for traveling from our world to Lysomnus, and he got it from his dad, that's only one human at a time. So why are these 'phantasms' or whatever they are trying to kill them? And if they had managed to kill either Deacon or any Talent before him, there wouldn't be any more humans here. Marcus wouldn't exist, right?"

Cornus and Davidia exchanged glances.

"Cassiope said there are other humans here in Lysomnus," Marcus said. "And since someone obviously came through their dimension and took my dad, it makes sense they'd be at risk too. And that person—that N—N—N person," he stopped himself as Cornus shook his head.

"She seems to be a human too."

"Whoa," Leopold breathed, looking at Sadie, whose dark eyes were wide as she stared at all of them.

CHAPTER EIGHT

A TALENT EMERGES

"I overheard the conversation the Teachers had about other humans being here, but Cassiope wouldn't tell me anything more. Do you know if they're like me and my dad?" Marcus asked.

"We—Cornus and I—do not know," Davidia said. "The Teachers have not told us much about them. The only reason we know as much as we do about them is because we saw them in Thicce Colpat one night."

"It is true." Cornus frowned. "I feel terribly guilty that I have kept this from you, Marcus. Cassiope instructed me to do so. It did not seem right to me, but I have followed her instructions until now."

"But why? Why don't they want us to know more about the other humans?"

"We do not know. We can only tell you what we have seen," Cornus answered.

"Then let's start with that," Marcus said.

The five of them returned to the wagon. Leopold pulled himself onto the seat and opened the box behind it. Marcus and Sadie sat on the front together; Cornus and Davidia shared the log where Cornus had been sitting when they had first come upon him.

Leopold handed a sartine down to Marcus. "Here's your

chance to try again, bro. Try again so we can all have a piece." Marcus held the large blue fruit between his left hand and his prosthesis. "What do I do? "

"You roll it between your hands and apply gentle pressure. You will feel when it is ready to open." Cornus frowned at Marcus, holding the large fruit awkwardly between his hand and the hook of his prosthesis. "I am sorry, Marcus. Give it to me and I will open it for you."

"No," Marcus said. "You don't need to do it for me. I will find a way."

Marcus thought for a moment, then set the sartine against the surface of the wagon. He rolled the sartine as Leopold tossed pellod to the others. Suddenly, he felt the fruit loosening under the palm of his left hand and pushed the fruit carefully against the cart as he rolled it. The sartine popped softly and split open into eight equal sections that unfurled like the petals of a flower, lying neatly on the cart. He picked one section up, eyeing it curiously, and bit into the sweet, juicy flesh.

Davidia and Cornus were staring. "That—that is a much better way to open a sartine!" Davidia exclaimed. "It is neatly on the surface, and nothing was dropped on the ground!"

Cornus nodded. "Sometimes, a section will fall when the fruit opens. I have never seen anything like this. That is quite an innovation. I do not know why no one ever thought of it before."

Sadie smiled at them both, putting a warm palm on Marcus's shoulder. "Necessity finds a new way when what you're used to doesn't work." She looked at Davidia. "I told you there was more to him than you believed." The Scrybb girl nodded, smiling.

"Okay," Marcus said, licking a trail of blue juice that had run down his arm, "let's talk about these humans."

Davidia spoke first. "All we learned from Cassiope is never to approach the eastern side of the continent during our Travels. No one from Thicce Colpat has been there for as long as anyone can remember. It is an exceedingly long journey and—"

"But Davidia and I know a little more," Cornus interrupted. "We saw them one night when we were supposed to be sleeping. We knew something was wrong because Cassiope was anxious all day. We were young and curious, so we promised each other we would stay up and find out what it was. We could not have dreamed what we would see."

Marcus was surprised that their rule-following friend had taken such a risk; then he looked at Cornus's hand, gripped tightly in Davidia's, and understood why the Scrybb boy had done it.

"The dormitory where the Scrybb children live is near the edge of Thicce Colpat, as you have seen. We snuck out and hid in the school. From there, we had an unobstructed view of the events of that night. Our Teachers gathered in the center of Thicce Colpat, and Cassiope approached from the west entrance of the bruwe. Following her was a group of creatures—people—unlike any we had heard of. They shared a similar physical form to us but appeared almost naked, as they had no leaves but only cloth coverings. They looked soft, like the skin of the pellod. The one in front was completely covered in billowy black cloth.

"Cassiope joined the other Teachers, and they stood facing the new people. We could not hear what was said, but the Teachers looked frightened." Cornus shook his head.

"We were so surprised and confused. Scrybb are afraid of very little other than fire. What could these soft people do to the Teachers that would cause such fear? Then, the strangers went to the bathhouse, and the Teachers returned to our dormitory. We were afraid to leave our hiding spot for fear we would be caught by either the Teachers or the strangers."

"It was a long and strange night for us," Davidia picked up the story. "The strangers came out of the bathhouse, covered in different wrappings than when they went inside. That is when we realized their cloth coverings were not part of them. They went into our banquet hall and feasted for what seemed like hours. At last, they entered the bunkhouse, and the bruwe became quiet. We felt brave enough to try to return to our dormitory."

"Where we were caught by Cassiope," sighed Cornus. "She was waiting for us inside the door. She sat us down and lectured us *forever* not to ever tell any of the other Scrybb children what we had seen. No one could know about the humans, as she said they were called. I asked about the smaller buildings they had gone into—the bathhouse and the bunkhouse—because, at that time, we did not know what they were. The Scrybb children are not allowed to enter either one."

"Deacon Talent has returned to Thicce Colpat since the time that we saw those first humans," Davidia said. "Cassiope told us that his family has been coming to Lysomnus for generations, but as young Scrybb, we were not allowed to go near Deacon. He was not welcome in our bruwe by every Scrybb."

"But when I met you, Cornus, it sounded like you knew my father and that he was some kind of famous person, or hero, or something," Marcus prompted.

"I do not believe that I said such a thing, Marcus. I am sorry if you thought that. I believe I said that he is very well known."

Marcus slid carefully off the wagon and began to pace slowly. "So, I'm getting the impression that the Scrybb don't care much for humans at all. Because of the humans that come to Thicce Colpat? What do they do to your people?"

"As we said before, we do not know any more than this."

"I feel so stupid." Marcus kicked a leaf on the ground. "I felt like everyone was helping us, and the whole time, they just wanted to get rid of us."

"That is not so," Cornus protested. "I want to help you. Cassiope gave me leave to help you, even though I am on my Travels, and she granted me permission to do so, clearly against the wishes of most of the other Teachers. And Abutilon and Buddleja helped us even though it is forbidden to do so while I am Traveling."

"Marcus," Davidia broke in. "There are Scrybb who want to support and help you. Please do not be angry. I know Cornus so well. He will do everything he possibly can to help you find your father."

"And what about the phantasms?" Marcus asked. "They're dangerous to those other humans, too, I assume?"

"Marcus, we just do not know. I would think they would be. We have always been told the <<null>> want to kill *any* human." Cornus sounded sorrowful as he looked at his friend.

Leopold walked back to the large, barren dirt field and leaned out to look back and forth along the tree line.

"Leopold!" Davidia cried out. "Stop!"

"I know, I won't walk out there. It's just hard to believe it's so dangerous, you know?"

Leopold turned back toward the others. Just as he did so, a dark shadow flitted across the dirt and gravel of the Brynar behind him. Sadie cried out and pointed at the sky. Startled, Cornus and Davidia ran to Leopold's side to look out from beneath the trees to see what had cast the shadow.

Leopold stepped farther out, craning his neck to look skyward. Davidia seized his arm and pulled him back under the trees. "Do not be foolish! If you step one foot on the Brynar, the <<null>> will come through and attack you."

Cornus walked out onto the barren dirt, looking up. Marcus half expected to hear the howling, screaming noise that had preceded the phantasm's appearance when he had walked out onto the Brynar on his first visit to Lysomnus, but nothing happened.

Cornus continued his scrutiny of the skies above as he walked farther out onto the Brynar. "I do not see anything. Perhaps it was just a cloud."

"Pretty fast cloud," Marcus said uncertainly.

"No way that was a cloud," said Sadie.

"Look!" Leopold pointed toward the other end of the Brynar, where an enormous flying creature appeared just above the trees. It dove swiftly toward Cornus, wide talons extended. The Scrybb boy was turning to see what the human boy was pointing at, but he was too slow to react. Leopold was abruptly knocked aside as Davidia shoved past him, dust puffing around her feet as she raced across the Brynar. She seized Cornus by the arm, whirling as she hurled him back toward the trees. The Scrybb boy landed hard, skidding across the dirt on his back. He rolled over and scrambled to his knees, watching helplessly as Davidia was seized from behind by the winged creature.

A single scream faded away as she soared into the sky, caught in the creature's talons.

"Davidia!" Cornus cried out.

There was only a pool of steaming red liquid where Davidia had been just a moment before. It glowed like lava as it slowly formed a black crust before their eyes. The humans stood just inside the trees, unable to step out and help Cornus.

"What was *that*?" Marcus gasped. Sadie shook her head, breathing shakily. Terror shone in her dark eyes when she looked up at him. Marcus wrapped his arms around her and pulled her against him. She squeezed him tightly, her tears dampening his shirt.

Cornus slowly rose to his feet. "I think that we are all in far more danger than we ever could have imagined." He walked over to look at the glowing material left by the flying creature. The others were terribly afraid that he would touch it since it appeared to be dangerously hot. However, he merely looked and then returned to the path to stand next to them. The others watched the skies anxiously the entire time it took for the small Scrybb to reach them.

"Cornus, I'm so sorry," Marcus said, releasing Sadie and wrapping his friend in an embrace. Cornus hugged him back, but they could all sense his immense grief. Sadie put a hand on his shoulder. It was obvious she was at a loss for words.

Marcus asked. "What was that thing? Do you know?"

"A fairy tale." Cornus sighed, his shoulders slumped. "As young Scrybb, we were told the legend of the Stondefel, the mighty stone demons of the Beornan Rokk. They are supposed to be able to eat molten rock and use their burning saliva to destroy their enemies. We were told the Stondefel would come to get us if we misbehaved. But it was just a story, a legend of the past. Or at least, so I thought."

"I hate to say it, Cornus, but it's starting to look like your legends might be true," Sadie said.

"How can we find Davidia?" Marcus asked. "I can only imagine how terrified she must be. Why would that thing—that Stondefel—take Davidia?"

"I don't think it meant to, Marcus," Leopold asserted. "It was going straight for Cornus. It only grabbed Davidia because she threw Cornus out of the way."

"But why would anyone want me?" Cornus rubbed his eyes. "I am no one. Just a young Scrybb barely beginning his Travels, and I am not even doing well at that."

"Cornus, you're a Scrybb who's helping *me* search for my father," Marcus pointed out. "Maybe someone wanted to take you for answers or stop you from helping me. Either is possible."

"But what are they going to do to Davidia?" Sadie asked, clearly frightened for Cornus's friend. "These Stondefel have molten saliva according to your legends because they eat molten rock—lava, I'd imagine. There's proof sitting right there in the Brynar." She pointed at the glowing residue.

"Maybe they won't do anything as soon as they realize they have the wrong Scrybb," Leopold offered hopefully.

"If she survives," Cornus uttered despondently.

"Hey," Marcus said, putting an arm around the Scrybb boy's shoulders and shaking him. "We aren't giving up on her. You said the Stondefel lived in the Beornan Rokk, according to the legend? Well, the legend seems to have gotten a lot right. So, the Beornan Rokk seems like a good place to start. And we're heading there anyway to talk to the Fyrtudo. We can ask *them* what they know about these

Stondefel. We just have to go faster to help your friend."

Cornus turned hopeful eyes up to Marcus. "You really think she might be okay?"

"I don't think she was the one they were after, so yeah, I think she's probably okay," Marcus said. *Hopefully they don't kill her just for being the wrong Scrybb*, he thought to himself. "Let's get moving. I just don't know how I'm going to get through the woods to get around this Brynar, much less help with a whole wagon. Maybe it would be better if I stayed behind."

"No," Cornus asserted firmly. "We will lose no more of our group. Once we make our way around the Brynar, you will stay on the wagon while we pull. It will be faster."

As they struggled to make their way through the woods around the Brynar, each of them at times contemplated leaving the unwieldy wagon behind. If they weren't so aware of how badly they needed it for Marcus, they might have done so. The undergrowth around the Brynar seemed unusually thick, with dense patches of briar, wayward gullies, and a few downed trees. Marcus was frustrated as his friends struggled with the wagon, which kept catching on every branch, root, and rock. While taking a break from working through the brush, he glared at the object that was causing them so much trouble. If only, he thought, he was strong enough to grab the wagon and throw it through the trees.

The whole thing flipped over and landed upside down, the handle flopping and nearly hitting Sadie. All four of them stared at it in astonishment.

"How—" Cornus started.

"What the—" Leopold said.

Sadie stared at the wagon, her mouth open.

"Uh...." Marcus muttered. "That was weird."

"Hey, man," Leopold asked, "how are you feeling? We've been working our way through these woods for a long time."

"Oh, you know," Marcus said. "I'm doing okay."

"I doubt that," Cornus said. "I have noticed that you are not able to move through the brush very well. It is time to rest and eat."

Leopold and Cornus turned the wagon over. Marcus slowly climbed on and leaned back on the seat, closing his eyes in relief.

Cornus was staring into the sky, a frown on his face. "Looks like rough weather coming." The others looked up to see dark clouds churning in the sky between the broad leaves of the trees. "Come on, let us get some water." Leopold followed the Scrybb boy into the woods.

Sadie climbed up to sit beside Marcus and put a gentle hand on his leg. "Marcus," she began hesitantly, "have you thought of using the Halfriez on yourself for your pain?"

"I don't know. It doesn't feel right," he admitted. "Maybe I could try it a little." He fumbled for the stone. Holding it against his back, he thought of his pain, and the stone heated up. The pain began to diminish, but something shifted in his back. He immediately stopped and put the stone back in his pocket. Sadie raised an eyebrow. "Why'd you stop?"

"The pain got better," Marcus said, "but something started to move. I think it was going to do something to the bones and metal that are fused together in my back. I don't know what would happen—things could get messed up."

"At least your pain is better." Sadie smiled. "I'm glad about that. I hate to see you hurting."

Marcus looked down at her. He could see the concern on her face. Little lines creased the skin between her eyes as she looked up at him. Knowing she was worried about him eased his pain in a way the Halfriez could never do. He'd never had a girl care about him before. And how he felt about Sadie was special; they'd only met a short time ago, but he already felt about Sadie like he never had about anyone. She didn't judge him for being disabled and had even spoken up in his defense.

He took the hand she had set on his leg in his left hand and squeezed lightly. It made him feel even better when she squeezed back, a smile easing the tension on her face. He looked at her dark eyes and her black hair, thinking about holding her hand as they walked together and—

"Marcus?"

He realized he was staring at her. "Sorry, I...I was just thinking about how much better I feel. Thanks for thinking of using the Halfriez; it was a good idea."

"Sure," she said, a smile on her face as she turned away.

Voices in the brush heralded the return of Leopold and Cornus. Marcus looked up as they came into the clearing to see tears sliding down the leaves on Cornus's face. He climbed clumsily off the surface of the wagon, walked over to his friend, and stooped to embrace him. "Cornus," he said, "you don't have to rush through every part of this journey. It's okay to take a break and talk about how worried you are."

"Davidia is my best friend!" Cornus cried out. "I cannot stand the thought of what might be happening to her right now." He buried his face in his hands, shoulders shaking as he cried even harder.

Slowly, Cornus's arms crept around Marcus, and the Scrybb boy wept against his chest. Sadie and Leopold looked relieved. Marcus knew that they had all been worried about Cornus and unsure how to help him, but he had been waiting for Cornus to be ready to begin grieving for his lost friend.

Cornus stepped back, mumbling and swiping embarrassedly at Marcus's wet shirt. He took a deep breath and said, "Thank you, Marcus. I do feel better. Now, we need to eat and drink some water."

Leopold had been holding the leaf cups of water and handed them to Sadie and Marcus. Marcus was glad that he and Sadie had gotten some time alone while Cornus had taken time to soak up water through his roots.

Cornus had restocked the produce box with fruit earlier that day, and they still had a few vegetables, so they were able to fill their hungry bellies.

After eating and quenching their thirst, they got ready to move on. Lifting the wagon again, Cornus, Sadie, and Leopold wrangled their way up a small rise to avoid another thick briar patch while Marcus followed behind. Leopold remarked that the forest was darker, and as if a faucet had been turned on above them, rain suddenly poured down from the sky. The three humans cried out with dismay as they were quickly soaked to the skin, making their clothes cling to them. Cornus, of course, felt little discomfort as water simply rolled off his leaves.

As well as being wet and tired, Marcus was still hungry in a way the produce couldn't seem to satisfy. His body was starting to crave other nutrients. He knew the others must be feeling even worse since they were doing all the heavy labor. While he was daydreaming, the wagon got stuck again. Leopold was pulling the front end while Cornus and Sadie pushed, and Marcus wished that the damned thing would just pull itself through the trees. The wagon flew forward, the rear wheels nearly hitting Leopold as it jolted forward.

"Dude, look out!" Marcus yelled, reaching out as if to try to catch it, even though it had already passed him. The flying thing stopped and lurched sideways, missing Leopold completely.

"How did that happen?" Cornus asked, staring at Marcus. "The wagon was going to hit him, and then it...did not?"

Leopold had turned around and was looking at the offending object lying upside down beside him. "What's going on, you guys? Are you trying to kill me?"

"Or something else is going on," Cornus said, looking at Marcus oddly.

"What, Cornus?"

"I think *you* had something to do with that. It is the second time the wagon has moved independently. You wanted to know why someone might want to use your father as bait to bring you to them? If you have power, that would certainly be a reason."

Marcus stared at Cornus. "Power? That's just—you mean like magic?"

Cornus shrugged. "I do not know what 'magic' is. I only know that I have heard members of the Talent family can have power. Look at what you can do just by coming here from your own world, just as your father did. If you can do that, why could you not wield another kind of power?"

Marcus stared at his own hand as if seeing it for the first

time. He looked up at Leopold, who shrugged and said, "Hey, we're in a different world with flying monsters and leafy people. Anything's possible."

"That sounds so crazy." Sadie shook her head. "You think Marcus has magic powers?"

"He did have the power to bring us here," Leopold pointed out, waving a hand at the world around them. "Not to mention healing me with that crystal cube thing. Is it so hard to believe?"

"Can you move the wagon again?" Cornus asked.

Marcus looked at it and shrugged. He tried to remember what he had done the other times the thing had seemed to move on its own, but nothing came to mind except a vague sense of frustration. He frowned, concentrating. He had wanted it to move. He held out his left hand and focused on the idea, willing something to happen.

One of the wheels began to spin slowly.

"Wow, Marcus, that's really impressive." Leopold snickered.

"Oh, shut up," Marcus snapped. "If you think it's so easy, you try it."

He watched while Leopold walked over and got ready to flip the wagon over.

"Just wait a second," Marcus said. "I want to try again." Leopold stepped back and crossed his arms with a sigh.

Marcus set his feet more firmly and held out his arm, trying to reach mentally through his outstretched fingers. The wheel started spinning again, fast enough that the wood creaked on its axle. Leopold rolled his eyes and went back to turning over the wagon.

Cornus went to help without a word. Sadie slowly took her own corner, giving Marcus a sympathetic look.

It was almost dark by the time Cornus said they were nearing the path on the far side of the Brynar. The rain had finally let up, and the shattered moon was shining through the patchy clouds, providing just enough light through the trees to help them push through the rest of the way to the path. The three humans had stayed warm from their exertions in the woods, though they looked forward to changing into dry clothes, while the Scrybb boy never seemed to get cold.

"Cornus," Marcus asked as the others finally set the wagon down on the path with relief, "have you ever heard of something new just showing up like that Brynar did? I mean, how could that happen?"

"No, I have not. It makes no sense to me."

"That area was all the Grenewud before, right?"

The Scrybb frowned. "Yes, and the path continued straight through. At least that is what I was told."

"Where did the trees go? Does someone have the power to create a Brynar wherever they want to? Are those the people who have my father?"

"I do not have answers for you, Marcus." Cornus shrugged helplessly. "I can only help you by finding other people in our world and asking them for answers." Cornus's eyes were dimmer than usual, and he moved with less enthusiasm, preparing for the night.

Marcus realized that the young Scrybb was still struggling with his grief and worry while trying to answer his questions. "Let us get some sleep tonight so we can continue with haste tomorrow toward the Fyrtudo."

Leopold climbed onto the wagon, handed down a pellod for each of them. and then took a bite of his own fruit. With his mouth full, he said to Marcus, "I think you're being kind of a jerk, bro."

Marcus stared at him. "Excuse me?"

"Dude just lost his best friend, and you're climbing all over his back about Brynars and power and trees," Leopold went on, gesturing with his pellod toward Cornus while juice ran down his arm. "Who cares? Why does it matter? Let's just get where we need to go, find Davidia and your dad, and go home."

Marcus's jaw clenched. He opened his mouth to snap at his friend. Ashamed, he realized he had just been thinking the same thing, and he felt awful.

"You're right," Marcus said, his face burning. "I'm sorry, Cornus. It's been a long day, and you didn't deserve that."

"Hey," Sadie said. "It might matter, Leopold. Cornus deserves our support, but we also need to know why these other things are happening. They might be part of what's going on with Marcus's dad and why Davidia was taken."

"It is all right, Leopold. And Sadie is correct. All things are important. Please, my friends, we need to rest now." Cornus's leaves drooped forlornly.

Everyone fell asleep quickly after the arduous day. However, after just a short time, Marcus was awakened by intense pain in his lower back and hips. On a normal day on Earth, he would walk short distances, between classrooms at school and around the house, with his cane. Longer distances required a wheelchair. He had done more walking today than he had done in the last several years back at home.

Marcus could see fairly well in the moonlight, and he struggled to a sitting position, leaning back against a tree. Across the path, he could see that Cornus was also awake. He wasn't surprised since the Scrybb was probably out of his mind with worry for Davidia. Leopold leaned sideways against a tree with his mouth hanging open, and Sadie was curled up on the ground, sound asleep.

Marcus noticed that Cornus had pulled up and was cleaning more wortang. As soon as he saw the vegetables, he realized how hungry he was. The thought of trying to get up and cross the path to get one was excruciating. Instead, Marcus wondered if he could try to move one like he had done with the wheel of the wagon earlier. Mouth watering, he held out his left hand and tried to imagine one of them in his grip. Nothing happened.

Marcus concentrated harder, trying to remember how he had felt when the wagon had moved on its own. Both times, he had been frustrated and lashed out with his emotions. He thought about how hungry he was and how badly he wanted to eat. With a burst of inspiration, he grabbed the Halfriez in his pocket. It had warmed and helped him sleep when he needed to return to Lysomnus, and it had gotten hot to help heal Leopold's broken leg. Maybe he could use it now to assist him in using this power that was starting to evolve within him.

Was it his imagination, or had a couple of the vegetables trembled and begun to move? He tried again, focusing with all his might. Without holding out his hand, he just concentrated with his mind on moving the vegetables. The Halfriez was warming in his clenched fingers.

Inch by inch, a single wortang rose shakily and drifted toward him. Halfway across the path, it dropped to the ground. Marcus sighed in frustration. Why had it fallen? He could feel himself getting angry, like he had when Leopold teased him about his failure in the woods the day before. But he refused to give up this time. He tried to calm down with a few deep breaths.

Concentrating on his hunger, he reached out again. The vegetable moved slowly into the air and fell. It took a third attempt to get it back into the air and moving toward him again. A few seconds later, the wortang was in his hand. Cornus, who had been watching intently, applauded and gave a small cheer, accidentally waking the others.

They all sat and talked about what this new power of Marcus's could mean.

"What does it feel like, dude?" Leopold asked, all of his former derision gone.

"I can't really describe it, honestly. I mean, there's the effort of concentration. That's not really any different than thinking hard during a test in school." Even Cornus could relate to that.

"You don't even feel different in your body?" Sadie asked. "When you heal someone, you've said it always feels warm."

"Well, I think that's the Halfriez itself. While it usually feels cold all the time, it warms up and feels hot when I use it for healing. My body doesn't feel warmer while I'm trying to use this power, but the Halfriez does. It's like I'm using it to boost me."

The others continued talking. Marcus tried moving more of the vegetables across the path to Leopold and Sadie. It took a lot of attempts, and several vegetables wobbled and fell to the path, but he did manage to deliver a few of them to his friends. It might have been an accident that a couple of Leopold's happened to fall on his head. As everyone finally laid down for the night, Marcus wondered if Deacon had some power like this. Would he have told Marcus about any of this if he hadn't been kidnapped? He wished more than anything that his dad had stayed up that night to tell him more about Lysomnus.

Marcus tried to find a comfortable position, hoping to get some rest. He was relieved to see that Cornus was finally asleep by the time his own eyes were feeling heavy.

When Sadie gently shook him awake in the morning, Marcus could not hold back a cry of pain. With the night's rest had come stiffness and pain in his entire back, hips, and legs, muscles in his body that hadn't been used this way in years and the injured areas that had been pushed far past their tolerance.

Leopold had to help Sadie get Marcus on his feet. "Bro, why don't you stay on the wagon? I think you should take it easy. You put a lot of strain on your bod yesterday."

Out of breath and shaking just from the pain of getting to his feet, Marcus was in no condition to argue. He was unable to walk to the wagon on his own and needed everyone's assistance to get up to the seat, where he couldn't hold back a sigh of relief. He was so ashamed of needing so much help that he couldn't bring himself to even look at Sadie. While she had stuck up for him and his resilience before, she had never seen just how bad it could get for him.

"Bro," Leopold said, familiar with Marcus at his worst. "You're going to be fine. A couple days of rest, and you'll be feeling a lot better. You just pushed way too far. I've known you for years, and I have *never* seen you push this hard. Or keep going through that kind of pain."

"There was no choice," Marcus said dully. "It was that or stay behind. I have to keep pushing so we can find my father and now Davidia. Sometimes, even though I'm in pain and it's hard to keep going, I have to find a way to make it through and do what needs to be done. Now we've made it, and I'm paying the price. I only hope I don't slow you all down." He dropped his face into his hand, embarrassed that Sadie should see him so weak and in need of assistance.

"Marcus." Sadie put a hand on his foot. He looked at her from the corner of his eye, then turned his head so he could see through the curls that tumbled over his face. "I don't feel any different about you. What you did yesterday... That was one of the toughest things I've ever seen. And I'm not talking about your power, either. You fought your way through the woods with us all day. Of course you're hurting today. Believe me, we've got sore muscles too. You pushed through more than you ever should have."

"I am also sorry you had to suffer, Marcus," Cornus said. "I do not know why that Brynar was there, but we should have been able to walk on a Scrybb path through that part of the Grenewud. Unfortunately, the danger was too great to the three of you. Now, we have lost an entire day, so we must get moving."

Leopold and Cornus took up the handle at the front and began to run, learning each other's pace. Leopold had to adjust his stride to match the shorter legs of the Scrybb boy, but even at his lesser height, Cornus was able to run at a pretty fast pace.

"Yah! Yah mule!" Leopold yelled. He cracked an imaginary whip over their own heads.

"What is a 'mule'?" Cornus asked.

"A mule is an animal with four legs and a long back," Sadie explained, jogging beside the cart. "They're very strong and can run faster than humans can. Our people used to ride them and use them to pull carts and wagons and other things."

"The people of your world are strange." Cornus frowned.

"You certainly like to take advantage of the labor of other creatures."

"Uh, yeah. I guess you're right," Leopold said. "I never thought of it like that before. But there are a lot of things that people can't do that strong animals like horses and mules helped us do before we built machines to do them."

"Mash—eenes?" Cornus turned to look at Leopold while continuing to run. "What are they?"

"Machines. Kind of like this wagon, but if it had a way to move on its own," Marcus answered for his friend. He noticed Leopold was finding it difficult to keep pace with Cornus, who wasn't having any trouble holding a conversation while pulling the cart at running speed.

"Such a strange world you must live in," Cornus said.

"Let's—ah—just—ah—run," Leopold panted. It was obvious he envied Cornus's lack of discomfort. Apparently, something about the Scrybb boy allowed him to run without becoming tired—at least at Leopold's pace.

"All right," Cornus agreed.

Marcus thought about it taking ten more days to reach the Fyrtudo. They had lost the entire previous day, making their way through the Grenewud around the Brynar. He hoped that Cornus had estimated the ten days at a pleasant walking pace. At first, Marcus thought that running without him slowing them down, they could cut the time down to at least half that. Now, watching his friend, he realized that Leopold could never keep this pace up for a few hours, much less several days.

How far away was Davidia by now? If her captors had wanted Cornus and not her, what might she be going through? What about his father? They had been holding Deacon captive for days. What had these kidnappers been doing to him? Would they ever find both captives if it took this long to get anywhere?

It quickly became obvious that running was going to wear Leopold out quickly. The human boy would never be able to run for ten days, even taking turns with Sadie. Marcus asked them to stop. "I want to try something," he said. "Can you fold the handle back?"

After they had done as he suggested, Marcus sat back on the wagon and wondered if he could use his newly discovered power to move it. It had gotten easier to move the vegetables as he continued last night, so he was sure he could move something bigger like this wagon if he tried.

At first, nothing happened, and he found himself sitting there on the seat feeling stupid, just as he had in the woods. Marcus refused to let disappointment take over. He closed his eyes and recalled the concentration he had used the night before and reached for the Halfriez in his pocket, letting it warm in his pocket as he focused. It wasn't anything physical but rather a mental gathering of power. He felt as if he were *willing* the wagon to do what he wanted it to do.

Marcus began working on moving the wagon again. He focused on *how* he would move it.

He could feel the wheels where they touched the ground. Moving himself and the wagon beneath him was really just a simple act of pushing the wheels against the ground. A smile played around the corners of his mouth as turning the wheels became the process of moving the entire conveyance in his head. He couldn't help but remember the look on Leopold's face yesterday in the woods when all Marcus had done was make one wheel spin. Now, as the wheels turned, they pushed against the ground and moved the wagon carrying Marcus and everything else on it. Marcus realized he was just doing what he had done in the woods—spinning the wheels. He hadn't had any surface for the wheels to push against then—and he sensed his power had somehow grown stronger now. The practice with the vegetables was like lifting weights; he had built up his mental power by using it.

To control the speed of the wagon, all he had to do was push the wheels faster or slower. Yesterday, he hadn't realized the actual physics of how he was moving them. Now that he had it figured out, it was much easier to control the speed.

With a shuddering jolt, the wagon started moving. Marcus hardly dared to breathe as it kept rolling forward in case it distracted him. Sadie walked alongside, looking up at Marcus, but he was afraid to look at her. The others followed behind.

"I don't think that either Sadie or Leopold will be able to keep running for the whole time, although it looks like you could, Cornus," Marcus said, keeping the power in his mind focused on the wheels. "But if I can keep the wagon moving with all of us on it, maybe we can still make good time."

"Unh!" Leopold grunted as the wagon stopped suddenly, and he ran into it belly first. "Gee, dude, a little warning might be nice."

Sadie laughed, trying to stifle it as best she could with one hand over her mouth. Leopold pretended to glare at her, but a grin quirked one corner of his mouth. Marcus smiled through the pain in his back as he turned to look at them.

"Sorry, man. It's not like I know what I'm doing. I'm trying." Marcus turned and started rolling forward again. This time, it was Sadie who tripped as he lost control and stopped suddenly, and her foot caught on one of the wheels. Leopold made no effort to control his laughter as he helped her back to her feet.

It took several abrupt stops and starts for Marcus to be able to keep the wagon moving. The jerks hurt, which he found motivating. If he could keep everything moving, it wouldn't hurt so much. He could keep it moving for a slightly longer stretch, then it would jerk to a stop. The others were walking around him, where they could avoid the sudden stops and starts. After several jolts that nearly knocked Marcus to the floor, he tried concentrating more diligently to keep the wagon from stopping so hard. Soon, it was gliding down the path and slowing smoothly to a stop.

"One of you should climb on," Marcus suggested. "I want to see if adding weight makes a difference to the effort it takes to keep it moving. It's a weird concept. *Is* it actually a matter of physics, where the weight of the object increases the work of my mind to move it?" He frowned. "I need to try it out."

Cornus, as the lightest, climbed on behind Marcus, and they started moving again. He felt no strain when moving the cart.

"How does it feel to have someone else on there with you, Marcus?" Sadie asked.

Marcus looked down at her where she walked beside the wagon. "'It's not any different," he said just as he jerked to a halt, throwing Cornus to the ground. Leopold laughed as he pulled Cornus to his feet and playfully dusted him off. "You okay, little bro?"

Marcus shook his head. "It looks like I'm going to have to start all over again, learning how to control stopping and starting while distracted." He was frustrated at the thought of all the work this would involve. The pressure of losing time weighed him down. He hoped they could make up some time when he learned to control moving with everyone on board. "Okay, this time, Cornus should sit behind the seat so he doesn't fall off if it stops suddenly again."

The others looked dubious, but Cornus climbed back up and sat behind the seat, hanging on as the cart started moving..

Leopold nudged Sadie.

"Hey, when we were at Marcus's house, you said something about your mom becoming an American citizen?"

"Yeah, what about it?" she said defensively.

"Sorry," Leopold said, breaking a dead twig off a tree. "I'm just curious. Does that mean she was Korean, and they met and got married there? And where were you born?"

The wagon stopped suddenly.

"Sorry, everyone," Marcus said, "I have to figure out how to keep going and listen at the same time."

"My grandmother lives in Korea, and my mother was born there and met my dad when he was stationed in Seoul. She moved here with him and became an American citizen."

Leopold looked at her with wide eyes. "So did you go through that with your mom?"

Sadie rolled her eyes. "No, Leopold. I was born on the American military base in Korea. It's considered to be American soil, so that automatically made me a citizen. My brother was born in California, but our family has spent a lot of time in Korea, even after my dad retired from the military."

"Hey!" Leopold shouted. "Marcus, you haven't stopped once since Cornus got back on!"

"That's because while you and Sadie kept talking, I concentrated on paying attention to moving the wagon while I was listening. I'm getting better at this," he said. "Why don't you guys try climbing on, and I'll see how it feels to move the wagon with all four of us on board?"

Things went well. Marcus continued to focus on keeping them moving on the path, which was remarkably smooth. The Scrybb obviously put a lot of work into maintaining these pathways through the Grenewud. Marcus wondered why they hadn't come across any of the Scrybb whose job it was to maintain these paths. Maybe they were working on other paths somewhere else.

Marcus felt no strain in his mind or increase in the pain in his body. When Cornus called for a stop to search for water and food, he found a different plant from any they'd yet seen, a tall yellow stalk hidden in the foliage growing by the path. He told the others it had been in the stew back in Thicce Colpat.

Cornus smiled as he handed it out. "This is allsop. I had hoped to find some. It is a difficult plant to grow, and I was told it could be found a distance away from the bruwe. There is a good opening to let the sun through here, which nourishes it."

The three humans found it delicious, despite its difference from their previous experience with it. In the stew, it had been savory with a soft, heavy consistency. It was sweet and chewy when eaten raw. Cornus said it was used in the stew for its thick consistency and because its sweet flavor countered the spice of the wortang. He also found another pellod tree, and the four of them restocked the storage box with the sweet vegetable and the fruit. Marcus was very grateful for Cornus, whose extensive knowledge of plants kept them stocked with food that could actually nourish them rather than only the fruit that the humans would have found had they been on their own.

"Cornus," Sadie asked, "How is it that there are pellod trees all along the path?"

The Scrybb smiled. "An astute observation, my friend. While we have been planting our seeds every time we stop to eat, often other Scrybb will carry the seeds with them as they Travel and plant them along the way so others will have food available to them. Pellod grow easily and quickly, so they are an excellent choice to leave for others. Sartine will grow, but much more slowly. The same goes for the vegetables.

Cornus and Leopold made the trip for water this time. While they were waiting, Sadie and Marcus twined their fingers together, and Sadie laid her head against Marcus's thigh. He suddenly found himself very glad he had brought Leopold and Sadie with him to Lysomnus.

The others returned with water and another edible surprise. Cornus found a tree that bore a small, hard-shelled fruit that resembled a nut by the stream while they filled the cups with water. The tixpits, as Cornus called them, were easily shelled, and the fruit inside was chewy and savory.

After everyone climbed back on the cart, Marcus was getting much better at moving them along without the sudden jerks. He was sure they had traveled farther than they would have if they'd been walking. Looking down at Cornus beside him, Marcus felt a stab of sorrow. He remembered the sight of Davidia's terrified face and the sound of her scream as she had disappeared into the sky. He knew Cornus had to be reliving the moment when Davidia threw him aside, when he watched helplessly as she was taken away.

The least Marcus could do was get them as quickly as possible to their next destination so his friend could get some answers.

When nightfall darkened the sky, they stopped to rest. Marcus realized that even riding all day had been hard on his body when he climbed down. A trip into the woods to attend to his toilet needs was exhausting, and he wished he didn't have to bother with such things. His back hurt from riding and all the jerking, and it was difficult to walk through the underbrush until he found a place he felt comfortably out of sight.

It took him so long that when he returned, the others were already asleep beside the path. He remembered Cornus saying there could be danger in the Grenewud, and after what had happened to Davidia, Marcus was even more concerned. He thought the least he could do was stay awake and watch over his friends for a little while as they slept. No matter how hard he tried, his eyes kept closing, and soon, he was fast asleep with his head on his pack.

CHAPTER NINE

THE FYRTUDO

Marcus found it much easier to keep the wagon rolling steadily the next morning. The most challenging part was keeping them progressing while he was distracted by talking or eating. As they moved along the path, Marcus concentrated on maintaining a steady speed and found that it took some effort. First, they'd go slow, then they would speed up until he felt as if the cart was almost out of his control. The looks of doubt he saw from the others didn't help. After hours of work, he found a balance and the wagon was moving at what felt like one constant speed, and he started to relax and listen to the others' conversation. He sighed with relief.

"Hey, Cornus," Leopold said, "how many Scrybb are in Thicce Colpat right now from your year in school? Are they all Traveling like you and Davidia?"

"Oh, ours is a small group. One of the smallest in several years—only twenty. I think most are done Traveling right now. I was the last to start. We are all very close friends—" He broke off, his voice thickening; it was obvious his thoughts had turned to Davidia and the tears were close.

With a jolt, the wagon jarred to a stop, Cornus fell off completely, landing on the ground, and Sadie slammed into the back of the seat, Leopold stayed on only because he was holding onto the back edge. Marcus slid forward, nearly falling off the seat. His cane clattered to the ground.

"What are you doing?" Cornus asked, wiping his wet cheeks as he stood up. He picked up Marcus's cane and threw it angrily onto the wagon.

"I'm so sorry." Marcus said. "I was distracted by your conversation again.. It's tough to keep this thing going at a steady pace while listening, and I'm not even trying to talk with you yet. Please be patient with me, and I think I can really get the hang of this. I've been working on it all morning."

"Well, I'd like to keep my body in one piece, thank you very much," Leopold retorted. He sighed. "Look, I get it, man. But please, try to keep us in one piece."

Sadie leaned from behind the seat, rubbing her shoulder, which had taken the brunt of the impact with the seat. "How is this making *you* feel? You're moving the whole wagon with this new power plus all of us, and now you're trying to control the speed. Isn't this going to wear you out? Are you tired?"

Marcus smiled at her. "I feel great. My body still hurts, of course, but using the power doesn't seem to be making it any worse. Even though I'm concentrating on moving the wagon with all our weight on it, I don't feel any mental strain."

Once everyone was settled comfortably again, Marcus began to move them, slowly at first and then faster, testing his ability to see just how fast he could go and maintain control.

"Whoa, Speed Racer!" Leopold exclaimed, sounding concerned. "Are you sure it's safe for you to go this fast? If you get distracted again—"

Marcus carefully eased them to a stop. "I wanted to test it. I know what I'm doing now—I've figured it out."

"I think it will be a problem if you smash us into a tree, Marcus. I hope you can stop quickly if it becomes necessary." Cornus looked at Marcus with some consternation.

"I can." Marcus slowed them down to a crawl.

"Marcus? What did you figure out? Can you tell us?" Sadie asked.

Marcus was happy to share what he had realized about the actual workings of his power on the wheels and how he was moving it. He thought all the practice was making his power stronger, and the Halfriez also seemed to act as a catalyst.

"Sounds like I was a big help, bro. In fact, I think we could say I was instrumental in figuring out how you could move this wagon," Leopold said.

Sadie pushed him, and he almost fell off. "Stop trying to take all the credit."

"Hey!" Leopold yelled as he caught himself.

Cornus looked up at Marcus. "This is a strong power, Marcus. We never had a chance to talk to any of the other Scrybb about your father. From what we saw and heard in the school in Thicce Colpat, there is one other human that has strong power, and my people were afraid of her."

"Yeah, she appeared out of thin air and started someone on fire," Marcus said, giving Cornus a dark look. "I'm moving a wagon. This doesn't seem like a strong power, Cornus. Maybe you should let me worry about it, okay?"

Cornus, Sadie, and Leopold still insisted that they walk at least part of each day, despite the extra time it would add to their travel time.

"You don't know anything about this power, man," Leopold said. "You could be melting your brains just by pushing too hard—even if you don't feel anything." Cornus and Sadie agreed.

Later that afternoon, they were all riding on the wagon when an animal ambled out of the underbrush and stopped in the middle of the path, looking aggressively at the approaching wagon. Marcus, trying to stop, lost control for the first time since that morning. As if he had cranked an invisible steering wheel, the wagon spun sideways, spewing up pebbles and dust. The entire thing began to tip away from the creature. Sadie screamed behind Marcus, and he grabbed Cornus in his left arm before the Scrybb could tumble to the ground.

Marcus pushed against the ground with all the mental force he could muster, and they slammed back down on all four wheels. Leopold lay sprawled on the path behind them where he had jumped off. Marcus turned his head to see Sadie's fingers curled around the edge of the wagon next to his seat, still clinging so hard, the skin had turned a bright white over her knuckles. Breathing heavily, Marcus set Cornus down while Leopold climbed back on, muttering under his breath. They turned to look at the creature, which was still standing in the path.

It was about the size of a Rottweiler with six legs, bushy black fur, a spiky tail that reminded him of the quills on a porcupine, and a mouthful of sharp-looking white teeth in a pointed muzzle. The beast snarled at them and raised its tail. Cornus ran toward it, forming leafy shields with his hands. The animal hissed and darted back into the trees.

"What was *that*?" Leopold asked, sounding truly afraid for the first time.

"A cantor. They do not often come out during the day. Scrybb often see them at night while Traveling. They are not dangerous to us because Cantor are meat-eaters. They eat other animals that live in the Grenewud."

"Thank you for scaring it off," Sadie said.

"I think we should continue to ride for now," said Cornus, "but perhaps at a safer speed."

Marcus was more than agreeable to that, glad to have his friends around him where they would be out of reach of cantors and other unknown creatures. He felt terrible about the accident, which had happened because of his overconfidence in his ability to stop. Now, realizing how easily he could have hurt any of them, he maintained a safer, more manageable speed.

"So, Cornus," Leopold asked, gulping nervously, "what other types of animal life might we expect to run into here in the Grenewud?" Marcus glanced at his friend, who had taken Cornus's previous position next to him; Cornus was riding on the front of the wagon, but was holding on firmly to the edge.

"Oh...ah, well, let me think. There are xinions. They are tall, six legged, and smell bad, I have been told. They have some type of long round tusk jutting from their mouths. They are leaf eaters but will try to impale other creatures with that tusk. They might be one thing the cantors eat. There is not much else living in this particular part of the Grenewud. Some flying creatures, I believe."

Several days later, all four of them were nearing the point of exhaustion. Cornus told them he had noticed marks on the path indicating they were nearing the bruwe of the Fyrtudo.

They all walked now, leaving the wagon in a small opening near the end of the path behind them. As they rounded the bend in the path, the relief Marcus felt was overwhelming. Sadie seized his hand with a small cry, and Leopold raised a fist of joy in the air. Marcus's relief was momentarily interrupted by the warmth in his chest as he stared at Sadie's hand holding his.

While they had been able to change clothes between those they'd carried in the packs and were only somewhat ragged in appearance, baths had been little more than the occasional rinse off in small streams.

"Jeez, I wish we'd had a little more warning," Leopold said, sniffing his armpit. "I *stink*."

"You got that right," Marcus laughed. He looked down at himself. His formerly sharp red shirt was smeared with dirt and torn in places.

Sadie laughed at them. "You both stink!"

"You're no bed of roses either, sweetheart," Marcus said.

Leopold snorted. "My man!" Marcus slapped him a sideways five.

Sadie flushed a deep red and stormed away.

"Oops," Marcus said to Leopold. "Guess I'm not very good at this yet." He walked to where Sadie was leaning against a tree in the shade.

"I'm sorry," he said, coming up to Sadie and putting his arm around her shoulders. Then, mindful of their previous discussion, he said self-consciously, "Maybe I should use my other arm? I don't use that one as much, so maybe that armpit isn't as stinky."

Sadie giggled even as she rubbed tears from her eyes, smearing dirt on her face.

Cornus had been listening to all of this very curiously.

"There is nothing to be done for it," he said. "Our business is urgent, so we must hope the Fyrtudo are not offended by our appearance and odor."

Marcus thought it was nice of Cornus to include himself since his leaves never changed their appearance, and he smelled just as fresh as he had when they had first met.

"C'mon, guys, let's get on with it," Leopold said.

As they walked out of the woods beneath another arch of trees, Marcus expected to get a first glimpse of a bustling bruwe, similar to Thicce Colpat.

Instead, they saw sunlight shining on a wide stone threshold with large boulders around the perimeter. Marcus followed Cornus onto the flat stone, blinking in the bright sun.

"Is this normal, Cornus? Aren't there usually people around in a bruwe? I don't even see any doors or anything." Marcus asked as they looked around. No one was in sight. At the far end of the terrace, the rock face of the Beornan Rokk soared above them, looming over even the tallest of the trees of the Grenewud. The jagged mountain face curved slightly as if protecting the flat stone where he stood. Cracks and crevices in the mountain gave evidence of some long-ago disaster that had altered its shape. Boulders that remained were scattered along the base of the mountains in both directions. Only the sun directly overhead brought light to the stone terrace they stood on.

Even in the bright sunshine, Marcus felt claustrophobic. The small path in the Grenewud had felt more like home and his tight-knit little group like family. Now he was anxious—frightened, even—of the unknown they faced in this new place that felt so threatening.

"I had no idea the Fyrtudo lived *this* close to the Beornan

Rokk," Cornus said in a low voice.

"But where are they?" Marcus murmured.

"And why are we whispering?" asked Leopold. "I thought these guys were supposed to be friendly."

"Yes, of course," replied Cornus. "I am merely being cautious." He took a few steps forward.

On both sides of the stone terrace where they stood, wide waterways flowed out from beneath the mountains, ending in shimmering pools that sent steam swirling into the air above them. Marcus carefully made his way over to the one on the left, noticing that the water had a slightly sulfurous smell. He turned back toward Leopold. "Hey, I think these might be hot springs!"

Leopold wasn't listening. He, Sadie, and Cornus were still as statues, staring straight ahead of themselves at the rock wall. Marcus turned to see what they were looking at.

A doorway had opened at the base of the mountain.

"Where did that come from?" Marcus asked. "I was only over there for a minute."

"It just opened like a second ago," Leopold said. "It didn't even make any noise!"

Marcus made his way over to the others, standing slightly in front of them. He felt protective of his friends and thought perhaps his newly discovered power could help him defend them in some way.

Walking slowly toward them were three great beings. The one in front looked like walking granite, and the other two were as brown as the deepest forests in the Grenewud. They were at least as large as Earth's elephants. Each had four long, thick legs ending with wide, four-toed feet. They had two heavily muscled arms extending from the front of their shoulders with large, thick-fingered hands. Their heavy, round bodies were plated with stony armor that covered not just their bodies but also their limbs, necks, and large heads.

Round green eyes gazed at the teens. From Marcus's perspective on the ground, their ducked heads and half-lidded eyes gave them an air of apprehension. Marcus stared upwards at a loose flap of a mouth on the underside of the creature's giant head. How could they talk without lips and visible facial muscles?

We communicate like this, child. Please tell me who you are.

Marcus jumped and looked around wildly. "What? Who said that?"

Be calm. It is I, Colflur. I am the Queen of Palaga, home of the Fyrtudo. This is how we speak. Your name, please.

"Oh!" he said. "It's them, the Fyrtudo!"

Leopold looked at Marcus. "Have you lost your mind? Who are you talking to?"

Apologies, I was speaking only to your leader. I now address you all and welcome you all to Palaga, bruwe of the Fyrtudo, Colflur said. *Please tell me your names. The presence of a Scrybb with you is reassuring, but I must hear your names.*

It was now the others' turn to jump and look about wildly.

"What–" Cornus exclaimed.

"Is that in my head?" Sadie said.

"Our leader?" Leopold said, a note of irritation in his voice.

Marcus looked at Colflur and gulped. "My—my name is Marcus Talent. These are my friends, Leopold Larson and Sadie Kim. Our Scrybb friend here is Cornus." Colflur visibly relaxed after he said their names; all the tension left her body, and she sighed with what seemed like relief.

Yes, children. This is how we communicate amongst ourselves and to everyone on Lysomnus. Welcome to you, as well, young Scrybb. You must be on your Travels.

Cornus bowed. "Thank you. Yes, I am on my Travels and have also been assigned to assist these humans. And I also need your help!"

Please come inside. You must meet King Tartarus. We will be happy to hear about each of you and help in any way we can.

Colflur turned and led them all back through the doors into Palaga.

As they walked inside, Marcus expected it to be completely dark, but once his eyes adjusted from the brightness outside, he found he could see well. The light dimmed as the doors closed, and Marcus looked back, waiting to hear a loud rumbling or grating sound. especially as he noticed it took two of the large Fyrtudo to push them together. Instead, as the last of the sunlight disappeared in the crack of the closing doors, there was almost no sound at all. Then Marcus remembered how he hadn't noticed that the doors had opened when he had been outside—he hadn't heard them while he was inspecting the steaming pool.

They entered a vast cavern, where the walls and high ceiling glowed a bright fluorescent green. The great area was full of Fyrtudo moving busily, some carrying tools that came from a large open room on the left while others led children to several different rooms. Many carried various dishes and disappeared into a closer room where delicious smells wafted out. The sound of hammering rang distantly down a hallway.

The large cavern was glowing with a green light, making everything visible. "Bioluminescent cave life," Sadie said, looking up at the glowing ceiling. "I did a report on it for science last year. Another symbiotic relationship, like the Vosfyren in Thicce Colpat."

Your friend is correct, Colflur said. *We live in harmony with other life in our caves under the mountain.*

They followed Colflur across the wide, cool cavern, approaching a large iron door with intricate gold scrolling. "I didn't realize that the Fyrtudo were ruled by royalty," Marcus said. He felt intimidated by the idea of meeting an actual King; it had been shocking enough to have the Queen of the Fyrtudo come out and tell him to call her by name!

I would not call it 'ruling,' young Marcus. It is simply our form of leadership. It takes a strong leader to serve the needs of a people like the Fyrtudo.

Colflur placed a hand on the door and pushed it open. Standing sideways to them in the room stood an enormous Fyrtudo. His bulk dwarfed everyone else in the room; his armored body looked dark, almost as if it had been smelted. He turned his head to look at them. *Hello Marcus, I am Tartarus, King of Palaga.*

The king was even larger than Colflur, with an enormous stone crown that appeared as if it were part of his head. While the others were various shades of gray or brown, the king's body was nearly black. This dark coloring started with the immense crown, covered his head and back, and only faded to gray down his limbs and chest. Another Fyrtudo—one of the brown ones who had greeted them outside with Colflur—was standing beside the king, and it appeared as if they were simply staring at each other. The room in which they stood was a significantly large space, but

Marcus felt almost claustrophobic in the space that was left once he and his friends entered. Colflur stayed behind them, holding the door open as if she knew he was nervous. Marcus half-expected to see the king of the Fyrtudo on an enormous throne, but then he realized how foolish that was. These giant creatures couldn't possibly sit in a chair.

He heard laughter inside his head. It sounded like many different people laughing and was quite disconcerting. "What's so funny?"

You broadcast your thoughts, young human. Everyone can hear you.

"Um. That's embarrassing," he muttered, his face getting hot. "Who's everyone? Just you three?"

Everyone who is close enough to hear your thoughts. You will have to learn how to keep your thoughts silent. It is a task even the young Fyrtudo must learn to master.

"I will start working on that immediately," Leopold said, winking at Sadie and giving Marcus an elbow.

Marcus was just glad they had finally made it to the Fyrtudo. He could finally start finding some answers about his father.

Yes, we are aware of the situation with your father. We are unsure of where he might be. Why anyone would attempt to harm Deacon Talent is unknown to us.

"The Scrybb didn't have any ideas either," Marcus felt his stomach drop in disappointment. He had hoped they would have the answers to at least some of his questions. "That's why we came here, to see you. They thought you might know something. Please, if there is something you know, tell me. I can take it."

We will do whatever we can to help you, Marcus. Deacon Talent is well-known and respected here in Palaga.

"You-you know him?" Marcus gulped. He hadn't expected to feel such relief at finding someone who reacted positively about his father. "What do you know about him?"

Deacon Talent is a powerful healer. He saved Colflur's life when she nearly died in childbirth.

Marcus was stunned. His father had power, too? There was so much his father hadn't taken the time to tell him. "What about the other humans? Could they have taken him?"

The king shifted his enormous bulk, appearing uncomfortable. *I cannot say much about them. We do not go where they are.*

"What did he say, Marcus?" Leopold asked.

"Does he know anything that can help us?" Sadie added.

"Please," interrupted Cornus. "What do you know of the Stondefel?'

We know them well, said Tartarus to them all. *After all, we share these mountains with them as home. Why?*

"Because one of them took my friend!" Cornus shouted, then burst into tears. Marcus wasn't surprised. The Scrybb had been struggling with his emotions for several days as they rushed to reach the Fyrtudo bruwe. He put an arm around his friend's shaking shoulders.

That is difficult to believe. The Stondefel do not harm the people.

"This one did. At least, it took his friend Davidia. We think it might have been trying to take Cornus here," Marcus said, indicating his weeping friend. He wanted to discuss the mysterious humans further, but it was obvious this issue had to be dealt with first. Leopold took over trying to comfort Cornus with little success. "We're really worried about her. I mean, they have molten drool, right? And she could burn so easily!"

We will go at once to their home in the upper caverns. I will have answers for this...this unacceptable behavior. Tartarus curled his hands into huge fists. He gestured for everyone to walk out before him. Once in the main cavern, he paced angrily. Marcus could see the king was trying to express his fury without success. Tartarus turned to the queen.

Colflur, you will accompany me. Marcus, I know all of you are tired and hungry, but do you think you and your friends can wait just a little longer before you rest and refresh yourselves?

"Yes, King Tartarus," Marcus said. He was eager to learn more, but he also felt nervous at the idea of confronting the Stondefel after what he had seen of them already.

Marcus, following Tartarus and Colflur, braced himself when he saw a much smaller Fyrtudo approaching at breakneck speed. The thought of an impact with a creature as solid as the Fyrtudo, even one close to the size of himself and his friends, unnerved him. He felt a little better when he saw a small smile on Sadie's face at the sight of the miniature Fyrtudo. The child was adorable, and slowed down as he neared them.

Father! Mother! he called loud enough for everyone in the cavern to hear. *I want to come!*

Now Marcus understood what the Fyrtudo meant when they said he was thinking loud enough for everyone to hear him. He would definitely have to work on keeping his thoughts to himself.

Growan, you must remain here, Tartarus said to the young Fyrtudo. *We are going where it is not safe.*

The child looked dejected as he stopped and turned away. *Oh, all right. I never get to come.*

You will. Learn patience, my son.

"Hey," Leopold said, dropping to one knee and holding a hand out to Growan. "I don't have to go with you, Marcus. Maybe this young fellow would like to show me around these caverns so I can learn a little bit about the Fyrtudo while you're gone? I would love to know what those wonderful smells are, and there are some really interesting sounds I think we could investigate."

Growan, Tartarus said to his son. *Would you like to show this human around Palaga? It is an important part of royal protocol.*

Yes, Father. The young Fyrtudo looked delighted, grasped Leopold's hand, and led him away.

Marcus was surprised that his friend wanted to stay behind, but he knew that Leopold was the type of guy who would help anyone in a pinch. He would keep the young Fyrtudo occupied while Marcus, Sadie, and Cornus accompanied the King and Queen.

Your friend will be well cared for, the king reassured Marcus.

"Thank you, Tartarus. Leopold is also great with children and loves to learn about new people and places. He will enjoy being here with Growan," Marcus followed the others to a dark tunnel all the way at the back of the great cavern.

Almost immediately, the light dimmed as the amount of bioluminescent life around them decreased, and Marcus saw the Fyrtudos' eyes light up with a reflective blue sheen, like a cat's did at night back on Earth. A warm breeze wafted gently past them toward the cavern. Marcus had expected the tunnels to be cool. Weren't caves always chilly or something? The odor of sulfur hung in the air. The tunnel floor rose at a slight incline, and Marcus felt the strain in his back almost immediately. He winced.

Colflur turned to him with concern. *I sense you are in pain, Marcus. You must ride on my back. Please, it is a long way, and I would not have you struggle and suffer pain during the journey.* She crouched low. *Sadie and Cornus, please feel welcome to join Marcus after you help him onto my back. Your weight will not be a burden to me.*

After Marcus was on Colflur's back, the others scrambled up and helped to support him on the curved surface. "Is this okay, Colflur? We aren't hurting you, are we?" Sadie asked.

You are perfectly fine. She sounded amused. *Our people are well-armored, and it would be quite difficult for you to do any harm to me.*

"We surely appreciate your kindness, good Queen," Cornus said.

"Yes, thank you," Marcus said, realizing he should have thought of thanking her right away.

I am happy to do it.

Underway once more, Marcus realized the Fyrtudo moved quite quickly without the smaller people to slow them down. Colflur's back did not feel like heavy armor; while smooth and warm like skin, the surface was harder than rock and slightly pebbly.

Occasionally, a swirl of air would waft toward him from a dark tunnel branching off from this main one. Sometimes, the Fyrtudo would pass one by while they turned into others. Marcus knew if he were in here by himself, he would soon be quite lost; the tunnel system was like a maze, with no obvious signposts that he could see. Yet the Fyrtudo chose lefts and rights quickly and decisively. Obviously, they knew these tunnels and these mountains very well.

"So, what are all these tunnels for?" he finally asked.

We are miners and forgers, Tartarus answered. *Our tunnels lead to different mines and to areas where our smiths forge tools and other items out of iron.*

"You mine for iron?" Marcus wanted to keep the conversation going. He hadn't eaten anything but fruit and raw vegetables for several days, and the rocking motion of riding on Colflur's back, along with the sulfurous smell in the tunnels, was making him a little motion sick.

We also mine for the emeristan, the rocks that stay hot. They are transported in specially made iron pots to people across Lysomnus to use for cooking and keeping warm. They stay hot for many months, even in water or when used for heating or cooking.

"There are so many tunnels here. How do you keep them straight?"

How do you know your way around your own world?

"Well, we have signs and stuff, and we have maps, which are like big pictures of places with the roads and stuff all marked on them." He decided not to try to explain GPS—that was just too complicated.

We also have 'signs'. These tunnels are marked, although you cannot see the marks with your eyes. Our eyes can. The tunnels we are traveling now are marked to stay away; these lead soon to the caverns of the Stondefel. While we are friendly with them, we do not approach them often. Their caverns are too near the burning mouths of the mountains.

"Burning mouths of the mountains?" Marcus was intrigued, but he felt Cornus shudder against him.

Yes. They are long vertical tunnels that lead deep into the ground. The mountains vomit hot molten rock into the air, and the Stondefel feed there as if it were a delicacy. I suppose it is to them.

"It sounds as if these mountains might be volcanoes?" Sadie suggested.

Deacon Talent used that same term to describe them.

Marcus suddenly missed his dad. Meeting all these people who had talked to Deacon, who knew him, made the fact that his dad had actually been kidnapped feel very real. The task of finding him felt overwhelming. Even these people who lived in Lysomnus and who knew his dad had no idea where he could be or what could have happened to him.

The tunnel soon began to angle up steeply. *We are nearly there*, Tartarus said. They slowed to a stop as they came to what looked like a solid wall at the end of the tunnel. Cornus and Marcus exchanged glances, wondering what would happen now that they had nowhere to go. Both Fyrtudo reached forward with their hands as they approached the wall. With strong, swift strokes, they dug at the stone, boring through it easily to reveal an open tunnel beyond.

"Wait! You mine with your *hands*?" Marcus cried out, watching this display.

Yes. We use some iron tools particularly when handling the emeristan, but we perform much of our mining with our hands. Unless we dig too close to the molten rock, that is.

"That's badass." He could sense amusement coming from both Fyrtudo as they made their way through the opening they had dug through the tunnel wall. Sadie sneezed as they passed through the dust cloud the Fyrtudos' digging had created. "Bless you," Marcus added, unable to control his silly smile or the blood flooding his face. He hoped he was doing a better job of keeping his thoughts to himself. Neither the king nor the queen said anything, so he assumed it was working.

Sadie glanced at him with a shy smile of her own. "Thank you, Marcus."

It was much hotter in these new tunnels. Sweat popped out on Marcus's skin almost instantly. "Why was there a wall between these tunnels? Are we not supposed to be here? And why is it so hot?"

"Are we in danger?" Sadie asked, glancing towards Cornus. Marcus could follow her line of thought—Cornus was much more flammable than they were, and any fire hazard here could be a real danger to the Scrybb.

It has been quite some time since we used these tunnels to visit the Stondefel, Tartarus said. *There is no protocol that keeps us from doing so, but this route takes us close to those vertical tunnels we told you about. We prefer to avoid the heat if possible, but in this situation, it is necessary to reach them quickly.*

Before long, they saw light through the thin wall at the end of the tunnel. It appeared to be daylight, but Marcus could hardly believe it. Had they been traveling long enough to reach the upper part of the mountains? A sound like claws scrabbling on stone reached his ears. The mental picture of those long, wicked talons he'd seen as Davidia was seized and carried off was right in the front of his mind.

When they exited the tunnel, Marcus realized they had not reached the top of the mountain. They were walking into a volcanic caldera. Where they stood was a rough surface covered with an ashy, chalk-colored substance. In some places, there were small, cone-shaped formations.

Rough paths were worn deep through the ash into the dark rock beneath. The steep sides of the caldera rose steeply all around them, soaring high above to the clear blue sky.

The Fyrtudo stopped, and Colflur lowered herself to allow Sadie, Marcus, and Cornus to climb down to the ground. *Remain here*, she said to them. *We will speak first and then bring you forward.* Marcus groaned, leaning on his cane for support. What he wouldn't give to lie down! He didn't think his body had ever hurt so badly. He thought again of using the Halfriez to take away some of his pain, but the thought of changing anything about his body was too big of a risk.

"It must not rain or snow here, at least up in these mountains," Sadie said under her breath., interrupting his thoughts.

Marcus glanced at her. "Why?"

"Because most caldera are filled with water." Her brow creased with puzzlement.

After Marcus climbed down from Colflur's back, he found himself facing away from Tartarus. When he turned around, the Fyrtudo had walked a short distance away, and Marcus got a good look at what kind of creature had snatched Davidia from the Brynar only a few days ago. He heard Cornus inhale sharply behind him and knew the Scrybb boy must be terrified. The beast pacing across the rocky bowl in front of them was easily the length of a house trailer. Its entire body looked as if it were carved from stone. Glowing red irises glittered beneath heavy brows; an aquiline nose stood out beneath. Behind lips like flexible bone were sharp teeth. Massive horns curled up from its head, and a second, smaller set of horns curved back over its bottom jaw. The torso was upright, with a massive chest and broad shoulders. Long arms ended in hands tipped with cruelly curved talons. The rest of its body was horizontal and segmented, making it look aerodynamic and almost delicate compared to the heavy torso. Marcus was reminded of a wasp, except wasps weren't made of stone. Six legs ended in taloned feet. Immense leathery wings spread open from the back of the beast. A long, thin tail lay behind it, with several small spikes extending in all directions near the tip.

Marcus found himself almost too terrified to breathe. These Stondefel were more dreadful than he'd dared to imagine. It felt as if his worst nightmares of Hell had come to life before him. He turned to see Sadie embracing Cornus, the Scrybb's face buried in her shoulder.

The enormous creature stopped pacing and looked down to face the Fyrtudo as soon as it caught sight of them. It faced Tartarus and began to speak in a harsh voice that grated as if the Stondefel had gravel in its throat.

"King Tartarus, Queen Colflur. I believe I know the purpose of your visit to our heights., The Stondefel of Lysomnus have been disgraced. Someone has corrupted several of our own brethren and is using them as a weapon against the people of Lysomnus."

Speaking so all could hear him, Tartarus said, *How can this be? The Stondefel* are *people of Lysomnus. To turn against any of us is to turn against yourselves.*

"And yet some have. Unfortunately, the minds of the young can be corrupted with promises of power. The Council remains intact, we believe, but we have not yet discovered how many of our younger brothers have betrayed us. Most of the young ones are missing."

Cornus stepped forward, shaking so much his leaves nearly drowned out his querulous voice. "My—my friend,

Davidia. She was taken by one—one of you..." his voice trailed away.

"Little Scrybb brother, please do not fear me." The Stondefel unfurled one taloned hand in supplication toward Cornus. "I am Anneberg, and I watch over the mining people, the Fyrtudo. I would never harm you or any of the people of Lysomnus. We will do everything we can to find her." His demonic face was as passive and friendly as such a face could be, but it was still pretty terrifying, Marcus thought.

"So—that other Stondefel did not bring her here?" Cornus spoke slightly louder now and was shaking a little less.

"No, I give you my word. We would never harm one of the people of Lysomnus. We have not seen several of our younger Stondefel in quite some time, and we believe they are hiding somewhere. One of them must have taken your friend."

"But would they hurt her?" Marcus broke in. "She is a Scrybb, after all, and she would be so vulnerable in the hands of a Stondefel, even by accident."

Anneberg cleared his throat, shifting his weight uneasily from foot to foot. "I do not believe so. We do not know why our younger brothers have chosen to separate themselves from us. It is as if someone is controlling them."

You would prefer not to acknowledge their responsibility for these actions, then.

"Of course they are *responsible*, Tartarus. I merely meant to say that I cannot think of any reasonable explanation for their behavior." Anneberg looked even more uncomfortable. He began to tap one of the long talons on his feet on the stone below him. The noise made Marcus uncomfortable.

I am curious. Was there any warning of this sudden breach between your Council and the younger Stondefel? Did none of you hear discussion of this defection?

"I do not believe so. None of us have any idea. They were here, and then they were gone. Now we have heard of some…violations. Like this abduction of the Scrybb girl." He shook his head. "It is senseless to us. We do not *harm*. We watch. We help."

"In all honesty, sir, we—I mean, the Scrybb—did not know you were real," Cornus admitted. "For us, you have been little more than a children's story, a tale of a time when Lysomnus needed watching over, and the mighty Stondefel would protect and rescue the people."

"Yes, we have been that. We *are* that." Anneberg nodded. "There are not many threats to the people of Lysomnus in these times. Or there did not used to be, anyway."

We need to know what threat to the people these younger Stondefel pose, said Tartarus. *We cannot defend Lysomnus if we do not know what the danger is.*

"I think the danger is clear," Cornus said, indicating Anneberg with a leafy hand. "How can any of the people of Lysomnus defend themselves—or each other—from Stondefel?"

"Cornus!" Sadie gasped.

"No, little sister," Anneberg broke in. "This young Scrybb is correct. There is little that most of the people of Lysomnus can do against one of us. Hide, perhaps, but defend? Fight back? That is unlikely."

The other great tragedy would be Stondefel against Stondefel, Colflur said softly.

Marcus felt dizzy and lost. He didn't know how to wrap his head around what was happening. His head ached, and he wanted to sit down and cry. He was supposed to be searching for his father, and now it sounded as if all Lysomnus might be going to war. Looking over at Cornus, he had the feeling that the Scrybb boy was feeling the same despair he was. Marcus stepped over and put an arm around Cornus' shoulders, squeezing gently. "We'll figure this out, little bro. I know it seems hopeless right now, but I know many tales about people who were stuck in hopeless situations and then got through all right."

"You do?" The Scrybb looked up at him hopefully while the king and queen huddled together, speaking with Anneberg. "Like what?"

"Well, one is kind of like this situation we have here. There was this princess who had been taken prisoner by this really bad guy, and these two good guys had to go rescue her. One had a special power, and the other one was just a brave guy, but they needed him because he had this really fast ship to escape with. They found the princess, and she was pretty tough too, so she ended up kind of escaping by herself."

"That is the most confusing story I have ever heard." Baffled, Cornus stared at Marcus, though he was at least standing up straight again.

"Well, I'm not sure I really told it right."

"You didn't," Sadie said, hands on her hips. "*Star Wars* is actually a nine-movie epic—well, ten, if you count *Rogue One*, the best of all of them. Almost all the powerful characters are women. They save everyone throughout the entire saga. Repeatedly."

"Uh, apparently, I have to see more than just *A New Hope*." Marcus felt thoroughly chastised, but Cornus now looked even more lost.

"I suggest we have a movie marathon as soon as we get home." Sadie smiled, looking at Marcus over Cornus's head.

"It's a date," Marcus said automatically, then flushed. What if that wasn't what Sadie had meant? Then he saw the way she was smiling at him, her eyes shining, and felt reassured.

The Fyrtudo and Anneberg were deep in discussion when a shadow flitted across the caldera. They all looked up to see another Stondefel flying down to land near Anneberg. He looked similar to Anneberg but was about half his size.

"Awar!" Anneberg exclaimed, sounding both relieved and delighted. "I thought I had lost you with the others!"

"I did leave with them at first, but I have decided that I will not be a part of what they are doing," the smaller Stondefel said. "I—" he glanced around at the others and stopped abruptly. "I must speak to you alone, Council Leader."

"Very well." Anneberg led Awar away from the others to the opposite side of the caldera.

"Will you be able to hear them?" Marcus asked Tartarus.

I will not because the Stondefel know how to keep their thoughts private and knowing that Awar wishes to speak to Anneberg privately, I avoid listening deliberately. It is courteous to do so.

"Oh. Yeah, that makes sense." Marcus felt a bit rude for asking the question. Still, he was curious to know what the Stondefel were talking about and what they might not wish to share with outsiders. He looked up at the Fyrtudo. "Can you teach me how to keep my thoughts private?"

It takes a lot of work. Colflur's softer voice said. *The children begin learning quite young, and as you saw, our Growan has still not mastered the skill. I think you may have an advantage if you try hard enough at your age*, she said, and Marcus knew she was talking to all of them now. *Every time you want to say something privately, imagine a wall around your mind, holding in your thoughts and sharing them only with the person you intend to.*

It sounded confusing to Marcus, but he would just have to practice.

When the Stondefel returned, Marcus felt as though Awar was watching him specifically. He could feel the Stondefel's eyes on him, making the sweat on the back of his neck turn cold, but when he looked directly at the smaller Stondefel, Awar was looking somewhere else.

"There is more danger than I even feared, and we will need to organize warnings to all the people of Lysomnus," Anneberg said. "To the Scrybb, to the Muirnati—those are the people who live in the Diluvium—and to the Cativera, who are the stock herders of the Zabanara grasslands. Awar and I will carry you back to the entrance of Palaga. You can prepare while we gather the Council."

"Carry us?" Marcus asked while Cornus and Sadie exchanged uneasy glances. "Can't we just go back down through the tunnels?"

There is no time, Tartarus said. *Fear not, children. The Stondefel will not hurt us.*

Anneberg launched himself into the air and seized both Fyrtudo in his talons. As massive as the Fyrtudo were, they appeared small as the Stondefel flew up and out of the caldera with them. Next, Awar lifted himself into the air, then reached for them, talons outstretched. They were all petrified and couldn't help flinching away.

"I give you my word I will never harm you in any way," Awar said. "Please trust me."

The three of them came closer. Awar reached out and carefully wrapped his taloned fingers around them. Marcus felt them squeeze tightly as the Stondefel lifted him off the ground, but as sharp as the talons appeared, they did not cut him. He looked more closely at one of them and saw a thick, translucent membrane covering it, protecting him from injury.

Cornus and Sadie gasped as the caldera dropped away quickly below them. A dizzying sweep of vertigo forced Marcus to take a steadying breath as the world spun away below his feet.

The air was cold as they rose above the Beornan Rokk. The caldera lay far below them now, just one of several visible volcanoes in a range of mountains both high and wide. They stretched the width of Lysomnus as far as he could see; to the north, they disappeared into a gray haze. His breath was sucked from him as they dove toward the Grenewud, and his stomach lurched unpleasantly as the trees grew from ant-sized to full trees in seconds, though the thrill of adrenaline was quickly taking over. Just as Marcus had started to actually enjoy the journey they were descending toward the stone terrace in front of Palaga, where Tartarus and Colflur were waiting for them.

"Whoo!" Marcus exclaimed as Awar released him gently from his talons. "Let's do that again!" Awar's gravelly chuckle vibrated through his bones.

Sadie was standing still, a dazed expression on her face.

"Please, let us not," moaned Cornus, weaving away from Awar's outstretched talons and dropping to the ground. "Oh…"

"Cornus!" Marcus exclaimed as he hurried to his friend's side. Sadie knelt by the Scrybb, looking concerned.

I think you all need food and rest, Colflur said.

Awar settled himself to one side of the terrace, wings folding to his back. "I will be here as soon as you are ready," he said to Tartarus.

As soon as we have these three back on their feet. Tartarus patted Marcus with one big hand. Marcus clutched his cane as he nearly fell over himself.

Now that the exhilaration of the ride was over, Marcus was feeling decidedly weak and ill. He wobbled as he walked toward the entrance to Palaga while Sadie braced his right side. Colflur carried Cornus, who was still groaning. Pulling himself to his full height, Marcus attempted to stride to show that he was able to walk on his own. It was a struggle, though, and he found himself leaning heavily on his cane.

As they entered Palaga, Leopold appeared, beaming widely. He looked clean and refreshed, and his clothes were different and looked neatly pressed.

"You're back!" he exclaimed as he joined the group. "That was pretty fast."

"Oh man," Marcus said, grinning at his friend. "You're never going to believe how we got back here."

He brought Leopold up to speed as they followed Tartarus and Colflur, enjoying his friend's exclamations upon hearing about the Stondefel and of the startling ride they'd just taken. The King and Queen led them to a wide arched opening on the right side of the cavern, which opened to show a room lined with tall, heavy tables made of a dark metal. Numerous Fyrtudo were lining up beside the tables; while the Fyrtudo clearly had no need of seating, they had courteously provided chairs for their small guests at the large table on a dais at one end of the room.

Cornus had recovered somewhat and was soon seated on

Marcus's right, with Sadie seated on Marcus's left. Leopold sat down on her left, declaring he wanted to grab a few more bites even though he had already eaten. Tartarus was standing at the center of the table with Colflur on his right. Their son, Growan, dashed in, climbing onto a small platform at the end of the table that was clearly just for him.

Marcus reached behind Sadie to poke Leopold. "Dude!" he whispered.

Leopold glanced over at him, an irritated look on his face. "What do you want, Marcus?"

"Who are all the Fyrtudo at the tables down there?"

"Most of them are the miners and forgers, along with their families. I think there are some teachers, but I'm not sure who everyone really is."

Everyone in Palaga shares in the work in an area of interest and skill. Tartarus's deep voice filled Marcus's head. Marcus wasn't too worried about not keeping his thoughts to himself because he had been genuinely interested in the people of Palaga.

More Fyrtudo entered the hall, carrying serving dishes that they placed on the tables. Marcus leaned forward curiously as lids were lifted, waiting hungrily for the steam to clear. He couldn't wait to try the food of the Fyrtudo. There were vegetables he recognized from their journey, but here, they were individually prepared, not raw or cooked into a rich stew as they had been in Thicce Colpat. The tixpits Cornus had shown them on the way were toasted, adding a richness to their savory flavor. Marcus could swear he tasted salt and guessed that the Fyrtudo, being miners, had probably discovered a vein of salt somewhere in the mountains. The Fyrtudo had their own way of cooking each variety of meat and used delicious spices Marcus had never tasted before.

"Dude, just wait till you see what they have for dessert here," Leopold said with a grin and his mouth full, chewing on a piece of roasted meat.

"Clearly, your bottomless stomach is still the same," Marcus laughed back.

Our servers have said that he eats as much as any Fyrtudo, Colflur interjected.

Even more than me! said Growan, and everyone laughed.

"Tartarus," Leopold said, leaning forward and looking over at the king, "Marcus tells me that these Stondefel have said there is some emergency and that all your people in Lysomnus must be notified. What is the emergency, and what can we do to help?"

Marcus looked out of the corner of his eye at Leopold, his mouthful of food preventing him from telling his friend to shut his mouth. If they got involved in this, how would they be able to find his father? Leopold was always first to volunteer to help anyone. When he looked back down the table, his eyes met those of Colflur. She held his gaze but said nothing. Marcus dropped his eyes, feeling ashamed. He knew he hadn't shielded his thoughts, and Colflur—and probably everyone else—had heard.

Awar tells Anneberg that the Stondefel who have defected are in league with someone very evil, the king said. *They are planning attacks on all the bruwe of Lysomnus. This also includes attacking members of their own Council.*

Audible gasps echoed about the room as the other Fyrtudo reacted. For these people who lived so close to the Stondefel and knew them to be friends, this must have felt like a terrible betrayal.

Marcus looked at Colflur again and his heart ached. He knew he had to help them to prevent this threat to Lysomnus in any way he could, even if it meant putting off finding his father. "Tartarus, what *can* we do to help? I can't do anything to find my father if Lysomnus is under attack, and I don't want to see any of the people of this world get hurt."

I believe we will need to take some time to formulate a plan to warn all the people of Lysomnus. According to Awar, there is still some time before the rebels enact their plan. Marcus, you all need to rest first. We can wait until then to coordinate.

Partway through the meal, Marcus felt overly full and suddenly exhausted. After the long days of traveling, developing his newly discovered power, the trip through the mountain tunnels, and the exciting flight down from the mountain heights, he couldn't take much more. He looked at Cornus. The Scrybb's shoulders slumped, and weariness showed in the droop of every leaf on his body. Marcus could swear Cornus's leaves had even started to lose their color. He pushed his chair back, ready to find a place to sleep.

"Wait, bro!" Leopold exclaimed, grabbing his arm. "You haven't had dessert yet!"

"Oh, Leopold," Marcus sighed. "I don't think I can eat anymore right now. I'm so tired."

"You'll have room for this," Leopold said enthusiastically.

One of the Fyrtudo placed a tray with some baked goods on the table in front of them. Leopold seized one and handed it to Marcus.

"Try this one," he advised. "There are berries here that we haven't tasted yet. They make pastries with them."

Marcus took it just so Leopold would stop pushing it under his nose. It was sticky, coated with something that felt like honey. When he licked it off his finger, it was sweet but with a smoky citrus aftertaste. Yellow berries inside burst into his mouth as he bit down. They were tart but complemented by the smoky sweetness that coated the pastry. "See? Delicious, right?" Leopold asked with his mouth full, having helped himself to another one of the pies.

When Marcus finished the pastry, he was so full he felt almost sick. The Fyrtudo who had been talking with the king earlier escorted him from the table. *I am Rotrukan. I will show you to the bathing chamber. You will sleep better if you are clean.*

Marcus just wanted to curl up and go to sleep, but he followed Rotrukan. They walked through the main chamber of Palaga and into a small room near the main door to the outside stone terrace. Inside was a large pool of steaming water.

The waters from beneath the Beornan Rokk flow through our kingdom along both borders. We use them in our iron forge, and where they come to the surface, they make for excellent bathing pools. This is just one of several we have here; your friend will be using another. Marcus knew Rotrukan must mean Sadie since Cornus had no need to bathe, and Leopold was already clean.

"Thank you, Rotrukan. What should I do with my clothes?" Marcus asked.

I will take them once you are in the pool. I will return with a towel and a robe for you to put on. Clean clothes will be provided for you after you rest.

Rotrukan politely looked in another direction while Marcus disrobed and removed his prosthesis as quickly as his pain and exhaustion would allow. He walked to the edge of the pool; when he looked into the water, he saw a set of steps that had been cut into the stone. He lowered himself into the steaming water, gasping a little at the heat, while Rotrukan gathered Marcus's things.

The heat sank into all of Marcus's muscles, relaxing the tension from the last few days. He sighed as the heat relieved some of the pain he'd been suffering. When he laid his head back on the side of the pool, he nearly nodded off. Forcing his eyes open, he cleaned the filth of several days' travel from himself with some soap he found on the edge of the pool. He turned at the sound of feet scraping on stone to find Rotrukan standing by the edge of the pool. The Fyrtudo held a towel in one hand and Marcus's cane—cleaned until it nearly shone—in the other, with a cloth draped over his arm. Seizing the towel as he climbed carefully out of the steaming basin, Marcus dried himself off quickly.

The cloth turned out to be a robe made of a heavy material that felt like cotton. A broad brocade followed the edge completely from one bottom hem to the other, even around the deep hood. Marcus found that when he pulled the hood up, it extended quite some distance beyond his head, leaving him with a limited field of vision. He thought it must be intended to hide the wearer's identity for some reason. Uncomfortable, he pushed it back. He noticed that Rotrukan sighed and appeared quite relieved as he did so.

Your arm—your 'prosthesis'?—is being cleaned and properly oiled. It will be ready for you when you have rested, sir.

"Oh, thank you, but Rotrukan, you can call me Marcus, you know."

Rotrukan looked slightly offended. *It would not be proper to call you by your first name.* He turned and gestured for Marcus to follow him from the cavern.

As they reentered the main hall, Marcus noticed a great deal of activity in and around the king's rooms in the back of the hall. He assumed preparations were already being made to warn the people of Lysomnus of the coming danger. With exhaustion weighing him down, he wondered where Leopold was.

Rotrukan led him to a small room that contained small, human-sized beds. Marcus could hardly keep his eyes open. As soon as he laid eyes on a soft pillow, he could feel his body crying out for sleep. Beyond caring about his nakedness, he pulled off the heavy robe and slid between the sheets of the nearest bed. His eyes closed before his head even touched the pillow.

CHAPTER TEN

THE PRICE OF HER NAME

Marcus heard noises before he was even aware he was awake. Voices murmured, but he couldn't quite make out what they were saying. Was his mom waking him up to go to school? No, he hadn't heard his alarm, so it must be the weekend or—

He opened his eyes and found himself in the bed in Palaga, where he had slept soundly. The memories of the past few days rushed in, and he remembered where he was. Leopold, Sadie, and Cornus were sitting in a row on the bed beside him, wearing identical smiles.

"What?" Marcus asked.

"You talk in your sleep," Leopold said, grinning.

"I do not!" Marcus denied hotly.

"Yes, you do. You say funny things," Cornus said and giggled behind a leafy hand.

"Did…did you just *laugh*?" Marcus said incredulously. "I didn't think you had a sense of humor!"

Cornus giggled again. "I do when you talk in your sleep!"

Blushing, Marcus rubbed his groggy eyes. "What did I say?"

Leopold, Sadie, and Cornus looked at each other and burst out laughing. "We can't tell you!"

Marcus snorted. "Fools." He decided to get up but

remembered a moment before throwing the covers back that he had climbed into bed naked. "Uh, would anyone happen to know where my clothes are?"

This question set off a fresh gale of laughter from his friends. "Why don't you get up and get them?" Leopold laughed, pointing at a shelf where neatly folded clothes waited.

"Come on, guys. Just grab them for me."

"Why can you not get them?" Cornus laughed again. "Were we not naked friends in the woods?"

At this, Leopold fell back on the bed with a whoop, tears squirting from the corners of his eyes. Sadie lost it completely and bent over her knees, giggling uncontrollably.

"Naked friends," Marcus muttered. "Doesn't count if one of you is covered with *leaves* all the time." He thought about rushing out to grab his clothes, then remembered he had the power to move things at will. Could he do it now, with a pile of separate items? He reached out carefully, and although it was a struggle to keep the pile together, he managed to guide the wobbling pile over to the bed. He was relieved to find a clean limb sock and his prosthesis, newly cleaned, on top. Soon, he had it on and was carefully sliding into his clothes under the covers, feeling much more comfortable.

"That's cheating," Leopold said. "You should have had to go get them."

"Oh, I would have gotten them for him before he tried to get out of bed," Sadie said, blushing to the roots of her black hair. "I'm not *that* mean."

Cornus's giggles were starting to die down. "I am sorry, Marcus, if I have hurt your feelings," he said, abashed. "I have never understood humor very well."

"It's all right, Cornus," Marcus replied. "It was nice to finally hear you laugh. It's *him* you have to watch out for," he went on, glaring at Leopold.

"Who, me?" Leopold asked, with a wide-eyed, innocent look on his face.

"Whatever, dude," Marcus rolled his eyes. "You're a menace, and you know it."

Once Marcus was up and dressed, he led the others out of the sleeping room. Gazing around, he tried to get his bearings. Since he wanted to check in with Tartarus, he headed for the massive doors with the iron scrolling on them set into the back wall of the cavern. He hoped he hadn't slept so long that he was too late to find out what was happening.

As he approached the door, he tried to project his thoughts toward the king, to request to come inside.

There is no need to shout, came the reply. *You are, of course, welcome.*

Marcus asked Leopold to open the door and was glad he had when he watched his friend push the enormous door open with some effort. "Sorry," he said to the king once he was inside. "I'm still learning about this thought-voice thing. Can the others come in, too?"

Colflur was standing in the room beside Tartarus this morning. Somehow, the day before, it had not seemed so crowded when Rotrukan was with the king. Marcus hadn't realized how much larger Colflur was than the other Fyrtudo. *Of course, they are welcome. Cornus in particular will be needed.*

"I will?" Cornus asked, appearing around the door. "Why will I be needed?"

Let us start at the beginning. The Stondefel who have left the Council have formed their own rebel group. One leads this group who is not Stondefel. That one—their name is one we cannot say—has coordinated a series of attacks on all the people of Lysomnus.

"But now that Awar has come back and told us about the attacks, the true Council of Stondefel can stop them, can't they?" Marcus asked.

Tartarus dipped his head to look Marcus in the eye. *Perhaps. The first planned attack was to be against the Council as they slept, to destroy any chance of protection the rest of the people would have. Now that we have received a warning, what will most likely happen is Stondefel fighting against Stondefel. That is something that has never happened before and* should *never happen. The only hope we have is that the group of defectors does not find out that Awar has betrayed them.*

"Won't they realize it when they find out he's gone?" Marcus asked.

He returned to them with a story of spying on this Council. Anneberg has given him some information to take back with him about suspicion of that attack. We can only hope he is believed. He is risking his life to save us all.

"What can we do in the meantime? Even if they don't find out about Awar, they're still going to attack everyone, right? What can we do about that?" Marcus felt sick at the thought of creatures as large and powerful as Anneberg attacking the Scrybb bruwe. He pictured the small amount of molten rock left behind when Davidia was taken from them. The damage even something that small could do to Thicce Colpat and the Grenewud was immeasurable.

Yes, Tartarus said, hearing Marcus's thoughts. *Their diet consists of molten rock, so their saliva is composed of it. They absorb the nutrient ores they need, and the rest of it can be used as a weapon. If they were to fight each other, to gut another, their molten stomach contents—would pour down on anything—or anyone—below. Along with their visible physical attributes, it is easy to see why these attacks would be so devastating.*

"Wait," said Marcus. "You said someone is on the Council of Stondefel that defected who isn't Stondefel? Who is that? Who else would want to help these other Stondefel attack their own people?"

I—I have already said too much. Tartarus spoke as if the words choked him. *It is too dangerous even to* think *of Nun the Wiser's name. There is always the fear that she could hear even our very thoughts.*

Tartarus! exclaimed Colflur. *You shouldn't have even* thought *her name. Even if it is just our thoughts, there is a risk she will hear.* The giant Fyrtudo queen was trembling, and her eyes were wide as she looked at her mate. Marcus felt even more fear at the terror expressed by the normally calm, steadfast queen.

Tartarus ducked his head. *You are correct, Colflur. I should be more careful with my thoughts. We must concentrate on our plans to aid the people of Lysomnus.*

Leopold stepped forward and said, "We need a coordinated warning so that all the people in danger receive the warning at the same time."

The king frowned. *How can such a thing be done?*

"Well, my good friend Marcus told me about a thrilling ride he took in the clutches of a giant flying demon. I figured we could begin by asking for rides to warn all the people of Lysomnus at once."

Marcus's jaw dropped. Leopold had come up with an excellent solution! That was, if the Stondefel were willing to provide transportation.

This is a good plan. However, we also need to develop solutions for the people to protect themselves and their homes from the attacks when they do come.

Marcus felt terrible as he watched Leopold's face fall. His friend's epiphany was a good one, but of course they still needed to find a way to defend every bruwe. Just knowing the attacks were coming would not be enough.

"I suppose we couldn't have a Stondefel on guard at each bruwe...." Leopold trailed off as he and everyone else in the room pictured the devastating results of a battle between two Stondefel over any of the bruwe of Thicce Colpat.

"What if we take the fight to them? And by them, I mean to whoever is causing all of this to begin with?" Marcus said. "Clearly, there was no rift between the Stondefel until this N —uh, person came along."

Tartarus immediately looked uncomfortable. Colflur would not meet Marcus's eye. *It is difficult not to say it. Thank you for catching yourself,* Colflur said. *Tartarus has already put us all at risk by saying it once.*

"Are you saying she can read minds?" Marcus asked incredulously.

She will hear her name whenever it is spoken in any *way, anywhere in Lysomnus.*

Cries of alarm and the stomping of heavy feet erupted outside of Tartarus's chambers. Marcus felt tension in the air, and it seemed as if time stood still for a second. Then, everyone rushed out to see what was happening.

Nun the Wiser stood in the center of the large chamber, looking just as Marcus remembered her from the classroom in Thicce Colpat. A large crowd of Fyrtudo had withdrawn as far away from her as they could.

Growan's neck was locked tightly in her grip. The

blackened talon-like nails of her left hand pierced his armored skin.

Growan! Colflur cried, rushing toward her son. Nun the Wiser pointed one bony finger at the queen, who stopped moving abruptly.

"Don't be foolish, Mother," she said harshly. Colflur stopped immediately. "I heard my name in someone's thoughts here." Colflur looked bitterly at Tartarus who was standing in the doorway of his room, glaring at Nun the Wiser angrily. "You people simply cannot stop talking about me. There are rules and a price to pay for breaking them."

She turned her head, and hidden in the depths of the black hood, Marcus could see glittering eyes staring at him. Growan whimpered; Nun the Wiser's sharp nails were cutting into his neck. despite his armored skin. Dark green blood pattered in droplets on the floor.

You must not harm the Prince! Rotrukan bellowed so loud, everyone jumped, including Nun the Wiser. The angry Fyrtudo rushed at her, hands outstretched. After regaining her composure, the woman flicked her bony hand at him. Rotrukan collapsed with a loud thump to the floor, sliding nearly to her feet. Growan shrieked at the sight of the lifeless body of his father's loyal friend.

With a grating cackle, Nun the Wiser released the young Fyrtudo. "That's the price you'll pay for today. I'm sure I'll be seeing some of you again soon." Before anyone could move, she vanished with a *pop* of collapsing air. Colflur rushed to Growan as he wrapped shaking arms around her leg.

A wail rose in the air as a Fyrtudo dropped to her knees beside Rotrukan, pulling his head into her lap. The rest of the people of the bruwe gathered around and began to hum.

"I'm so sorry," Marcus said. Leopold tried to comfort Growan. Marcus stared at the dead Fyrtudo's body as he knelt beside Leopold to heal Growan's injuries. He looked up at Tartarus. "I wish there was something I could do for Rotrukan, but death is beyond healing." Tears rolled down his face.

Tartarus put a hand on Marcus's shoulder. *Thank you for what you have done for my son. Now we must mourn Rotrukan. Please, go outside, where you will find Awar waiting to help you continue planning to warn the people of Lysomnus. I do not mean to rush you, but the loss of our friend is something we must deal with ourselves.*

Marcus heard Leopold gasp behind him as the other boy got his first glimpse of Awar. The stone doors closed behind them. Awar was on his feet and pacing as he waited, and the sight of the young Stondefel was impressive. The double horns on his face seemed more intimidating here than even those of the larger Anneberg had up in the caldera.

When he caught sight of Marcus, Awar stopped pacing. "Marcus Talent, I have some of the answers you seek. As one who was part of the original rebellion, I have been privy to much. I know where the rebel Stondefel are hiding. I know the plan of attacks. I know the location of the young rebels and their human leader. I assume all these things will be of interest to you."

"Okay, so where are the young Stondefel hiding?"

"They are near where the humans live. No one will find them because no one goes there. Their leader has an incredible amount of power, as you've seen. She isn't afraid to use it to hurt others and is always looking for anyone else with power in order to control and use them."

"Power..." Marcus looked at Cornus, Sadie, and Leopold.

They all looked as surprised as he felt.

"You've seen examples of her power," Awar said. "As an original member of the rebels, I've seen examples of other abilities that she has. That much power makes her incredibly dangerous."

They all looked up to see Tartarus approaching them. *I had to come out—you need my help. My people understand. The fate of the whole of Lysomnus is at stake.*

"If she and the other humans are so dangerous, then why do you have clothing, soap, beds, and bathing facilities? The Scrybb have them as well. It looks as if you treat them like guests in your homes! I have to know—are there more humans than just her? Is my father involved in this?" Gripping his cane tightly, Marcus paced along the flat stone, ignoring the pain in his anger.

Sadie put a hand on Marcus's arm, but Marcus jerked away.

They are certainly not guests, Tartarus said harshly with an angry look on his face. His body stiffened, and his hands balled into tight fists. *Our people were forced generations ago to allow those humans to bathe in our pools, to add rooms for them to sleep in, and they brought the clothing and told us to store it and care for it. When they come here, we must serve them and treat them like they are guests. They receive the best food and eat first. They treat us with disrespect and go into every chamber in Palaga, including my own rooms.*

"Marcus, man–" Leopold said in a warning tone of voice, gripping him by the elbow tightly. Marcus knew he had already said too much to these people who had been abused by the humans and their leader.

"Tartarus, if my father was such a beloved friend to the Fyrtudo, why didn't he do anything to help you?"

Deacon is a close friend of the Muirnati as well. He knew of these transgressions and chose to either not come to Lysomnus or stay in Fisc when he knew the humans were coming to our bruwe or that of any other people of Lysomnus. It had become a source of contention between Deacon and the Scrybb, particularly as his father, Malcolm, was a good friend of theirs. I do not believe Malcolm or previous members of the Talent line were aware of the other humans here. It was kept a secret because of our shame.

Marcus looked up at Awar and asked, "And do these humans come up to the caldera of the Stondefel, demanding to be fed and bathed? Do even the Stondefel bow down before these humans?"

"We never had contact with them prior to this betrayal by our young brothers, young lord. We kept to the skies and the Beornan Rokk. Honestly, the good people of Lysomnus had not told us about the humans and their mistreatment at their hands. We had no knowledge of the humans' power. Their leader just recently made her way up into the Beornan Rokk and found one foolish young Stondefel, and now we find ourselves in a terrible plight. I am ashamed to admit that I even joined the rebels. My brother, Anneberg, has told me none of the other Stondefel have ever seen the other humans before. We have never flown to the eastern side of the continent—perhaps a previous generation was warned to stay away by that powerful human.

The Talents have always had power of some kind, each generation. It has long been our hope that, eventually, one Talent would develop a strong enough power to rival that of the one who has plagued us for all this time, Tartarus broke in.

"This explains something that happened to me while we were traveling here. I started noticing that I could move things just by thinking about them. It's not much, and it was hard to do at first, but at least it makes sense now why I can do it."

I don't believe that Deacon's healing power was very strong right away. The Halfriez passed down to him by his father was useful when he first traveled here. He had to practice building up his power to become proficient at it, Tartarus said.

I am curious about something, Colflur spoke up. *Why is the child of the most powerful healer in all Lysomnus living with such painful disabilities?*

"I don't think my dad can do any of the things he does here back on our planet. At least, he never has that I know of. My mom and I are both scarred from the accident that caused this," Marcus gestured at his body, "and he's never given any indication that he could do something about it."

But what about the Halfriez? Why didn't he use it to heal you?

"Huh. He *did* use the Halfriez to heal the injuries to my arm when I first returned from Lysomnus," he said thoughtfully. "I don't know. Maybe it's not powerful enough in our world to heal major injuries like we had right after the accident, or he didn't want to try to explain himself."

"Maybe he just didn't want to," Leopold said. Marcus stared at him, taken aback.

But what about you *using the Halfriez? Why haven't you used it since you arrived here to heal yourself?*

Marcus paused. "I did try using it once to help my pain, and it did help some," he said slowly, looking at Sadie. "But then it felt like some of the fusions I had done after my accident were changing. I don't know if I want to change myself."

"Look," Leopold interrupted, "we need to talk about

warning the rest of the people of Lysomnus. If the Stondefel are willing, they could take us to the bruwe of the other people to at least warn them so they know what could happen. Even though we don't know how to protect them yet."

Your friend is correct. We should warn the people. Awar, will you speak to Anneberg? Tartarus asked.

"Of course." The Stondefel stood, opened his great, leathery wings, and launched himself with a leap of his powerful legs. Dust flew everywhere from the first downstroke of his wings.

Leopold waved his hand in front of his face, sputtering. "You'd think he'd warn us!"

"It hardly seems necessary, considering." Cornus said. "A giant creature with enormous wings is going to generate a lot of wind when he takes off from the ground."

"Oh good, stuffy Cornus is back," Leopold said, rolling his eyes. Sadie giggled.

"Well, make a stupid observation, receive a stupid comment," Cornus said, shooting a sly glance at Leopold. Marcus and Sadie burst out laughing as their friend was left speechless.

CHAPTER ELEVEN

SPLITTING UP

The three humans and Cornus returned with King Tartarus to his chambers. All were willing to travel to the other bruwe. At first, Marcus expected that Cornus would want to return to Thicce Colpat to warn his own people, but Cornus insisted that he must not. His Travels were to continue for a year, and he did not want to return to his bruwe yet again while he was supposed to be completing them.

Leopold said he would return to Thicce Colpat. After all, he had spent a full day visiting with the Scrybb while Marcus slept. He felt he had made some friends while he was there and would like to see them again. Sadie wanted to go back, too, but Leopold was insistent that he should go alone. "Why do boys always insist on getting their own way?" Sadie grumbled. "Well, perhaps I'll stay here and discuss what might be done about the potential attacks with King Tartarus and Queen Colflur while you three are off gallivanting around."

"And since you'll be flying," Marcus said to Leopold, "you won't have to worry about that Brynar."

Brynar? asked Tartarus.

"Yes, there is a new one on the path between Thicce Colpat and Palaga," Cornus said. "That is where we said

Davidia was taken, remember?"

My apologies for forgetting. So much has happened. I don't understand where that could have come from. I have never heard of such a thing. At least you have not had anymore trouble with the <<null>>. I know they are always waiting for humans to step foot on a Brynar.

Marcus looked at his arm, running his finger along the prosthesis thoughtfully. "I do have one question about them —the phantasms, we call them. Would they pass a message for someone else? Like a human?"

What? Absolutely no, I would say not. The <<null>> will immediately kill any human they see. Why do you ask?

"Because when I was still back at home, I received a message through an interdimensional portal like the ones the phantasms use. That's how I knew my father had been taken."

Marcus, are you aware of what happens when you arrive here in Lysomnus?

He frowned, confused by the question. "Um, I've always just woken up on the ground. I travel here in my sleep."

When you arrive, you come through an interdimensional portal identical to the ones used by the <<null>>.

Marcus was stunned. "What? That doesn't make any sense." He turned to look at Cornus. "Wait a minute. Both times I arrived here, you showed up shortly after and said that you 'heard' me arrive. Is that what you meant?"

"Oh, Marcus. I thought you knew, I suppose. That your father might have told you?" Cornus looked dreadfully uncomfortable, his orange eyes dimming and his facial leaves drooping.

"So you hear that same terrible screaming sound of a hole in reality every time I come here?"

"Yes. But we were taught by Cassiope, you and the people of your bloodline always arrive at a safe distance from any bruwe. It is our duty to find you and offer assistance."

It is the duty of all the people of Lysomnus to do so. Most of us consider it an honor.

Cornus looked uncomfortable, and Marcus remembered how the Scrybb had started treating the three of them differently and then complained about all humans, including Deacon and himself.

It is possible that whoever has your father might have the ability to use them in the same way that you do. It could even be N—that powerful human herself. This makes me even more certain the humans are involved with your father's disappearance since they have power and could likely do such a thing as create a portal. We have seen several of them use power when they come here, although nothing as strong as— well, the leader herself.

"Is this why the phantasms are after humans? Because we use the same interdimensional portals that they do?" Marcus wondered.

We know very little about them, Marcus. Tartarus shrugged. *This may be something we can discuss at a later time.*

"I understand." Marcus sighed. "Okay. Who are the other people of Lysomnus we need to warn?"

The Muirnati are the people who live on the shores of the Diluvium. Their bruwe is called Fisc and is under the waters of the ocean. The Cativera are the stock herders who live on the Zabanara plains. They live under the ground in their bruwe, Grasian. Their stock, the Struthtaur, live in the grasslands, so the Cativera spend much of their time above ground to care for them and protect them.

"Oh, is that where the meat comes from? Do you trade with them for the meat?" Sadie asked.

We trade with the Muirnati for fish and the Cativera for meat.

"Fish? I haven't eaten any fish yet," Marcus said.

You have eaten fish every time you have dined with us. The white meat that you enjoyed is the fish we receive from the Muirnati.

"I thought that was chicken! Well, I suppose you wouldn't have chicken here, but a kind of bird anyway. It sure was delicious. So, where should each of us go, Cornus and I?"

The Cativera will need to be approached on foot. It would not be prudent for a Stondefel to fly in over their bruwe or their fields because of the Struthtaur.

Marcus was torn. He wanted the opportunity to meet both of the other races of Lysomnus. However, he thought that it would be better if Cornus went to the Cativera since it would be quite challenging for him to walk the distance required. The Scrybb was delighted with the idea, and it was decided. Marcus would go to Fisc to warn the Muirnati while Cornus visited the Cativera.

I will speak to Awar about which Stondefel will assist with travel, said Tartarus. *He is the liaison between the Stondefel and us for now. You will not need to bring supplies with you; the Muirnati and the Cativera will be happy to host you both. They are friendly and generous people.*

Everyone made their way to the dining hall for the midday meal. Cornus walked ahead with Tartarus, discussing his entry to the territory of the Cativera. Leopold carefully draped his arm around Marcus's shoulders.

"Well, broham, I'll bet you didn't see this coming when

you came back to good ol' Lysomnus!"

"Hardly. Remember, we came here to find my dad. I feel like we're getting further and further away from that goal every day." Marcus felt a terrible weight in his chest.

"Have you ever considered that he might be the captive of these other humans that live here in Lysomnus?" Sadie suggested from behind them.

Marcus frowned. "Tartarus did mention that the message I received might have come from one of the humans since it seems likely only one of them would have had the power to send me a message through a portal."

Leopold nodded, his arm sliding off Marcus's shoulders. "That does make sense."

"It stands to reason." Sadie continued. "All the clues seem to be pointing in that direction. No one wants to discuss the humans and their leader with us, but they're the ones who're causing all the trouble here in Lysomnus. It makes sense they would be the ones who took your father at the same time. It might actually be part of some larger plot that all ties together."

"I guess that makes sense." Marcus stopped walking and thought for a minute. "What I really don't get is why they would take him and send a message to invite me to come after him. They have him if they need his healing power, but all I have is some weak ability to move things around, and they don't even know about that. Why would they want me?"

"I don't know, Marcus. Perhaps they don't know anything specific about your power but only guess that you *have* some kind of power and want control of it." Sadie chewed her lip pensively as she walked with them.

"Let me ask you a question," Leopold said. "Have you

thought more about healing yourself with the Halfriez? You saw what it did to my leg. It might be able to fix your back."

Marcus rubbed the back of his neck. "People keep asking me that, but I really don't know if that's something I want to do."

"You keep saying that, but I wish you'd think more about it. It would be nice to see you be able to do things without suffering so much pain all the time."

The group fell silent as they walked the rest of the way to the dining hall, each lost in their own thoughts. As usual, the food was delicious, and now that he was feeling well-rested, Marcus found he was able to appreciate each dish thoroughly, including the desserts Leopold had raved about before. Rather than reaching out to serve himself the majority of the food, he carefully used his newfound power to bring most of the morsels to his plate. He wanted to use every opportunity to practice. A cacophony of thoughts filled his head as he did so, and he looked up to see most of the Fyrtudo in the room staring at him.

Growan was staring, too.

How is that happening? The young Fyrtudo's thoughts were unblocked and quite loud.

Marcus, is this an example of your power? Tartarus asked.

"Yes, after I learned to use it to move the wagon, I've been trying to practice using it as much as I can to get better and have more control. I'm sorry if I startled anyone." Most of the Fyrtudo in the room nodded and turned back to their meals. Marcus was reassured. Since they knew of Deacon's healing power, he figured they understood he would have some kind of power, too.

Colfur turned to the prince, and Marcus knew she was explaining Marcus's power to her son.

A good idea. I know your father also had to practice to become more skilled. He was more impatient, though. You seem to be working at a good pace.

"Tartarus," Marcus began after swallowing a delicious mouthful of pastry. "Are there strict protocols I must observe when meeting with the Muirnati?"

They are the most flexible of all the people of Lysomnus. Remain polite, of course. You can meet with any of them, and whichever Muirnati you find will take you to their meeting place to spread your message. I think you will quite like them. I have met with them once, but it is difficult for me to visit with them effectively. You will understand more when you get there.

Once they finished eating, everyone involved in the plan was to meet outside with Awar. Marcus felt uncomfortable just getting up from the table and walking away, leaving his dirty dishes for someone else to clean up for him.

Please do not worry, Colflur said to him. *It is the duty of the kitchen staff, and they would be more uncomfortable if you tried to help them do their job.*

Marcus felt reassured but realized he kept forgetting to put a block in place to keep his thoughts to himself.

Once they had all arrived outside, Awar landed with a sudden flurry of wind and whirling dust. While everyone else coughed, Marcus tried something he had thought of earlier. Since he was able to push things, could he use his power to push the dust away from his face? He concentrated. It was too difficult to block the dust itself—it contained too many tiny particles to push away. He had to construct a kind of shield around his face to block the dust. The Halfriez grew warm in his hand as he concentrated, trying to think about blocking all the particles flying toward him. It worked, but it felt completely different than what he had done before. So far, he had turned the wheels on the cart, lifted food through the air, and now created a barrier around himself to keep dust away. He had kept it away from his face, anyway. Was he manifesting various aspects of the same power, he wondered? Or was there more to this than he thought?

"Colflur has called me and says you are ready for your rides," Awar said as he tucked his leathery wings to his back. He smirked and said to Tartarus, "She also says you were supposed to be coordinating who among the Stondefel would take these boys to each bruwe, but of course you have been too busy. We have handled that business for you." He laughed, a sound like rocks being clashed together.

Tartarus harrumphed. *Colflur is a good partner for taking care of these things for me. We have been discussing other important matters. I believe that more is involved in all of this than we first imagined.*

Awar snorted. "I'm quite sure you are correct, but we need to get these warnings taken care of before anything else, Tartarus."

You are right. Who will take each of the boys to their destinations? Upon hearing this statement, Marcus realized Sadie had been right. The only girl in their group had been left out of these visits. He wanted to say something, but it was too late.

"I will take Leopold to Thicce Colpat, as there is a smaller area for landing near their bruwe," Awar said. "Anneberg will take Cornus to Grasian, and Agatho will take Marcus to Fisc. We are all ready to leave. I will take Leopold now and fly to Thicce Colpat."

"So, uh, when we take this flight...Marcus kind of told me about you bringing him down here, Awar, and I was wondering, um, could we try it a different way?" Leopold stammered, flushing a deep red as everyone looked at him.

"What do you mean, Leopold?" Awar asked, sounding puzzled. "We had no problems bringing the others down here from the caldera."

"Well, I'm not really thrilled about the idea of flying above the forest while being clutched in those talons. It was just a short drop to bring everyone down here. But it would be a lot more comfortable to sit, uh, please don't kill me"— Leopold ducked behind his raised hands—"on your back and use some kind of harness to keep from falling off. If you don't mind."

"That is an excellent idea!' Awar laughed. "It would be much easier than holding onto you and trying to remember not to cut you in half!"

The boys exchanged nervous glances.

"I would never do that, of course. I only jest. Please provide an example of this 'harness' you would like to use, and I will discuss the idea with Anneberg and Agatho." He flew off again. As he did so, Marcus again worked on using his power to control the dust flying around the terrace. This time, he was able to keep it completely away from himself, and he smiled, pleased he could avoid small particles stinging his eyes or dusting his clothes.

Leopold asked Tartarus if they had any rope. Cornus was able to answer this question, as the Scrybb created ropes and traded them with the Fyrtudo. He asked Tartarus if they could have some brought to the stone terrace to work out the harnesses. Cornus, who was more accustomed to working with the ropes, stood behind Leopold and twisted them into a shape that would fit his body while reaching forward to wrap around Leopold's torso as well. Once they had the shape worked out, they stepped out of the completed harness and began to expand the torso section to fit on the much larger Stondefel.

When Awar returned, two larger Stondefel could be seen circling in the sky above. Once he landed, he confirmed that he and the other Stondefel were happy to wear the harnesses if they were comfortable enough. Leopold cracked a joke that although the Stondefel were made of stone, they were apparently not so tough; in response, Awar tapped Leopold gently on the head with a sheathed talon, knocking him to the ground while everyone laughed.

CHAPTER TWELVE

THE LOST LANGUAGES OF LYSOMNUS

Sadie

S adie came out to watch while they got everything ready. Then she grabbed Leopold by the arm. "Can I talk to you for a minute before you leave?"

"Sure," he said, his bright blue eyes quizzical.

They walked to the edge of the terrace, nearly enveloped by the steam of the sulfurous river. "I just wanted to ask you... Look, I know you and Marcus are best friends. I really like him. Like, *really* like him. And I don't want that to interfere with your friendship or anything."

"Interfere?" Leopold laughed. "Sadie, I couldn't be happier for Marcus to finally find someone special. And you don't have to be worried about me tragically falling in love with you, too, like some kind of devastating love triangle. I think you're cool, Sadie, but I'm gay. Don't worry," he added, "Marcus already knows." He glanced over at Awar, who was tapping a talon impatiently. Giving Sadie a quick hug, he said, "Sorry, but I gotta run!"

Sadie was left staring after him, startled. After each pair of Stondefel and human flew away, she turned to Colflur and Tartarus. "What can we possibly do to protect Lysomnus in case the Stondefel really do attack each other?"

It is unimaginable, child, said Colflur, wringing her hands nervously. She was absently shifting her weight from foot to foot. *The people of our world could well be destroyed.*

"Has anything like this happened in the past?" Sadie wondered out loud.

There is one place we can certainly find out, the Queen said, leading Sadie to a room to the left of the massive cavern of Palaga. Inside was an enormous library. Shelves made of light-colored wood surrounded the room, and tall stacks of more beautiful shelves stood just behind some high tables made of even more wood polished to a high shine. These stacks were full of books that looked older than any Sadie had ever seen before. Light bounced off the wood, and Sadie looked up to see where it came from. A single window was bored through the rock high above, and the sun that shone through reflected off a curved piece of metal hung at an angle in front of it to another and then to several more around the room. Each was highly polished. The books themselves had thick, leathery covers, some with English titles, and some were in languages that appeared different from any Sadie had ever seen. Hieroglyphs or other markings delineated words or characters, while pictures accompanied them. Sadie pulled one off the shelf.

"I knew it! Your world did have different languages in the past. It didn't make sense to me that such different people of one world would all speak the same language. I wonder what changed—" She covered her mouth as she looked up at Colflur in horror.

What is it, my dear? What has you so disturbed?

"The humans!" Sadie gasped. "While they have been forcing your people to give them your goods and anything else they want when they come to your bruwe, I wonder if they somehow forced everyone to learn English sometime in the past."

That would be terrible. Colflur sounded concerned, but doubtful. *But—we have used this language all my life, and it is what my parents taught me, and I believe their parents knew it too.*

"Do you know how long the humans have been here, on Lysomnus?" Sadie turned another page in the book she was perusing.

I do not know. I know that the Talents have been coming for many generations, but I know little of the other humans or their leader.

"This book appears to show Fyrtudo using a different written language, Colflur," Sadie said, indicating the graphics on the page she had turned to. The Queen came closer and peered at the picture and the hieroglyphics below, her eyes widening.

These markings are similar to the ones we use to mark directions in our tunnels. Those are much more rudimentary, but these... I can almost make some sense of them. Some of them are the same. I don't think we've ever looked at any of these other books before.

"I think this might have been your people's original written language. Perhaps you used both telepathic language and written words, and the written language has been forgotten since then.

"How long have these books been in your library, Colflur? Do you know why no teachers use these books?"

I believe they probably use only the basic language texts because we cannot read these or any others in here that are not. Other than the ones I saw like our cave markings, I cannot read it at all.

Can you make any noises through your mouth, Colflur?" Sadie asked curiously.

The Fyrtudo nodded. *We hum to the children, and we can call out warnings in the tunnels. We use no words, though. Now, I am starting to wonder if we ever spoke.*

"I would like to know if there's someone you have—a teacher, perhaps, who could look at these texts and match your tunnel symbols with the markings used in the hieroglyphics? It could be the beginning of figuring out a language or something, recovering the original that was lost. I'd be willing to work with them to help figure it out." Sadie was excited. "Do you have books from any of the other people of Lysomnus here in your library? I speak and read different languages on Earth, the world we come from, because my family comes from a different part of our planet than Marcus and Leopold's. They were easy for me to learn, and I really enjoyed it. I would love to try to learn some of these." She walked to the shelves and ran her fingers lightly along several spines.

I'm sure you could find them here. This is the only library ever built on Lysomnus, and somewhere along the way, the art of printing words on paper was lost. We keep the books safe for all the people of our world here. Some people used to send Travelers here to study, but that was generations ago, Colflur said, her expression melancholy. *However, I will certainly find a teacher and set them the task of trying to translate our old language from our tunnel symbols with you.*

Sadie pulled out some books at random and pulled herself up onto a table, sitting cross-legged. She began looking through each book, noting which of Lysomnus's people were depicted in the pages inside, and separated them into piles.

"There are books here with pictures of the Scrybb, and a *very* unique looking language in them. I simply cannot imagine how it would sound. This one"—she pointed with one finger to the cracked leather cover—"has interesting creatures in it. There are both large, powerful-looking wingless birds and strange animals pictured! They look like nothing I've ever seen. Quite dignified, the ones with the spears. Are these both people of your world?"

Not both, laughed Colflur, looking at the pictures. *The first are Struthtaur; they are not people. They are herd animals and the source of the meat we have at dinner and also leather. The others are the Cativera, the people of Grasian whom Cornus has gone to meet.*

"Oh!" Sadie said. "*That* should be interesting! I wonder what their language was like. It's so hard to tell by looking in these books. And such a shame that all these languages have been lost. Oh," she said, remembering her original task, "but I'm supposed to be looking for a solution for our Stondefel problem!"

She climbed back down and walked to a different section, discovered that the books contained there were in English, and began looking through them. Colflur watched her for a moment, then left to find a teacher. Soon, Sadie had found several that referenced the Stondefel and stacked them up, making her way back to the table. Once in place, she buried herself in reading, hoping to find something—anything—that would help them out of their current predicament.

CHAPTER THIRTEEN

FISC

Marcus

Rejoining the others, Leopold helped Cornus try the harness they had designed on Awar; he had some suggestions for minor changes but declared it a success. Cornus and Leopold quickly braided two adjustable larger versions for the other Stondefel, and then Leopold climbed aboard Awar's back and tightened his harness. As Awar stood from his crouching position, Leopold grinned. Marcus knew his thrill-ride-loving friend would thoroughly enjoy his trip.

With a thrust of his powerful legs, Awar vaulted into the air. Those left on the ground covered their faces against the flurry of dust blown around by the first downdraft of the Stondefel's leathery wings. Marcus extended the shield around him to see how much space he was able to keep clear. He definitely felt like he was getting better with his power. Before the cloud had settled, Anneberg had landed on the terrace, creating his own dust cloud.

Marcus was taken aback by the difference in Anneberg's size upon seeing him land on the stone terrace. He had forgotten how enormous the full-grown Stondefel was after being around Awar. He saw Cornus hastily making changes to the harnesses he had made for the larger Stondefel and guessed he was not the only one who had forgotten just how big Anneberg was.

Cornus climbed up and got the harness properly placed and secured. Anneberg said, "I want you to know how sorry the Stondefel are about what happened to your friend, young Cornus. It is an atrocity that any Stondefel would hurt one of the people, and we will do everything we can to help you find her and bring her home."

For the first time in the presence of a Stondefel, Cornus smiled. "Thank you, Anneberg. I cannot tell you what it means to me to hear you say that." Then he climbed into the harness, tightened it, and turned to Marcus. "Did you see the placement and fit of the harness?"

"I did." Marcus nodded to reassure the Scrybb. "I'll be able to put my harness on Agatho with Sadie's help. See you soon."

When Anneberg departed, Marcus was prepared for the dust storm, which was quite a bit fiercer with the much larger spread of Anneberg's wings. The Halfriez warmed in his pocket as he pushed the shield out to surround Sadie, who was standing nearby. She looked around, confused that the swirling dust was not touching her. She looked at Marcus, and he winked. She smiled in appreciation.

The Stondefel circling in the sky above waited until the dust had settled before landing on the stone terrace. This Stondefel, Agatho, was slightly shorter in length than Anneberg, but broader in chest and girth. Marcus walked over to him and smiled. "Hello. I'm Marcus."

"Hello, Marcus Talent. I am Agatho." the massive creature rumbled with a bow of his head. "It is a pleasure to meet you, and I am honored to escort you on this errand. Let us hope that we are able to save lives and avoid conflict with our brothers."

"I agree wholeheartedly. Nothing could be more important right now."

Marcus held up the harness. Agatho nodded, and Sadie climbed up to help get it placed correctly and tightened down. Marcus was glad to have her help since he was finding it difficult to get the harness into place with his prosthesis. He found a natural seat behind the juncture of Agatho's upper torso and segmented body.

Once they had the harness tight, with his cane tied down and secure, Sadie kissed him, her mouth lingering on his before she climbed down. Marcus touched his lips in wonder and smiled down at her. Her dark eyes shone as she gazed up at him, a pink flush coloring her cheeks.

The abrupt feeling of Agatho vaulting into the sky was like nothing Marcus had ever experienced. Even being carried by Awar from the caldera couldn't compare. The force of taking off pressed Agatho against him, and he gripped the rope around Agatho's chest in his left hand and pulled himself in tight until the force eased. As Agatho reached his desired altitude, he banked to one side, circling the stone terrace below. Marcus couldn't make out the Fyrtudo, even though he thought their dark backs would be visible on the much lighter stone terrace. Marcus gulped. They must be very high. "Can you see Tartarus?" he shouted to Agatho to overcome the wind.

"I can," the Stondefel replied.

"You must have incredible vision!"

"When you are a creature designed for flight, you must have eyes that can see far," Agatho rumbled.

Marcus stared down, enjoying the view of Lysomnus

from above. The high, craggy peaks of the Beornan Rokk stretched across the top of the land mass within his sight, and the dense forests of the Grenewud spanned much of the rest. Light lines crossed through the dark trees in a meandering pattern that Marcus realized were the pathways maintained by the Scrybb. Barren patches of dirt stood out like ugly scars that soon disappeared as they traveled to the southeast. As Agatho flew on, Marcus noticed a growing gray haze in the distance that turned blue beneath hazy clouds as they approached. This must be the Diluvium, he thought. Their destination–Fisc–was a bruwe on the shore of this world's ocean.

Marcus was freezing. The air up this high was incredibly cold. He was grateful that Agatho's body radiated heat, so at least he was shielded from the wind and had a source of warmth. To distract himself, he tried to get to know Agatho better..

"Agatho," Marcus called out against the wind, "Is the Diluvium the only ocean of this world? Or are there others?" He raised his prosthesis and tried to push back the hair whipped into his eyes by the wind. It was a futile attempt. His black curls were out of control, and he was afraid to let go with his left hand.

"It is the singular ocean. Beyond the Beornan Rokk, there is ice. To the south and west of here are the Zabanara plains where the Cativera live, and the Diluvium laps the shores around this entire land mass."

The Diluvium grew larger in Marcus's view as Agatho began to descend. The Grenewud had faded to a dim shadow to the north, while the Diluvium covered his entire eastern view of Lysomnus. The blue expanse was not smooth but churned turbulently beneath a dark mass of storm clouds. Lightning flickered inside the clouds, and the rumble of thunder reached them even at this distance.

"We must make it to Fisc before that storm hits," Agatho called. "It is dangerous for you to be exposed to that kind of weather."

"What about you?" Marcus couldn't imagine the Stondefel trying to fly through a violent thunderstorm.

"I can fly away and return once it has passed," Agatho said. "It is imperative our message reaches the bruwe as soon as possible. I will drop you off nearby and then leave."

Marcus gulped at the idea of entering a strange bruwe on his own. He had managed to offend the Scrybb almost immediately when he first entered Thicce Colpat. He hoped he would do better this time.

Agatho had altered his course, following the shoreline of the Diluvium. As they flew lower, they passed over the edge of a grassy plains area. The shoreline was a combination of the boulders he and the others had seen when they first arrived, and smooth gray sand extending to the water.

Agatho landed on a wide expanse of sandy shoreline. "Quickly! Climb down, Marcus, and leave the harness on. Fisc is just around this bend. A few Muirnati noticed me as I flew in, so your arrival should not be too much of a surprise. I must go. Waste no time—that storm will come swiftly!"

Marcus worked his way out of the harness, pulling his cane out and stepping down carefully. The Stondefel launched himself immediately back into the air, showering Marcus with sand.

The air was noticeably warmer, and Marcus sighed in relief. They might have to think about warmer clothing for air travel! He started to brush himself off as best he could, then stopped, thinking about how he had pushed the dust away from himself. Could he do the same thing here? He stopped and concentrated. He focused on the sand, and once he felt it, he pushed it away as he had the dust on the stone entrance to Palaga. Sand flew off his clothes and out of his hair. Marcus smiled to himself in satisfaction.

The smile slipped as soon as he started walking. His back hurt worse than it had since he had walked on the Scrybb path. It must have been that first jerk on Agatho's back during takeoff. Grimacing in pain, he began to make his way along the rocky, sandy beach. The Fyrtudo had treated him as though he were an equal. The Scrybb had been hostile by the time he and his friends had left. What would the Muirnati be like?

When he rounded the bend, he stopped in confusion. He saw nothing here to indicate how to find the Muirnati. The only thing in view was a half-circle of tall, flat rocks standing independently a short distance back from the water's edge. Agatho had suggested he should find the Muirnati easily, so they had to be nearby.

He walked closer to inspect the rock formation. The tall stones stood vertically in a half-circle, with gaps between them. They must be protecting something. Marcus approached the rock formation and peered between two of them. He saw a tunnel opening in the sand with water at the surface. The tunnel entrance itself was lined with jagged gray rock, similar to what lay around on the beach. As Marcus stared, a face appeared in the tunnel and peered up at him. He jerked backward, nearly falling over. A jolt of pain shot up his back as he caught his balance.

"Come closer!" a voice cried out. The person he'd seen lifted herself halfway out of the tunnel and rested her hip on the rocky edge. Her smoothly scaled skin was teal in color, and random dark stripes crossed her body. Her ears and nose were little more than flaps. Her yellow eyes were much larger than human eyes, round and luminous. When she opened her mouth, he saw rows of small, sharp, pointed teeth. Gills fluttered above the ridges of her collarbones. "Come with me," she said, reaching out one hand to him. There was webbing between her fingers, which were much longer than human fingers, and fin-like material stretched between her arms and the sides of her body.

"Okay," Marcus said, stepping around the edge of the rock. He edged close to the tunnel. "My name is Marcus. I came here with an important message."

"We thought a message was forthcoming when we saw the Stondefel in the sky," she said. "I'm Pelamis. Come with me into Fisc so you can share your message with everyone."

Marcus eyed the tunnel entrance, half-full of surging water. "I don't know how this will work," he said. "I can't swim that far without breathing underwater."

"Neither could your father, and he was a frequent visitor," the Muirnati woman laughed. "I have a special mask for you to wear. Don't worry." She reached down and pulled an item from under the water.

Feeling intensely relieved, Marcus took the mask and inspected it. It looked like transparent glass but was quite flexible, and when he put it on, it fit tightly to his skin, as if it was part of his body. There were slits along the bottom near his mouth, and when he breathed, he could hear air hissing in and out of the mask. After removing his shirt and prosthesis, Marcus toed off his boots to leave beside his cane.

With some trepidation, Marcus lowered himself into the cold seawater. He gasped as the chilled water soaked through his pants. He entered the tunnel headfirst behind Pelamis. As he followed her, it quickly became very dark; dark enough that the rocks lining the tunnel faded out of sight. Anxiety swiftly built pressure in his stomach.

The Muirnati woman was just ahead of him; he felt a little calmer when he noticed she glowed in the darkness, providing some illumination. He noticed that her legs were also connected by webbing, and a long, narrow fin rose along each one beginning just behind her ankles. He held his breath at first by instinct, but finally, he had to breathe. There was a hissing noise through the slits at the bottom of the mask, and air rushed into his lungs.

The trip through the tunnel felt extraordinarily long, even though he was following Pelamis. The water was very cold, and he was freezing; his back hurt, and his limbs felt heavy. With Pelamis providing the only light, he felt as if the tunnel were closing around him. He wanted to stop swimming and let himself sink, but he kept his eyes on Pelamis and told himself there was warmth ahead if he could just keep going. He almost gave up when he finally saw light glowing ahead of them.

Marcus felt immense relief as he exited the tunnel. It ended abruptly after a sharp upward turn, and Marcus broke through the surface of the water. Pelamis was right next to him, smiling as she watched him look around with interest. The bruwe of the Muirnati was open to the sky above. He looked up, expecting to see the storm clouds he had seen when Agatho dropped him off, but the light gray clouds here were calm, and light rain splashed the surface of the water.

Pelamis gestured for him to follow her. She led him to another tunnel entrance. This one descended straight down, which Marcus found frightening, but at least the journey was short. Before his anxiety could rise too high, the tunnel curved to the side and ended by opening into a small pool. After he and Pelamis broke the surface, she told him to take the mask off while gesturing to the side of his face.

Marcus removed the mask, peeling it from the side as Pelamis had indicated. The pool dominated the center of the room, but the floor around it was wide and dry, and the whole interior was curved and pale green, reminding him of the curvature of a seashell. There were no windows, but the green curve of the room glowed just like Pelamis did. The shell must be bioluminescent, like Pelamis's body and so many other things he'd encountered in Lysomnus so far. There was a bed with comfortable-looking bedding built into the curve of the shell and a shelf with folded smooth, gray, rubbery-looking material. It had a shimmery look to it, like the scales on Pelamis's body.

Pelamis remained in the water. When her head emerged from the water, clear membranes retracted from her eyes. Her ears and nose flaps opened as she came out of the water. "Marcus, I formally welcome you to Fisc. The Muirnati are honored to have you here in our bruwe."

"Thank you, Pelamis." He bowed his head. "I'm honored to meet you."

"I must tell you that I volunteered to come and guide you when we saw you walking down the beach. Your father, Deacon, is well known to me. He told me—told us—all about you. And you resemble him."

"I do?" Marcus had always been told he looked like his mother; no one had ever said he looked like his father. It felt weird, and he wondered how often this Muirnati woman had seen Deacon to notice any resemblance between father and son.

"Yes," Pelamis replied. "You have his curls and his height, and I see him in the bones beneath your skin."

"Ah, okay. Um, thank you?" Marcus's face was hot, but he wasn't sure why.

"You need to get out of your wet pants and warm up," Pelamis said, gracefully changing the subject. "I am hopeful one of the suits on the shelf will fit you. You will be able to swim much more comfortably once you are out of those wet, heavy items and have a suit to keep you warm! The door there"—she indicated a narrow door with a long-fingered hand—"leads to a room for you to refresh yourself and change. I will wait here for you, and then we can go to the Shoal."

"The Shoal?"

"Yes, it's where all Muirnati meet when there is something important to discuss."

Marcus looked at the clothing on the shelf over the bed. There was only one in each size.

While perusing the suits, Marcus said, "This seems odd to me. At both the bruwe of the Scrybb and Fyrtudo, the rooms where the humans forced the bruwe to allow them to stay are full of many different styles and sizes of clothing. Many people stay in each room in both places. Why is it different here in Fisc?"

"Oh, Marcus. This is not a room where the humans of Lysomnus reside when they come with their forceful ways and hateful hearts to Fisc. This is your father's home."

Surprise ran through Marcus's body. "My father has his own home in Fisc?" he croaked out the words.

"Yes. Oh, Marcus, I have wanted to meet you for a long time" Pelamis said quickly. "There is much more to tell you, but we must get you to the Shoal first. Then we can talk more about your father." Strong emotions crossed Pelamis's face, but it was obvious she wasn't ready to say more just yet.

"Okay," he said, his voice rasping out of a throat so dry he almost wanted a drink of the seawater in the pool. "Are you sure one of these suits will fit me? My father is a pretty big guy." In fact, looking around, Marcus couldn't imagine how his father would even stand up in this place.

"Oh," Pelamis said with a smile, a flush coloring her blue-green skin with red. "When your father first came to Lysomnus, he was not a large person. In fact, he wasn't much bigger than you are right now. Why don't you try one on?"

Marcus grabbed a couple of the smaller suits from the shelf. They were full-body suits and felt both rubbery and slippery at the same time. He went through the door Pelamis had indicated, finding a bathroom so like one back home, he would have been astonished had he not already found himself over his limit for surprises for the day. There was a shower stall, a sink, and an actual toilet. Several days of using the woods for a bathroom made using a real toilet a novelty again. Even the facilities in Palaga hadn't made him feel quite this way. Somehow, it brought home the reality that his father had actually lived here; only a human would need a toilet in an ocean bruwe inhabited by fish people.

He was happy to strip off his wet pants. They were soaked and cold, and he was thoroughly chilled. Once they were off, he checked out the shower, fearing it might only pipe in cold seawater. He was pleasantly surprised to feel hot, fresh water spraying from the showerhead. Marcus didn't need to clean up—he had just bathed in Palaga the night before—but he was freezing from swimming in the ocean.

Stepping under the spray, he stood there for a few minutes and let the hot water pour over him. Hot water was a luxury he had been lucky to find at all three bruwes in Lysomnus. Although now that he thought about it, that was only due to the interference of humans in each place, and in two of them, that interference was the use of force and cruelty. It sickened him to think of humans treating the people of Lysomnus that way.

At least here in Fisc, it appeared the only human who visited might be his father. But Pelamis—why had she blushed when talking about Deacon? He had the feeling she knew his father more closely than he wanted to believe. He also had the feeling that perhaps even the Muirnati were somehow not free of the humans' tyranny.

Turning off the water and stepping out of the shower, he glanced around and saw a thick towel on a shelf over the toilet. He dried himself off thoroughly and then began working himself into one of the rubbery, one-piece bodysuits. The first one was clearly going to be too large, so he decided to try the other one and hoped it would fit better.

The first thing he had to do was work his feet into the suit. His own feet were just a little too small, so they didn't fit snugly. And apparently, he was a bit taller, too, so it was a tight fit. He thought it would be an uncomfortable, cold, rubbery feeling suit, but the interior was soft and even a little slippery. Finally, he sat down on the toilet with his butt in the suit, braced his feet against the wall, and stretched the suit to get it to give enough to allow him to put his residual arm in first and then his left arm. He groaned with the pain of pushing against his back. He struggled to reach down and grasp the zipper. As he pulled it up, it formed together, and he couldn't see the line where it had been a moment before.

When he reached the neck, it looked as if it were one solid suit with no seams. Yet if he grasped the tiny tab at his neck, he could pull it back down, and it would separate again. The right arm hung loose where his own was missing, so he just tucked it up inside as best he could.

He left the bathroom to find Pelamis waiting in the water for him. "Good! You will be much more comfortable now," she said. "Just put your wet clothing by the edge of the pool, and it will be cleaned and dried for you, along with what you left on the beach." Marcus wondered what kind of drying methods would be used by people who lived underwater but didn't ask in case he offended Pelamis. The Stikke slid easily over the sleeve of the suit, but he was unsure what to do with the Halfriez. He fumbled it out of his pants pocket and stared down at the close-fitting suit.

"Marcus, what are you doing?"

"Trying to figure out what to do with the Halfriez." He held up the crystal cube.

"Oh, there is a small pocket." Pelamis reached out and pulled a small zipper on the chest of the suit. She also did a better job of folding the empty right arm in a way that made it more watertight. Marcus slipped the Halfriez inside and closed the pocket. The cube made a small bulge in the suit. "We will need to swim much farther this time. The Shoal is farther away than Fisc is from the shoreline." Marcus groaned internally at the thought of another long distance swim. He was already in so much pain.

When he eased himself back into the pool, he stayed warm and dry. Between the mask and the suit, it would be much more comfortable to swim around Fisc now. Pelamis plunged into the water, and Marcus followed.

First, they swam back up to the bruwe, where Pelamis

called out to other Muirnati nearby. She asked them to pass on the message to come to the Shoal and then told Marcus to follow her carefully. He dreaded the long swim ahead as he dove beneath the surface and followed her. Following Pelamis was difficult because he tried to kind of wiggle his body and legs like she did, and it hurt and was very tiring. He was glad of the mask that made it possible to breathe while trying to keep up. Suddenly, he wondered, could he move *himself?* He closed his eyes and thought of his body gliding through the water without the struggle of using his arms and legs. Putting his left hand over the Halfriez, he felt the heat grow even within the rubbery suit. He realized he was holding his breath, and relaxed as he felt water flowing through his hair. When he opened his eyes, he had almost caught up to Pelamis! He tried to slow down and saw her pulling away. He practiced moving his body slower and faster behind her until they reached the surface of the water.

When they finally stopped swimming and Marcus was able to look around, he saw a set of massive bones curving far above the Diluvium. Each bone was wider than he was tall, and they disappeared into the depths below and continued out of sight into the clouds above. The skeleton arched overhead in a long formation that spoke of the beast that must have died here a long time ago—a beast he couldn't even imagine, given the size of its skeleton. When he looked up, rain pelted his mask. The storm that had worried Agatho appeared to be nearly over.

"Pelamis," Marcus asked, pulling his mask off, "why is there a tunnel to enter Fisc? I'm sure the Muirnati are more than capable of traveling through the sea in your own bruwe. I know the Talents have traveled here for a long time, but surely it wasn't necessary to build tunnels just for us."

She looked at him uncomfortably. "I'm sure by now you've heard of the humans who take advantage of the different people of Lysomnus, even within our own bruwe. The Muirnati were forced to install the tunnels for their use a long time ago. There are empty homes in our bruwe similar to your father's, where those people stay when they come here."

Marcus frowned. "Did my dad know about this?"

Pelamis looked away. "Yes, but he said there was nothing he could do. Usually, he wasn't here when she and her people came. If he was, he would stay in his own home —the place I showed you."

"How convenient for him." For the first time, Marcus felt a stirring of real anger toward his father. Deacon really *had* known of the humans and their predation of the Lysomnians and had done nothing to help them.

Before too long, many Muirnati began surfacing and lining up in rows around the large area. Marcus realized that there were many more Muirnati living in Fisc than he had thought. Pelamis kept her place beside Marcus. In a low voice, he asked, "Is there a specific Muirnati leader I need to address? Or a Council of some kind?"

"No," she chuckled. "The Shoal is composed of all our adult Muirnati. We make all decisions as one people— together. Simply share your message when I tell you it is time."

Marcus nodded and watched as more Muirnati swam up and began to line up in rows with the others. At last, when the rows were complete and no new Muirnati arrived, Pelamis asked loudly, "Is everyone here?" Everyone looked around themselves and back to Pelamis. Affirmative calls came to her. "Everyone has a place to be and another

Muirnati to be near when they come to the Shoal, Marcus," Pelamis explained. "That way, when we have a gathering, we can determine that everyone is present." Marcus looked around. There were more Muirnati than he could count in the water around them. He could see how their system would ensure that they could keep track of everyone.

"People of Fisc!" Pelamis called out. "This is Marcus Talent, son of Deacon Talent!" A murmur spread through the crowd. "He has come with a message for us!" She lifted one webbed hand and beckoned him forward.

"Yes, um, hello! I, um, I'm here with a warning about a possible attack." Marcus's voice steadied as he remembered the reason he was here. "The Stondefel have split apart. Some of the younger ones have left to join a rebellion. They have plans to attack every bruwe in Lysomnus!"

Loud cries and exclamations swept through the Shoal.

"When will this happen?"

"How could this child know? Maybe he's lying!"

"How can we possibly protect ourselves against the Stondefel?"

Pelamis waved her hands to get their attention. "This is not how we act, people of Fisc. This boy deserves our respect and attention."

Marcus spoke again as she nodded at him. "Fortunately, one of the younger Stondefel has infiltrated the rebels to spy on them and help us. We have knowledge of their plans. All the bruwe of Lysomnus are receiving warnings, just like this, right now, and the Council of Stondefel is meeting in hopes of producing a solution for ending this rebellion peacefully."

A Muirnati man with a thick yellow body and black stripes swam forward. His yellow eyes were on Marcus's the entire time he closed the distance between them, his lips pressed tightly together. Marcus felt as if the man's eyes were burning right through him. "A war between the Stondefel themselves could cause terrible damage, not only to them but to all of us! If those who are sworn to protect us are destroyed, all of Lysomnus would be lost."

"Of course, that is the worst possible outcome," Marcus replied, "but now that we know about the plot, their Council plans to stop it."

"How?" The man held up his long-fingered hand. His features were creased with worry and anger.

Marcus gulped. He felt as if the man blamed him personally for the danger to Fisc. "I'm sorry, sir, I don't have all the answers right now. I was sent here to warn the Muirnati, the same way my friends are warning the Scrybb and the Cativera at this very moment. If the Council has a solution, I know they will advise us, and you, what to do next." Marcus squirmed under the man's glare.

"Where is Deacon Talent?" A woman called out. "Why isn't he here to warn us about the danger?"

"If you remember," Pelamis answered loudly, "Deacon told us when he was here last time that he would—that he would not be able to return." Marcus looked at her with concern as her voice hitched with emotion.

"Are you all right?" he murmured.

"Yes, I will be fine," she said in a voice intended just for Marcus. "Do not worry about me."

Raising her voice again, she said, "The Muirnati, of all the people of Lysomnus, are the safest in Lysomnus with our bruwe in the Diluvium. That does not mean we are not in danger. We must discuss better defenses and where to flee if it comes to that."

Voices called out suggestions, and soon, utter chaos broke out. Pelamis, with the help of the man who had confronted Marcus earlier, regained control with large shells that made an immense sound when blown. The sound immediately silenced the arguing Muirnati.

"We must maintain order, everyone. The Shoal works best when we all work together. Now, let us organize into groups and discuss ideas." The Muirnati man took over efficiently, swimming from one area to another and grouping the Muirnati as he went.

"Now, that certainly worked out well, didn't it?" Pelamis chuckled. "Maximus does very well once he has a goal in mind. Let's leave them all to it. We need to talk. Put your mask back on." She nodded at Maximus, pointing back toward the bruwe. He nodded back to her.

Marcus replaced the mask and then started to swim behind her. It was easier this time to move himself through the water. He didn't have any of the issues he'd had when first working with the cart. His speed was easy to control. This time, when they surfaced in the bruwe, Pelamis led him to a different part of Fisc. Inside, he found just another pool, a wide ledge, and some shelves for storing things.

Sitting on the ledge cross-legged was a Muirnati girl who looked close to his age. There was no webbing between her legs and she had only the long fin behind her legs. She was holding a net in her long-fingered hands. There was no webbing between her fingers or her arms, either. Marcus realized that while the blue-green of her skin was the same color as Pelamis, this girl had dark red hair tucked behind her ears. None of the Mirnati he had seen in the Shoal had hair *or* ears. She had red freckles instead of the stripes Pelamis had on her body. Pelamis called out softly, "Boehlkea."

When the girl looked up, Marcus saw large, deep blue eyes, rather than the yellow eyes he had seen on every other Muirnati at the Shoal, and a small nose that protruded from her face! Her beautiful features were somehow familiar. He looked at Pelamis, confused, while Boehlkea studied Marcus, her large eyes full of curiosity.

"This is Marcus," Pelamis said. "Deacon's son. And Marcus, Boehlkea is my daughter."

"Hello, Boehlkea. It's nice to meet you." Looking at the girl, Marcus had the weirdest feeling that he had seen her somewhere before.

"Hello, Marcus. I've heard so much about you."

Marcus felt as though he was at a disadvantage; these people knew who he was already, and he was just finding out they existed.

"Is it... I'm sorry, is it really rude to ask why Boehlkea looks different from you? I know I haven't been here long and just met you, but..." His sentence trailed off as he flushed with embarrassment.

"Of course not, Marcus. It's natural for you to be curious. I brought you here to meet Boehlkea for a reason."

The girl rolled her eyes. "Mother, just tell him."

Pelamis grasped the edge of the pool, clenching her jaw, and looked Marcus directly in the eyes. She looked incredibly nervous. "Okay. Marcus, Boehlkea is Deacon's daughter."

Marcus was overcome with astonishment. He stared at Boehlkea's blue eyes, the nose that protruded from her face, and the red hair that covered her head. Now he saw why she had appeared so familiar to him. It was the shadow of his father he saw in her.

Pelamis laid a hand on his arm. "I'm sorry if you are upset

by this news. Deacon often worried about the fact that he could not tell you about your family here in Lysomnus. He told me of your longing for a brother or sister, and how he had to stop himself from telling you of Boehlkea."

"How old are you?" he asked Boehlkea.

"I'm sixteen, the same age as you. My father told me constantly about the things you were doing, how we are different, how we are alike."

It was true—Marcus *had* always wanted a sibling but not like this, kept secret in another world. He felt sick.

"But what about my mom? How could he betray her like that?"

Redness crept up Boehlkea's neck into her face, and her lips wrinkled back from even white teeth, so different from the sharp teeth in her mother's mouth. "*Your* mom? What about *my* mom?" Boehlkea threw the net, now crumpled in one hand, into the pool, where it sank slowly to the bottom. "She and my father were together most of their lives, but then my father mated with some other woman—a human in his 'home' world, claiming he had to do it for 'appearances.' Oh, and don't forget the precious Talent *bloodline. I* wasn't good enough. What do you think that was like for us? For me?" Her voice had risen to a shout.

Pelamis pulled herself out of the water and wrapped her arms around her daughter. "Shhh, Boehlkea. It's all right. You know it had to happen that way; we've talked about this a hundred times."

"But it's not fair! He always went back to *them*! And now he can't come here anymore because of Marcus!"

"Hey, whoa," Marcus said, holding his arms up. "I didn't ask to come here. I wasn't given a choice. He didn't even tell me about any of this until I'd already come here once and been attacked by a phantasm."

Pelamis and Boehlkea looked at him. "A what?"

Marcus sighed. "I can't say the name Lysomnians call it. It attacks humans in the Brynar."

"Oh, the <<null>>," they said simultaneously.

"Wait...you were attacked by one and survived?" Pelamis added.

Marcus told them about the phantasm that had erupted from the portal on the Brynar when he had first come to Lysomnus. He told them about how it had torn off the prosthetic arm he had been wearing. He mentioned the gashes he had sustained and Deacon using the Halfriez to heal them. He realized that the Muirnati hadn't even really seemed to notice his residual limb.

"Hey. You guys don't seem surprised by how I look," Marcus said.

"Deacon told us about the accident and how badly you and your mother were hurt," Pelamis said. "He was quite upset. It frustrated him a great deal that he had so much healing power here in our world but wasn't able to do anything to help you in yours. I think he hoped that when you were able to start traveling here, you could use the Halfriez and heal yourself."

A sob came from Boehlkea, and tears pooled in her blue eyes. "My father never said anything to me about Marcus healing himself. It sounds like he cared more about his other child than me," she said to Pelamis. "You sure are being nice to Marcus, especially since it's his fault we'll never see my father again." She glared at Marcus.

"I didn't even know about this world, let alone that I could travel here," Marcus said defensively. "He told me that first night about where I'd gone and why, and he said he would tell me all about Lysomnus the next day before I came back, but by then, he was gone."

"Gone? Gone where?" Both Pelamis and Boehlkea looked alarmed.

"Oh, right," Marcus said, realizing that these two Muirnati—Deacon's Lysomnus family—were the only people in Lysomnus who would care as much about what had happened to Deacon as he did. He told them about finding Deacon missing, the message he'd received about the kidnapping, and how he'd accidentally brought Leopold and Sadie with him when he'd returned.

"Who would do such a thing?" Pelamis asked while the tears in Boehlkea's eyes spilled over. "Kidnap Deacon, I mean?"

Marcus sighed. "There was some speculation during our meeting with the Fyrtudo and the Stondefel that it might have something to do with the humans who live here in Lysomnus. Their leader, Nun the Wiser, is believed to be working with the rebel Stondefel." He clapped his hand over his mouth just as Pelamis and Boehlkea shrieked. "Oh my God, I'm so sorry."

"Please, Marcus, don't ever say that name." Pelamis looked frightened as she embraced her weeping daughter. "Don't cry, my love. If they want Marcus to come after him, they won't hurt Deacon."

"I'm sorry," Marcus said. "It just slipped out. I was so overwhelmed by all of this. But I've seen several examples of what she does when her name is mentioned."

"Maybe this time we got lucky," Pelamis said.

"What if my father's kidnapping is some kind of trick or trap?" Boehlkea said, still crying.

"I did think of that already." Marcus went on to give

them all the details of his adventures in Lysomnus. "But finding him is still a priority."

"Marcus, what does your mother think about all of this? Have you told her anything now that your father is missing?"

"I haven't been back since I came back here. I left her a note, but my father hasn't ever told her anything about Lysomnus—none of us are supposed to tell anyone in our world."

Pelamis looked concerned. "Marcus, how have you managed to stay in Lysomnus for so long without returning to your own planet? Your father had to go back at least every couple of days. And he stayed that long very rarely. He didn't say why, but I got the feeling it had something to do with how time passes in our world and yours."

Marcus held up the arm with the Stikke on it. "He gave me this bracelet the first night I traveled here and told me I could use it to keep from returning to Lysomnus until I was ready. I figured since it could keep me from going one way, it could do the same thing the other way, and so far, it has."

"Marcus, I never saw your father wearing that here. Not ever, and I spent more time with him than anyone in Lysomnus." Pelamis shook her head slowly.

"Well, he never got the chance to tell me *anything* about Lysomnus, so I don't know what he did to come here, or stay here, *or* go back. I don't want to do anything by accident because I don't know how to do anything on my own." Marcus's temper was rising. "I'm sorry if it sounds like I don't want to listen to you, but I have to stay here until I find and rescue him."

"Alright, I understand."

"Hey," Boehlkea broke in. "Deacon is *my* father too. Why can't I go along to help? Just because I didn't get any secret messages doesn't mean I'm not important."

Marcus was surprised. "I'm sorry, I assumed that you had to stay in the Diluvium to survive."

"Most Muirnati do and are unable to leave it," she said, "I, however, do not suffer that limitation."

"That's true to a point, Boehlkea," her mother said. "You still have to submerge yourself in water every day, or you will slowly suffocate. You cannot go on a journey that takes you away from the safety of the Diluvium."

Boehlkea frowned. "Any water, mom. I can find water anywhere. I want to go along and help find my father."

"The answer is no, Boehlkea." Pelamis's tone left no room for discussion.

Boehlkea looked as though she might burst into tears again, but instead, she dove into the tunnel and disappeared.

Pelamis sighed. "She's been so upset since Deacon told us he would be unable to return. I knew it would be hard on her, particularly at this age. It hasn't been easy for me either."

Marcus cleared his throat. "Well, I should probably make my way back to Agatho and Palaga." He was unwilling to discuss his newly discovered sister any further. "We're supposed to return to the Council and continue planning from there. If the storm is over, he will be waiting for me on the beach."

"It has nearly passed. I can feel it. Please be sure to have someone let us know what new plans are made," she said. "We will be doing what we can to ensure the safety of our people in case of an attack in the meantime. Put your mask back on, and I will accompany you to the beach."

When they resurfaced in the main bruwe, Marcus heard screams. Muirnati were swimming about, agitated. In the sky above, Nun the Wiser floated, glaring down.

"Oh, no," Marcus breathed. Guilt tore through him as he heard her raspy voice. He knew she was in Fisc because he had slipped and said her name.

"Who was it? Who said my name? You all know the price!" Boehlkea was nearby, her arms wrapped around a shaking Muirnati girl whose face was buried in Boehlkea's neck.

"Boehlkea!" Pelamis swam toward her daughter.

"The lover of Deacon Talent!" Nun the Wiser shouted hoarsely. "I have long ignored your dalliance, but perhaps it is time to punish you for tainting the Talent bloodline."

With a quick gesture, Nun the Wiser disappeared. A scream nearby caught Marcus's attention, and he looked to see the girl who had been crying in Boehlkea's arms swimming alone, her arms empty.

Pelamis was sobbing, webbed hands over her face. The girl wrapped her arms around Pelamis and wept, too.

Marcus swam over to her and put a trembling hand on her arm. "Pelamis," he said, "I swear I'm going to do everything I can to find Boehlkea and bring her home. This is my fault."

"Please," said the girl with her arms around Pelamis. "I don't know what to do without Boehlkea." She looked pleadingly at Marcus. "If you have a way to bring her back to us, please do it."

"I'm not going to be like my father and ignore this. I'll save her—you'll see."

Pelamis raised hopeful eyes to meet his own. "Let's get you back on dry land," she said.

She led him back through the dark tunnel, and they finally resurfaced in the tunnel inside the ring of stones on the beach. "I will be waiting to hear anything about Boehlkea. Please, send me a message if you can." She grasped his face and left a gentle kiss on one cheek. Then she pointed to a nearby flat rock and a bundle that lay on it. "There are your clothes. If you leave the suit and mask here, I will have them clean and ready when you return."

Pelamis disappeared back down into the tunnel. Marcus climbed out and walked to the rock, which was dry, although the sand around it was still damp from the rain. Grabbing the bundle, he found not only a package containing his clean, dry clothes but another with some dried meat. He dressed slowly, disheartened by the loss of the sister whom he had just met. It made him feel even worse knowing it was his fault. He cried out in pain as he sat and lifted his feet to pull on his socks and then stood to stomp into his boots. His body hurt all over from swimming. He still had to walk down the beach to reach Agatho.

Carefully rounding the end of the stones, he headed for the spot where Agatho had dropped him off. His cane frequently sank into the damp sand and threw him off balance. Hunger rose, prompting him to stop to unwrap and take a bite of the fish, which was saltier than the kind he'd eaten in Palaga and had a different texture.

Agatho hadn't returned to the beach yet, although the rain had stopped, and the clouds were breaking above. While he was waiting, Marcus looked at the enormous boulders that stood where the sand ended. He decided to see if he could lift them, as he had the food before. One lifted into the air, sand and dirt falling back to the ground beneath it. It quavered for a moment, then fell back to the ground.

Disappointed, Marcus hung his head. Then he threw his shoulders back. *I'm not giving up just because I dropped a stupid rock.* He tried again.

This time, he was able to hold it in the air, although it wobbled as much as the vegetables had when he first tried to lift them on the path. The boulder fell. *One more time.* Making a fist, Marcus raised it as he forced his will at the rock, and it flew into the air. It hung as if he was holding it in place with his arm. Marcus whooped. Was his power like a muscle? Using it was building it up, making it stronger?

He tried to lift a second rock while holding the first one in place. The first rock stayed in the air, but the second boulder shook as it rose. Marcus concentrated harder. He imagined a cushion of air beneath the rocks, holding them up. Now, both rocks were shaking. With a crash, they fell to the ground. Marcus shook his head. He really thought he had it there for a moment. Maybe more practice would help.

A dark shadow swooped along the sand as Agatho arrived, landing close to Marcus so he wouldn't have to walk much farther. Marcus was in a lot of pain from getting dressed and walking in the sand. He was exhausted from swimming in the ocean and the emotional toll of the day. With each step, his feet sunk into the sand, and he forced himself to pull it out and go on. As he neared Agatho, he looked up at the Stondefel's back and the height of the outstretched leg he would have to climb to get there.

He closed his eyes and focused on his own body. He had moved himself through the Diluvium—could he *lift* himself? It couldn't be much different than maneuvering his body through the water. Feeling the full weight of his body moving while out of the water took more effort, but once he had a good hold, he lifted himself slowly off the ground.

He kept his eyes closed because he was afraid if he saw the ground beneath him, he might lose his concentration and drop himself as he had the boulders. Once he was in the air, he had to open his eyes to see where Agatho was. Maintaining control with a firm grip on the warming Halfriez in his left hand, he lowered himself into the seat behind the Stondefel's torso and began to work himself into the harness.

"That was quite impressive, Marcus. Your power is getting stronger all the time."

"I have been practicing whenever I get the chance. We are all meeting back at Palaga, aren't we, Agatho?" Marcus realized he didn't really know what came next.

"Yes, little brother. We want to wait until everyone has returned from their missions and then decide our next move together."

This time, Agatho flew a different route. They headed away from the Diluvium along the edge of the Grenewud. The edge of a great plain came into view ahead, which stretched to the south for as far as Marcus could see. Below them in the skies, he saw birds soaring through the air. He wondered if they in any way resembled the birds back on Earth, but they were too far below to tell. He tried to imagine what creatures the birds might be hunting in the grasses below. He realized there was a lot of merit in the Scrybb method of traveling; walking through the world definitely let a person really get to know it well and see every part of it.

Before long, Agatho banked to his left and began to head to the north again. Marcus knew they were making their way back to Palaga. It seemed to take forever to cross the deep green of the Grenewud. Occasionally, he saw a brown area that must be one of the Brynar patches. It made him wonder how many there were and if they were only in the Grenewud or if there were others in that plains area and along the Diluvium's shores.

Finally, he saw the growing shadow of the Beornan Rokk north of the Grenewud. "Hey, Agatho," Marcus shouted, "why did you fly a different way this time?"

'Have to follow the air currents," the massive Stondefel replied. "Even Stondefel will wear out if we fight the wind."

When they reached Palaga, Agatho seemed to drop right out of the sky, taking Marcus's breath away and leaving his stomach among the clouds. "Sorry," Agatho rumbled at Marcus's startled shout. "Not used to having passengers yet."

Marcus worked his way out of the harness once they were on the ground and, rather than clumsily and painfully making his way down Agatho's leg to the ground, he carefully moved himself again using his power. This time, the short trip was a little wobbly, and he assumed it must be his exhaustion from the exertions of the day.

Tartarus and Colflur had emerged from the cavern of Palaga with Sadie. *You have returned!* Tartarus exclaimed. *You are the first.*

"Really? I thought I took a long time to do everything at Fisc, and I was sure I'd be the last to get back here," Marcus said, looking up at the darkening sky.

No, we have had no word from anyone else yet. All we can do is wait.

"I must return to the Council," Agatho rumbled. "Although we will have no word of the renegades until Awar is able to return to them, we may yet devise some plan to avoid conflict."

Marcus carefully reached out with his mind to untie the harness from the Stondefel's shoulders. He was feeling increasingly confident about this power and each nuance of it, from when he had first felt the wheels turn to holding back the dust and now to moving his own body. "Thank you for your assistance," he said.

"Young one, it is I who must thank you," the Stondefel replied. "You have volunteered to help our world with no hesitation. You fly with us with no fear. Your father is missing, and yet you hold off on that important pursuit for this one. No, it is we who owe you a debt for this."

Marcus felt tears burn in his eyes and an unexpected lump in his throat at Agatho's words.

Agatho launched himself back into the air, headed for the peaks of the Beornan Rokk. Marcus kept the entire terrace clear of dust this time, using the pushing ability of his power to keep the dust away. It was easier each time he did it, just as it was when he practiced with lifting objects and moving them through the air. It must be that. Strengthening his power with practice. Waiting for the others gave him the perfect opportunity to spend some time with Sadie. He told her everything that had happened and the new things he had discovered about his power.

If only he could use it to end this terrible conflict somehow.

CHAPTER FOURTEEN

RETURN TO THICCE COLPAT

Leopold

Leopold climbed onto Awar's back and tightened the harness around his body. With a thrust of his powerful legs, Awar vaulted into the air.

Leopold whooped as Awar flew into the sky above Palaga. He had always loved adrenaline-inducing rides like roller coasters, and he'd dreamed of bungee jumping and skydiving. Riding on the back of a Stondefel outdid *all* of those fantasies. Awar rumbled laughter at the excitement of his passenger. There were a few air pockets as he flew along, and he allowed himself to drop when he hit them, giving Leopold the most exciting ride he could.

This flight was a short one since the Scrybb lived close to the Fyrtudo. Their proximity to the Beornan Rokk made Leopold suspicious of the fact that the Scrybb thought the Stondefel were a fairy tale. The Fyrtudo knew of the Stondefel and traded with the Scrybb. How could the topic not come up during trade? He frowned, considering the problem. Perhaps the adults knew and withheld the knowledge of the truth from the children until adulthood, as they did with the existence of humans.

All too soon, the ride was over, and Awar was circling to land in a green field close to Thicce Colpat. Leopold realized he had wasted some of the ride thinking about his visit to the Scrybb rather than enjoying the experience and was a little upset with himself as he climbed down. Awar poked him with one huge knuckle and said he'd wait for him in this field. There shouldn't be any worry about any of the Scrybb finding Awar here while Leopold was sharing his warning in the bruwe, as the field was currently fallow.

Leopold walked to the edge of the field and saw the familiar arch that marked a path to Thicce Colpat. He turned to wave to Awar, but the Stondefel was back in the shadows under the massive trees so that Leopold couldn't see him. Hopefully that meant the Scrybb wouldn't either.

As he walked to the bruwe, Leopold passed several other paths that led to fields that were being actively farmed. He could hear voices and other noises that he assumed were the hand-built mechanicals that were used to aid in fieldwork. Having now used one of the wagons hand-built by Scrybb Crafters, Leopold could attest to the quality of their craftsmanship—even when Marcus had nearly crashed it.

The beauty of this world was one thing he hadn't taken the time to really appreciate, he thought. The air was so clear and clean. It was amazing how he hadn't noticed the reek of his own world until he came to Lysomnus with Marcus. The water in the streams was so crystal clear he'd drunk it without even thinking about the fact that on Earth, a person could die from drinking directly from a stream— and that was the water in the most isolated parts of his world, never mind the urban areas, where drinking from a stream was unthinkable.

As he passed one of the paths, he noticed that it ended

rather abruptly in a Brynar. He wondered if this one had been there for a long time or if it was new, like the one where they had lost Davidia. The Scrybb had said nothing to Leopold and his human friends about Brynar the entire time they had stayed in Thicce Colpat.

After a brief walk, Leopold found himself at the edge of Thicce Colpat. It was the middle of the day, so he knew that most of the Scrybb would be busy working. During the time he had spent here waiting for Marcus to wake up, he had spent time with different Scrybb to see what they did. One had shown him their implement construction, another their farming, a third the cooking. The cooking was his favorite, as he had gotten to sample several different dishes during the process.

The Teachers were the ones in charge. They were always present in the bruwe, raised the children, and made decisions for their people; it made sense to find a Teacher first to help spread the warning.

As he approached the school, Cassiope emerged from the door, the spiny needles covering her body bouncing a bit as she strode firmly toward him. "Leopold!" she exclaimed. She looked around apprehensively. "What are you doing back here alone? Has something happened to Cornus?"

"No, ma'am," Leopold said, a little surprised she asked about Cornus but not Marcus and Sadie. "Cornus is fine, and the others as well. I have come with a warning for your people. Something terrible is going to happen. The Stondefel—"

"Stop! Do not say that name here!" Cassiope stepped forward and pressed one needle-covered hand firmly over Leopold's mouth. "It is heresy to mention those beasts."

Leopold pried her hand off his face with difficulty. "You have to listen to me," he insisted. "This is *important.* The

Stondefel and the Fyrtudo are working together because some of the young Stondefel have—"

She clenched her jaw. "I am so *tired* of humans and their tricks and manipulations. Please refrain from spreading your lies here." She spun around, stormed back into the school, and slammed the door.

Leopold was left standing in the center of the bruwe with his mouth hanging open. He wasn't quite sure what to do. Of all the reactions he had imagined, this was the absolute last thing he had expected.

From behind him, he heard someone go, "*Pssssst.*"

He turned around slowly.

He heard it again. "*Pssssst.*" A leaf-covered hand reached out from the door of the bunkhouse where he and the others had stayed while here in Thicce Colpat and made a beckoning gesture. The whole situation was so ridiculous, Leopold couldn't help laughing.

"*Pssssst.*" He repeated to himself as he made his way to the bunkhouse, still giggling. "Who actually says *Pssssst?*"

When he reached the porch, he saw Abutilon standing inside the door. The orange flowers interspersed along his heart-shaped leaves really did look like tattoos in the dim light. The Scrybb man waved to him urgently. "Quickly, come inside!"

"Okay, okay." As he slipped in, Buddleja closed it firmly from behind.

"Did we really just see you fly in and land in Far Field on a Stondefel? We were sure that we saw a legend come to life!" Abutilon was so excited, his leaves were rustling.

"Yes, you did see me riding a Stondefel. He's my friend, and his name is Awar." Leopold's chuckles faded away, and the seriousness of his task came back full force. "Look, I came to talk to the Scrybb about a very serious situation that will threaten everyone in Lysomnus. The Scrybb are in grave danger," he said.

"In danger? Yes, from you flying over Thicce Colpat on a Stondefel and causing riots!" The Scrybb man stared at Leopold, his eyes wide. "Fortunately, I think Buddleja and I were the only ones who saw you."

"Why? Abutilon, are you going to tell me that the Scrybb don't know about the Stondefel? Or is it like Cornus and Davidia told us, you all think the Stondefel are just some old bedtime story?"

"What they told you is accurate. Most of us were told as children that the Stondefel used to exist to protect all Lysomnus but that they disappeared long ago. Now, they are just bedtime stories. I cannot believe we just saw one, to be honest. It is so exciting!"

"How is it that none of you find out the truth during your Travels?" Leopold persisted. "The Fyrtudo know them well, and you live so close to them! I don't understand."

Abutilon looked down at his feet. "It has not ever come up during trading or Travels, to be honest. The Teachers are quite firm with the young Travelers and the Traders not to discuss anything but Scrybb business with the other people of Lysomnus. But please, tell me—why would a *Stondefel* let you ride on his back?"

"That's why I'm here. All the people of Lysomnus are in danger. A group of Stondefel have rebelled and left to follow the leader of the humans, and they are planning to attack the bruwes! Awar—the one I came here with—left the rebels to warn the Stondefel Council and brought me here to warn the Scrybb. But when I tried to speak to Cassiope just now, she wouldn't even let me tell her what was happening.

She just got angry and called me a liar."

Abutilon and Buddleja looked horrified. Buddleja's leaves trembled with agitation. "I do not—I cannot—how will we get them to listen, Abutilon?" She looked up at her mate in desperation.

"We have to think of something. We cannot just let those stuffy, stubborn old Teachers continue to let their closed minds endanger us all." Abutilon looked determined as he opened the door and strode toward the school.

"I'm going to consult with Awar and see what he thinks," Leopold said.

"That sounds good. Perhaps we can talk the Teachers into coming to Far Field and prove that what you are saying is true," Abutilon called as Leopold raced off.

It seemed to take much longer to get back to Awar than it had to get to Thicce Colpat, even though Leopold ran as fast as he could. Leopold was breathless by the time he returned.

Awar walked out from under the trees where he had been waiting. "Is our goal achieved? Have they received and heeded our warning?"

Leopold shook his head, bending over with his hands on his knees. "No, I'm afraid not." He blew upward to try to get the hair out of his eyes. The blond strands kept catching on his eyelashes, his sweaty forehead holding them in place. "Most of them don't believe that the Stondefel even exist anymore, and when I tried to talk about it to one of the Teachers, she accused me of lying."

Awar rumbled angrily. "This will not do. Disbelief will only result in death. They will be screaming while they burn, wishing they had listened more closely to our warning."

"At least two of them do believe me. In fact, they saw us

land here today. They're trying to convince the Teachers to come out here to this field to see you and learn the truth. Then we can give them the warning."

Leopold was startled when Buddleja ran into the field. She skidded to a halt as she saw the Stondefel standing behind Leopold. Awar watched her curiously. "Leopold!" she called out.

"What is it, Buddleja?"

"I cannot believe it. The Teachers will not come to Far Field. They have seized Abutilon, accusing him of being 'influenced by humans' and lying about the Stondefel. I ran as fast as I could to find you!" She wrapped her arms around Leopold, weeping.

"*That is enough!*" roared Awar. He carefully grasped Buddleja and Leopold in his taloned hands and leapt into the air. He hopped the short distance from the field to the bruwe, a single flap of his wings landing him lightly in the heart of the Thicce Colpat.

Several Teachers, including Cassiope, were tying Abutilon to a post near the place Awar had just landed. They all turned when they heard Buddleja cry out at the sight of her mate's treatment.

"Why are you ignoring the warning this young human has delivered?" Awar rumbled angrily.

"Warning about what? He just brings more human lies." Cassiope spat as she tightened a rope across Abutilon's chest. Another Scrybb was tying a rope around Abutilon's legs. Several others stood back, calling out angrily.

"You have been warned about an imminent attack. But you refuse to listen. Rebel Stondefel *are* coming." As Awar raised his voice, Leopold attempted to move closer to Abutilon, but Scrybb began to crowd in front of him.

"Stondefel are a bedtime story. We will have no such tales spread about our bruwe by humans or our own people." Cassiope stepped down from the dais where Abutilon was now completely immobilized.

"There is a Stondefel right here in the middle of your own bruwe!" Leopold shouted, holding one hand out to indicate Awar. "He's right here, talking to you!"

Cassiope and the other Teachers turned to look at Awar. "That thing does not look so dangerous to me," she said. "Nothing like what a *real* Stondefel is supposed to be. This is just another trick being played by a manipulative human. Humans clearly can no longer be trusted."

Awar, nearly shaking with rage, began to drool. The molten liquid hissed as it hit the ground behind Leopold. Buddleja turned to see what the noise was and screamed in terror. She ran to Abutilon's side, pulling at the ropes that held him in place on the post.

"Easy, Awar," Leopold muttered to the Stondefel. "We're supposed to be the good guys here."

Awar attempted to control his drooling. Leopold looked around to see that most of the windows were full of Scrybb faces. Maybe the Scrybb would become believers now that they could see Awar for themselves. "Cassiope, I thought you might want to know," Leopold said, "that Davidia was taken by one of the renegade Stondefel. It happened so fast, we couldn't save her."

A look of concern crossed the Teacher's face as Buddleja cried out behind her at Leopold's words; then her face smoothed out. "I am sure this is just another of your lies. You humans are all the same. Manipulative, cruel, willing to do anything to get your own way. Take your false beast and leave."

"Cassiope, this is a serious warning." Leopold's temper was rising. "Stondefel could attack Thicce Colpat any day now. You have to be prepared to protect yourselves."

"Get out," the Teacher hissed. "Get out and don't come back."

Leopold was grief-stricken. The Scrybb were the first people he had met here in Lysomnus. They had saved him and made him feel welcome. He pressed a hand to his chest as tears filled his eyes; it felt like his heart was breaking.

He turned to Awar and mounted the Stondefel. As he was getting the harness back into place, he heard noises all around him: yelling, running, banging, and clanking. A large crowd of Scrybb were now running into the square. Most of them had objects in their hands.

Awar sensed the danger too late. As he tensed to vault into the air, the Scrybb—many with only rocks and branches—threw their implements, using them as weapons. Most just bounced off harmlessly, but others did damage. A dagger sliced into Leopold's thigh. He threw his arm up just in time to block a heavy iron pot from hitting him in the head. His elbow throbbed as the pot clanged to the ground. Awar grunted as something hit him in the chest; a heavy wagon rolled over his foot and snapped off a talon, and the Scrybb standing on the wagon narrowly missed his eye with another dagger. He finally launched himself into the air to fly away.

It was the last blow that did the most damage. As Awar pushed his wings down to try to gain altitude, a sharp, heavy piece of wood pierced through his wing sail. Leopold heard a crack as the spear flipped and its weight snapped the main bone in Awar's wing. The Stondefel bellowed in pain, a sound that made Leopold wince. Just as Awar had gained enough height to fly, he was forced to try to glide. It was impossible to flap the broken wing. He spread his good wing and tried to maneuver through the air without losing the altitude he had gained, but his body wobbled gracelessly, and Leopold could do nothing but hold on. Awar tried to glide as far away as possible toward Palaga. It was clear that he wasn't sure how he could land safely with one wing, and attempting to move the other was too agonizing.

Leopold realized that Awar was going to have to land somewhere in the Grenewud no matter what and held on grimly. The Stondefel flapped his good wing and extended his taloned feet, grabbing the top of a tree in his talons and jolting them to a stop. Leopold could only hold on helplessly as Awar tumbled into a large clearing, groaning as he attempted to pull in his broken wing.

Leopold immediately dismounted to look at the wing. Dark blood ringed the tattered hole of the leathery sail material, which appeared to have torn even more during the glide away from the Scrybb bruwe. The massive bone that had swept the length of the beautiful wing just before the attack was now cracked and broken. Unfortunately, it wasn't broken cleanly; the segment that led to the end of the wing now jutting up toward the sky, the break jagged and ugly. Black blood trickled from inside the bone and from beneath the leathery skin that was torn all around it. Awar moaned with pain as Leopold moved the wing slightly to look at it.

"I'm so sorry, Awar," he said. "I don't know what to do."

"I am not sure how far we made it toward Palaga," Awar rumbled. "I flew as far as I could, but I know we are still many days' walk away for you. I am too big to walk the Scrybb paths, and the trees of the Grenewud are far too tall for me to try to push through."

"If only Marcus was here, he could use the Halfriez on you. Then you could be as good as if you had never been hurt." Leopold wished he had something as powerful as the Halfriez to use on his friend. Even if it didn't fix everything, it could make the pain a lot better.

"I think, for now, we will have to plan to spend the night here. I expected you to be fed by the Scrybb, but I think that we may both have to sleep with empty bellies tonight and figure out what to do in the morning. I only hope that the others will worry when we do not return and come looking for us."

"Can you wait that long in so much pain, Awar?" Leopold bit his lip, feeling helpless. "I know it must be terrible. I'm so sorry."

"Perhaps. I will try. You will be waiting with me, and that is helpful."

Leopold lay down to rest between Awar's legs, using some moss he'd found as a pillow. He wanted to keep himself from falling asleep. He watched as Awar stared up at the sky, knowing every second must be dragging by as if it were an hour. He watched the sky darken and the stars come out with his friend, keeping one hand on his leg to offer some comfort.

Suddenly, the stars above were completely blacked out.

CHAPTER FIFTEEN

GRASIAN

Cornus

C ornus had initially felt nothing but horror upon seeing the Stondefel up close, particularly after what happened to Davidia. However, now that he had gotten to know them, listened to them, and had them reach out to him with an apology, he could not hold on to his anger and fear. Anneberg was a massive creature, but he clearly cared deeply about his role in Lysomnus as a protector of its people. As they flew, he told Cornus of flying high to watch over each bruwe and the people within, and his curiosity about the people. "We know the Muirnati, the Cativera, and the Fyrtudo, but I don't know where along the way we lost contact with the Scrybb. I have been so tempted to try to reestablish contact."

"I don't know why my people allowed the Stondefel to become a myth," Cornus wondered out loud. "It is strange to me that any people of Lysomnus, particularly one that protects the others, would be left out of our learning. Especially to use your people as a way to scare children into behaving."

"Perhaps it *is* fear. We have been told to avoid being seen by the Scrybb, so I always fly very high. I can still see everything, but I know I cannot be seen in return. It saddens me that the people are all separated from each other now. It was not always so." Anneberg's voice, always deep and gravelly, seemed heavier with grief.

"I do not believe the Scrybb were always so... so reclusive. Our Travels are meant to help us learn about our world and get to know the other people in it, but I think most of the other young Scrybb are staying on the paths in the Grenewud for the entire year. It is so isolating to do so. We should get to know the other people of our world."

"I very much like the Cativera, the people you are going to visit. I do not get much opportunity to see them because they are stock breeders and herders. The Struthtaur they raise for meat are terrified of Stondefel and will stampede and kill their silly selves if I go near them, so I must meet the Cativera outside of the stock fields. They often see me when I fly near and land and someone will come to meet me. I think you will like them too. I am glad that you will have this opportunity, though I wish the reason for your visit was different."

Cornus remembered what the Fyrtudo had told him about the Cativera. They were taller than adult Scrybb, so they would tower over Cornus, who was short even among his people. The stock animals the Cativera raised—the Struthtaur—were tall animals with long, thick legs. One had to be careful because they were extremely fast and could also kick with those legs. They had even been known to disembowel some people with their sharp claws! Even though that wasn't a danger to a Scrybb with thick, protective vines, Cornus was still wary. He was quite sure it would not be pleasant to be kicked by a very tall animal.

Cornus noted the end of the Grenewud in the south and the beginning of the plains. "What is the name of the plains region where the Cativera live?" He was embarrassed to have to ask.

"It is the Zabanara region," Anneberg called back. "It will not take too long to reach the landing site. Notice the red roads that run through the fields."

Cornus felt disoriented as the Stondefel circled and dropped quickly to the open field below. All too soon, they had landed, and Cornus was climbing down to the ground. After flying for four hours, he found it a little disorienting to walk on land again.

"What do you know of the Cativera, young Scrybb?" Anneberg asked.

"Most of what I have learned is about trade and their stock," Cornus replied. "Anything more is supposed to be learned from our Travels."

"Hmmm," rumbled Anneberg. "That seems a foolish way to teach Traveling children about interactions with the plains people, particularly when you say your people do not come here often. The Cativera are easily offended, and you can upset them just by approaching their territory in the incorrect manner."

"Oh," Cornus said anxiously. "I planned to simply walk to their bruwe. Just like we do with everyone else."

"That will not work with the Cativera, Cornus. If you blindly walk through the fields or make too much noise, you will startle the Struthtaur. That will result either in an attack or a stampede."

"What shall I do?" Cornus wished he had gone to visit the Muirnati instead.

"Your situation is not as dire as it seems. I have brought

you very close to the trade road. You must walk silently up the road until one of the Cativera spots you. They will notify the others, who will keep the Struthtaur under control. And they will escort you into Grasian." The confidence in Anneberg's voice went a long way toward helping Cornus feel better about approaching the Cativera. "I will warn you, though, communication will be difficult until you meet with the Monarch."

"And you will be right here when I return?" Cornus asked Anneberg. He was a little surprised at how quickly he had gone from desperate fear of the Stondefel to trust, at least regarding Anneberg.

"Yes, young one. I will be here waiting for you."

Cornus looked around but did not see the road that Anneberg had mentioned. He looked up at the Stondefel, who pointed in the correct direction. Cornus made his way through the tall grass and soon saw the red clay road. He looked back at Anneberg, unsure of which way to go down the road. The Stondefel sighed and pointed to Cornus's right.

Dust rose from his footsteps as he ambled slowly along the road, unsure of what to expect. He was afraid of alarming the Struthtaur, though there was no sign of another living creature. Silence rang in his ears, and he could see nothing through the tall grass on the side of the road.

Then again, it seemed likely that Anneberg would have avoided flying anywhere near the Struthtaur. If they stampeded easily because a person walked into the fields where they lived, he could only imagine what would happen if a Stondefel were to fly overhead. It must be some distance to where they and the Cativera herders were.

He had gotten so used to having his human friends with him, he had forgotten what it was like to be alone. He missed his friends. Marcus was a serious boy, dark and quiet. Leopold, on the other hand, was more upbeat, bright and full of laughter and wit. Sadie was sweet and funny, smart and quick to help. They had all embraced him as a friend almost immediately. He felt ashamed of the way he had gotten angry with Marcus on his second arrival to Lysomnus. Cornus knew he had been arrogant as a Traveler and had been impatient with the boy he had met who was ignorant of this world.

Now he was alone again, and it was too quiet. Cornus had always been awkward around others; Davidia was the one Scrybb who could draw him out of his shell, even in Thicce Colpat. He marveled that he had been able to laugh and even joke with his human friends. It was wonderful, and he credited Davidia with teaching him how to be open to that.

He longed for Davidia's return and the chance to laugh with her again. Through all their years together, she had been his best friend, and watching her soar screaming into the sky as she was taken away from him had been terrifying. His heart hurt all the time, thinking of her somewhere, lost and alone. Was she being mistreated, waiting for someone to help her? This plan might lead to her rescue, and he felt a lot of hope. Hope he was almost afraid to let himself feel in case the worst happened.

Deep in his thoughts, Cornus jumped when someone stepped onto the road a short distance ahead of him. No one had told Cornus what to expect when meeting the Cativera, so he had no preconceptions. What he saw was not one of the Struthtaur, he was sure. Those were tall armless creatures. This person was not.

The Cativera stood upright but looked quite different from any other people Cornus had met so far, nor did it resemble the humans. It stood on the ball of its foot in what looked to Cornus like a very uncomfortable position. The foot had six long toes. Above the foot, a narrow leg angled to a knee that was quite backward from any Cornus had ever seen! Then it rose up to a round hip, muscles rippling all along the leg. A split tail waved from its lower back. A heavily muscled upper body rippled under dun-colored fur that nearly matched the prairie grasses all around them. The Cativera's round, furry ears were on the top of its head, swiveling constantly in all directions. They were quite large. Round black eyes met Cornus's. A flat brown nose flared above a stern mouth. He noticed with some alarm that it was much taller than he was and carried a spear in one hand.

"Um...hello," Cornus began but stopped abruptly when the Cativera put an outstretched hand up, claws tipping each of six fur-covered fingers. Movement from the corner of his eye made him look around, and he saw numerous other Cativera appear above the grasses all around him. He would have laughed at the comical display, but the serious look on the face of the Cativera in front of him stopped him. A quick beckoning gesture urged him to approach.

The Cativera waited until Cornus was near to mutter quietly, "What be ya need ayon?"

Ayon? Cornus thought. Hoping it meant something like *here*, Cornus answered quietly, "I have an urgent message for the people of your bruwe."

The Cativera stuck the spear point-first into the ground and raised both arms over its head, maneuvering its hands and fingers in a series of gestures. Several of the other Cativera gestured back and disappeared. The one beside Cornus grasped the spear and gestured for him to follow.

Because the Cativera did not speak again, Cornus also kept quiet. After they rounded a curve in the road, they came upon a large carved stone structure on the left of the road. A Cativera with a round belly stood at the top; Cornus thought the Cativera must have traded with the Fyrtudo for the handiwork on the massive stonework. Numerous steps led up to a platform, which allowed the Cativera standing up there to see a long way. Cornus wondered uneasily if the creature had been up there when he and Anneberg had landed.

Cornus's escort stopped and gestured to the Cativera at the top of the stairs, who nodded and pointed straight in the direction of Anneberg, then gestured again. Cornus swallowed with agitation. He wished he understood what the gestures meant. Now they were gesturing again! It was all very uncomfortable.

The Cativera next to him laid a clawed hand on his shoulder. "Be clim upon the upper, ye. See it all an why quit must be," the Cativera muttered quietly in Cornus's ear.

Cornus was quite mystified about what was meant by this until the creature gestured for him to approach the stone stairs, and the one on the platform gestured for him to climb up.

The stairs were obviously made for longer legs than his. He struggled to pull himself up each step, and by the time he reached the top, he was quite out of breath. He sat on the top step, trying to regain control of his breathing. The Cativera stood solemnly beside him, waiting. When he was able to gain his feet again, he gasped.

The view was amazing! He could see the grass-covered plains all around them. The road wound its way through the grass; it was really the only thing that broke it up until it reached an area that was little more than a wide, grassless place in the Zabanara, as Anneberg had called it.

Speaking of Anneberg, Cornus turned and looked the way he had come and realized the Stondefel was quite visible where he waited in the grass. He looked up at the Cativera, who were, for the first time, smiling. The tension in his body eased now that he felt they weren't upset with him.

"Ye see na Cativera know ye kim," the first Cativera laughed quietly. The second one chuckled as well. Cornus noticed they still kept their voices low. He looked at the fields carefully, and now he saw the Struthtaur dotting the grasses along both sides of the road. There were hundreds of the tall birds, some close enough that he could see their loose, leathery skin and the bright blue of their heads even as they fed.

"Talk quit, or Struthtaur run. Hard for sim to catch all nit, and Struthtaur dit."

Cornus thought he might be catching on to their way of talking a little bit. No long i sounds? He was sure there was far more to it than that, but he was hopeful they would understand him.

They communicated with each other with elaborate gestures, which Cornus guessed must be a silent first language for them because of the Struthtaur. Finally, his escort gestured to him to climb down, which he did very carefully. The second Cativera waved in a way Cornus hadn't seen before to them both as they walked away.

They continued down the road in the direction of the open, grassless area. Cornus had thought that might be their bruwe, but the rock platform had given enough of an aerial view for him to see that there were no habitations there. He hadn't seen anything further away either, so he was quite puzzled.

However, when they reached the open area, the Cativera stopped. This time, it turned to Cornus, put a hand on its own chest, and announced at a more normal volume, "Suri."

"Suri? Is that your name?"

The Cativera nodded. "Is alrit now."

"To talk?" Another nod. Cornus sighed, his anxiety easing. "What a relief! My name is Cornus." The Scrybb boy felt almost as if he had been holding his breath since leaving Anneberg's side.

"Cornus. Grasian is here." Suri smiled.

"Your bruwe is here? Where?" Cornus looked around, but all he saw was the road, the red dirt, and the surrounding grass.

"Wait." Suri smiled and whistled loudly.

All around them, holes opened in the packed dirt, and Cativera large and small climbed out. Dust puffed up around the openings as feet landed on the surface. Most of the Cativera looked to be young, and a few appeared quite elderly, but there were several adults as well. The tallest of them approached Suri and Cornus.

"Cornus, sa is Cata. Monarch." Suri bent and opened long arms wide.

Cornus bowed also, saying, "Monarch Cata, it is my honor."

"Cornus, you are my guest," the Monarch said. This Cativera was much taller than the others, wearing a sash of flat metal pieces. "Please stand."

He straightened quickly, looking at the Monarch and

wondering why this new Cativera didn't speak in the same stilted way as Suri, even though this one still had a strong accent.

"It's quite alright," Cata said. "I know what you want to ask. As the Monarch, it is my duty to learn to speak the language of all Lysomnus, as well as both of our own," At the same time, the Monarch was gesturing to Suri. The other Cativera darted away. "We will prepare a welcoming feast for you."

"Oh my," Cornus said, flustered. "That is not really necessary. I am really just here to deliver a message."

"A message it is important for me to hear, I am quite certain," Cata said. "But we do not often receive guests who are not just here for trade. It will be fun for us to have a celebration for your visit."

"Well, okay. Just to eat and visit," Cornus said. He was torn between the pressure to return as soon as possible and staying to have a celebration thrown in his honor. Even if it was just because he happened to show up. Being the center of attention wasn't something he was used to.

Cata took his arm and led him to one of the large holes from which the Cativera had emerged. "Let me show you around the bruwe," Cata said. "Grasian is unique, and I don't often have an opportunity to show it off."

"Actually, that may tie into the message I am here to deliver," Cornus gulped.

"Really?"

"Yes." They were at the entrance. A clever door had slid back under the surface, allowing access. Cornus saw that there were steps here, but unlike the ones at the watchtower, these were much smaller and carved into the firm red clay of this region. Even his short legs were able to manage them. As he stepped down, Suri appeared at the bottom and quickly gestured to the Monarch. Cata laughed as Suri disappeared again.

"Oh, I am sorry about the trouble you had with our tower stairs. All the stairs in Grasian itself are designed so that children can get in and out of the bruwe easily. There isn't need outside of the bruwe. We've never shown that tower view to someone who wasn't Cativera before."

Despite his discomfort at being compared to children, Cornus said, "I am very honored to be the first to see it. It is a magnificent view."

Cata smiled at him. "Oh, of course. It's wonderful to have you here, Cornus. I can't remember the last time a Scrybb was here without a wagon, waiting impatiently to bargain and rush off again!"

The bruwe of the Cativera reminded him somewhat of Palaga's mining tunnels. From the bottom of the stairs, multiple round tunnels led through the clay in various directions. However, these tunnels were smaller and brightly lit. Vents and openings in the ceiling allowed plenty of light, but he saw they could be quickly closed to protect the people within.

There were several places where recessed shelves held items that looked quite interesting to Cornus; he wished he had time to stop and look. Cata led him down a wide tunnel that was taking them away from the noise and bustle of the main entrance. As they passed one tunnel, the smell of baking bread wafted out; he couldn't help but pause and sniff.

Cornus returned to their conversation. "Have any young Scrybb like myself come through while Traveling?"

"Oh, no. Not for many years. We assumed it was for safety's sake, times being what they are. We keep a close eye on our children also. The Fyrtudo are all mature adults who come to trade, and they trade with the Muirnati for us. I don't remember seeing a Scrybb in a long time. No, children are not safe to go out."

"Can you tell me what the children of Lysomnus are not safe *from*? I have not even told you why I am here yet, what my warning is about."

Cata looked uncomfortable. "I really shouldn't be talking about this with you, Cornus. You are really still a child yourself."

"Are you concerned about the humans? The humans who are forcing all the people of Lysomnus to give them things and treat them in special ways?"

Cata looked around quickly. "Shh! You must stop talking about this here. Someone might hear." The Cativeran Monarch led him further down the tunnel, then turned down another, until they reached a round wooden door with ornate scrolling. The door swung into a round room carved into the same reddish earth as the tunnels. Once they were inside, Cata closed the door firmly and locked it. Lowering powerful haunches to a backless chair behind a stone table, the Cativera's split tail draped behind the seat to the floor. Cata gestured for Cornus to sit on a tree stump that had been burnished and carved decoratively.

"I always feel safer to talk here, Cornus. The humans do come to Grasian, and we do have special rooms here for them to bathe and sleep. We are forced to feed them before ourselves and give them what they want rather than any fair trading. But they are *dangerous*, Cornus. They have power and do things that hurt people. Their leader is the worst of all. That one has caused great harm to us and, I'm sure, to the other people of Lysomnus."

"Why is it that she punishes everyone who says her name?" Cornus asked. He didn't understand. He had never heard of this person until that day in the school in his bruwe when the Teachers were attacked.

"It's about power and control, Cornus. Each bruwe must have accommodations for her and her followers to use whenever they appear. We don't like it, but there is no choice. If we say her name when she is not in our bruwe, she believes we are plotting against her, and she will appear and retaliate against us."

"Cata, the warning I was sent here to give is a serious one." Cornus swallowed nervously. "The Stondefel have divided. Many of the young ones have left to follow—that person"—Cornus gulped—"although one of them came back and is spying for the Council now. He says the rebels are planning attacks on all the bruwes of Lysomnus at the same time." He stopped, feeling a little breathless.

Cata mewled and covered a furry face with clawed fingers. "This is a disaster. We have no way to protect the Struthtaur. They cannot come into our tunnels. We could not build stone shelters for them in time."

"Awar—he's our spy—hopes that now that the Council knows about the attacks, the rebels will call them off. Or if not, the Council will have time to prepare and stop them."

"Stondefel against Stondefel? That would not be much better. We would lose Lysomnus's best protection and good people. And the damage would still be done. Can you imagine a battle between Stondefel over the Grenewud? Or the great grass plains of the Zabanara?" The Cativera placed furry hands flat on the table. "I can't understand why the Stondefel would do such a thing."

"We were told that the human leader made her way up into the Beornan Rokk and turned one of the Stondefel against his elders. And it escalated from there."

"Those humans again!" Cata made a fist out of one clawed hand and pounded it on one muscular thigh. "They are all evil! They are all trouble!"

"Well, not *all* of them," Cornus said. "Deacon Talent is not evil, I am told. And I have human friends who—"

"Deacon Talent never spent any time down *here*," Cata spat. "He was too arrogant. He wasn't going to spend any time with *groundhogs*, as he put it. Whatever that means. And he made fun of how my people talk rather than trying to learn our language."

Cornus was aghast. It seemed Deacon Talent had shown different sides to each of the people in Lysomnus. He shifted on his stool. "Well, anyway... the warnings are going out to all the bruwes today. In fact, I am sure the other ones have all received their warnings by now."

"And we are so grateful to you for delivering the message to us. We will start our planning as soon as we can."

"I should probably start heading back to Anneberg so I can return to Palaga," Cornus said.

"Yes, soon, but first, you have a celebration to attend, Cornus. Like it or not, you are our new favorite guest!" Cata got up, opened the door, and gestured. Suri entered, swept Cornus onto strong shoulders, and dashed through the tunnels until they reached the stairs. Cornus gasped in surprise, then found himself laughing with joy.

"Head dun, Cornus!" Suri called.

Cornus ducked, just missing bashing the top of his leafy head on the tunnel entrance. It was already evening outside. He laughed and waved his arms as Suri raced around, careful not to take Cornus close to an enormous bonfire. All the children of the bruwe were soon following, whooping and gesturing madly. They dragged indulgent adults into the line, one by one.

Cata's scream brought the activity to a sudden halt. Cornus looked just as Suri was lowering him to the ground to see a hooded figure standing in front of the Monarch, hands raised.

"The people of Grasian have dared to speak my name. It is a day for challenging me, it seems."

"No one has!" Cata cried. "There must be a mistake."

A Caivera wailed, burying their head in their partner's shoulder. "I didn't mean to!"

Nun the Wiser laughed. "Even the voice of one person is enough to start a conspiracy. I'll not tolerate any insolence. I've taken one of your own, as well. They'll be joining me at my own bruwe now."

Nun the Wiser disappeared. The Cativera began to look around anxiously, trying to figure out who might be missing.

"The herders are not all back yet," Cata said. "We will have to wait and see if someone doesn't return." The Monarch wiped at their eyes, trying to regain some aspect of control.

"Cata, I think we should skip any type of celebration," Cornus said, feeling dejected after what had happened. "You don't even know who is missing yet."

"No, Cornus," Cata said, snuffling. "I will not allow that person to feel responsible for the cancellation of our festivities. The fire is lit, and we will continue at least with a bountiful meal. We will know soon enough who has been taken."

From the fields, the day's herders began to trickle in.

Finding release from the silence of their day, they were soon finding seats in a circle around the fire chatting loudly. As a chant started up, some even stood and began an organized dance. Cornus wanted to join in, but he was afraid of the flames and still worried about who had been taken by Nun the Wiser. It gave him chills just thinking about the name.

After everyone was danced out, rumbling stomachs took over. Suri gave Cornus a plate and utensils. The young Scrybb boy joined the line with everyone else to help himself to roast meat, root vegetables he recognized from back home, and the bread he had smelled baking earlier. He wondered if they grew the grain for this around here somewhere; he didn't recognize the aroma or texture from home. He saw pellod, sections of sartine, and sweet pastries but wasn't ready for dessert just yet.

While eating, Cornus sat with Suri and learned a few of the gestures they used. It was fun to learn a completely different way to talk. Some of the younger children who were still just learning sat nearby and copied them. Cornus suddenly thought of Sadie and the sign languages she had told them about that she used to communicate with her brother. He knew she would be fascinated to learn of this sign language used by the Cativera.

"Suri," Cornus asked, "where is the Cativera who was on the tower? I have not seen her yet. I noticed she was pregnant. Is she your mate?"

The Cativera children seated around Cornus sat staring at him with mouths agape. They looked from Suri to Cornus and back again, and Cornus noticed that they looked confused. Suri signed to the children. Then they called out to Cata, who came and joined their group. They looked at Suri, who signed rapidly to the Monarch.

"Oh!" the leader of the Cativera exclaimed. "I understand why you would be confused, Cornus. The Cativera have no gender as most of the people of Lysomnus understand it. We have no 'male' or 'female'. There are many mated couples here, but we never know who a fertile Cativera might be. Those who do conceive are considered extremely fortunate. You met Tini today, who is pregnant. They are one of our blessed members, soon to be bearing a child."

Cornus was bewildered. He had never heard of such a thing. It was fascinating, however, to learn of such different people of his world. He noticed Suri was sitting up a little straighter. The Cativera pointed at their chest. "Tini wit Suri. Tey mi mit."

Cornus nodded. "Congratulations, Suri." The Cativera beamed with pride.

After the celebration had died down and it was nearly fully dark, Cornus looked for Suri to thank them for the warm welcome, but the Cativera was standing motionless at the edge of Grasian, staring into the darkness.

Instead, he found Cata. "I want to thank you for everything. I have never felt so accepted in my life." He felt the sting of tears and knew he would miss this place he had visited for only a day.

"Cornus, the good fortune is ours. Please come back and visit us for longer. It has been many years since anyone took the time to learn our language. You are early in your Travels, and we would love to host you for a significant portion of them." Cata's voice was sincere, and Cornus knew that he would have to come back here just as soon as he could.

He had learned from Suri the gesture to use for leaving. It didn't mean 'goodbye,' but instead 'I will return when I can.' He stood at the edge of the light from the bonfire and used the gesture, indicating everyone in the bruwe. When everyone stood and made the gesture that meant 'Please come back' to him, he could not control his tears. He was glad he had a bit of a walk to work through his emotions.

Even though it was dark now, the air was still warm, and a breeze carried a sweet aroma to him that was unfamiliar. It was a lovely floral scent, but not recognizing it made him realize just how far he was from home, where he knew the smell of every plant and tree. Rustling noises in the tall grasses near the road made him aware that he wasn't alone; the Struthtaur and the Cativera who watched over them in the night were all around him.

As he passed the stone stairs again, Cornus looked up to see if Tini was still at the top, watching over the herd. No one was there. He thought back and realized Tini had never returned to the bruwe, either. Now he realized why Suri had been staring down the dark road. Eyes wide with fear, he covered his mouth and nearly turned to run back to Grasian. Then he continued on to the clearing where he had left the Stondefel. The Cativera would soon realize Tini was gone— the best thing he could do was return to Palaga and discover what the next step in the plan might be.

Anneberg was waiting in the same place, but even in the dark, Cornus could see he'd a large section of grass down with his pacing. "What took so long? It sounded like you had a party!"

Cornus had forgotten that Stondefel had such good hearing. "I could not be rude. I had to stay when invited." He stood up a bit straighter while making this pronouncement.

"I'm sure it's fine," Anneberg said. "We'll just probably

be the last ones back, that's all." He waited for Cornus to climb up and adjust the harness as he found a comfortable seat. Then he vaulted into the dark sky.

Cornus gazed in wonder at the land below, so different from how it all looked during the day. The Diluvium seemed to glow, although that might have to do with the light of Lysomnus's shattered moon. As they flew on, Cornus smiled at the sight of the familiar Grenewud. Although it covered nearly two-thirds of his world, he felt at home anywhere in it. His people had built paths throughout and seeded fruit and root vegetables everywhere within it. While there were still some dangerous creatures lurking within, it was unlikely a Scrybb could be hurt by them. He gazed down at the trees, imagining the paths running through them that Scrybb had created.

Below them, in a clearing, he thought he saw a large pile of stones and then realized what it might be. "Anneberg, did you see that?"

"Hm? See what where?" the Stondefel rumbled. "I was admiring the stars. They are so beautiful at night...."

"In that clearing back there. I am quite sure I saw a Stondefel lying there!"

"Stondefel don't sleep on the cold ground, Cornus. We only sleep on warm rock in the mountains."

Cornus was absolutely sure of what he had seen. "Please circle back around, Anneberg. I know I saw a Stondefel!"

"All right, all right. Here we go." Anneberg turned in a wide loop that brought him directly over the clearing that Cornus was pointing to. He gasped. "It's Awar!"

CHAPTER SIXTEEN

POWER EVOLVES

Marcus was practicing lifting boulders on the stone terrace of Palaga when Anneberg bellowed from above. He had finally gotten to the point where he could lift multiple boulders at the same time. Just before Anneberg called down, he had smashed all the boulders he was lifting together. Dust and small pieces of rock tumbled to the ground, adding to the pile that had collected from earlier attempts and successes. Marcus was excited about how much easier it was to do these bigger exercises and what he was accomplishing. He wondered just how big of a rock he could lift at this point. However, he was feeling a little tired.

"Marcus," Anneberg rumbled. "We need you to accompany us. And bring the Halfriez with you!"

Marcus held up his left hand, where the cube was in his tight grip, warm from use during practice. "I have it."

Anneberg lowered himself as close to the ground as he could and reached for Marcus.

"Just wait there, Anneberg!" Marcus called out. He wasn't thrilled about the idea of being carried in talons again, especially in the cold night air. Instead, he lifted himself through the air and put himself on Anneberg's back behind Cornus.

"Marcus—" Cornus said as he watched his friend rise through the air to land on Anneberg's back behind him, "You have become more powerful! But we do not have the double harness with us."

"If it's as urgent as it sounds, let's just go," Marcus said. "I will hold myself in place." He closed his eyes and concentrated on staying on Anneberg's back. He still held onto Cornus and his rope harness, just in case, and hoped it was a short journey.

It was just a few minutes until they were hovering over a small clearing in the woods where Awar and Leopold stood, looking up at them. Even from here, Marcus could see the dark blood coating Awar's wing. He lowered himself into the clearing to see what he could do for the injured Stondefel.

Marcus carefully looked over the injury. Fortunately, the shattered moon had risen high in the sky, so he had some light to see by.

"Hey, Awar," Marcus said. "I know it will be more painful right at first, but I think your wing will heal a lot better if we can actually straighten out the bone here and hold it and your wingsail in place before I start to heal it. Leopold and I are going to try to straighten it out."

Awar was trying to turn his upper body around to see the wing, and it was doing some funny things to his face. Leopold looked away so he would not laugh at an inopportune time. Marcus gave him a dirty look, knowing his friend all too well.

"Yes, just do what you have to do. I can stand the pain if it will help me fly again," Awar said.

Marcus looked around. "Leopold! What are you doing? Get over here and help me straighten out this bone."

Leopold had walked to the trees, probably so Awar would not see the look on his face.

Marcus asked Awar to bend one leg so he could climb up on it and gestured to Leopold to do the same. The bone was so large and heavy, Marcus needed Leopold to help move it back into position. Once they had it nearly straight, Marcus closed his eyes, frowning as he concentrated, and the bone slid back into place. Leopold did his best to hold the outer end of it up so it wouldn't fall again.

Awar was bellowing with pain, and both boys' hands were coated with black blood by the time the bone was in place and ready to be healed. Marcus pressed one slick hand against the bone. Marcus felt the healing heat in his hand, and the bone started moving. He indicated with his head that Leopold could let go. A few minutes later, the wingbone straightened and thickened at the break. Leopold made a strange face and bent to the ground. Marcus ignored him and kept working as the torn skin of the wing had reappeared as if out of nowhere and reconnected to the wing. Finally, his hand cooled down.

Awar sighed in relief. "I am most grateful, Marcus Talent. Not only was the pain terrible, but I grieved at the thought of never flying again. You have healed both of those hurts."

"I'm glad to be able to do it," Marcus said. "I only wish it was something I could do myself instead of depending on this Halfriez."

"Uh, Marcus?" Leopold said. "I think you did." Marcus looked down to see Leopold holding the crystal cube in his hand. "I just found this lying on the ground. You must have dropped it because your hands were so slick with Awar's blood."

"I'm not sure, man," Marcus said. "I don't know when I dropped it."

"Marcus," Awar said, "Leopold is also injured, although he may not have said anything. Please help him as well."

"It's not that bad," Leopold shrugged. He sat on Awar's leg so Marcus could look at it.

"Let me see it," Marcus said, inspecting the wound. "Dude, this is a deep cut!"

"I guess this is the time to find out if you really can do it without the Halfriez," Leopold said holding the cube behind his back.

Marcus wiped as much of Awar's blood off his left hand onto his pants as he could. He pressed his palm to Leopold's leg, concentrating on healing his friend. His hand warmed up instantly. He could almost feel the layers of muscle and skin closing from the inside out. Leopold gasped.

"What is it? Does it hurt?" Marcus asked concernedly.

"No—that's just it. My thigh is better, but there's been a mild ache ever since I broke my ankle, but now it's gone!"

Marcus grasped his friend's ankle and pulled up his pants leg. The faint scarring that had been left after he originally healed Leopold's broken leg was gone.

"It's healed more," he said quietly. "I thought that wasn't possible."

"I think we're learning a lot of things are possible. Maybe it has something to do with your new power," Leopold answered.

"I would agree," rumbled Anneberg from above them. "This power seems to be growing stronger very quickly."

"Let's get back to Palaga," Marcus said, rising painfully to his feet. He really didn't want to talk about his power, not right now. He realized just how exhausted he was after healing Awar, especially after all the boulder smashing earlier. It was scary that he had been getting so powerful so fast.

"Awar, are you sure you feel up to flying both of us there?" Leopold asked. "One of us can ride on Anneberg with Cornus."

"Oh, absolutely," the Stondefel flapped his wings. "I feel amazing right now!"

The boys waved Anneberg off, Leopold climbed back into the harness, and Marcus lifted himself into place. Awar launched into the air. The flight back was a short one. Even gliding on one wing, Awar had managed to glide quite a distance away from Thicce Colpat with his injury.

They landed on the stone terrace outside Palaga. Awar said it was time for him to return to the rebels again, or his long absence would be noticed. He had more false information from the Stondefel Council to share with them to allay any suspicions they might have about him. Marcus knew that Leopold would miss Awar.

Leopold removed Awar's harness and climbed down the Stondefel's leg. Marcus watched in silence as Awar pushed Leopold gently with one of his talons. "I will miss you, boy. When I return, I will find new ways to scare you in the air."

Leopold snorted. "You can try!" he said in a choked voice, but Marcus could see the tears in his friend's eyes. The Stondefel vaulted into the air and flew off, disappearing into the dark.

Marcus couldn't maintain the shield as Anneberg landed. He was just too tired now. Leopold wiped angrily at his wet eyes and climbed up to remove the harness from Anneberg, and everyone moved to allow him room to take off.

Please bring everyone to my chambers, Tartarus said to Marcus. *I would like to hear how each bruwe responded to our warnings.* Marcus told the others to follow him. He saw a nervous look on Leopold's face just as he noticed an anxious look on Cornus's face directly behind his best friend.

Once everyone was inside the King's chambers, Tartarus said to everyone, *I think each of you must share in turn your experiences as you visited each of the people of Lysomnus. I think we should begin with Marcus.*

"I'm so sorry, but would it be all right if I took the night to sleep?" Marcus said. "I'm really tired. Especially after healing Awar. I need to rest."

Of course. My apologies to all of you. You have traveled and had emotional days. Please rest. We will meet again in the morning.

Marcus was relieved to bathe and wash the rest of Awar's black blood from his body, face, and hair. After a light dinner, he collapsed into his soft bed and relished the comfort as he pulled up the blankets.

The next morning, after a hearty meal, everyone was back in Tartarus's chambers, ready to discuss their experiences from the previous day.

Marcus, I think we should begin with you and your trip to the Muirnati, Tartarus said.

"All right," Marcus said, taking a deep breath. He began with meeting Pelamis in the tunnel on the beach. He wondered for a moment if he could leave out the part about his father having another family in Fisc. Instead, he decided to reveal everything that had happened while he was in the Muirnati bruwe. Tartarus and Colflur said nothing, but Leopold could not seem to hold back a muttered comment Marcus couldn't hear.

It sounds like the Muirnati have taken the warning well and are going to do what they can to prepare for a potential attack. It is alarming that the human leader has taken another prisoner, and I am sorry to hear it was your sister, Marcus, Tartarus said when Marcus had finished.

I believe we should hear from Cornus next, Tartarus said.

Cornus told them about all the adventures he had had while visiting Grasian, including the language of gestures used by the Cativera.

"How fascinating, Cornus!" exclaimed Sadie. "I think I saw something about their sign language when I was reading about the languages of Lysomnus. I'd love to learn some of it if you can teach me!"

"In all honesty, I felt ashamed of my people while I was there. We have not been taught very much about them. I had to ask Anneberg for the name of that region of Lysomnus; I did not even remember that much. And Scrybb, on their travels, have not been making their way to Grasian. The only Scrybb who have been getting to the Cativera are those who need to trade for meat, and they haven't gone there in a long time. And yet again, the human leader took a member of their people. I am very afraid it was the pregnant Cativera I met!"

This is very frightening, Coflur said. *There have been repercussions in the past, but nothing like these events. I hope none of these people are being hurt in any way.*

"Did they say anything about my father there? Does he visit often like he did at Fisc and here in Palaga?" Marcus asked.

Cornus was looking at him uncomfortably. He looked away as if unsure how to answer the question.

Tartarus broke in just before Cornus's lack of response

became an awkward moment. *This is neither the time nor the place to deal with such things. We must hear from Leopold regarding the Scrybb. I fear his tale will not be a good one, given the damage done to Awar.*

"I think my trip was not only a waste of time but caused more harm than good," Leopold began. He told them everything that had happened during his visit to Thicce Colpat.

The room filled with gasps of horror when Leopold told them all about the Scrybb tying Abutilon to a post. How all the angry Scrybb had flooded the square to attack Awar and had broken his wing while he tried to fly away.

"I cannot believe my people would do such terrible things," Cornus looked sick. "What they are doing to Abutilon is something that was done in dark times of the past. I never expected to hear of this happening in my lifetime!"

"What does it mean, Cornus?" Leopold asked. "Buddleja was horrified when she saw them tying him up to that post."

"Scrybb require large quantities of water. I showed each of you when we found a stream that I needed to stay in the water for a while. While we can drink water and sustain ourselves for a couple of days, we need to pull water in through our roots to stay properly hydrated." He held his foot up, and several long roots unfurled and waved about.

"When they tied Abutilon to that post, they made it so he could not hydrate. Even if they allow Buddleja to bring him water to drink—which I doubt—he will suffer and die in a matter of days. It is a cruel and painful torture."

"I don't understand. Why are they doing this? They saw Awar; they *know* Stondefel exist!" Marcus pounded a clenched fist on his own thigh in frustration, sending a jolt of pain through his thigh and into his back. He ignored the pain in his anger.

"They accused me of somehow 'creating' him, as if I had some way to do that," Leopold said. "Cassiope hates humans even more now and wouldn't believe anything I said!"

When people are determined to believe something, they will do everything in their power to ignore anything that might disprove that belief, Tartarus said. *It sounds as if they have already convinced themselves that Awar was not a* real *Stondefel. He is smaller by half than most Stondefel, and they were* able to injure him more easily than they would believe a *legendary Stondefel should be.*

"We need to do something about Abutilon. We can't just leave him to die, especially after he was trying to help us." Leopold's voice quavered, his eyes filling with tears.

"And my people need to heed the warning, at least to try to protect themselves in some way in case the rebel Stondefel really do attack them. They are so vulnerable right now," Cornus shuddered, clearly thinking of all the exposed wood and plants that would burn easily in an attack. Not to mention the Scrybb themselves.

Let us return to the terrace, Tartarus said. *I believe we may find a potential solution to both problems there. Anneberg has told me he requires our presence.*

When they exited the doors of Palaga, they found Anneberg waiting.

"I need one of you to join me," Anneberg rumbled. "We must return to Thicce Colpat to remind these hardheaded Scrybb that the Stondefel exist and are to be respected! We will also be rescuing your friends," he said to Leopold.

"Leopold should stay in Palaga this time. I'll go instead,"

Marcus said, stepping forward. "After all, it's my family that's somehow involved in this."

While they flew to Thicce Colpat, Anneberg told Marcus the plan—he intended to use the element of surprise and his own massive size to prove to the stubborn Scrybb that the Stondefel were no fairy tale, and convince them of the potential danger of an attack. When they arrived over Thicce Colpat, Anneberg landed with an enormous crash right in the middle of the bruwe. Many Scrybb were about, full of excitement after the thrill of driving Awar away. When Anneberg's immense body slammed to the ground, the bruwe rumbled as if a small quake had shaken the area. Dust flew up from beneath the Stondefel's feet, and several Scrybb were knocked to the ground. Shouts and screams erupted all around them. "What is the meaning of the Scrybbs' treatment of my brother?" Anneberg roared. Buddleja, who had been sleeping on the ground at the captive Abutilon's feet, woke with a scream, leaping to her feet to wrap her arms around her lover's legs.

Cassiope acted extremely foolish for the way she strode directly out from the student dorms to face Anneberg. She looked very small standing there, leaning far back to stare up at the Stondefel's face with her hands on her hips. "For such a terrifying legend, your *brother* certainly was easy to defeat," she declared.

"My *young* brother was here to help you, not to attack. Be assured that had he intended to harm you, this bruwe could have been destroyed without him setting a talon on the ground. Your disbelief and your unwarranted attack on Awar were criminal."

Marcus could feel anger thrumming through the body beneath him.

"What have the Stondefel ever done for the Scrybb?" Cassiope asked. "We have never seen you, not as long as anyone can remember. We owe you nothing."

"Even if we had not spent countless years protecting you from dangers outside of your bruwe you never even knew about, you owed us the respect to listen to a warning. The human was a recent guest, and you could not even give him the respect to listen—"

"Listen to fairy tales?" she scoffed. "Humans are worthless. They respect no one and hurt everyone. We regret the hospitality we showed the three who were here. They repaid us by turning our own Scrybb against us, by coming back with warnings of 'imminent danger' and then flying on a half-sized fake to try to convince us. We are not fools. Their fake was easily chased away!"

Marcus was shaking with anger. How could Cassiope continue to disbelieve in Stondefel when there was one right in front of her? True, Awar had been smaller, and they were able to injure him, but Anneberg was quite a different matter.

Anneberg reached down and grasped Cassiope between two of his talons. He lifted her until she was even with his face. She could obviously feel the heat of his breath as he spoke, see the horns that swept back from his massive face and his red eyes. "Do you deny even still that *I* exist, Scrybb? Even now, staring directly into my face?

"O—Obviously, there is some merit to the legend," she stammered. "But this 'warning' is clearly intended to convince us to leave our bruwe and our goods open to thievery of some kind. Why else would you want us to go into hiding?"

Anneberg let Cassiope go. She screamed as she fell, twisting to try to avoid the certain death landing on the ground from this height would cause. Marcus cried out. The watching crowd of Scrybb gasped, and several of them screamed in fear. Just before she could hit the ground, Anneberg caught her. "Cassiope, the other Stondefel and I on the Council are not your enemies. We are your friends. I would never hurt you, but you should be very frightened right now. The Stondefel who left and now stand against us would not hesitate to burn your bruwe to ashes and all of you with it. We have guarded Lysomnus for many of your lifetimes. But these younger Stondefel are following the lead of a very dangerous human who is planning the destruction of all the people of Lysomnus. Prepare yourselves for the worst."

Anneberg looked around at the rest of the Scrybb, who were frozen in place with fear. Marcus saw Berberis and Malberis at the back of the crowd, arms wrapped tightly around each other. Anneberg rumbled again. "And do not think you can injure me as you did Awar. I do not have his vulnerability, nor do I have his patience."

He reached out one taloned hand and snapped the post where Abutilon was tied before carefully picking up Buddleja. "These two will not remain here to suffer your cruelty," he added before launching himself into the air. Marcus was quite sure that the Stondefel didn't *really* need the extra flap of his wings to gain more altitude, but it definitely caused a lot more wind to blow around the bruwe; he saw a few Scrybb knocked off their feet as Anneberg flew away.

"I don't think you needed me to come along at all, Anneberg!" Marcus shouted as they soared through the air.

"I thought that they might still have some regard for you, particularly as you are the son of Deacon Talent." Anneberg's voice was still edged with anger. "He is esteemed by the Fyrtudo and the Muirnati."

"Yeah, I didn't really get that feeling while I was in Thicce Colpat. I don't think the Scrybb really care for humans at all. In fact, it sounded like the only reason they helped us when we first arrived was because Leopold was hurt so badly. I wish my dad had taken the time to tell me more about this world and what he knew of its people. I think he ignored the Scrybb and didn't do anything to try to develop a better relationship with them." Anneberg rumbled beneath him thoughtfully.

As they landed, Anneberg cradled Buddleja and Abutilon in his hands so they would not be jarred. It was intriguing to see the care taken by the Stondefel, who had been imagined as dangerous enemies by the Teachers.

And yet it was the Scrybb, not the Stondefel, who had acted cruelly.

A Fyrtudo led Abutilon inside so he could root himself in fresh water. Buddleja followed behind, obviously nervous about being around so many strange people. After removing the harness, Marcus lowered himself down to the terrace, where Tartarus, Colflur, Leopold, Sadie, and Cornus were all standing around in the early morning light. Anneberg leaned forward, listening intently to the group's conversation.

An enormous thunderclap roared above them. Startled, the group looked up. Massive boulders whistled through the air above them, falling at immense speed, while a dust cloud billowed out, covering the ground. The entire mountainside was collapsing. There was no time to run.

Marcus reacted instinctively, raising his arms above himself as if to catch all the falling rocks and he *pushed* with all his might. Immediately, not just his hand, but also his chest grew so hot he was uncomfortable.

The mountainside returned to place as if nothing had happened. The slight hiss of the sulfur pools was the only sound at first, then Leopold cleared his throat, and the Fyrtudo shuffled their feet, breaking the silence.

Everyone stared at Marcus. Marcus looked at his own hand in disbelief. He had no idea what he had just done.

"What—?" Leopold started to ask, but Marcus shook his head.

"I don't know what I did!" Marcus continued to stare at his hand. "I just wanted to stop us all from getting killed. I wasn't thinking." For the first time, he felt the effort of using the power *within* his body.

We knew you had power, and you have been practicing with it, Tartarus said. *I am, however, astounded at the strength you have just demonstrated. I am also most grateful as you have just saved all our lives.*

"So, did you use your power to push things back in time?" Sadie pondered. "Or are you just strong enough that you actually pushed the mountain back into place?"

"Would not the rock still be loose and ready to fall if he had just pushed it back up there?" Cornus suggested. "The time suggestion would make more sense to me."

"No, then we would just be stuck in a time loop," Leopold said. "The rock falling, us screaming, Marcus pushing it back. The rock would fall again, we'd all scream, Marcus would push it again."

"Okay, okay, we get it, science nerd," Marcus said, rolling his eyes.

Perhaps you can physically change things when you want to, Colflur ventured, *so you changed the falling rock back to its original form, which would be the mountainside.*

"That makes more sense," said Sadie, "but he's been just moving things around before now. He's never done anything that big before. Is it possible to have more than one power?"

"Well," Marcus admitted, "I have been lifting very large boulders and smashing them together." He pointed at the pile of rocks just off to the side of the terrace.

Is that *what all that noise has been?* Colflur said. *People have been asking about it. It sounded too close to be coming from the forges.*

I do not know, Tartarus said. *We know very little about human power. Deacon Talent only has healing power that we are aware of. And his father, Malcolm, helped the Scrybb and the Cativera with his power to make plants grow very quickly. Both of those were very useful, but nothing close to the extent of what Marcus can do.*

"Well, Marcus *did* heal a pretty major injury for Awar," Leopold said, frowning. "And he wasn't even using the Halfriez because he had dropped it and didn't realize. Marcus can also move himself—he's been doing it to get on and off the Stondefel."

"Um—yeah," Marcus said. "I did it in Fisc, too, when I was in a lot of pain while swimming. I was able to move myself through the water and keep up with Pelamis."

This would all indicate more than one power or at least more than one way to use a strong power, Tartarus said.

"As interesting as all this is," Anneberg interrupted, "I need to fly up to the Caldera to find out what just happened up there."

He took off immediately. The others expected to cough as dust flew in their faces, but Marcus blocked it, and the flying dust stayed away from them all, giving them clear air to breathe.

"That's another way you've been using your power," Sadie said. "You've been keeping the dust away from everyone when the Stondefel fly."

Tartarus approached Marcus's left side. *I would venture to guess that now that it has manifested, Marcus will master his power quickly.*

"I hope you are right. When I was pushing the wagon on the way here, it never felt any more difficult, no matter how many of us were sitting on it," Marcus said. "And then when I was lifting boulders or healing Awar, I noticed I was tired after. Now, after what I just did, I feel okay."

I have only heard of one human with a power that has the capability of reaching out to affect places where they are not, Tartarus said. *And I believe that power takes a toll on them when they use it.*

She also takes revenge on those who talk about them, Colflur said worriedly.

At that moment, Nun the Wiser appeared on the verge of the stone terrace. From the depths of her overhanging hood, her glittering eyes stared directly at Marcus. Wind blew inexplicably from nowhere to swirl her cloak around her body like an ephemeral shadow. He stared back, confused as to why she had appeared at all. "No one said your name," he blurted.

"No," she said harshly, pointing one bony finger at Marcus. "As I anticipated, your power has finally manifested, Marcus Talent. See you soon." She laughed and disappeared.

CHAPTER SEVENTEEN

HOSTAGE

A shadow flitted over them from above. Startled, Marcus looked up to see Anneberg dropping toward them at a tremendous rate—so fast that Marcus sucked in a sharp breath, sure the Stondefel was going to crash into the terrace. At the last minute, Anneberg opened his wings, stalling his rapid drop. Without hesitation, he reached out with one hand and seized Marcus in his talons.

"Get inside now!" The Stondefel shouted at the others.

As Anneberg banked and beat his wings to gain altitude, another shadow loomed overhead. Another massive Stondefel was directly behind Anneberg. The newcomer reached out, slashing at Anneberg's wings with his sharp talons. Anneberg let out a shriek so loud it felt as if it was tearing through Marcus's brain.

A second unknown Stondefel appeared and seized Anneberg's arm and one of his legs, squeezing with razor-sharp talons. The three of them tumbled through the air, making Marcus dizzy and disoriented. Black blood poured from Anneberg's wounds, and the other Stondefel squeezed harder until Anneberg was finally forced to open his talons and release Marcus. The second Stondefel caught Marcus as he dropped from Anneberg's grasp. Then the murderous beast released Anneberg, tossing his torn and bleeding body toward the ground far below.

Marcus reached out desperately with his left hand, trying to heal Anneberg before he crashed to the ground below. He concentrated on the sensations he had felt when healing Awar—the straightening of the bone, the torn skin of the wing. He reached out with his power as he had with the mountain and could feel the slippery blood of Anneberg's wing injuries and concentrated on healing them.

The sensation of heat filled his body. His friend needed to fly first. He was overjoyed to see the Stondefel flapping his wings and flying normally. While still maintaining contact, he did what he could for Anneberg's remaining injuries, then disengaged.

"Who are you?" Marcus shouted at the Stondefel, who now carried him. He struggled, but to no avail. "Traitor! Take me back to my friends!"

He thought about doing something to this horrible creature to make him let go, but a glance at the ground below told him that would be a very bad idea. Perhaps he should wait until they landed before he attempted an attack.

The Grenewud was swiftly falling behind them as they traveled southeast, and Marcus now noticed that he was over a part of Lysomnus he had never seen. Below him stretched grass the color of wheat, which rippled over red soil. It was terrifying to see the land so far below him, knowing that only the grip of the Stondefel kept him from plummeting to the ground. There were no signs of habitation below, but that didn't mean there wasn't any.

As the flight dragged on, Marcus fell asleep despite the cold. He was exhausted from stopping the mountain and using so much power to heal Anneberg. The air was so cold at this altitude, and the Stondefel's hand didn't radiate heat the way Agatho's body had.

Marcus didn't know how long he slept before the cold woke him up again. He wondered if the Stondefel was taking him so far away that no one would be able to find him. A haze appeared ahead. As the gray dissipated, blue water shone beneath the sun. It looked like the Diluvium had when he first saw it on the western coast near Fisc.

Finally, they began to descend, though Marcus saw they weren't heading directly for the bruwe but instead toward a clearing in the grass where he could make out numerous figures. They weren't large enough to be more Stondefel, and his terror grew once he realized the truth: he was being brought to the notorious humans of Lysomnus. He wasn't ready to face Nun the Wiser.

It was only a matter of minutes until the Stondefel carrying Marcus landed on the ground, though his captor's talons remained locked firmly, and the protective sheath the Stondefel usually used when carrying delicate cargo was no longer covering the talons. Marcus concentrated on remaining as still as possible; he'd seen how they'd sliced through Anneberg's rock-hard skin, so his own would surely part like the flesh of the pellod with a single touch. He grimaced, finding it difficult to stand upright. His cane was back on the stone terrace of Palaga where he had dropped it.

The din of a crowd grew closer, and a crowd of people approached over the small rise in front of him.

"Ahazu, you may release your prisoner," an unseen woman called out.

Marcus breathed a sigh of relief as the massive talons opened one by one and were gone.

A woman with curly blond hair and green eyes was standing in front of him. He recognized her immediately.

She was a substitute teacher at his school! Marcus gaped at her in surprise. She gaped back, mocking him.

"Surprised to see me? Yeah, I'll bet you are. You Talents, so arrogantly thinking you're the only ones who can travel between worlds."

"*You're* the one who can open a portal between the dimensions?" Marcus was shocked. Of all the people who could have shown up at this very moment, Ms. Martin was the last person he would ever have guessed. She was one of the nicest teachers at his school, friendly to him and all the other kids. She usually dressed in casual clothes. Now, she was wearing a long white robe that looked like linen, cinched at the waist, with a green cloth belt and a hood draped down the back.

"But what. How..." he spluttered.

"Did you get my message?" She smirked. "I sent it directly."

"Oh, I got it." Marcus was furious. This traitor had planted herself in his life—had even tricked him into *liking* her. "What have you done with my father?"

"We're keeping him somewhere *safe*. You just behave yourself, or who knows what might happen."

The other humans approached behind her, dressed in different variations of the clothes he had seen in the rooms in Thicce Colpat and Palaga. "Ms. Martin—" Marcus began. She whipped around, green eyes glaring at him. "Don't call me that," she snapped. "My name is Eris."

"Were you even a teacher in my world? Or was that all just a ruse to get close to my family?"

"What do you think? I don't even like kids. But now that we have you and your father, I won't need to go back to your hideous world ever again." She wrinkled her nose. "It *stinks* there."

"I don't understand why you'd kidnap either me or my dad. Just because we can come to Lysomnus? You can already do that, and my father couldn't even come here anymore now that I'd inherited the power."

"Your line of Talents knows so little about your own abilities. Somewhere along the line, someone forgot to pass on the *full* knowledge of what you're capable of, and you've all been fumbling along ever since, thinking you had to stop traveling to Lysomnus once the next generation started *accidentally* traveling in their sleep. Half of you never figure out you have any other power. Your father only found his healing power when he thought he had his Halfriez in his hand and then realized he had dropped it."

"*My* line of Talents? What does that even mean? How do you *know* so much about us?" Marcus glared at her. He felt spied upon, betrayed. He thought of all the times this woman, in the guise of his teacher, had sat down with him to discuss a project he was working on or an assignment he was struggling with. Deep down, she must have been laughing at him the whole time. He felt sick.

"My family should be the one that gets all the respect in Lysomnus. We have more power than any of you Talents, and we've actually lived in this world for generations. Now's our chance to make Lysomnus our own. With a little help from someone else you know, of course."

The crowd parted respectfully as a cloaked figure emerged. Eris stepped back as Nun the Wiser approached.

Marcus's heart hammered in his chest. Nun the Wiser was even more terrifying up close. The hood she wore was so deep her face could not be seen, just the thick, dark red hair that flowed from within to hang to her waist, which was belted with ropes of black beads.

Her hoarse voice emanated from within the hood, harsh as a whisper but loud enough to overpower anyone else who might be talking. "I am Nun the Wiser. Eris is my child, and I am the leader here. You are here to serve me."

Marcus was terrified, but he didn't want to give any of them the satisfaction of knowing it. "I know who you are," he said, his voice steady, "and I have heard of how you intimidate and bully the people of Lysomnus. Why would I ever do anything to serve you?"

"Because you want to save your father and your friends. If I have them in my possession, you will do whatever I want you to do. Just as your father will do whatever I tell him to do."

Marcus thought of his father and how strong he was. "I don't think so. My dad wouldn't just cave in when someone tried to coerce him."

Nun the Wiser's voice became even more hoarse and forceful, "You say this because you believe I will not actually *do* anything to your father. You know nothing of me or what I will do to get what I want out of you. Deacon knows what I am willing to do to get what I want."

"Am I supposed to just believe your threats?" Marcus held his left hand in a tight fist to ensure that it would not shake to show any fear.

Nun the Wiser turned and gestured with her skeletal hand. Awar's limp body rose from behind the rise and spun in the air.

Marcus couldn't hold back a cry of anguish when he saw the body of the young Stondefel, who had been taking a dangerous risk by betraying the rebels. The risk had proved fatal, and Marcus felt devastated to see Awar's lifeless body.

As Marcus looked at the Stondefel's wings hanging loosely, he couldn't help but remember healing one of them just the day before. As much as he tried to hide his emotions, tears burned his eyes as he looked at what was left of the friendly young Stondefel.

"You see that I am not afraid to take a life when I find it necessary," Nun the Wiser croaked. A derisive chuckle rolled out of the depths of the cowled hood. "You seem surprised to see this young Stondefel dead. I don't take betrayal lightly."

"Betrayal?" Marcus scoffed, though hot, angry tears trickled down his cheeks. "Where is the betrayal in trying to save the lives of the people of Lysomnus?"

"I hope his death proves that I am quite willing to do what is necessary to get what I want," she said, ignoring Marcus's question. "You have learned something new about yourself recently. I must warn you right now against using your power in any way unless I allow you to do so."

"Where is my father?" Marcus shouted. "How am I supposed to know that you really have him? You sent me a stupid note, and I'm supposed to just believe you?"

Eris narrowed her green eyes at him, obviously incensed that he would doubt her.

"Stupid boy," she spat at him. "How dare you?"

Nun the Wiser put her skeletal hand on Eris's shoulder. "Easy, daughter," she rasped. "We will take care of this right now."

She waved her other hand, and a large man dragged Marcus's father through the crowd and threw him roughly to the ground at Nun the Wiser's feet. Marcus was surprised; there wasn't a single visible mark on his father. Deacon looked as healthy as he had the last time Marcus had seen him, except for the red scruff on his jawline.

"Dad?" Marcus said. Despite his appearance, Deacon looked miserable. "Aren't you glad to see me?"

"You shouldn't be here, Marcus. I hoped you wouldn't come." Deacon's voice was quavery with emotion and sadness. The look he gave Marcus was the same one he used when he was disappointed by something Marcus had done. Marcus was devastated. He thought Deacon might at least be proud that his son had made it all this way.

Nun the Wiser reached up and slid the hood back from her head. Her face was gaunt, the skin so tight and sunken her skull was visible beneath. Her red hair was thin and patchy, leaving bald spots on the top and sides of her head. She placed her skeletal white hand on Deacon's head and looked up at Marcus. "This is the time of your testing, boy. You recently used your power to affect the world around you, but you will no longer attempt to use this power of your own will. You may use it at my command and my command only. If you attempt to do anything else, your father will pay the price."

Marcus gritted his teeth. "While you claim that you killed Awar and can do many other things, I have only seen you do one thing—appear and disappear. Why should I fear you?"

The crowd behind Nun the Wiser gasped.

"You doubt me, boy? Let us all show you what you should fear!" Nun turned and gestured to the humans. "Go on. Show him the powers you wield!"

Each person, in turn, stepped forward and demonstrated an ability. One man formed a fireball in his palm, then threw it at Marcus as if they were playing catch. Marcus ducked, and a tree behind him exploded. Flaming branches landed everywhere around them. A teenage girl touched the ground, and a torrent of water flowed in a small river. Lightning crackled from one man's fingertip, riding the water in a deadly current. Another man turned into a wolf, with jaws strong enough to bite through a thick branch from the tree that had blown apart. A woman touched a tree, and it instantly became a pile of deadly, sharpened spears.

Others followed. The man who had pushed Deacon through the crowd picked up one of the spears and easily broke it into small pieces. Eris went last. She opened a screaming hole in dimensions, reached through, and pulled back Marcus's cell phone.

"Good thing mommy's not home right now, eh?" she laughed.

Marcus's heart raced with fear that he knew he could not show. It felt like a terrible risk to force Nun the Wiser to demonstrate her own abilities, but there had to be a reason she hadn't used her power yet. "I see their power," he said, jerking his chin towards the crowd. "What I don't see is your power. You threaten my father if I don't follow your commands, yet you personally have done nothing to prove why I should listen to you."

Nun the Wiser stepped away from Deacon, now raising her skeletal hand into the air. "You doubt me, *boy?* I will show you why Nun the Wiser is to be feared above all others."

The humans backed away uneasily while the Stondefel that had been resting leapt into the air and raced away. Marcus began to wonder if it had been a bad idea to provoke her. Nun the Wiser pointed both hands down the beach at Awar's body. To Marcus's horror, the body rose into the air and began to spin.

Eris stepped forward, dismay apparent on her face. "Mother, this is too much!"

"I will not be questioned, Eris!" Nun the Wiser's hands moved as though they conducted a symphony.

Awar's body jerked from side to side. Finally, his head lifted, and his eyes opened, though they were blank and white. The Stondefel flapped his wings, rising into the air. His movements were stiff and ungainly, all former grace gone. "What do you command?" Awar asked. Even his voice sounded wrong, as if it was being forced out of his body.

"Go back to the Council of Beornan Rokk," Nun the Wiser said. "Tell them we are still planning the attacks on all Lysomnus, that we don't know about the warnings the bruwes received. When you get the chance, attack the bush bruwe yourself." She smirked. "Try not to destroy *my* buildings there if you can help it."

"At your command." Awar turned and flew away.

Nun the Wiser turned back toward Marcus. The long red hair on one side of her head fell out in a cascade, landing in a pile on the ground. "As you see, even death cannot take you beyond my reach. Awar is now my creature and will act solely on my orders."

Marcus couldn't believe the Stondefel's dead body was being used in such an evil way. This was clearly more power than any one person should have. "But I thought each human only had one power. If your power is to bring someone back from the dead, why is that a problem for me?"

"You misunderstand, child. My power is different from these other humans. I can do many different things, even change the very landscape of this planet.. There are many possibilities I can choose from when it comes to your father. None of them are pleasant."

Marcus looked at Eris, who was on her knees, cradling the hair that had fallen to the ground. "But at what cost? It looks like it hurts you when you do these things. Are you killing yourself just to gain control of my power?"

"No, boy. You have forgotten one important thing. While coercing the son with the father is one side of the coin, coercing the father with the son is the other. And your father has not said one word to me about the cost, or doubting my power, or refusing to work for me."

Marcus looked at his father, who was still on his knees before Nun the Wiser with his head down. It was true; he hadn't heard a single word of defiance from his dad.

"Your father knows that I've told him a lot of lies while he's been in our prison because you are here," Nun the Wiser continued. "However, now that I've proven my power, he knows that I can do anything *to* Lysomnus or anyone on the planet."

"Are you saying it was you that put that Brynar in front of us in the Grenewud?"

"A little fun." She shrugged. "I had hoped one of your friends would venture out and meet a <<null>> or two, but they were too cautious. Never mind, we still managed to catch one of your friends. No matter. Now, your father will do what I've been asking him to do since we first brought him here. If he refuses, then he will be forced to watch me change you in unthinkable ways." Nun the Wiser looked down at Deacon, who was still staring down at the ground. "Ready, Deacon? I'm quite sure this time you will grant my heart's fondest wish."

Without looking up, Deacon closed his eyes and reached up with his hands. Nun the Wiser seized both, one in her well-fleshed hand and one in her hand of bone. As Marcus watched, he finally figured out what Nun the Wiser wanted his father to do, why they had wanted him and his father all along.

"No, Dad!" he cried.

It was too late. He could see flesh reappearing on the bones of the skeletal hand clasped in Deacon's. As if in an optical illusion, the evil woman's long red hair sprung from her skull and grew back, full and lush. Her face filled in, and the flesh regained a healthy tone. The glitter in her eyes returned to a lovely shade of green. He hadn't realized how gaunt the figure beneath the robe appeared until he saw the shape of her body fill in beneath her robes.

Nun the Wiser was a beautiful woman, restored to full health.

Deacon gasped, let go, and collapsed to the sand. His pale, freckled skin was now a sickly gray. Marcus sank to his knees by his father's side, terrified he would find that the big man was dead. To his relief, Deacon was breathing normally. Marcus glared up at Nun the Wiser. "You won't find me so easy to manipulate," he spat through gritted teeth.

"That's funny, while I look at you crouched down in the sand next to your father." Nun the Wiser walked away with a bounce in her step, rubbing the fingers of her newly repaired hand together.

Marcus put his hands over his face and bit back a sob. Everything was falling apart. His friends wouldn't know that Awar was now their enemy. Thicce Colpat could be going up in flames even now. He wondered just how far his reach really was with this power. Could Nun the Wiser really tell if he was using it? If he used it on something far away and she didn't see the effects, would she know?

Even if there were consequences, he needed to find out. Peeking through his fingers, he could see Nun the Wiser talking to Eris a short distance away. Most of the humans were drifting away, now that their leader had obtained her objective. He assumed they'd be heading back to their bruwe. No one was paying him any attention. He kept his hands over his face and tried to picture Awar. The young Stondefel was a fast flier and should have made it a good distance over the plains now. If Marcus could stop Awar now, their friends would never see him and wouldn't receive the wrong information.

Once he had pictured Awar in his head, he reached out with his mind. Several times, his mind fastened on a flying creature, only to discover it was some kind of bird. He broke those connections and reached farther. He finally got a glimpse of the plains far below and knew he was seeing through Awar's eyes.

Everything he could feel in Awar's head was wrong. This was not the Awar he had known. There was no thought in the body—just a blankness and the drive to destroy. Death had stolen the brave Stondefel from them, and Nun the Wiser's evil resurrection had replaced him with this horrible undead creature.

He reached out and *pulled* at the dark life force within Awar's body.Heat seared through his chest. In his distant mind's eye, Marcus could see the Stondefel's body spinning, falling to the ground. He quickly disengaged. Weariness surged through him—he only hoped he would still have enough strength to handle whatever else Nun the Wiser might have planned for him. He looked around. At least it appeared as if she hadn't noticed that he'd used his power.

Deacon groaned. Marcus put a hand on his shoulder.

"Dad, are you all right?"

"Yeah, I've just never had to heal a whole person with so much damage before," his father said weakly. "Took most of my strength to do it."

"You shouldn't have!" Marcus cried out in a harsh whisper. "You should have let that evil creature die!"

"Nun the Wiser wasn't going to die today, Marcus. I had to do what I did to save you. She would have killed you if I hadn't done it."

Marcus sat back on his heels despite the pain it caused him. "No, you didn't. I'm just one person. It's not worth losing everyone else on this planet just to save me!"

Deacon looked up at him and clasped his forearm in one big hand. "It is to me, son. The Talent line has to go on."

"What do we have here? A touching father-son reunion?" Eris laughed and pushed Marcus' shoulder with her foot, knocking him onto his back on the sand. "Get up, spawn. Your daddy has a cell to get back to."

"You're still going to lock him up? Why? He did what you wanted!" Marcus brushed the sand off himself as he worked his way painfully to his feet. Behind him, Deacon pushed himself to a sitting position and grimaced.

"This isn't a resort." Eris snapped. "You stay where we tell you to stay."

"If you think I'm going to do anything you want, you'd better start to change how you're treating us," Marcus growled.

"Now comes out the true nature of the beast. You think you have the power to make demands?"

"I didn't say that. Don't you think it will be easier to get me to work with you if you treat us with some kindness? Look at how well it worked for you back on Earth." Marcus shouted at her.

"On Earth?" Deacon stared up at Marcus. "What do you mean?"

"Eris pretended to be a substitute teacher at my school—in fact, she was one of my favorites," Marcus told his father. A startled look crossed Eris's face.

Marcus turned back to Eris. "So, the same thing could work here. Treat us better and give us a better place to live—some incentives to do what you want, maybe."

"Hmmm. Let me talk to my mother."

"What are you doing, Marcus?" Deacon asked in a low voice. "I thought you said you were never going to do what they wanted?"

"Be quiet, Dad. They don't know that. I've got some ideas on how to learn more about my own power and help you at the same time."

Eris came back. "My mother is going to let you live in a house in our bruwe. You'll even have some surprise roommates. You'll be locked in there except when you're working for us. One of our people is going there now to put bars on the windows and the door."

"See?" Marcus said. "I told you."

Deacon closed his eyes. "Oh, thank goodness."

"Dad?" Marcus put a hand on his dad's shoulder. "What is it?"

"At least I don't have to go back down into their prison. It's little more than a dark hole in the ground."

"Leverage, Dad. Do you know when the bigger Stondefel joined them? Awar said that only the younger and smaller ones rebelled and left, but those two today were the biggest I've seen, bigger than Anneberg!"

Deacon looked at Marcus as if he'd gone crazy. "You speak

of the Stondefel as if you know them, as if they are your friends. Yet you've only been here on Lysomnus a short time. I have traveled here almost all my life and only now have seen them while they've been working with Nun the Wiser." He shook his head. "I saw no need to meet with terrifying demons made of stone."

Marcus doubted this since both the Muirnati and Fyrtudo were friendly with the Stondefel, but he let the lie go for now.

"The Stondefel have become a part of our mission, and we've become part of theirs. I have so much to tell you." Marcus didn't think his father was quite ready to find out that not only was his son friends with the Stondefel but had ridden on their backs in flight.

"I'm sorry, Marcus. I don't know anything except what they've told me, and I think that's mostly been lies. I—"

"All right." Eris was back, this time with the bulky man and two other humans. "Garrett and I will be escorting you to your little house in the bruwe now that it's all prepared for you." She chuckled as she gestured for them to follow. Marcus waited for his father to get to his feet.

He was in so much pain, he didn't think he could walk all the way to the human bruwe, especially without his cane. He was in so much pain, he didn't even find it humiliating when Garrett picked Marcus up and carried him. He only wished his dad was carrying him—but maybe Deacon was still too weak.

The entrance to the underground prison where Deacon had been held was near the edge of the bruwe, which was set up as a grid, with parallel and perpendicular streets. Unlike the bathhouse and bunkhouse he had seen in Thicce Colpat, the homes here in the human bruwe were made of wood, but they were not properly cared for. Some of the logs had split from lack of care, and Marcus saw rotting wood in several places, creating a foul smell. The other odors he smelled were more noticeable now that they were in the bruwe; spoiled food was the most prominent, and piles of garbage could be seen near some of the houses as they walked past.

The house that had been prepared for them was a small one right in the center of the bruwe by a large open area. There were bars on all the windows and the door. Garrett stepped in and set Marcus down carefully on his feet. Deacon followed Garrett inside.

"Gentlemen, your quarters," Eris said, "I hope you find them to your liking. Spend your time getting comfortable; you'll be here a while." She closed the door behind herself, and they heard the solid *chunk* of the bars being locked.

Marcus slowly lowered himself to a stained wooden bench, the only furniture in the room. Outlines and drag marks on the floor indicated where other furniture had once sat before being hastily removed. He might have bargained to get them a house instead of an uncomfortable prison, but it was clearly just a minor win. He saw no kitchen area and no storage for food, but the presence of two doors that opened off from this small room gave him some hope. Deacon sat on the floor with his back against the wall, his hands hanging limply between his knees.

Marcus pulled one leg onto the bench, clenching his teeth against the pain. He propped his elbow on his thigh and covered his eyes. Scalding tears rolled down his face. Every time he closed his eyes, the image of Awar's lifeless body appeared. The loss of his friend made his chest hurt. Even worse was the memory of using his power to jerk the wretched animation from what remained of his friend's body, knowing he had left it to plummet to the ground below. His grief for Awar brought thoughts of Leopold to mind since he knew just how close his friend had been to the young Stondefel. Leopold would be heartbroken when he learned of Awar's death. Thinking of Leopold made him envision Sadie's beautiful face.

For a moment, he touched his lips and remembered the unexpected moment when she had kissed him. Marcus realized he had never felt as alone as he did right now. He had no idea how far away his friends were or if he would ever see them again. Awar was the only one who had known where this place was.

Wiping his eyes, he sniffed and looked over at his father. Deacon was staring at the barred window and seemed unaware of his son's grief. As Marcus lowered his foot back to the ground, he groaned in pain. He was unable to stifle another cry when he pushed himself to his feet. Despite his son's obvious pain, Deacon never looked away from the window.

Marcus shuffled slowly to the door on the left. He had never missed his cane more. Holding himself upright without it was impossible, adding yet another agony to the difficulty of movement. Another glance told him his father would be of no help. The big man was still on the floor, now staring up at the small, barred window as if to specifically avoid looking at his struggling son.

Marcus opened the door to find a bathroom with a tiny shower, a toilet, and a shelf with soap and some clothing and towels. He took a moment to use the facilities, then stepped out and closed the door. He used the wall to shuffle to the other door. As the door swung open, he gasped.

Davidia, most of her flowers and leaves missing, was sitting on a bench with her feet in a trough full of water. The remaining leaves on her face fluttered as she opened her dim orange eyes and turned her head in Marcus's direction. Lying immersed in the trough was Boehlkea, the scales on her face pale. She, too, opened her eyes and looked at him. Marcus could not help crying at the state of both of them. A third person sat in the room—a very obviously pregnant creature, obviously exhausted. Marcus could almost see the outlines of their bones through their skin. He shook his head in disgust at the way the captives had been treated.

"Marcus!" Davidia and Boehlkea tried to smile, but they were obviously tired and probably underfed.

"You're here! And safe!" he tried to sound positive.

"This is Tini," Davidia gestured weakly to the pregnant creature. "They're Cativeran."

"I'm so glad to see you all." Marcus blurted, relief flooding his chest. "They haven't been treating you very well, have they?"

"Not really," Boehlkea said.

Marcus sat on the edge of the tub and called out. "Dad! Boehlkea is here!"

"Really, Dad is here too?" Boehlkea said, with some excitement in her voice, "Can he come in here?"

They waited, but Deacon didn't come in, and there was no reply from the other room.

Marcus sighed and squeezed his sister's hand. "I'll go tell him you're in here. I'm sure he'll want to come see you," he said, backing out and gently closing the door.

FACE OFF

Deacon was on his feet now, hands behind his back. He was staring out the barred window at the moon.

Marcus turned around, leaning against the door. "Dad, didn't you hear me? Boehlkea is in this room. She'd like it if you would go in and see her."

Deacon turned to look at him. "I must not have heard you. Um...when did you meet Boehlkea?"

Marcus was surprised by his dad's excuse. In this tiny house? He didn't hear Marcus call out?

"I traveled to Fisc to warn them about the possibility of an attack on their bruwe by a rebel Stondefel. Nun the Wiser showed up at Fisc while I was there trying to warn their people of the possibility of a war. She's been showing up every time someone says her name and either attacking someone or kidnapping someone from the bruwe."

"You've been to Fisc?" Deacon said, alarmed, his cheeks reddening.

"Yes, and I met Pelamis and Boehlkea there." Marcus hesitated. "I know that Boehlkea is my sister."

Deacon swallowed hard.

"Pelamis was beside herself with worry when I left. She hoped I'd be able to find and rescue you."

"Well, here I am. I'm glad they brought me out of that

horrible prison underground, even if it was just to heal Nun the Wiser. And I don't regret doing that," he said, with a sharp look at his son, "because it saved your life." He wrinkled his nose as he pulled at his filthy shirt. "I've been down there in the dark in these same clothes for weeks. I feel disgusting and smell worse."

"Well, you'll be happy to hear there's a bathroom," Marcus pointed at the other door with his prosthesis, "that actually has a shower with soap and a change of clothes for each of us. After you talk with Boehlkea, you can get cleaned up."

Marcus was shocked when Deacon turned and walked straight to the bathroom door. "Dad, what about Boehlkea? She's waiting for you!"

"She'll be fine, son. There's plenty of time to visit after I get clean. Then I'll feel better." He closed the door behind him. A few seconds later, Marcus heard the shower start. He stepped back into the room where the hostages were waiting. Pain tore at his chest as he saw the eager look on his sister's face, that changed to disappointment at the sight of Marcus.

"I'm sorry, Boehlkea. Dad will be just a few more minutes. He didn't want to come in all dirty and smelly from living all this time in prison." Marcus felt terrible just saying the words to her. He knew they were lies. "He wants to be clean when he sees you." A crooked smile matched the tears that stood in her eyes at his words.

They waited in awkward silence until the sound of the shower abruptly ceased.

"Sounds like he's almost done. As soon as he comes out, I'll make him come even if I have to drag him in here." Davidia put a hand on Boehlkea's arm as Marcus stepped out of the room again.

Deacon came out of the bathroom in cuffed black pants and a white button-down, steam billowing out behind him. With too-long fingernails, he scratched at the scruff on his cheeks. "I wish I had a razor. Never did like letting my beard grow out."

Marcus gestured to the other door. "Dad. Your daughter is waiting."

"Oh, right," Deacon said.

Boehlkea had climbed out of the trough and was waiting with an anxious look on her face. "Father!" she cried out and dashed forward. Throwing her arms around Deacon, she closed her eyes in happiness. Marcus could see her arms trembling as she embraced the big man. "I thought I'd never see you again!"

Deacon grasped Boehlkea's arms and carefully pushed her away from his body. "I just showered, Boehlkea. You're getting me all wet."

Marcus could see the hurt on his sister's face and felt as if his chest was being squeezed. Heat rose in his face. "What's wrong with you, Dad? You nearly killed yourself to heal Nun the Wiser when she threatened to hurt me and now you push your daughter away because of a wet shirt?"

Deacon sighed. "You have to understand, Marcus. You're my son, the one who has to carry on the Talent legacy and pass it on to the next generation. I do love Boehlkea, but she's just a half-breed who can never do that. I could only ever see her in Fisc while wearing a wetsuit. I didn't have to worry about things like getting my clothes wet or slimy."

Boehlkea burst into tears, burying her face in her hands. Marcus moved closer, embracing her clumsily. Davidia stood up. "You've got some nerve," she said, nearly spitting with fury, "coming to *our* world and treating *our* people like this. Lysomnus isn't some playground for humans."

"Humin git!" Tini exclaimed.

"One of those Cativera *animals*!" Deacon snorted in disgust, as if he hadn't even noticed Tini until they spoke.

Marcus's teeth clenched together so hard his jaw hurt. None of these people deserved to be treated this way. Marcus grasped his father's arm and led him out of the room. Deacon gave way and followed easily, as Marcus had expected, knowing his father understood his son's limited abilities.

"Look, Dad," Marcus began, "I've been learning as I go since you never told me anything about this world. And I've learned stuff about *you*, too, while I've been here." He sat down on the bench carefully. "And I have to admit, I'm starting to feel like you're not the person I thought you were. I don't think you've taken the time to understand or treat Lysomnus or its people the way they deserve while you've been traveling here. You avoided telling me about it when I started traveling, which left me clueless. You have a secret family here, and I don't think that's a common Talent practice. You work all the time to avoid seeing your family at home."

Deacon glared at Marcus angrily, but Marcus thought he could see shame hidden beneath the anger. "You don't know everything about life yet, Marcus. Just wait until you've had to make the decisions I have."

"Like what? Having two families and avoiding both of them? Why did you marry Mom and have me at all if you were going to ignore us all the time?" Marcus asked. "Stick to the things you like, such as the family you created here? They at least *thought* you cared about them, although I'm starting to wonder. They knew that we existed on Earth, at least."

"I never had a choice about *any* of this! Do you think I *wanted* to travel to Lysomnus? I wasn't given a choice! Then I found someone I cared about here, and we finally had a child. But that doesn't even matter because she's not a full human and can't carry on the bloodline, so I *still* had to marry someone back home so I could have a child to carry on our precious bloodline. And then I *couldn't tell you or your mother anything*!" Deacon yelled, his face flushing.

Marcus swallowed hard, trying to get past the lump in his throat. He felt unloved and unwanted by the man he'd looked up to his whole life. Why hadn't he seen his father for who he truly was?

"You're a bigot, Dad. A weak man who puts himself and his own wants ahead of an entire world. I'm ashamed of you." He could barely speak, he was so choked up. He wrapped the fingers of his left hand around the hook of his prosthesis to keep himself from saying anything worse.

"Stop it, Marcus! I won't have you speak to me that way!"

"If you had just taken the time to talk to me that first night..." Marcus held up the wrist with the Stikke on it and shook it gently. "I've been wearing this since I came back to Lysomnus. I haven't returned home once. I don't know what I would say to Mom. I miss her so much, but what would I say about where I've been and where you are?"

Deacon's face darkened further, his mouth pursing in an angry line. "It's not safe to wear the Stikke that long, Marcus! And you accuse *me* of not caring about family?"

"How real are your feelings for Mom, anyway? Did you marry her just to have an heir to this?" He waved his hand, gesturing to indicate the world around them.

Deacon's eyes widened in shock. "What the hell kind of question is that, Marcus?"

"You have a *family* here, Dad! A woman you were bonded with for years before you married Mom! Pelamis had no choice but to accept it, and Mom never even knew."

"Marcus, right now, we need to focus on what's important, and that's getting home safely."

Marcus looked at him sharply. "You're kidding, right?"

"Of course not! It's quite clear that Nun the Wiser is very interested in your power, whatever it is. You're going to take off that Stikke and go back home tonight."

Stay calm, Marcus told himself as he took a deep breath and looked up at the ceiling. During his time in Lysomnus, he'd realized how valuable this world really was and the lengths he would personally go to in order to save its people. There was no use trying to convince his dad. He slid the Stikke off his wrist.

"Great, son." Deacon smiled. "I'm glad you're seeing things clearly now. Tonight, I'm sure you'll be able to make it back home. I know Nun the Wiser thinks you'll try to protect me, but you need to leave so she can't use me against you."

"No, Dad. That's not what's going to happen. I'm not going back to Earth. The people of Lysomnus are in danger because of these humans, so if there is any way that I can help them, I'm going to do it."

"Damn it, Marcus!" Deacon's fists clenched. "This isn't a game!"

"I'm well aware of that. And the gift of power that we gain here is something we should be using to help these people, particularly when someone is hurting them."

Deacon sighed. "I've used my healing power to help people, but I couldn't have used it to save this entire world."

"Refusing to heal Nun the Wiser today would have made a difference. Using her power for decades has clearly taken an immense toll on her body. She would have died eventually if you hadn't healed her. Instead, you let her threaten you into doing it."

Deacon avoided his gaze. "I couldn't take the risk of losing the family line."

Marcus threw his arms into the air in exasperation. His prosthesis nearly hit the low ceiling. "It's so clear you don't care about me at all," he snapped. "Just the continuation of the 'Talent family line."

"Someday, you'll realize just how important it really is, Marcus."

"You know what's important? Friends, Dad. Remember Cornus? The Scrybb I met when I first came here? It's a good thing I did make a friend because when I returned, Leopold broke his leg, and the Scrybb helped us out. I was able to use the Halfriez to heal it."

"*Leopold* is here? How did you manage that one? What a mess you've made of this, Marcus! In all *my* years here, no one was ever bothered by these other humans. My visits were quiet and fun." Deacon cleared his throat, evidently trying to resume his position of authority. "You're only on your second visit, and now this world is in the middle of a war."

"Plenty of people were 'bothered' by these humans—you just didn't want to know about it." Marcus shook his head, still angry but also saddened by his father's willful ignorance. "You know what, Dad? You've made this decision much easier for me," Marcus said. He closed his eyes, concentrating as he felt the heat from his power building inside him. He heard the beginning of the howl that accompanied the portal between Lysomnus and his own world and knew it would be audible to the entire bruwe.

He had to keep the humans away long enough to help his friends in the next room. As the portal opened, Marcus created a shield around it. The growing howl cut off abruptly.

"Son, what are you doing? Hey, stop it!" Deacon yelled.

Marcus ignored his father and quickly worked to expand the portal. Then he opened his eyes, looked at Deacon, and concentrated on *pushing*. He released the portal and the shield with relief as soon as his father disappeared into it, crying out his name.

Marcus grimaced as he used his left hand to push himself to his feet. He limped back to the room where the others were and opened the door to find them all staring at him; fear was evident on all of their faces.

Marcus reached out and embraced his sister. "What was that noise? We could hear you arguing." Boehlkea pulled back, her eyes searching his face.

"I'm sorry you didn't get to say goodbye, but I've sent our father home," Marcus said. Tears filled his sister's eyes and trickled down her beautiful face. She pressed herself against him, sobbing. "And now I'm going to do the same for you."

"Do you know how to do that?" she asked, her voice muffled by his shirt. "Is it safe?"

"I'll be careful, don't worry." Closing his eyes, he pictured the tunnel entrance where he had first entered the Muirnati bruwe. He concentrated on placing her on the sand right next to the tunnel opening. Putting her into the water of the Diluvium seemed too risky. What if another Muirnati were in that same place? One or both of them could be hurt. In his mind, he saw her standing on the firm sand inside the ring of stones by the tunnel. His arms collapsed against his own body as her body left the room.

He turned to Tini, who gestured cautiously. "Go hom?" they asked.

Marcus looked at Davidia, who shrugged.

He held out a hand, and Tini took it with one paw. As he pulled them close, he noticed the difference between the Cativera's more muscular body, swollen with pregnancy, and Boehklea's slender form. Tini also had smooth hair covering their body, while Boehlkea had cool, smooth scales.

Marcus thought of what Cornus had told them about Grasian. The young Scrybb was excellent at describing things; Marcus could picture every detail of what his friend had said. But where should he put the Cativera? Cornus had described the stone steps where he had first met Tini clearly. Marcus felt fatigue clutching at him and fought it. It was imperative to get Tini and Davidia to safety. He pictured the stairs and carefully felt Tini's body, and he also remembered to include the life within them. Marcus concentrated, and they were gone. He had put them at the bottom of the stairs so they didn't have to strain too much to get home. He was nearly spent. After stopping Awar, opening the portal and shielding it, and sending Boehlkea and Tini home, he hoped he had enough left for one last trick.

He looked at Davidia, barren of most of her leaves. The vines of her body, interlaced with twig-like structures in some places, framed the structure of her body as a human skeleton would. It reminded him of the bodies of the Scrybb back in Thicce Colpat, which were used to grow the

Vosfyren. Those vines and twigs were covered with small buds, like those of trees in springtime.

"I think I have an idea, Davidia. You just have to trust me, okay?" Marcus held out his hands to the Scrybb girl.

Davidia looked at him forlornly. She held out her hands and wrapped her fingers around his. Marcus gently squeezed her hands and closed his eyes. He traced her hands with his fingers, feeling them with his mind. He could feel all the soft bumps on her hand where each individual leaf would grow.

He concentrated on one of these at first, feeling for the bud to unfurl into a delicate, dewy leaf. Davidia inhaled sharply, startling Marcus into opening his eyes. He realized that although he and Davidia were just friends, this was an incredibly intimate process. He was sensing every part of her, and she could feel it too. That first bud had surprised them both. "Hold on, Davidia," he whispered. "Just a little more."

He expanded his thoughts to her entire hand and along her arm, and he realized he could sense every bud on her entire being. As if in a dream, Marcus bloomed her. He could think of no better word for it. Davidia gasped as leaves and flowers burst open all over her body at once.

Her face was full of wonder. "Marcus, how are you doing these things?"

"After you were taken, I discovered I can..." He wasn't quite sure how to describe it. "Well, I can affect things in different ways."

Davidia pulled her hand from his. "Affect things? What do you mean?"

Marcus spent a few minutes explaining everything that had happened—the first time he'd moved the wagon, his practice, the way he'd learned to prevent dust blowing around. "And I healed Awar and, uh..." Marcus stopped, remembering that the only thing she knew about the Stondefel was that one of them had kidnapped her. He sat down next to her. "Davidia, look. Not all the Stondefel are bad." He rubbed his sweaty hand on his thigh. "I think you really need to know everything that has happened since."

He filled her in on everything that occurred after she was taken by the Stondefel. She cried out and put her hands over her mouth when he told her about the actions of the Scrybb when Leopold and Awar arrived to warn them. "I can't believe it," she said, "though you know my only experience with the Stondefel was when I was kidnapped and brought here. You can see why it is hard for me to think of them as anything but dangerous beasts."

"I'm so sorry, Davidia." Marcus ran a hand through his hair, feeling exhausted. "I wish you could have met Awar. He was so brave."

Exhaustion made him dizzy, and he held up his hand. "Davidia, if I'm going to send you home, it has to be now. I don't have much strength left."

He pulled her close, happy to feel the rustle of leaves against him. He closed his eyes, not picturing Thicce Colpat but the terrace of Palaga, where his friends would be. He decided to put her just to the side of the Scrybb path to be sure no one would be there. With a breath, she was gone.

Marcus crawled out to the main room and collapsed to the floor in a shaft of moonlight. Thanks to the shield he had put around the portal, he knew no one had heard anything. He should have hours to rest before anyone discovered Deacon and the others were gone. The floor was hard, but

Marcus was exhausted. As soon as he closed his eyes, he was asleep.

The next thing he knew, morning sunlight streamed through the doorway as someone opened it and shoved several trays inside. "Breakfast is served!" a man's voice shouted. "Eat heartily because you'll be working fer Nun the Wiser t'day!" Marcus held a hand up and squinted into the bright light, but it was behind the man, and he could see nothing but a dark shape.

He was relieved when the door slammed shut and he heard the bars lock once again. The man hadn't noticed Deacon's absence, then. He had to pull himself over to see what was on the trays—his entire body was made of pain, it felt like. Sleeping on the floor had probably been the worst thing for him.

The food wasn't nearly as good as what he had been eating at the other bruwe of Lysomnus, but he needed nourishment after the energy he had used yesterday. He began to eat as quickly as he could. They could come at any second and discover that the others were gone. There were five trays of food—apparently, they had decided to start feeding everyone again. Marcus managed to finish what would have been his own tray and his father's before he started to feel full. He had a mouth full of fish when he heard the clank of the bars again.

When the man who stepped in cried out that the others were missing, Marcus heard people running toward the house. He thought about trying to see if he could somehow send himself away, but he knew one way or another, he had to stay and finish this for the good of all Lysomnus.

Garrett came in and seized Marcus roughly. Then the big man stepped outside and dropped him to the ground, where he landed on his hands and knees. Agony rippled up his hips to his back, and he held back tears as his prosthesis jammed against his residual arm.

Garrett stormed back out of the house. "The other prisoners aren't in there."

Eris's green eyes glared at Marcus, and her mouth pursed unattractively as her face flushed with anger. She darted over and dealt Marcus a kick in the ribs. "What did you do, you piece of garbage?"

"Eris!" Nun the Wiser snapped. "We will get no answers that way. Get up, boy."

Eris grabbed Marcus by his left arm, fingers digging deeply into the nerves in his armpit. He moved as slowly as possible, hanging most of his body weight so she had to do most of the work to lift him. He finally put his feet on the ground when he heard her grunt with effort before she could call Garrett—who would hurt him on purpose—to help her.

"Child," Nun the Wiser said almost sweetly, sounding nothing like her previous harsh hiss. "Where are the other prisoners?"

"You're the one with the power to bring back the dead," Marcus replied. "Surely you can figure out where a couple of escaped prisoners are." He looked at her newly restored beauty. "Oh, I get it. You don't want to use your power if you don't have to because it'll hurt you."

"You know nothing," Nun the Wiser spat. "I spent many years using my power before I reached the condition in which you saw me." Her full lips curved in an unflattering smirk. "You haven't noticed anything odd while using your own power? Perhaps it is your pain that keeps you from feeling it. Yes, boy, I am sure we are more alike than you realize. Using this much power has a price." She raised an eyebrow. "By now, the bruwes are burning, and the people of Lysomnus are concerned with more important things than you. Come, tell me where the prisoners are."

"You're wrong, Nunny," Marcus said, grinning. She had no idea she'd been foiled. "No attacks have taken place. Your message never made it through."

"That's impossible!" Eris cried out. "My mother sent that dead traitor to burn down the Scrybb bruwe, and by now, he's given your friends false information."

Marcus laughed, never taking his eyes from Nun the Wiser's green ones. "If you're so powerful, check on your messenger. See if the bruwe are burning. I know you can check for yourself."

For the first time, Marcus saw Nun the Wiser lose control of the arrogant countenance she so carefully kept under control. Even the minor change in the set of her lips brought him joy.

"Then I will have to destroy you and your power. I cannot allow someone so strong to live."

She stepped forward, boring into Marcus's eyes with her own. Marcus gulped as he stared back, knowing this was the most important confrontation of his life. Pain lanced through his eyes. He was revolted to feel the sensation of cold fingers poking around inside his head, as if Nun the Wiser was digging through his memories. Nausea curled through his stomach, and he pressed his hand to his face with a cry. It was surely only a matter of seconds before Nun the Wiser found the source of his power and took it away.

With a groan of effort, Marcus pushed back against the eerie sensation. In a way, his adversary was teaching him the method of attack she was using on him. Marcus had learned how to control his power quickly, and as he felt what she was doing, he tried to do exactly what she was doing to him. Just as when he had figured out how to turn the wheels on the cart when he first discovered his power, he now reached out as Nun the Wiser did when she reached into his own mind.

He sent his own mental fingers into her head. The quickest way was through the soft globes of her eyes. The crowd muttered as Nun the Wiser gasped loudly. It was incredibly difficult, there was no ease to it as there had been when using his power before. This was no comparison to moving mountains, reaching out to flying Stondefel, or shielding portals he had created. He had to focus from deep inside himself, concentrating on holding his power against hers, while at the same time, he continued to force his way into her mind, to find her source of power before she found his.

His consciousness was abruptly surrounded by cold blackness. It was an insidious, slimy feeling, as if his mind had slipped into a bowl of rancid oil. The sensation made it difficult to gain any control of his surroundings, which pulsed with rich, ancient power. The perception made him aware of just how young he was and how new his power was in comparison to hers.

Could he search through the powerful mind of his adversary and learn more about her? He immediately imagined fingers of his own reaching out of the slimy pool and finding her memories as if he were looking at the pages of a photo album. Marcus could feel Nun the Wiser pushing at his fingers and imagined creating a shield around the source of his power at the center of his mind as he searched hers. He turned back to the memories. The heavy sensation of the memories told him they contained decades. Marcus lifted the heavy weight to find the beginning of the memories. It took a lot of concentration and power, and his shield slipped.

With a cry of victory, Nun the Wiser pushed against the shield to stop Marcus, and he divided his concentration between her memories and the shield. She battered at the shield, and he knew he had to make this quick. The first memories began with a younger version of Nun the Wiser walking arm-in-arm through the Grenewud with another red-haired young woman who looked just like her, but whose hair was of a lighter hue.

This younger version of Nun the Wiser reminded him of his father. She had the same reddish freckles, the same deep shade of red hair. In the next set of memories, the other girl was pregnant, and the two girls were arguing. Tears flowed down the other girl's face as she turned and disappeared into a portal. He saw Nun the Wiser traveling between Earth and Lysomnus. So the girls must be Talents, too. As she returned, she often brought people wearing old-fashioned clothing with her. Many of them were struggling and looked unhappy.

Marcus needed to move on. He left the memories behind and returned to the slimy pool to find Nun the Wiser's source of power. He could feel his own body weakening as it tired from using so much power. How much longer could he keep this up? He was afraid his weakness would give Nun the Wiser the opening she needed to defeat him. He was nearly forced to drop his shield as he moved away from her memories.

He was stunned when he sensed *her* exhaustion as he exposed himself. She had continued to fight so hard to force her way through his shield, she had exhausted herself! Marcus realized he had left himself vulnerable, and Nun the Wiser could have killed him while he was distracted, but instead she focused entirely on attacking the core of his power behind his shield. She was so determined to destroy him, she had worn herself down.

Moving quickly now, he pushed his mental hand back into the cold, oily slime at the center of Nun the Wiser's mind. If evil had a physical feeling, this was it. His mind was slipping below the surface of liquid tar, and it felt like he was drowning in the thick slime. Marcus needed to finish this and get out. He never wanted to experience this sensation again.

A feeling of pressure at the center of his own mind made him realize that she was very close to the source of his own power, and his shield had finally fallen. Fear made his heart pound; if he didn't hurry, he could lose either his power or his life at any second, but even the slightest misstep inside her head could cost him dearly. Only staying calm would get him through this battle safely.

Finally, he found it. Her power existed as a dark core resting in the black pool. Marcus reached out with the fingers he had imagined into existence as he searched her mind. He could feel Nun the Wiser's mind searching closer within his own mind and began to panic. He pushed the fear away, regaining control of his own power.

Marcus squeezed his mental hand into a fist, feeling the core squelch. The moment Marcus felt he had a strong hold on it, he pulled with every bit of power he had left and squeezed harder at the same time. Something that felt like stretchy material snapped free as the core exploded in his clenched fist.

Screams brought his attention back to the physical world. He opened his eyes, not sure what he might find. He was trembling with exhaustion. His entire body was drenched in sweat, heat from inside overloading his physical form. Nun the Wiser was in a heap on the ground.

Eris screamed with grief, dropping to her knees and pulling Nun the Wiser's head into her lap, weeping into an armful of black robe and red hair. Finally, she lifted her head and stared at Marcus. "Murderer! She's dead!"

Marcus was stunned. He had only meant to destroy that awful core of power to stop Nun the Wiser and save himself. He had been acting out of pure desperation. Those stretchy fibers must have represented Nun the Wiser's life force, and when Marcus had pulled at the core of her power, snapping them had killed her. He thought about what Nun the Wiser had said about his own power and wondered if the same thing would have happened to him if he had lost their terrible battle—he might well be the one lying dead on the ground right now.

Eris was on her feet, green eyes blazing. She slapped Marcus across the face with one hand, and with the other hand, she was already opening a portal. "Let's see how *you* feel about losing a mother, Marcus! I can sense where *your* mother is right now!"

Instinctively, Marcus closed his left hand into a fist. He half expected to see it covered in the dark, slimy remnants of Nun the Wiser's mental core, but it looked perfectly normal. Eris shrieked as the opening portal closed.

"How did you do that?" She glared at him. "It doesn't matter." She turned to the humans behind her, her cheeks still wet with tears. "It's time to get revenge!"

A fireball flew over the crowd and nearly hit Marcus in

the face. He ducked, flicking out with his power at the same time. The fireball sailed by close enough for him to feel the heat and smell of his own singed hair. *I can't fight them all,* he thought, panicked. *This might be it.* He flinched as a spear hit the ground next to his foot. A river of water came roaring out of the group of humans, hitting Marcus hard enough to knock him off his feet. The cold water soaked his clothes immediately and made him gasp, and he rolled away from it just in time to avoid the sparking electricity that came crackling along its surface.

Marcus tried to climb to his knees and push out with his own power, but he was so exhausted from his battle with Nun the Wiser, he couldn't get his body to follow his commands. As he was trying to push the crowd back so he could defend himself, he heard an enormous thud behind him. Before he could respond, he was surrounded by enormous talons. Had Anneberg found him somehow? He looked up hopefully, only to see Ahazu's face snarling down at him. He heard Eris laugh.

He heard a stony voice rumble, "Forgot about us, didn't you?" His heart sank; he *had* forgotten about the rebel Stondefel. The last time he'd seen them, they'd been flying away as Nun the Wiser lifted Awar's corpse.

The talons holding him began to squeeze more tightly, the sheaths around the razor-like inner surfaces pulling back. Panicking, Marcus threw up a barrier between himself and the talons. They stopped closing in on him, and the Stondefel growled in frustration. Marcus pushed a little harder, forcing the talons to slowly open. One of them began to bend backward, and a cry of pain rumbled from above him.

He was preparing to step out of the Stondefel's opening

talons when he felt a hand on the back of his neck and heard a woman's voice whisper, *"Sleep"*.

Everything went dark.

CHAPTER NINETEEN

JOINING THE FIGHT

Leopold

Leopold watched with relief as Anneberg managed to land back on the stone terrace in front of Palaga. Sadie was wrapped in Leopold's arms, tears streaming down her face. She had run to his side as soon as Marcus disappeared in the hands of the strange Stondefel. As they had watched the rebel Stondefel attack and fly away with Marcus, Leopold had seen Anneberg's deadly injuries and the blood pouring down from his body. He had expected to see Anneberg plummet to his death. Instead, he had started flying again, and here he was, with only a few small gashes remaining on his arm, but his wings and the deepest wounds on his legs were completely healed.

"Anneberg, what happened? You were flying toward us so fast I thought you were going to crash!"

"When I arrived in my Caldera to find out what happened after the mountain exploded, I found two strange Stondefel up there," he explained. "I knew they had come for Marcus. Once he stopped the mountain from collapsing, they knew exactly what he was and where. I barely had time to beat them down here. Still, I did not expect them to attack me."

Leopold looked at the slashes on the Stondefel's leg. "I'm surprised it was just your leg and arm. It could have been your wings!"

Anneberg unfurled his wing and looked at it again. "It was."

Leopold cocked his head, surprised. "Then how did you manage to fly back here?"

"I think it was Marcus. After the other Stondefel took him from me, I was falling. My wings were useless, torn to shreds. I was in agonizing pain. But then the pain started to fade, and I could fly again. I wanted to chase them, to get Marcus back, but they were too far away by then. I lost him." Anneberg's shoulders slumped, and he struggled to keep back the tears that had pooled in his eyes.

Leopold gave Anneberg's stony leg a smack, then shook his stinging hand. "Don't be a fool. It's not your fault. You almost died trying to save him, and if he didn't have the power to heal you, you probably would have. Stop blaming yourself."

Anneberg looked around at the people on the stone terrace. "I don't know where those Stondefel came from. I think they were rebels, but I'd thought only the young Stondefel left to join them. Those Stondefel were bigger than Agatho or me."

Leopold looked up as a shadow crossed the terrace. "Speaking of Agatho...." Leopold watched with a smile as Anneberg scrambled to try to make room for the other Stondefel. He backed into the path under the trees of the Grenewud, where they led up to the terrace, wincing as he heard each one crashing to the ground beneath his weight. There simply wasn't room for two massive Stondefel on the stone plateau. Trying to cause minimal damage to the

Grenewud behind him, Anneberg backed up just far enough to give Agatho room to land.

"Brother," Agatho said to Anneberg after bowing to the crowd formally, "I am relieved to see you safe. Losing young Marcus is a devastating blow."

Leopold agreed, feeling his own throat thicken with emotion as the truth of losing his best friend really hit him. Anneberg's near death and injuries had distracted him, but now he felt the devastation of losing Marcus and having no idea where his best friend might be. He hugged Sadie more tightly, letting the tears fall.

Sadie finally pulled back and wiped at her face, looking up at Leopold. "I'm sorry," she said. "I got your shirt all wet."

"It's okay," Leopold replied. "I got your hair all wet." They both smiled through their tears.

He knew his friend would do everything he could to get back to them, but he also knew that if Marcus found his father when he arrived, he would be fighting to free his dad, despite everything he had learned about Deacon.

Is Awar not late returning as well? Tartarus asked.

"I fear that our young brother may have been discovered by the enemy," Agatho said, tapping a talon on the stone. His stony eyebrows furrowed. "The two strange Stondefel caused an explosion. Had that plan worked, they could have killed Marcus and most, if not all, of you as well." Agatho looked up at the craggy mountainside that had cascaded down toward the terrace not long ago.

I believe this was a test to see if Marcus had developed his full power, Tartarus said, stepping from the shadows beneath Agatho. *Nun the Wiser must have suspected that he had such an ability and thought it worth the risk of killing him to evaluate it.*

"Even if he has that kind of power, what good would it do them?" Sadie asked. "How could they control him if he's that strong? He was able to stop an entire mountain from collapsing!"

Tartarus sighed. *Nun the Wiser has similar strength and power. If the humans have Marcus's father, they only have to threaten to harm Deacon to force Marcus to do their bidding.*

Colflur said, *Tartarus, should you be taking such a chance by saying her name again?*

I do not think it matters anymore. She has what she wants now. Everyone knew Tartarus meant Marcus.

"How do we find Marcus? I mean, we should try to rescue him, should we not?" Cornus asked.

The silence lasted a beat too long. Tartarus shuffled uncomfortably.

"Even if we knew where he was," Agatho said, "we still have the problem of Nun the Wiser and her abilities. Several of the other humans also have power, though none as strong as her."

"Then what are we supposed to do?" Leopold burst out. "We can't just sit around. If Marcus is distracting her in some way, then I say we take advantage of that!"

Agatho placed one stony hand on Leopold's shoulder. "I know how hard it is, Leopold. Sometimes, all we can do is wait. It is what we Stondefel are forced to do while Awar is with the rebels."

Colflur ducked her head to look Leopold in the eyes. *These seem like the darkest of times, when it feels like our enemies are winning and we are helpless to fight back. We can only be patient and see what comes next.*

Everyone debated for hours. Leopold, Sadie, and Cornus were insistent in their desire to rescue Marcus. They were so adamant, they insisted on sleeping on the terrace. Meals were brought to the terrace for them while they continued the discussion.

Abruptly, a figure appeared out of nowhere at the edge of the terrace. Sadie clutched Leopold's arm, suddenly terrified that Nun the Wiser had heard them talking about her and arrived to do... she couldn't even imagine what. Leopold pushed her behind him protectively.

"Davidia!" Cornus exclaimed, running to the pretty Scrybb girl as she walked toward them. He embraced her tightly. Davidia hugged him back enthusiastically, and they both laughed with joy.

"Where have you been, Davidia? We were all so worried!" Leopold said.

"What happened? How did you *get* here?" Sadie asked.

"Oh," Davidia exclaimed. "It's a lot to tell, but I think the most important part is Marcus. Marcus is alive, and he—oh, he saved my life."

"Tell us everything," Cornus pleaded.

Davidia began with the day she was taken by the Stondefel, then described her days held captive by the humans, and finished by explaining that the humans had brought Deacon and Marcus to the small house where she and the other captives had been moved. "Marcus has such power; it is unbelievable," she said. "He sent his father home through a portal, then he sent Boehlkea and Tini home, then he helped me." Leopold saw Cornus twitch in surprise at the mention of Tini. "I honestly thought I would die after my time in prison. Without light and with very little food or water, all my leaves had fallen off. I was so weak. Marcus came to me, and he held my hands, and suddenly, my leaves just grew back. Then he told me to trust him, and the next thing I knew, I was here."

Everyone was awed by Davidia's story. Leopold looked around at everyone on the terrace: Cornus, holding hands with Davidia; Abutilon with one arm around Buddleja's waist; Tartarus and Colflur standing side by side. Agatho and Anneberg leaned down to listen. Sadie stood next to him. When Leopold glanced at her, she reached out and took his hand, squeezing tightly.

"Everyone keeps saying that we have to be patient and wait," Leopold said, "but I don't agree. We have to try to save Marcus. I know the human leader is powerful, and the other humans might be as well, but I know how Marcus thinks. He sent everyone away because he thinks he can save Lysomnus by himself if Nun the Wiser has no leverage to use against him."

"Of course we want to help Marcus," Abutilon said. "But it would be dangerous to go to the bruwe of the humans, even if we knew exactly where we were going or what to do when we got there."

"When Marcus, Sadie, and I first arrived here in Lysomnus," Leopold said. "his only goal was finding his dad. But the more Marcus got to know this world, and the more he saw its people in danger, the more he wanted to help save everyone and stop the war. Now we know he found his father, which is what he came to Lysomnus to do.

"But according to Davidia," Leopold pointed at the Scrybb girl, "he's still there. Why did he stay? He could have gone home with his father and come back for Sadie and me. I'll tell you why. He stayed there alone to face the humans and their powerful leader." He took a deep breath. "I won't abandon him while he stays there to fight for Lysomnus. I'm not afraid of the danger to myself.

"Even if it costs my life, I need to go and help my friend. I may not have any special abilities, but I have another power—our friendship. Anytime we are together, we are stronger. Imagine how strong we all would be if we stood together with Marcus against the humans."

He looked around, catching everyone's eye in turn. "It's possible I will die," he continued. "That is a cost worth paying to fight for Lysomnus and Marcus. But I don't believe that we will *lose*, not if we all fight together."

Anneberg pulled himself up to his full height. "I agree with you, Leopold. I will fight beside you and carry anyone who will join us."

Agatho agreed immediately and at the same time as the other Stondefel. Abutilon and Buddleja said they would go, looking frightened but determined as they clutched each other's hands tightly. Tartarus and Colflur said they must go to help Marcus, who was an important person to Lysomnus.

Besides, Colflur said, *he is dear to me already.*

Leopold looked at Cornus. "Of course I will go," Cornus said, upset that Leopold would even think he had to ask. "Marcus has become a cherished friend." Then he smiled. "And I need the destination to add to my Travels! No Scrybb has yet gone as far as the bruwe of the humans."

"Excuse me, Cornus, but you are wrong," Davidia said, putting her hands on her hips. "I was there already. And I am going back with you because there is no chance I will stay behind while everyone else goes to help Marcus."

Cornus sighed and rolled his eyes but didn't argue.

Once the trip was decided upon, it didn't take long for everyone to get ready. New harnesses were braided to hold more people on the Stondefel. "What about weapons?" Leopold asked. The Lysomnians looked at each other uneasily.

We do not use weapons, Tartarus said. *Other than the Cativera, who use spears to protect their flocks from natural predators.*

Leopold shrugged, but it made him feel even more uneasy to go up against the humans with no way to fight them other than their own hands. It was fine for the Stondefel and the Fyrtudo, and even the Scrybb, who could make shields out of their vines, but he and Sadie were depending on their own hand-to-hand skills. "Then I guess we'll just go." He rubbed sweaty palms nervously on his pants.

"Do we even know where we're going?" Sadie asked. The Stondefel looked at her.

"We know the human bruwe is on the east coast of Lysomnus," Anneberg said. "We will fly to the coast and search along the shore until we find it. There is no other way without Awar."

Without any more discussion, they arranged themselves on the backs of the Stondefel. Abutilon, Buddleja, and Sadie were seated on Agatho, while Leopold, Davidia, and Cornus were with Anneberg.

As they began to climb on and organize themselves, Growan came running out of Palaga. He dashed to Colflur's side. *Momma, where are you going? I want to come!*

No, son, Colflur replied with pain in her voice. *It isn't safe for you.*

Nothing is ever safe for me! I'm tired of being left behind. How will I learn to be a strong Fyrtudo like Father if I'm never allowed to come along?

Tartarus put his hand on his son's head with love. *My son, I hope to take you along on many journeys, learning all there is to know about Lysomnus. However, today is not the day for you to join us. If something happens to us, you must be here to carry on as leader of the Fyrtudo.*

Growan hung his head for a moment. Then he raised it and took a deep breath. *I will stay here and take care of Palaga.*

The Stondefel each seized one of the Fyrtudo and launched into the sky.

CHAPTER TWENTY

FRIENDS TO THE END

Marcus regained consciousness on a hard floor. Keeping his eyes closed, he didn't move, unsure if there was anyone in the room keeping watch over him. The smell of old dirt filled his nose, and he had to fight back a sneeze. After listening for breathing or sounds of movement and hearing none, he opened his eyes to find the room empty. Morning sunlight streamed through the window, leaving striped shadows on the floor where the bars blocked the light. It was possible that the humans expected him to remain asleep until the woman who put him to sleep came to wake him again. If so, he had a little time to figure out his next move.

If only he had some help taking care of those enormous Stondefel, he might have been able to focus on the humans. He wondered what kind of people they were; were they all faithful followers of Nun the Wiser, or had they been forced to follow her?

Those with power were the ones who had attacked after his battle with Nun the Wiser, but none of the other humans had been there, and he didn't want to assume that all the humans would stand against him.

His body went cold as he thought of her, his adversary. At the time, all he'd been focusing on was saving his own life and his power, but now that it was quiet and he had time to think, he realized that he had actually killed another person. Her dead body had been lying on the ground after their battle. He could tell himself he hadn't used a weapon to kill her, but he had. His power was strong—strong enough to take a life.

The feeling of the core of her power and the strings of her life force tearing away in his grip rose up in his mind. The image was there every time he closed his eyes. He held up his arms and looked at his hand and the hook of his prosthesis, but part of him could see the hand that had existed in his mind when he killed Nun the Wiser the day before. Tears filled his eyes and ran down his cheeks. He retched, but his stomach was empty, and nothing came up.

Marcus knew he would need to use his power again today. He wondered if it was really taking a physical toll on him as it had on Nun the Wiser when he used it. He was tired but no more than usual when waking up after a night's sleep.

His body hurt all over, but a lot of that was from sleeping on the hard floor for a second night. Nun the Wiser had clearly been affected by using a power as great as hers, but that was over an extremely long time of using it haphazardly.

Perhaps once he was through all of this and used it sparingly, the same thing wouldn't happen to him. There was no way to know. With his disabilities, there might be no way to know for some time. For now, Marcus didn't have a choice. He would worry about it later and restrict his usage once he was free of danger and these humans.

He was surprised to see the trays of food from the

previous day were still there. They must have just tossed him in here after he was knocked out and closed the door. The bread and fruit were still good, so he ate as much as he could to restore his energy, ignoring the nausea that made him feel sick.

He began to feel with his mind for any humans nearby. Now that he was calm, it was easy to do. There was no immediate need to hurry, as he had needed to do with the mountain, Anneberg's injuries, the shielded portal, and his battle with Nun the Wiser. It was quiet, and he supposed everyone must still be sleeping.

It was an interesting experience to take his time and search the bruwe from mind to mind. He was searching for specific people. When he brushed a mind that wasn't one of them, he ignored it and moved on. The now-familiar sensation of warmth filled his body as he used his power.

A familiar mind lit up as he searched, and he focused on it. He would not be able to describe it, but he was sure the mind he sensed was Eris. There was something about the feel of her energy that resembled her personality, like a particular scent.

Marcus probed until he isolated the power within her as he had with her mother, but he trembled at the thought of killing another person. He felt carefully around her core of power. There was no webbing of life force connected to her power and he was fairly confident she would survive the termination. A little mental snip, as with a pair of scissors, and it was done.

It was so easy to destroy Eris's power that Marcus was astonished. He was much more careful than he had been with Nun the Wiser. Her ability was much weaker than her mother's had been, and taking it away felt as if he had just broken a connection. Nun the Wiser had felt him probing just as he had felt her probing in his mind.

Eris had not given off any reactions while he took her power away. He didn't believe she even knew he had been inside her head. He continued his search until he found the mind of the woman who put him to sleep. Hers, Eris's, and Garrett's powers were the most dangerous to him but just as easy to disconnect. The sleep power was one he could not allow to be used on him again. Finally, he discovered Garrett's mind with its power of increased strength and took that, too.

Groaning with the effort, Marcus used his left hand to push himself to his knees. Fortunately, he had been lying on his side and not his back. While that would have rendered him nearly unable to move at all, he still felt like a pile of broken sticks. Every movement made him feel as if bones were grating against each other beneath his skin. He balanced some of his weight on his left hand and then slowly crawled to the bench and pulled himself up to a sitting position.

Just as he made it to his feet, there was a flurry of activity outside. Marcus hobbled to the window. A Stondefel landed right in the middle of the bruwe. At first, he thought it was the one who had held him captive earlier and wondered what would be in store for him next. Then he saw Tartarus step out from the opening talons of the Stondefel's hands, followed by Leopold and Cornus climbing to the ground.

"Hey!" he called out. Marcus moved over to the door and pulled it open, only to find himself staring through the locked bars over the doorway. He shook them in frustration. He pushed at the bars, but they didn't move. "What the..." He was taken aback by his inability to move them. Someone must have used power to lock the bars to the house, to keep Marcus from escaping, knowing how powerful he was. How would he get out? Marcus tried pushing at the bars again, with no luck.

Then he remembered when Garrett had carried him through the bruwe—how dilapidated and poorly cared for most of the houses were. He pushed the wall with his hand. Soft, as he had thought. He lowered his head and concentrated on the wall. Logs blew outward, sending splinters flying into the air. He walked out through the wall in time to see Davidia climbing down from Anneberg's back.

"What are *you* doing here?" he said to her. "I sent you away to get you *out* of danger!"

Leopold ran up and grabbed him in a bear hug, lifting him off the ground. "Marcus! I thought I'd never see you again, man! We're here to help!" Marcus groaned and gasped for air to croak, "Leopold, please stop. You're hurting me."

"Oh—sorry, bro," Leopold said, looking abashed. "Guess I was so excited to see you, I got a little carried away. I got everyone together, and we came to help you out. You probably handled it all already, but you never know when you need your best friend by your side. I've always got your back."

Smiling, Cornus handed Marcus the cane he had been sorely missing. Sadie gave him a much gentler hug, looking into his eyes and kissing him softly on the mouth. She looked up. "We need to move so Agatho can land." They all moved out of the way.

As soon as Anneberg cleared the square, Agatho landed. He set Colflur gently on the ground while Abutilon and Buddleja climbed down from his back.

"I can't believe you're all here." Marcus felt relief squeeze his chest. Tears filled his eyes as he remembered how alone he had felt, thinking he would never see any of his friends again. "You're putting yourselves in terrible danger! I wanted you all far away and safe."

"It was our choice to come here and help you, Marcus. You can't always do things on your own. Even with your power, you need your friends by your side to help you." Sadie said as she clutched his hand. Together, they watched Agatho launch himself into the air. The two Stondefel began to circle in the sky.

"What are they doing?" Marcus asked.

"Looking for the rebels. They want to prevent a battle and hope to talk to them first," Abutilon explained as the Stondefel flew away.

"I hope they're successful. The two large Stondefel here are enormous and extremely dangerous," Marcus said.

Sadie seized Marcus's arm. "We need to be prepared! Where are the humans?"

"I think they're all asleep in their houses," he said. "I woke up, and it was just…silent. I'm surprised no one has come out, hearing you all arrive. You haven't exactly been quiet."

How did you survive a confrontation with Nun the Wiser, Marcus? Tartarus asked, concerned.

"Well, um, it was kind of an accident," Marcus said, feeling a flush warm his face. "I didn't know that her power was so tightly bound to her life force. She started probing in my mind, so I did the same to her. I found the source of her power in her mind and destroyed it, but that also killed her."

Tartarus looked stunned. *Nun the Wiser is* dead?

"Yes." Both Fyrtudo stared at Marcus, wordless with

astonishment. Cries began to rise from the houses around them.

"We're being attacked!" A voice called out.

"The murderer is escaping!"

"Eris!"

"Someone get Ravenna!"

Humans rushed from all the houses in the bruwe, and their group was quickly surrounded by a large crowd. Eris stepped forward. "So, you managed to wake up from Ravenna's sleep spell all on your own? It doesn't matter. We have many other ways to control you, Marcus. In fact, you've just brought us eight of them."

"Don't touch my friends!" Marcus shouted as a line of humans stepped forward to seize them. He pushed them all back into the crowd. Then he looked back at Eris. "I think you will find that things have changed somewhat. You no longer have the power to harm me or my friends." His voice was calm and steady. "It's time for all of this to end."

Eris threw her head back and laughed. "You think that just because you have power, you can defeat all of us? Even my mother knew that she needed our help. It wasn't until she had me, with my ability to create portals, that our plan was finally formulated to overtake this world.

"I know exactly how to get to you," she sneered. "If we all attack you at once, you can't stop me from bringing your mother here. Torturing her will be my pleasure, and it will ensure your full cooperation."

Marcus watched with slight trepidation as Eris attempted to open an interdimensional hole. Eris's power had been strong, and he wasn't completely confident he had actually taken it away.

Eris stood with one hand outstretched, her green eyes

closed. As he watched, a small furrow of concentration wrinkled her smooth brow. Her mouth turned down in an unattractive bow of effort. Finally, she stopped and opened her eyes.

"What have you done?" she shrieked as she stormed toward Marcus. Leopold and Cornus moved to stand in front of him. "I cannot find my power. It's just… blank!"

"I took your power away, Eris. The fact that you use it to harm others means you don't deserve to have it. Every human power should be considered a gift and used only to help others, not harm them."

Eris screamed in fury. She whirled on the humans behind her. "Are you going to help me or just stand there like fools? Are you all cowards?"

Marcus watched the crowd, but no one said anything. No one moved, either. Finally, the people who had shouldered their way to the front of the crowd the first time returned. Marcus recognized them as the others who had attacked him before. He realized he should have taken the time to find them all while they slept. He had been too focused on the ones he thought were the biggest threats.

"Be careful!" he cried out. "These humans have power that can hurt you!" He saw his friends move into guarded positions; Cornus and the other Scrybb ducked behind the Fyrtudo, worried about fire.

Water surged toward them. Sadie stepped forward, undaunted. Marcus cried out in alarm and pulled her aside just as electricity sparked its way along the turgid stream.

Fireballs shot toward them all, but Colflur and Tartarus reached out and batted them back toward the crowd. As people ducked away from the dangerous projectiles, Marcus began to reach out and feel for the minds of those with power. One by one, he found them and slowly took away their abilities.

Marcus realized that Ravenna was not among those with abilities in the group in front of him. He whirled around to see the black-haired woman creeping stealthily toward him, hands extended. He smiled at her. A second later, her hands were on his neck, and she whispered *sleep* in his face. She stared at Marcus, baffled, as he smiled.

"That's right, Ravenna. Your days of putting people to sleep are over." Snarling, she squeezed his throat, unwilling to stop attacking him even without her power. Sadie slapped Ravenna hard enough to rock her head back, and the woman let go of Marcus and grabbed Sadie by her hair. Sadie pulled her hair free and whirled, kicking Ravenna in the chest, and Abutilon and Buddleja grabbed Ravenna's arms and pulled her away. Both Scrybb grinned at Marcus.

"We've got your back," Abutilon laughed. He looked as if he were having the time of his life. Then his orange eyes widened in horror as he stared at something behind Marcus. He opened his mouth as if to cry out a warning just as Marcus felt arms wrap around him tightly, knocking his cane from his hand. He heard a grunt as he felt a hard thump that jolted his own body. The arms slowly slid away.

"*Leopold!*" Sadie shrieked.

Marcus turned around with dread to see his best friend sliding to the ground, a wooden spear jutting from his back. Blood spread slowly from underneath his body.

Marcus stared across the square to see the woman who created spears from wood. He saw her in a small opening in the crowd, a stack of spears at her feet, a gap in the wall of the house behind her. A log was missing from the structure. Beside her was Garrett, spear in hand, ready to hurl the projectile at his next victim. Although Marcus had taken his power of increased strength away, Garrett was still an extraordinarily strong man.

Furious, Marcus *pushed*; Garrett flew back against the house so hard he dropped to the ground, unmoving. The spear he'd been holding clattered to the ground. Then Marcus snatched the woman's power, not caring if he hurt her or not, and she fell to the ground, gripping the sides of her head as blood burst from her nose.

Marcus dropped to his knees as Tartarus pulled the spear from Leopold's body.

"You stupid fool! Why?" Tears already dripping from his nose, Marcus pressed his hand against Leopold's back, unmindful of the blood soaking his friend's shirt and coating his skin. Sadie knelt beside him, sobbing. Blood poured from his friend's back as he pressed down.

"Why isn't it working?" Marcus yelled, pressing the hook of his prosthesis against his hand and trying to press his power through both arms into Leopold's body.

Calm yourself, Colflur said. *You cannot heal him when you are so upset.*

Marcus closed his eyes and took a deep breath. He ignored the tears that poured from his eyes and splashed into the blood. Leopold's skin grew hot as warmth flowed down Marcus's arm, and the hole in Leopold's back grew smaller. "Turn him over," Marcus said, watching a rivulet of blood still trickling.

"Are you sure, Marcus?" Cornus asked. Marcus nodded. When Cornus and Sadie gently rolled Leopold onto his back, another gaping hole poured blood from his abdomen.

I should not have pulled the spear out, Tartarus said. *It appears I only made things worse.*

Marcus wiped his running nose on his sleeve and placed his hand directly over the bloody, ragged hole. Leopold moaned as more blood poured out from the pressure. The group around him was silent as they watched, and Marcus knew they were hoping, as desperately as he was, that he could heal Leopold's grievous wound.

He squeezed his eyes shut and tried to remember how he had healed Leopold's broken ankle. He pictured Awar's broken wing. He thought of Anneberg, falling through the sky and healing him across the distance as he was taken by the rebel Stondefel.

I can do this, he thought, sending his mind into Leopold's abdomen as he had into Nun the Wiser's head. He could see the damaged organs, blood everywhere. His mind found a severed artery and pushed as much blood back against the flow as possible before sealing the tear. Next, the bundle of intestines curled around and around itself in a messy pile. Marcus took time to find each individual tear and seal it. His mind searched slowly along the length of the ropy stuff, searching through the blood. When he felt confident he had repaired all of the intestinal injuries, he sent his mental power around the rest of Leopold's abdominal cavity.

A sudden cry distracted him—Cornus stood between Marcus and a leaping wolf, hands held out in wide shields. The wolf bounced off, and Tartarus thrust the spear through it, pinning it to the ground. Marcus nodded, set his shoulders, and turned back to Leopold.

A kidney was torn and weeping blood. Marcus hung his head as he concentrated on repairing the final organ. At last, he pulled back and opened his eyes, watching the pale skin around the wound knit itself back together.

Leopold lay still with his eyes closed. His chest rose and fell slowly. Sadie felt his neck for a pulse. She nodded.

"I don't get it," Marcus said, "I don't think I missed anything. Maybe he has brain damage from blood loss?" He reached forward.

A hand grabbed his arm. "Don't be tinkering around inside my head, bro."

"What—" Marcus looked at Leopold's face to see one blue eye staring at him. "You...you were fine as soon as I finished healing you!"

"Just keeping you on your toes, man. By the way, my back still hurts. Did you miss something?"

Sadie slapped him on the arm. "That wasn't funny, Leopold!" She was still wiping tears from her eyes, but relief was evident in the small smile on her face.

Leopold tried to sit up. "Whoa," he said. "My head is spinning."

"Maybe you should take your time," Sadie said, one hand on his shoulder. "You lost a lot of blood. For a moment there, we thought we were going to lose you."

"It takes more than that to keep ol' Leopold down," he cracked, but Sadie saw the fear in his eyes. He knew how close he had come to death. Yet she had seen him leap in front of Marcus to save him from the spear without hesitation. He had meant every word he had said back on the terrace of Palaga.

Leopold stood up and pulled Marcus to his feet. Cornus handed Marcus his cane again and hugged Leopold hard around the waist.

"Ow!" Leopold put a hand on his back. "There really is something back there that still hurts, man."

"Turn around." Marcus saw the small hole that had still

been bleeding when they had turned his friend over. It was a small matter to heal it now.

The line of his friends in front of him parted, and he saw several angry members of the crowd dragging away those who had been stripped of their powers. It was obvious these people had been held against their will by Nun the Wiser and the others with power. The dead wolf—the man who could change form—had been the last.

"How could you do that? I almost lost you!" He shouted at Leopold. He couldn't believe his best friend had taken a spear for him.

"If I hadn't, it would be you lying on the ground, Marcus. And there's no one here to heal you. *You* would have died. Do you think I could live with that?"

Marcus shook his head. "I understand that, but what if *you* had died before I could heal you? Garrett threw that spear, and he was strong. I'm surprised it didn't go right through you and into me."

"I pulled myself back before it could hurt you. It would have been worth it if I died. I decided that before we all came here."

He threw his arms around Marcus, who hugged him back tightly.

"Thanks for saving me," Marcus said.

"Same, bro," Leopold said right back.

'Excuse me," said another voice, and a hand tapped Leopold's shoulder. He released Marcus and turned to see Sadie. She pushed in between the two boys to wrap her own arms around Marcus and embrace him tightly.

Marcus leaned down and kissed her. His emotions were all mixed up from everything that had happened, but having everyone there made him feel so much better.

Davidia skipped up to them and tossed leafy arms around their shoulders. "You guys are so cute! Almost as cute as Abutilon and Buddleja."

Voices cried out, and several people pointed at the sky. Marcus looked up to see Stondefel approaching. Two of them were locked together in battle. As they reached the skies above the bruwe, they spun in the sky, arms and legs locked around each other. Their spiked tails swung through the bruwe as they swept through the air. People screamed all around him. A third Stondefel dipped toward the combatants, reaching out, trying to pull them to safer heights above the people on the ground.

As the Lysomnians had feared all along, Stondefel against Stondefel meant death for those caught below the battle. Molten saliva began pouring down upon the bruwe.

The glowing fluid came down in thick, red-hot loops, hissing as it landed. People screamed and scrambled to get out of the way but ended up running into each other instead. Marcus saw people fall, getting trampled by the crowd. He cried out in horror as he watched a woman drop to the ground with a mass of the superheated liquid covering her head.

The screams became a cacophony as more people were struck by sizzling drops of the liquid rock. From above, Marcus recognized Agatho desperately trying to stop the vicious battle between Anneberg and Ahazu. The fourth Stondefol hovered above as if unsure what to do. Marcus reached up and struggled to create and hold a shield over the bruwe to catch the molten material and stop it from falling onto them.

Anneberg was struggling to break free of Ahazu's grip, but the talons squeezing his legs were tearing through his rock-hard skin. Black blood began to pour down, sliding along Marcus's shield. A swing of his spiked tail pierced Ahazu's side, sending more blood cascading down in a torrent. Anneberg had Ahazu's hand in a tight grip, fingers folded together to keep the other Stondefel's talons from clawing at his own torso.

Marcus was struggling to hold the shield in place. Healing Leopold had taken a lot of effort. Now he was trying to hold a shield large enough to cover an entire bruwe. He thought about reducing it to cover just the square where the people were but looked down a street and saw a child standing near a house, crying. He didn't know how many people like that kid were in the outer bruwe, exposed. He pushed as hard as he could to keep the shield up—and collapsed to the ground. The shield disappeared.

As the battle raged on above, black blood soaked the ground and drenched the crowd. Hissing red liquid dropped haphazardly onto people below the battle. The crowd broke apart as people screamed and ran to find a place to hide, only to find several houses on fire. A swooping tail dropped along a street and swung up with people impaled on several of its spikes.

Marcus felt large hands lift him and looked up to see Tartarus's large head above him. He was sheltered by the king's head and looked to see Sadie and Leopold beneath Colflur. He hoped the others were beneath Tartarus, but he couldn't see.

Finally, just as Tartarus looked over at Colflur, Marcus saw just enough of the sky to see Anneberg pull Ahazu away from the bruwe and rip the talons of his left foot into Ahazu's belly. More molten material cascaded down, but now it was safely hitting the ground away from everyone.

Ahazu shrieked and let go of Anneberg. He and Agatho grasped the rebel firmly in their talons. He screamed in fury and pain. They flew off with the struggling Standefol away over the Diluvium. Marcus looked around. Everywhere, he saw people who had been burned, stepped on, or impaled. "Where are the worst injuries?" he asked. Leopold, who was kneeling next to a man with a severely burned arm, waved him over. The woman who lay beside them was the one who had been engulfed with molten rock. Marcus was glad she had died instantly from the grievous injury; at least her suffering was over.

Marcus healed the man quickly and then looked to his friends to direct him to the next patient. Sadie comforted a woman whose leg had been broken when she was trampled. Davidia called him to help a man with burns down his back where the Stondefel's saliva had splashed. Colflur had a burn on her own hand but pressed Marcus to heal a woman whose face had been burned.

Another man had been badly raked by tail spikes; Marcus shook his head as he saw there was nothing that could be done besides easing the man's pain. The head injury he had sustained had caused too much damage. A woman had a burned face from a drop of saliva. Several people had sustained injuries from the spikes of Ahazu's tail as it swung through the bruwe.

Many of those impaled were similar to the injury Leopold had sustained—damaged organs and muscles, blood loss. It took so much power to complete these repairs that Marcus turned away from each one more exhausted. Burns were damaged skin, often so deep Marcus had to delve several layers inside and heal each layer as he returned to the surface of the person's skin. It seemed like every time one person was healed, he would look up to see someone else calling him. Person after person was healed until Marcus began to feel dizzy and sick from all the terrible injuries he had helped.

He was just looking around worriedly for Cornus, whom he hadn't seen in a while, when he spotted the Scrybb boy on the opposite side of the square. He was kneeling with his back to the activity. Marcus assumed he had found another injured person. It was odd Cornus hadn't called for help yet. Perhaps the injury wasn't that bad.

He looked around. No one was looking for him at the moment, so he walked over to Cornus. As he reached Cornus, he saw what his friend was staring at; on the dusty ground in front of him lay Abutilon and Buddleja—or what was left of them.

They must have been caught by some of the molten rock. The couple had held onto each other as their leaves curled and their bodies shriveled. Marcus knelt clumsily, wrapped his arm around his friend, and wept alongside him. A scream erupted behind them as Davidia saw the dead couple. She dropped beside Cornus and cried as if she would never stop. Cornus let go of Marcus and wrapped his arms around Davidia, still weeping. Leopold and Sadie soon joined them with cries of grief.

The humans of the bruwe were removing their own dead. When they saw what had happened, they left, giving the people who had saved them some space as they mourned their friends. Tartarus and Colflur had approached and wrapped their arms around as many shoulders as they could, trying to offer as much comfort as possible.

When Anneberg and Agatho returned from their flight over the Diluvium, the news of the death of the Scrybb couple upset Anneberg so much, he refused to talk about it. Alastor, the remaining rebel Stondefol, expressed a genuine desire to return to his brothers, so Marcus agreed to fly with Agatho to try to help him. His enormous size was unnatural for his age, both Anneberg and Agatho agreed. He had been about Awar's size and age when he left, and they feared something terrible had been done to him by Nun the Wiser or one of her minions.

"What happened to the other young rebel Stondefol, Anneberg?" Marcus asked as they flew to where Alastor waited.

'We don't know," Anneberg said, his voice heavy and gravelly. "There is no sign of them, and we fear the worst has happened."

"I'm so sorry," Marcus said, then lapsed into silence. What else was there to say to someone who had just lost half of his people?

Marcus remained seated on Agatho's back so he could be taken to safety immediately if anything were to go wrong. Anneberg posted himself on the other side of Alastor. He put his arm around Alastor's shoulder and told him what Marcus was going to do.

Marcus closed his eyes and felt tentatively inside Alastor's mind. He found a miasma of confusion. The Stondefel had not been ready to be pushed to maturity. Alastor seemed puzzled and sad. He didn't understand what had happened to him. The things he had done were mostly because he had been following the orders of his friend, Ahazu. Marcus realized that Alastor had a disability, and it was not something that needed to be fixed.

Next, he found a small gland deep within the brain of the Stondefel. He sensed it had something to do with the growth of all Stondefel. After feeling it, Marcus asked Agatho if he could feel for the gland in his brain. Agatho nodded. Marcus found it easily, now that he knew where it was in Alastor's brain. In Agatho's brain, it had a small bit of hormone in it, one that Marcus sensed had something to do with growth. Feeling Alastor's gland, Marcus realized that rather than a normal release to slowly reach adulthood, all of Alastor's hormone had been released at once; this had forced him to enormous growth at an excelled rate. No matter what Marcus tried, there was no reversing what had been done to him. Alastor would be a gentle giant for the rest of his life.

He opened his eyes. "There's nothing I can do. Years have been stolen from his life. He has a disability in his mind, and I will not fix it. It isn't hurting him, and I don't think the growth is causing any hostility like it did with Ahazu."

Anneberg put a hand on Alastor's shoulder. "I am grateful that we have saved this one." Then he hesitated as if dreading the answer to his question. "Marcus, where is Awar?"

Marcus's voice hitched with agony as he told Anneberg what had happened to their brave young brother. The look of agonizing grief on their faces tore at his heart.

CHAPTER TWENTY-ONE

HOME

Marcus looked at the Halfriez in his hand. He was curious about the true nature of the piece—it certainly healed well, but it also seemed to work for other purposes. He realized that, since he didn't need it anymore, he could give it to someone else to use for minor injuries. Then again, since it was a Talent legacy, maybe he would hold onto it. Maybe when he had the time, he could experiment with it to discover the full extent of its power.

In the meantime, Garrett, Ravenna, and Eris were all being held in the same small house. Marcus didn't know if he agreed with the idea of keeping them imprisoned, especially now that they had no powers, but he wasn't sure what the right thing to do might be. It felt right to leave the decision up to the humans of the bruwe since they had taken control of the powerless humans as soon as they realized they were no longer a threat.

Now, his goal was to get everyone else home. The Stondefel were more than willing to carry whoever needed a ride, though the older two felt it best if Alastor flew home with no passengers.

Cornus and Davidia had a long discussion about the best way to return Abutilon and Buddleja's bodies home to Thicce Colpat. Davidia's Travel year was over, so she could return with no repercussions. Abutilon and Buddleja had fled Thicce Colpat with Anneberg, Marcus riding on his back. They decided that returning the couple with Davidia, Marcus, and Anneberg would be the right thing to do.

Once things had calmed down, Marcus discovered that Tartarus had been struck by a headful of molten rock during the terrible battle. Fortunately, the Fyrtudo's black rock crown was melded to his rock-like head, and he had felt nothing. Colflur still insisted on inspecting every inch of him before finally allowing Marcus to heal her own arm.

Marcus was just heading back toward the group where the others had gathered when he heard Leopold and Sadie talking. He stopped just behind Tartarus's leg and put up a mental block to keep his thoughts private. He felt guilty eavesdropping, but he was curious. "What do you think he's going to do?" Leopold asked Sadie. "I mean, I know he's going to keep coming here, but how do *we* just go back to regular life after all this?"

"I can't imagine, honestly," she said thoughtfully. "I wish there were some way to keep coming back here with him. What I found about languages in the Palaga Library was fascinating—I would love to keep working on that research. And I wanted to learn the sign language of the Cativera too, that would be so cool. But I know it's impossible. We have to go home and go back to our everyday lives."

"You really like him a lot, don't you?" Leopold said softly.

"Yeah." She murmured. "Yeah, I do. I mean, not because of his power, or because he brought us to some beautiful new planet, or any of that, although that's all pretty neat. But he's an amazing guy, you know?"

A smile creased Marcus's face. He felt like crying with happiness. It hadn't been that long, but he was pretty sure he was in love with Sadie. Hearing her say those things about him, that she liked him despite his disabilities *or* his power, felt pretty amazing.

"Yeah, I do know." Leopold laughed. "He's been my best friend for, like, eleven years. I'm glad you like Marcus. A lot of people look down on him because of his disabilities, but it's nice that someone finally sees him for who he really is."

"I wasn't sure at first if he liked me, to be honest."

"I'm pretty sure he likes you, Sadie," Leopold said. "I've never seen him so happy. And I've certainly never seen him doing so much *kissing*." Leopold made a gagging noise.

"Oh, knock it off," she said. Marcus could picture a pink flush coloring her golden skin. "All we can do is wait and see."

Marcus sensed their conversation was coming to an end, so he walked away. He didn't want to get caught eavesdropping. To look purposeful walking, he headed into the bruwe.

The humans asked Marcus to join them. They wanted his advice on what they should do next.

"You aren't ideally located here," he mused. "I know the point of this location was to keep you isolated from the rest of the people of Lysomnus, but now that Nun the Wiser is gone, you need to consider things like travel and trade. What do you have to offer to the other people of Lysomnus? If you want to move, you need to work that out with the people who live in other areas as well."

One of the women spoke up. "Who is going to lead us now? And who will tell us how we will travel?"

"It's up to you to decide how you want to handle that.

Some people have a Council—a group of people who make decisions together. That might be best for you right now, rather than one or two people who tell you what to do. You've lived under a tyrant for too long." He sighed, running a hand through his hair. "Your method of travel is up to you, and the only thing you need to decide is what impact you might have on the lands you travel through and the people who live there."

The humans looked dumbfounded. Marcus guessed they had been under Nun the Wiser's thumb for so long, the idea of democracy hadn't even occurred to them.

"Keep working on this. I'm leaving for a while, but I will be back to help if you need it." They stared up at him. Marcus bit his lip, thinking. He was only sixteen, and yet these adults wanted his advice; they expected to be led and controlled by the person with the most power. They needed to start thinking for themselves. "Start with the bruwe. Clear the streets of garbage and make repairs to the buildings."

Anneberg was waiting for him as he left the bruwe. "We're waiting for you, Marcus. We are ready to take everyone home."

"It's long past time, isn't it?" Marcus asked, squinting against the sun as he looked up at the massive Stondefel. It occurred to him as they walked toward the others that a person could get used to just about anything. Even traveling to another planet, and riding on a stone demon the size of a house trailer.

Tartarus and Colflur were welcomed warmly upon their return home, and a mighty feast was put on. Palaga loved its king and queen and had waited silently in fear while they faced down their enemy. Their return was greeted with a day-long celebration that rumbled the Beornan Rokk all the way up to the Caldera. Everyone stuffed themselves until they were too full for another bite. Growan, who realized during his father's absence that he needed to prepare for his own maturity, was more dignified and had left his childish antics behind. Marcus and Leopold agreed they rather missed the excited young prince they first met.

Leopold came out to the terrace and stood in the dark next to Marcus. "So, when is it our turn?" he asked. "Got to be soon, right?"

Marcus glanced at him. The light of the shattered moon highlighted the planes of Leopold's face, as he looked up at the sky. Then he turned to Marcus. "Lot of stars up there, Marcus. But they aren't *our* stars. Know what I mean?"

"I know, man. But this place, this planet...it feels like home to me. More than ours ever did."

Leopold looked directly into Marcus's eyes and asked, "Are you sure it's not just the power that you have here?"

Marcus raised an eyebrow. "That's not fair."

"I think it's a perfectly fair question. You have an insane amount of power here. Maybe more than anyone should ever have. I can see why you wouldn't want to give that up."

"Okay," Marcus admitted. "It is a lot of power. But I don't intend to *use* it, not unless I absolutely have—"

"Oh, I'm sure you don't," Leopold cut him off. "Everyone starts off with good intentions. But then it's 'oh, just this once,' or 'maybe it won't hurt,' and 'just one more time,' and next thing you know, you're running the world."

"Are you sure you aren't just jealous?"

Leopold's jaw clenched, and his mouth tightened. "Man, I can't believe you'd even ask me that."

"Really? Because your best friend happens to have this

superpower in a world you can't even get to unless he takes you?"

"What the hell, Marcus! All I've done is defend you since I got here. Helped you. Tried to save this world with you. Saved your damned *life*! Not once did I ask you to take me home, or give up on your quest, or—or anything."

Marcus realized they were standing face to face, shouting at each other. He stepped back and took a deep breath.

"You're right. I'm sorry, man. I shouldn't have said that. You just hurt me with that 'running the world' bit."

"Yeah, I'm sorry too, bro." Leopold clapped him lightly on the shoulder and shook his head. "Can I ask you a question?"

"Sure, anything."

"You've had that healing stone since before you even knew you had any abilities of your own. You saw what it did to me. Why haven't you used it on yourself, Marcus? Don't you want to be normal, not have your disabilities? All that pain?"

Marcus looked down at the ground and took a deep breath. "You know, that subject has come up several times since I arrived here in Lysomnus. I've thought a lot about it. And you know what? I don't need to 'heal' myself because there isn't anything wrong with me. Sure, I'm disabled. I have pain. But I *am* normal, just the way I am. Being disabled doesn't make me not normal. Some of the things I've faced here in this world, I don't know if I could have handled if I hadn't been through the things I've already dealt with in my life." He sighed. "So no, I don't want to heal myself. I want to stay who I am because everything I've been through has made me what I am, and I would never change that."

"You're right," Leopold said. "I was wrong to ask you. You're one of the strongest people I know, dude. I wonder if that's why your power is so strong?"

Marcus shrugged. "Honestly, I'm not sure. I just know that for the first time in my life, I feel completely comfortable with myself. Whether I'm on Lysomnus or Earth, whether I have power or not."

Leopold laughed. "Maybe it is time for me to go home. Don't know what I'll tell my parents." His expression grew thoughtful. "I wonder what your dad told *your* mom? Especially since you've been gone so long."

"I can't even imagine. I guess once we get through this last part in Thicce Colpat, I'll find out. I have to go home and face my dad first, but coming here frequently is still going to be a part of the rest of my life."

Leopold clapped him on the shoulder again. "Let's get some rest, bro. One more thing to do in the morning, and then we can go home."

Marcus was up early the next morning, waiting to go. Sadie walked out to wait with him. He wrapped his arm around her, and she laid her head on his shoulder. After a couple of minutes, Marcus pulled back to face her. He shook his head to get the curls out of his eyes as he looked down at her.

"I want to thank you," he said, looking earnestly into her beautiful black eyes.

"For what, Marcus?"

"For seeing me for who I am and not everything on the outside that everyone else has always judged me for. For sticking up for me."

"Oh, Marcus," she wrapped her arms around him gently. "You're an awesome person. Anyone who can't see that is a fool." She looked up at him again, chin on his chest.

Marcus cupped his hand on the back of her head and kissed her. She kissed him back with a fervor he hadn't expected. Pressure and heat built in his chest until he thought he might explode. He never wanted this moment to end.

Tartarus spoke to them both. *My apologies, but Marcus must go. Davidia has been waiting a long time.* The kiss broke apart, and Marcus looked at Sadie's flushed face.

"I love you," he said.

"I love you, too." Marcus's hazel eyes widened. He knew Sadie liked him, but he never expected to hear her say that she loved him. She gave him one more gentle kiss. "Now go take care of your friends." She went inside.

Marcus had been dreading this part of the day. The Scrybb had been hostile and violent the last time he'd been in Thicce Colpat. Davidia was devastated by the loss of Abutilon and Buddleja. Marcus remembered that she and Buddleja were somehow related. Cornus was also broken-hearted, but as much as it hurt, he wouldn't return with them to his bruwe. Anneberg had volunteered to take everyone who was going. Davidia and Marcus were seated on his back with the wrapped remains of the fallen couple.

As soon as everyone was ready, the Stondefel launched himself into the sky. It was a short flight, and before he'd readied himself to face the Scrybb, Marcus felt Anneberg descending toward what the Scrybb called Far Field, which was the only place where the Stondefel could comfortably land when they weren't crashing into the bruwe. It was depressing how easy it was for Davidia to carry the remains of Abutilon and Buddleja with only a little assistance from Marcus. It didn't take long to reach Thicce Colpat. Since it was very early in the morning, there were several Scrybb about. One of them was Cassiope, who was on her way to the school.

"Excuse me, what are you doing here?" she said angrily, storming toward them.

"Cassiope, stop." Davidia, who had just laid the wrapped remains of her friends on the ground, put her hands up. "This is a sad day for Thicce Colpat."

The Scrybb woman stopped and indicated the bundle that Marcus was untying. "What is this? More of your tricks?"

Without speaking, Marcus and Davidia pulled back the wrapping to reveal the bodies of Abutilon and Buddleja. Cassiope shrieked and dropped to her knees. Scrybb came running from every direction at the noise. As they saw the remains of Abutilon and Buddleja, many of them began to weep.

"What...what happened?" A Scrybb man asked in a hushed tone from behind Marcus.

"They died in the battle to save Lysomnus," Davidia said. She told everyone the story of how the Scrybb couple had been a part of the battle and added that the smaller Stondefel, who had been wounded here in Thicce Colpat, had also been killed by Nun the Wiser.

Cassiope looked up at Marcus. "How could I have been so blind?"

"It's not all your fault," he said, his tone somber. "Nun the Wiser and her followers tainted many things in Lysomnus. They abused people. No one can blame you for wanting to shut humans out after how they treated you."

"But—but the Stondefel," she wept. "If I had only listened. I sent them away with hate in my heart. We hurt one of them, and now we can never make up for that. And we tortured Abutilon on *my orders*! But the whole time, he and Buddleja were the ones who believed in the truth and did the right thing. I cannot—"

"Cassiope," Marcus interrupted. "The hardest part of doing something wrong is that you have to live with it. Perhaps someday you will be able to forgive yourself. Until then, all you can do is try to change and be a better person."

He held out his hand to her, and she took it, rising shakily to her feet. "We will start by honoring them," she declared. "We will add the tale of their heroism to the Teaching of our children." She gave Marcus a sideways look. He knew she meant that the Stondefel would also now be a part of their Teaching as well. He nodded his approval. It wouldn't bring the dead Scrybb back, but their deaths would make a difference here.

He waved goodbye to Davidia, who blew him a farewell kiss and walked back down the path to Far Field, where Anneberg was waiting for them.

"After this, we'll have to get used to making our own way around Lysomnus," Marcus said. "We can't continue to expect Stondefel to be our beasts of burden."

"I don't mind," Anneberg rumbled, amused. "It is enjoyable to share the thrill of flying with someone who can't do it on their own."

"Still, if everyone keeps doing it, no one will want to walk around and use the trade routes. That's an important way to learn about this planet, too." He climbed into the harness.

"Ready?"

"Yes," said Marcus. "Let's go."

When Anneberg dropped Marcus on Palaga's stone terrace, Leopold and Sadie were waiting for him. "I think it's finally our turn, Marcus," Sadie said, her smile tinged with sadness.

"Yeah, dude, we gotta get home too," Leopold said. They both looked almost as exhausted as Marcus felt.

It is time for you all to return to your world, Tartarus said. *We hope you will be able to come back and visit us often. We consider you all friends. Marcus, you are an important part of Lysomnus and will need to return and spend time with us.*

"I definitely plan to do that, Tartarus. Now that I know I don't have to wait to go to sleep to come back, I'll definitely come as often as I can. And whenever these two can make it work," he indicated Sadie and Leopold, "I'll bring them along too."

"I want to come back soon, but I definitely need to see my family and spend time with them first. I can't imagine what explanation we're going to come up with for our long absence," Sadie said. "Then I plan to come back and work on those languages!"

"Me too," Leopold said. "Only I'm not going to study when I'm here. I don't even like studying back home!"

Marcus and Sadie couldn't help laughing.

You will all be missed very much while you are gone. I know Growan will miss you most of all, Leopold, Tartarus said. *We look forward to your return.* The King of the Fyrtudo turned and walked through the gates of Palaga, which slid closed behind him.

Marcus turned to his friends and smiled.

"Man, I know no one back home would ever believe what we've done. Well, except for my dad," he frowned, thinking of the complicated relationship he would now have to navigate. "Okay, are you guys ready?"

He handed his cane to Leopold, then held out his left hand and his prosthesis. Leopold grabbed the prosthesis, and Sadie took Marcus' other hand, squeezing tightly. Marcus closed his eyes, picturing his backyard. The portal appeared in an instant, as easy as snapping his fingers. How far he had come in such a short span of time.

Together, they stepped through, and the portal collapsed behind them.

A
DISCOVERY
OF
TALENTS

PRONUNCIATION OF NAMES AND PLACES

Lysomnus - LYe SOM nus
Bruwe - BROO way
Thicce Colpat - THEEkuh COLE pat
Berberis - BURR ber ISS
Cativera - CAT ih VEER ah
Halfriez - HAL freeze
Stikke - STEE kuh
Brynar - BRYE nar
Vosfyren - Vose FYE ren
Cassiope - Cas SIGH oh pee
Abutilon - Ah BEU til on
Buddleja - Boo duh LAY ah
Fyrtudo - Fear TOO doh
Beornan Rokk - Be YORE nan ROKE
Stondefel - STONE duh FEL
Palaga - Pah LA ga
Colflur - COLE Fleur
Tartarus - TAR tar ROOS
Rotrukan - RO troo kan
Anneberg - ANN eh berg
Muirnati - Mooweer NAH tee
Agatho - AG gah tho
Pelamis - PEL ah mis
Boehlkea - Bel KEY ah
Zabanara - ZAH bah NAR ah
Grasian - GRASS ee AN
Suri- SOO ree
Ahazu - Ah HA zoo
Alastor - AL a STORE

ACKNOWLEDGMENTS

Lysomnus is a dream that wouldn't have come to fruition without the involvement of so many hands. First and foremost, the inspiration for this book belongs to my son and to the mother of my grandson, who came up with the idea of me writing a book for kids. At that time it was supposed to be younger kids, but as I played with the idea it expanded into first a nightmare (hence the phantasm) and then just exploded into the entire world it wanted to be over the course of three months.

So I'll start with them. Thanks to Denny, my son, and to Sabrina, for inspiring the first idea.

Next, I have to thank Elizabeth Roderick, who encouraged me to give fiction a try in the first place when I was burned out on nonfiction. She also edited an early draft and gave me a lot of helpful tips.

I owe a lot to Elyse (a certain Brave Little Teapot, you know who you are) who brought me in on one of the most important group writer's projects Having the fortune to be a part of The Dark Side of Purity allowed me to work with some of the greatest women and genderqueer writers I've had the fortune to meet.

Lindz McCleod edited this book for me over the period of a year, while obtaining a PhD and writing about a hundred of her own projects. *A Discovery of Talents* would not be the book it is today without her help and patience.

Alexandria Anderson volunteered to jump in and proofread the very final draft of this book when it was obvious it was absolutely needed. Her help was critical and perfected the last draft before formatting. She added many of the details that made this book immeasurably more readable.

A.M. Weald typeset and formatted the book for me. She's been an invaluable resource and friend throughout this entire process. I also depended on her beautiful book *Even If We're Broken* to help me through the most stressful of times toward the end.

Disability, queer, and marginalized representation is incredibly important to me and should be to everyone, particularly at this time in history. Every person who worked on this book represents a marginalized group, whether it is via disability, LGBTQIA+, or BIPoC.

I'd also like to thank my beta readers and my sensitivity readers. Your input was invaluable in the completion of this book.

To Ethan, for a very honest review when it was what I needed to make this book as good as I thought it was, and to help me bring the final copy to as good as it really could be.

Also to my youngest kiddo for calling me and yelling at me when they were reading and certain characters didn't make it.I'm sure some of you who read the book are angry or sad too, Believe me, those deaths tore my heart apart.

Thank you to the partner I had for 32 years, who was willing to read my book when reading books was something he really, really didn't want to do, and then liking it.

And lastly, to the baby, the best of us—I love you the morst.

Phoenix

ABOUT THE AUTHOR

Phoenix McDonald was born in Richmond, Virginia, and spent most of his childhood moving around the country with his parents before settling in Wisconsin. After raising two beautiful children, he found his dream career in Respiratory Therapy. Unfortunately, physical disability and grade II brain cancer forced him to give up his career. Not to be stopped, he took up writing. In 2020, he moved to Portland, Oregon to be near his grandson and found himself at last to be at home.

A lifelong fan of speculative fiction, Phoenix writes YA fantasy novels, and horror and scifi short stories. After publishing many short stories, *A Discovery of Talents* is Phoenix's first published novel.

Learn more at therealphoenixrises.com.

OTHER WORKS BY THE AUTHOR

"The Talent Continuum, Book Two: The Crystal Island" (2025)

"Sight and Sound" and "Smuggler's Blues" in A Cold Christmas and the Darkest of Winters anthology pub by Cinnabar Moth

"Karma" in Bomemilk II anthology pub by Gutslut Press

Creative Nonfiction "The High Wire" in Yuzu Press November 2021 Edition

"In the Dark Places" in Toilet Zone 3 anthology pub by Hellbound Books 2022

Poem "Childhood Demons" in Raven Review's winter 2022 issue

"The Last Glass" short story in Featured Creators section of Full House Literary's April 2022 edition

"Skeleton in the Closet" in 206 word stories flash fiction anthology pub by Bag of Bones

"Life Support" in Hell Hath Only Fury anthology pub by S.H Cooper and Oli A. White

"Legacy" in The Future's So Bright anthology pub by Water Dragon Publishing October 2022

"The Earth is Not Your Home" in Expat V (EXPVT) anthology pub by Expat Press Jan 2023

"The House of Cups" in The Dark Side of Purity anthology pub by Band of Bards May 2023

"Childhood Sweethearts" in No One Should Kiss a Frog anthology pub by MacKenzie Publishing June 2023

"Message in a Bottle" in Colp-Desert/Dessert anthology pub by Gypsum Sound Tales August 2023

"Dory's Sacrifice" in From the Yonder Volume IV pub by War Monkey Publications Fall 2023

"Raising Hell in Blockbuster" in Captured pub by Inky Bones Press August 2024